PASSIONATE KNIGHT

She fought him like a wildcat, but he was much too strong for her. In the dim light of the chill bedchamber, Lyon Beauchane took control and unsheathed his dagger. "Not a sound, m'lady, or I will kill you," he said, his tone soft and decisive at the same time.

It was an idle threat. A knight could not kill his own princess, no matter what offense she had committed.

Princess Jade curled her knees beneath herself on the bed, folding her hands in her lap after pulling her nightgown well over her knees. "What do you want of me?" she whispered, not looking up.

The anger that had blazed in Lyon only a second earlier vanished instantly. When Jade had adjusted her nightgown, the thin white silk was pulled low and tight across her bosom. Now, in the dim moonlight, he was able to see the velvety inner swells of her breasts in the cut of the neckline.

His mouth went dry. "I don't wish to hurt you. I wish only to talk. Do you understand?"

Jade looked up and into the face of the intruder, thinking that surely this was the most handsome executioner the world had ever produced. Then she noticed the direction of his gaze, and her heart began to pound furiously in her breast . . .

DANA RANSOM'S RED-HOT HEARTFIRES!

ALEXANDRA'S ECSTASY   (2773, $3.75)

Alexandra had known Tucker for all her seventeen years, but all at once she realized her childhood friend was the man capable of tempting her to leave innocence behind!

LIAR'S PROMISE   (2881, $4.25)

Kathryn Mallory's sincere questions about her father's ship to the disreputable Captain Brady Rogan were met with mocking indifference. Then he noticed her trim waist, angelic face and Kathryn won the wrong kind of attention!

LOVE'S GLORIOUS GAMBLE   (2497, $3.75)

Nothing could match the true thrill that coursed through Gloria Daniels when she first spotted the gambler, Sterling Caulder. Experiencing his embrace, feeling his lips against hers would be a risk, but she was willing to chance it all!

WILD, SAVAGE LOVE   (3055, $4.25)

Evangeline, set free from Indians, discovered liberty had its price to pay when her uncle sold her into marriage to Royce Tanner. Dreaming of her return to the people she loved, she vowed never to submit to her husband's caress.

WILD WYOMING LOVE   (3427, $4.25)

Lucille Blessing had no time for the new marshal Sam Zachary. His mocking and arrogant manner grated her nerves, yet she longed to ease the tension she knew he held inside. She knew that if he wanted her, she could never say no!

ROBIN GIDEON

ROYAL ECSTASY

ZEBRA BOOKS
KENSINGTON PUBLISHING CORP.

For George & Loraine and Carol & Bob—
fine folk who spent a bundle on our wedding . . .
and all they get is this dedication.—RG

ZEBRA BOOKS

are published by

Kensington Publishing Corp.
475 Park Avenue South
New York, NY 10016

First printing: August, 1992

Printed in the United States of America

Chapter 1

England

Lord Charles Frederick looked at the young knight who had just entered the room, and immediately felt a sense of confidence that he had not felt earlier. Sir Lyon Beauchane had just returned from six years of fighting the wars, and it was easy to see that his many battles had hardened Lyon without breaking him, either in body or in spirit. Tall, narrow-waisted and broad-shouldered, he walked with a purpose, his head held high and proud. He had the bearing of a man who had never taken a step backward for anyone or anything, and never would.

Lord Charles glanced over to his friend and associate, Baron Timish von Mueller. The two elderly men exchanged a glance, and without words confirmed their belief that this knight was the man necessary to put sanity and peace back into the region, and prevent the bloody, costly war that would, in the end, accomplish little more than carnage.

"Sir Lyon Beauchane, I am glad to see you again," Lord Charles said in his commanding voice that sprang from his barrel chest. He stood six-foot-five and weighed nearly three hundred pounds. In his younger years, he had been a formidable warrior; now he was comfortable running his vast estate and hiring young blood such as the knight, Lyon Beauchane, to do his physical fighting for him. "It has been many years."

Lyon stepped forward, the cape trailing behind him. At six feet, he was taller than most men, though not nearly as tall as Lord Charles. His sandy blond hair curled over the high stiff collar of his shirt, and fluffed slightly with the speed of his stride. His eyes were icy blue, and he tended to keep his head cocked slightly to the right when he talked to people, hiding the knife scar near his left ear. His mouth was wide, and not quite full lipped, and his nose was faintly hawkish.

It was the blue eyes that darted right and left, taking in the entire room in a glance, assessing possible dangers, that first impressed Lord Charles. He knew there were many strong knights and mercenaries to be had for the right amount of gold, but there were very few fighting men with a truly keen intelligence and a grasp of realities that encompassed a world larger and greater than just their immediate surroundings. Lyon, it appeared, possessed the physical, psychological, and emotional qualities necessary to have at least a chance of surviving the arduous task they would ask of him.

"The battles have not taken away your strength, I see," Lord Charles said as the younger man approached.

"Battles kill men or make them stronger," Lyon replied, coming to a stop. "There is no other way for men of action."

There was the faintest edge to Lyon's voice, a slight challenge in the timbre which Lord Charles and the Baron both noticed, though neither knew the warrior well enough to feel confident in making any interpretation. Still, it was that edge that made Lord Charles's eyes narrow as he studied Lyon once more.

"You're curious as to why we've asked you to come here before returning to Castle Crosse," Baron von Mueller said, his German accent thick, though his English was perfectly understandable.

"That surprises you?" Lyon asked, cocking an eyebrow.

"I would have been surprised only if you weren't curious." The baron smiled, moving a little closer to Lyon, looking up at him. The baron was almost the exact opposite of his good friend, Lord Charles, standing barely over five feet tall. "You do not know us well yet, my friend, but you will find out that Charles and I have little time and no patience for men who lack a curious, grasping mind." He made a face. "Dullards waste my time, and I am a busy man."

If there had been a hint of challenge in Lyon's tone earlier, now there was a matching hint of a smile. He, too, had little time for posturing intellects.

Three chairs had been placed in the center of the room, along with a large pitcher of hearty wine with three heavily bejeweled goblets. With a wave of Lord Charles's hand, the three men took their seats. It was not lost on Lyon that the chairs were placed in a triangle, indicating that the three men were at least nominally equals, rather than having one chair facing the other two, which would have indicated varying social stations. This pleased Lyon, though none would

7

have known this from his expression, which remained blank and inscrutable.

Wine was poured and glasses passed around. Lord Charles explained that the servants had been dismissed for "privacy, and fidelity to our cause."

Lord Charles and Baron von Mueller exchanged a look, and then the Englishman, clearly the more talkative of the two, cleared his throat softly; took a drink of his wine; then began speaking, his eyes meeting and holding the young knight's.

"You have been fighting abroad for six years now, and it has been that long since either the baron or myself have spoken to you, though we have on occasion heard stories of your heroism and bravery from Prince William, your lord."

"I did only what was expected of me," Lyon said. Though he spoke in a normal volume, the commanding quality of it was enormous, particularly for a man not yet close to advanced years. "King Henry bid me to fight; Prince William bid me to fight; so fight I did, leading my men."

"Yes, fight and win," Baron von Mueller said, studying the man over the rim of his goblet.

"As you know, Prince William died on the field of battle nearly six months ago, and since that time his fiefdom has been run by Princess Jade, though some suspect that the real person making the decisions is Bishop Fields," Lord Charles affirmed.

"Or it could be Sheriff Sean Dunne. He's a foul man," von Mueller cut in.

For the first time, Lyon's expression was easy to read. At the mention of Bishop Nathan Fields's name, his face twisted into a disrespectful scowl, though he

8

kept his words to himself.

"She's done the damndest things," the baron continued. "She's raised the taxes on her peasants to such a level that they have no hope of paying them. This put the peasants in low spirits, and troubled peasants have a way of becoming a plague. I don't want my serfs agitated because Princess Jade Crosse cannot see the difference between decent profit and foul greed."

Lyon nodded faintly. He had heard rumors of what changes had been made since the death of Prince William Crosse, but rumors were always circulating, particularly on the field of battle, so he paid them little mind until now. He knew Baron von Mueller and Lord Charles Frederick to be men of honesty and virtue. They were not gossipmongers, nor men who saw problems where there were none. If they saw stormy skies on the horizon, it was prudent to prepare for bad weather.

"Recently, Crosse soldiers have taken to taxing those who must cross the land. The baron himself was forced to pay a tax to come here for this meeting."

"A passage tax is not unheard of," Lyon commented. Princess Jade's property abutted the sea, and was surrounded on either side by von Mueller's and Lord Charles's fiefdoms, so it was necessary to cross Crosse land to visit.

"True, not unheard of," Lord Charles replied. "But such a tax was never levied when Prince William was alive. You know, as well as I, the tolerance we have all shown. A passage tax? And how would you respond as a member of Princess Jade's court to pay a tax to come here tonight?"

9

Lyon swirled the rich red wine in his goblet, staring into the scarlet liquid, his thoughts far away, though he listened intently to every word being spoken.

"She's been using that damnable sheriff to do her bidding."

Lyon concluded von Mueller had a personal grudge against Sheriff Sean Dunne. It wouldn't surprise him. There were many good reasons to hate the sheriff.

A hint of a smile turned the edges of Lyon's mouth upward. "I'd have thought someone would have run him through by now."

"Worse luck that no one has," von Mueller said through clenched teeth. When he was angry, his accent became more pronounced, his English less distinct. "If I wasn't a peaceable man of the law, I'd see to it that Dunne and Knight Rawlings both dangled from the end of a rope."

Lyon nodded absently. Sheriff Dunne was a corrupt, depraved man, and Lyon had always hated him. And Garth Rawlings was a knight for Prince William who had gone through training with Lyon. Lyon had consistently reached the top marks among the knights, with Rawlings always coming in second place. The open enmity and jealousy that Rawlings felt for Lyon was no mystery to anyone who knew them.

"How many serfs has Garth killed to date?" Lyon asked.

"Too many," von Mueller replied quickly.

"One is too many," Lord Charles added, and with nothing more than a look indicated that many serfs had fallen to Sir Rawlings's sword, dagger, or arrow.

"He has always had a taste for blood," Lyon explained. "He enjoys it as other men enjoy women."

10

Lyon looked into Lord Charles's blue eyes and asked, "But what has that to do with me now? Rawlings was an abomination when I left six years ago. It is no surprise to hear that he's an abomination now. Why is it you've gone to such extraordinary lengths to see that I speak with you before returning to my home? After all, Castle Crosse is my home, and Princess Jade with the death of Prince William is now the owner of my allegiance."

"The baron and I are on the verge of warfare with your fiefdom. We have sent agents to speak with Princess Jade, but she refused to speak with any of them. The last man that Timish sent to speak with Princess Jade never returned. His body was found eventually. The wolves had gotten to it by then. Bishop Fields said he'd never reached Castle Crosse, and Sheriff Dunne promised a thorough investigation into his death, but no answers have been found."

Baron von Mueller said, "When our agents could not reach Princess Jade, I went to see her myself. Bishop Fields said she wasn't seeing anyone and that included me. And then the bastard had Sheriff Dunne and Rawlings escort me to the edge of the enfeoffment." A muscle ticked in the baron's cheek at the ugly memory. "I've never been treated so disgracefully in my entire life."

"We want you to speak with Princess Jade," Lord Charles cut in, absently tugging at his beard. "Find out if this is her doing, and see what it will take to make her stop."

"It's her land," Lyon said. "She can do with it, and with her own villeins, whatever she wills. The law and King Henry so decree it. What right do you have to tell

11

her how she must treat her subjects . . . one of whom happens to be me?"

"Aye, that she can. But when her knights begin raiding my villages, and the villages in von Mueller's fiefdom, then it is time she is stopped."

Lyon's eyes narrowed. This was a serious statement. "And the Crown knows of this? You have proof it is Rawlings acting on Princess Jade's orders?"

"Nay. Even if we did have the proof, we wouldn't go to the Crown with it. Whenever the Queen Mary and her Court gets involved, there's nothing but trouble for everyone. Besides, I'm a man who handles his own problems, and if Princess Jade has become my trouble, then not even the King Henry will be able to save her," Lord Charles mumbled.

An abundance of energy, mixed with his anger toward Princess Jade, and frustration at the situation in general, forced the baron to his feet. He began pacing the room, flinging his arms about as he spoke.

"Since the death of her husband, she has turned into an absolute tyrant! I'll grant you, good sir, she is young and beautiful, and she no doubt suffered mightily while her husband Prince William was alive. He was a feeble old fool! No one who knew him during his final days would ever tell you he was anything but a fool, trying to relive his youth for reasons only God Himself can completely understand. But whatever demons haunt Princess Jade, they cannot be sufficient to warrant her behavior.

"Lord Charles and I are reasonable men. We will listen to reason and behave peaceably if she will listen to reason and behave peaceably. But if I have one more village attacked in the night by riders who then seem to vanish into thin air, if my villeins suffer one more atrocity by hooded men who ride away always in the direction of Castle Crosse, then I guarantee you, Lyon Beauchane, that I will assemble the largest, most finely trained army of soldiers, mercenaries, and archers that this island has ever seen. And I shall personally lead the attack upon Castle Crosse myself!"

"Let's not let our blood boil too hotly," Lord Charles said with a hint of a smile, despite the seriousness of the conversation. "Leading a battle, Timish? You're beginning to sound like Prince William. He led a charge in a futile, silly war, and now he's feeding the worms."

With a shrug of his shoulders, Baron von Mueller forced himself to calm down. He poured himself another goblet of the rich red wine, then took his seat once more.

"What we're asking of you," Lord Charles said to Lyon, "is to use whatever skills and wiles you possess to speak with Princess Jade personally to find out why she is behaving so inappropriately. You know the castle better than we do. Perhaps you can accomplish what we cannot. We're not asking you to be a traitor. We're asking you to do what you can to prevent a war that will benefit no one, and surely cause the death of many fine young men."

Von Mueller said quietly, "It is almost always the young men who die in war, is it not?"

Lyon rose from his chair, placing the goblet upon a small round table. He had hardly touched his wine, though his palate told him it was of exquisite quality. "I will do what I can."

"What will you do? How will you arrange to see Princess Jade when those before you have failed?"

Lord Charles inquired.

Lyon shook his head, sending his blond hair passing back and forth over the collar of his cape. "That is my concern, not yours. I will tell you what it is you need to know."

Lyon left, and when the men were alone in the great room once again, Lord Charles began laughing. "You know, Timish, if that young man were a knight for me, I think I'd probably want to strangle him."

Baron von Mueller was smiling by this time. "He probably spoke to Prince William as disrespectfully as he spoke to us."

"Aye. But he is a strong, brave young man. If there is anyone who can speak with Prince William's widow and make her see the light of day, Lyon Beauchane is the man."

Princess Jade Crosse stood before the window of her bedchamber, staring out to the empty sea and the darkness beyond. She loathed her new bedchamber, which faced out to sea instead of landward. Before, when William was alive, she had enjoyed being able to look upon the people within the high boulder wall of Crosse Castle. She enjoyed watching them as they worked and played, especially in the early morning hours. Jade often waved to the people, and she was always greeted then with a wave and a smile in return. It had seemed, back then, that the people liked Jade, and that they were happy their new princess had once been a commoner, just like themselves. She felt a closeness to her people, and they felt more than mere fealty to her. Or so she had always believed.

14

And then her husband was killed, and the people she had always thought of as "her people" had turned into an angry, rebellious mob. Bishop Nathan Fields had even directed Mary Ellen, Jade's personal maid, to move all of her royal bedchamber belongings into another bedchamber to shield her from the unpleasantries now happening within the walls of her castle, and further out, within the realm of her fiefdom.

"Will m'lady be needing anything else?" Mary Ellen asked, standing near the bedchamber door. She clearly was not interested in doing anything more for Jade, and wanted to retire for the evening. She made only a minimal attempt to hide her feelings.

Jade looked at her maid. She disliked Mary Ellen, who had been assigned to her by Bishop Fields shortly after Jade became a widow. The bishop had said he no longer trusted Jade's maids, assistants, or dressmaids, stating that with William's death Jade would do well to start anew completely. Against Jade's wishes, the bishop had all of Jade's retinue removed from their posts and sent away to all parts of England, making it impossible for Jade to retrieve them.

Jade had considered those women her friends. The new maids who now worked for her always had a faint contempt in their tone when they spoke to her, and Jade suspected they were really just spies working for Bishop Fields.

She felt desperately lonely. Lonely as she had never really felt before in her life. Though only twenty-four, she felt old, too. Older than she ever dreamed she'd be. How had a young girl become a princess, once adored by her husband the prince and her subjects, only to become the object of scorn and derision? Why would she need to take a seaside bedchamber to protect her delicate sensibilities from the wrath of her subjects? How had a young girl of fourteen, chosen to become the bride of a man in his fifties, become a lonely widow just ten years later?

"Ma'am, will there be anything more?" Mary Ellen said, cutting into Jade's worried thoughts. Now there was no attempt at all by Mary Ellen to hide her annoyance at being kept on duty.

"No, that will be all. Good evening."

"Yes, m'lady," Mary Ellen said, barely giving the customary curtsy before exiting the bedchamber.

Alone at last, Jade breathed a sigh of relief. Only a few years earlier, she hadn't particularly cared for being by herself. Now, that aloneness was something she accepted and understood. Though she cared for it no more than she ever had, at least it was less painful than being with people she knew respected her not a whit.

It seemed as though so many things had changed in her life since her seemingly calm days of youth, when she had no responsibility other than to experience as much joy and laughter as possible, and complete whatever chores around the house Mama deemed necessary.

The first big change was when she got married to Prince William Crosse. Overnight she went from being a poor fourteen-year-old girl from a small village to a princess in control of vast riches, with total dominion over the lives of the peasants living on the property that had been in her husband's family for more than three hundred years.

The second major change came when Prince William

16

decided that he needed to prove his manhood upon the field of battle. Though Jade could not tell anyone of her marital problems, Prince William had become impotent within two years of her wedding ceremony. Since he felt himself incapable of proving his manhood in the bedroom, he turned to war to regain his masculinity. By this time, he was well into his fifties. The sensible members of his retinue realized that Prince William was doing much worse than merely flirting with disaster; he was begging for a savage and bloody death.

When the news finally came to Jade, she was saddened at her husband's death, but she was smart enough to realize that she had lost him much earlier.

At one time Jade had taken great pride in wearing the fine, expensive gowns that Prince William had commissioned for her. She enjoyed the approving looks that her husband gave her, and she was pleased when he commented how this dress or that gown brought out the color in her eyes or hair. And though she had never for an instant flirted with any of the guards at Castle Crosse, or any of the numerous men who comprised her husband's retinue and advisers, she did take secret pleasure when she caught one of the young men paying a bit more attention to her than normal as she walked by.

But lately, she did not want to look good for anyone, not even herself, and though she was only partially aware of it, a sinewy depression was settling into her bones.

Jade stripped out of her gown and carefully slipped the broad, clothbound holder into it, then hung the garment up in the closet of her bedchamber. She had been a poor girl for too many years to casually cast the gown aside until morning, leaving it for Mary Ellen or one of the other maids to tend to.

She listlessly removed the rest of her clothing, then pulled on the plain white nightgown. The nightgown was very old, she'd had it since the year of her wedding. It was plain, almost completely unadorned with lace or edging or even small bows near the slender shoulder straps, or a sash of any kind around the waist. The silk had started out soft, and over the years and after innumerable wearing and many cleansings had gotten even softer.

Prince William hadn't liked the nightgown, stating that it was too plain for Jade's ravishing beauty, and that it was becoming frayed at the edges, and elsewhere. Jade didn't care. She liked the nightgown precisely because it was plain and old and simple, unadorned with anything frivolous. It was soft and comfortable, and the only real shape to the garment was Jade herself.

She turned back the blankets to her bed. Jade Crosse had no need to dress in anything fancier because no man would see her.

She closed her eyes and listened to the sea crashing against the rocks far below. She hated this bed-chamber. All she could hear was the sea, a constant reminder of her loneliness and her stark solitude. In her other bedchamber, which had faced the main court-yard of Castle Crosse, there was always the sound of children playing, sellers displaying chicken and geese, and a thousand ever-cheerful sounds of people going about their day's business. Even after Prince William's death, those sounds had let her know that she was not truly alone in this world.

With a sigh, Jade closed her eyes, hoping that sleep would come easily to her. It seldom did these days. Whenever she closed her eyes, she would begin to think of the way things were now and the way they were back then. Then she would be wide awake, turning this thought or that memory over and over in her head for hours. And when she finally arose for the day, she would feel as though she hadn't slept a wink, and go through the day nearly a sleepyhead.

Jade desperately needed peaceful, dreamless sleep. She had so few things left in her life that gave her any pleasure, and in lieu of actual happiness, she readily accepted the peaceful nothingness of dreamless sleep.

Lyon Beauchane stood at the edge of the water, the waves breaking near his polished boots, his clothes and cape covered in a fine mist of salt water. He looked up at the rocky face of the earth and beyond that to the formidable wall of the castle. He wondered once again whether or not he was really doing the right thing on this blustery, warm summer's evening.

Lyon Beauchane, knight of the Castle Crosse, hero of wars fought for the Crown and country, as well as for Prince William, felt uncomfortable about scaling the rock face, then the eastward wall of the castle, all to surreptitiously enter Castle Crosse like a common criminal. There was just something inherently shameful about it, possibly cowardly, that bothered Lyon.

But what if Lord Charles and Baron von Mueller were right? What of the rumor circulated that there would be a price upon his head should he return from the wars in fighting condition? What if Jade did have men put to death who approached her for an audience?

Lyon wouldn't pretend that he knew his princess well. He had seen her several times, of course, at special activities for which Prince William loved to show her off to other noblemen. But he had not seen her in six years.

In those seven years, Lyon knew that he had changed. The wars had changed him, hardened him in positive and negative ways. He was a more capable soldier now, and a better leader of men. The years and the experience of countless battles had given him that.

But was he a better man for what he now knew?

The last time he had seen Princess Jade, she was the child bride of his prince, a beautiful young girl with a promising figure that had yet to actually blossom the way he suspected it would. Her soft amber eyes, even back then at the tender age of seventeen, held great sympathy and compassion in them. Anyone spying upon Jade while she looked upon her people would see the love and devotion she felt for them reflected in her eyes, in her countenance, in the proud way she held her head upon her shoulders.

Her youth mattered little back then. The serfs saw Princess Jade as their personal protector from a sometimes cruel and always distant nobility, and from a prince who occasionally issued orders that made little or no sense, but had to be followed under penalty of death.

Lyon dismissed these thoughts and worries from his mind as he tugged at the gauntlet of his gloves, making sure that the leather fingers were tight against his skin. Then he tossed his beautifully tailored, ebony black cape back over both shoulders and began making his way up the cliff's edge. He tried to recall how he had accomplished exactly this feat many years earlier when, on a faintly intoxicated evening with other knights-in-training, he bet everyone that he could climb the wall. On that night, he had climbed into a larder where, among other precious items, dried mutton and wineskins of wine were kept. Now that seaward room was the bedchamber for Princess Jade Crosse.

Slowly, steadily, by the light of the moon, Lyon chose his handholds and footholds in the rock face carefully, his long black cape fluttering softly behind him like the gigantic wings of a mighty raven.

Chapter 2

Lyon was sweating. Little rivulets ran down his cheeks and made his long blond hair stick to his temples. His fingers inside the kid gloves ached from holding his weight for nearly an hour. His toes hurt, too, from all the time that he had spent clutching onto the side of the castle, his toes wedged between the bricks to give him some support and stability during his arduous ascent.

But he was almost there. Less than twenty feet to go and he would be at the window ledge to Princess Jade's bedchamber.

In his mind he went over options of action that he could take. Somehow, he had to keep her quiet so that the guards would not be alerted. Once that was accomplished, he needed to convince the princess that he really meant her no harm. He only wanted to talk with her. If she resisted, that would mean that she was aware of the changes that had been happening in her kingdom since the death of Prince William. Of course, considering the circumstances surrounding their first conversation in seven years, she might react suspiciously, and that wouldn't necessarily indicate any guilt on her part.

Stop thinking about it now, or you'll end up smashed on the rocks below, Lyon thought, mentally upbraiding himself for letting his mind wander. Scaling the castle wall required all his concentration if he was to succeed.

When he was almost within reach of the marble railing along the balcony to Jade's bedchamber, the moon disappeared behind an angry-looking blue cloud, and Lyon was suddenly plunged into a darkness so completely that he could not see enough to make his next move.

Stifling a curse, he pressed his cheek against the rough surface of the castle wall and waited, his fingers throbbing with tension, his thighs knotted, solid as the rocks to which he clung. And two hundred feet below, the waves crashed against the rocks, waiting perhaps impatiently for Lyon to make one errant misstep, and with that mistake, shatter his body and then steal it out to sea.

The seconds ticked by with exaggerated sloth. Lyon waited, praying for the moonlight to again illuminate the path he needed to take. He had been straining his muscles for nearly an hour without a single moment's relief, and now, within a few feet of his destination, he could not help but wonder if all his efforts had been in vain.

Lyon couldn't take much more. If the moon did not reappear from behind the angry black cloud, he would not be able to see where he could wedge the toes of his boots into the castle wall, nor would he see where to grab to hoist himself higher.

Miraculously the moon reappeared.

Lyon muttered a thanks to the gods as the eerie, golden glow of the moon showed him exactly the moves he should make to reach Jade's balcony. He took just two more steps, dragging himself upward with his muscled belly scraping against the wall, then grabbed the smooth, sharp edge of the balcony.

First he pulled himself up so that he could look into the window. The bedchamber was dark, as he expected it to be. Then Lyon pulled himself higher and, with much less noise than the wind whistling along the castle from the sea, tossed a leg over the balcony and pulled himself over the edge.

Lyon drew the slender dagger from the sheath at his belt as he crouched in the darkness, his heart hammering in his chest, all the muscles in his body aching with the exertion of the climb. Though his restless nature and instinct urged him to move directly into Jade's bedchamber, he remained kneeling outside on the balcony.

A minute passed, then two, and when five minutes had ticked by, Lyon's body was again refreshed; his muscles, toned and conditioned to perfection, again ready to do whatever was required of them.

In the darkness, a smile creased Lyon's mouth. His teeth, even and straight, gleamed white in the moonlight. The dimple in his left cheek, which he disliked and his *amours* found so delightfully boyish and charming, appeared.

On silent feet, he crept closer to the open window to look into the bedchamber. Idly, in the back of his mind, it occurred to Lyon that either Lord Charles or Baron von Mueller had a spy within the heavily fortified walls of Castle Crosse. Without a spy, how else would they have known that the suddenly obstinate Princess Jade had decided to move her bedchamber? This awareness didn't particularly surprise Lyon, but it did make him wonder whether there had been spies while he lived within the castle as a knight-in-residence, and whether there were any spies among his own superior fighting force.

A faint breeze played with the lacy yellow curtain, briefly pushing it inward into the room, then billowing it outward into Lyon's face.

Squinting his eyes to better see in the dark interior of the bedchamber, Lyon felt the racing of his heart. He knew with absolute certainty that he was a man of action, and that he simply was not ready to accept the life of a wealthy, serene squire. At least not yet. Not while there were wars to be fought and the hot blood of a soldier and knight still roiled in his veins. Someday he would settle down and seek comforts such as those he looked in upon, but not now, not yet.

He saw the bed, and was only mildly surprised that it was the largest bed he had ever seen. Though Lyon had shared the bed of several princesses so far in his life, he had never before seen one who had so large a bed, or so few possessions surrounding it.

The bed was massive, almost as though it was an altar, a religious shrine of some sort. The fact that there were very few other items of furniture in the room added to the illusion that the bed was a religious ornament of some sort.

The room appeared very large and ornate, but it seemed barren somehow, desolate and infinitely unhappy. The slumbering form of the princess, alone in that spacious bed with only a light cotton sheet to keep her warm, added to the sense of aloneness that pervaded the room.

Lyon twisted the handle of the dagger in his hand. He hoped it wouldn't be necessary to use force with Princess Jade. He had always believed that violence solved very few problems, and he found violence toward women was especially repugnant. But he also accepted the grim reality that often in life a man isn't given a choice on whether he wants to fight or not, that it is thrust upon him, and the only possible way he has out of his predicament is to fight his way out.

With his left hand, he brushed the curtain aside. His boots, the leather soft as butter, were soundless against the marble balcony. Princess Jade, in the bed, was fifteen feet away.

Lyon took another step, and at that exact moment, Jade muttered under her breath and sat upright in bed, twisting to kick her feet out beneath the blankets over the edge.

Every muscle in Lyon's body tensed and coiled. Like a gigantic wolf, he instinctively prepared himself for exactly the right moment to strike. But Jade, still unaware of his presence, had her back toward the silent intruder.

Lyon had hoped to catch her sleeping so that he could awaken her with a hand over the mouth, insuring her silence. Now, everything had changed. He was still more than ten feet away, and since she was now sitting at the edge of the bed, he would either need to walk around the bed or climb over it in order to get to her.

Either way he went gave Jade plenty of time to

scream. If she screamed, Lyon was a dead man, and he knew it.

He could not possibly scale down the wall quickly enough to escape, and making a leap for the water below would be suicide, since he would surely end up dashed against the rocks.

The seconds ticked by. Jade, calm and sleepy, rolled her head slowly around on her shoulders to loosen the tension-tightened muscles; Lyon crouched, unable to move forward without being heard, unable to retreat without being seen before the night could hide him.

Lyon watched as Jade pushed fingers through her long, faintly wavy blond hair. She whispered a sigh, and then twisted on the mattress, raising one knee up on it, as though she could not decide whether she should return to sleep or not. Lyon, now looking at her in profile, was confronted with the conflicting reality that he was looking at one of the most beautiful women in the world, but one who was possibly evil to the core.

Even in the plain silk nightgown she wore, she was an exquisite creature, especially with the glow of the moon playing over her features and giving her beauty an angelic quality.

Thoughts raced through Lyon's mind, chaotic and disjointed, moving from one extreme to another. How incredibly unseemly was it for a knight to have lustful thoughts about his own princess? he wondered. How foolish was he to be thinking lustful thoughts when death was just one short, feminine scream away?

Princess Jade pushed her hair back away from her forehead again. He watched her breasts rise up as she moved her hand backward to smooth away the troublesome but entirely appealing wavy tresses. When she dropped her hand sleepily into her lap, the breasts swayed slightly, briefly, enticingly. The thin, plain silk nightgown did absolutely nothing to mask or restrict Jade's physical charms. Even in the thin golden moonlight that streamed over Lyon's broad shoulders to touch lightly upon Jade, he could see the blunted rise that her nipples made in the silk.

Would they rise up to his touch? Were they sensitive?

Lyon clamped his jaws shut angrily with such force that his teeth hurt. What in the name of the Devil and all that must be avoided to preserve the blessed Soul was he doing thinking such wicked thoughts at a time like this?

Lyon had never lacked for female companionship, so it was entirely unlike him to be so thunderstruck by beauty.

Jade sighed again. Lyon realized then that he was holding his own breath for fear of discovery.

She turned just a fraction of an inch. Perhaps she had seen Lyon. Perhaps she was just stretching. Either way, it mattered little in the outcome. Lyon, with his life already greatly in jeopardy, made his move.

Better to die rushing into the fray than running away like a coward, he thought as he launched himself at his princess.

Chapter 3

Time seemed to move at a snail's pace, and Lyon was able to see and experience every subtle nuance of the attack.

He took just one long stride toward Jade, then leapt, launching his body over her huge mattress, his arms outstretched, tossing the deadly dagger aside to free both hands.

Jade either sensed or heard his presence, and the speed of her reflexes surprised him, though she wasn't fast enough to escape cleanly. As she looked over her shoulder at the pouncing figure, her eyes exploded wide, filled with fear and surprisingly anger.

She tried to get her feet to the floor, but the mattress was so high that she was required to hop completely off the bed to get footing. With her weight well back on the mattress, the quick forward movement was impossible.

Lyon's right hand caught Jade's shoulder, the strong fingers curling around smooth flesh, jerking her backward. At the same time, his left hand clamped tightly over her mouth as he pulled her down onto the mattress, dragging her toward the center of the bed.

"Silence!" Lyon hissed through clenched teeth, figuring that the princess, once caught, would immediately crease her struggles.

Lyon Beauchane, knight to the Castle Crosse, gave his loyalty to Princess Jade Crosse. That didn't really mean he knew her all that well; not if he assumed she would quit fighting so easily.

Instead of trying to get away, Jade spun on the bed, her bare feet flying as she tried simultaneously to kick him and to pull his hand off her mouth.

Lyon pulled her in tighter, her back now firmly against his ribs, his arm nearly completely encircling her. He tried to trap her legs with his own, but she was thrashing about too frantically for him to succeed on the first attempt. His hand over her mouth was tight, too tight, he thought, believing it a crime to ever be violent with a woman, and a sin to bruise such golden flesh. But he dared not release even an ounce of pressure or Jade would surely be able to pull free just enough to scream for the armed guards who would be stationed just outside the bedchamber door at all times.

Jade kicked her legs high again so that only her shoulders remained on the bed, trying this time to turn her body within the steel circle of Lyon's arm. She flailed blindly with her tiny fists, and was rewarded when she struck something solid and heard the muted grunt of pain.

"You're a wildcat, you are, m'lady," Lyon whispered angrily, his ears ringing from the punch he'd taken in the temple.

When she tried to open her mouth beneath his hand,

30

Lyon knew that she was going to bite him. Only the size of his hand, and the great strength of it, enabled him to squeeze her firmly enough to prevent her teeth from sinking deeply into flesh and bone.

Though the fight had lasted only three or four seconds, it seemed a decade to Lyon. All his senses, charged for battle and heightened by the tempting visions of feminine perfection preceding his attack, were ready for action of any variety. With Jade's thrashing body in his arms, he was vividly aware of the heat of her body, and the thinness of the silk nightgown that covered her. As she windmilled her fists, occasionally managing to strike him on the head or cheek or ear, he was keenly aware of the weight and firmness of her breasts against his forearm. When she kicked her feet high in the air for the third time in her attempt to spin free, Lyon watched, his chin near her shoulder, as the pale cream silk fell around her waist. For a moment in the moonlight he glimpsed the small, triangular thatch of soft brown hair that hid her womanhood.

It was seeing her so intimately that warned Lyon he had to end the fight now, before it was too late. He had not previously taken Jade's threat seriously, just as he had not fully realized the importance of his own mental dalliances when he looked at her. But now he knew how dangerous her beauty was, since it made him forget the danger he was truly in. His left hand came away from her waist, but before she could do more than spin in his grasp to face him on the bed, he had recovered his dagger and touched the sharp silver blade lightly to her throat.

"Not a sound, m'lady, or I will kill you," Lyon said, his tone soft and decisive at the same time, indicating that he really would carry out his threat unless Jade followed his every command.

It was all an idle threat. Lyon could not kill his own princess, no matter what offense she had committed. He did not, however, do anything to indicate this as he looked straight into her large, round, frightened eyes.

Lyon was on his back, with Jade laying halfway upon him. He pushed her off him gently, rolling her onto her back on the mattress. She pushed her nightgown down from her waist, but it was still bunched up at the tops of her thighs, and Lyon did not miss the opportunity to take a long look at them.

"Remain very quiet," he said, moving just enough so that he was free to move if necessary, yet close enough to Jade so that he could whisper to her. "I don't wish to hurt you. I wish only to talk. Do you understand?"

Jade's heart was pounding furiously in her breast. She looked into the eyes of the intruder, thinking at first that surely this was the most handsome executioner the world had ever produced. His looks, though, could not soften the fact that he had the razor-sharp blade of a dagger lightly touching her throat, and with not much more pressure and a quick flick of his wrist he could silently kill her.

She placed her hands lightly on his chest, then recoiled, not wanting to touch this intruder. Suddenly, her brows furrowed, and her eyes flew open wide once again.

"Knight Beauchane! Lyon Beauchane!" she whispered, stunned that a knight would do such a dastardly thing as sneak into her bedchamber and assault her. In her confusion, it didn't even occur to Jade to question how he had gotten into her room.

"The very same," Lyon said, pleased that she still recognized him after all these years. "And you will please excuse the bluntness of this visit, m'lady, but I really must speak with you. You have been keeping yourself rather detached from us lowly servants lately."

He smiled then, and his dimple showed itself. Jade looked at that dimple, then into his sparkling blue eyes, and wondered what bizarre circumstances had converged that would have forced a knight of Sir Lyon's standing to behave in such a criminal fashion. Surely, he had to know that sneaking into her bedchamber in the black of night was an offense that warranted a public execution at worst, or a severe flogging in the public square, at the very least.

She did not like being so near him, especially when she wore so little, but she did not dare do anything that might upset him. Though he smiled at her, he kept the blade of the dagger very near her throat. Jade, without ever taking her gaze from Lyon's, slipped her hands down the front of her body and as covertly as possible pushed the bottom of her nightgown down to the tops of her knees. She still was a long way from being modestly attired, but she didn't feel quite so vulnerable with the nightgown covering her thighs.

"What do you want from me?" she asked. Then, though she knew it was a mistake, her stubbornness came to the forefront, and she said, "You'll be sorry you came back. I don't know what you have planned, but you'll never get away with it."

She saw the anger spark in his blue eyes and knew that she had made a mistake by challenging the traitorous knight, but Jade did not care. If she was going to be killed, then she would rather die regal and

33

defiant in spirit.

She had never begged, and she would not start now.

"Choose your words carefully, m'lady," Lyon replied. He pushed himself to a sitting position, moving lithely. Despite his size, his moves were quick and light, like a cat. "There have been people who have suffered greatly because they did not choose their words prudently when addressing me. And keep your voice down. I do not wish to be disturbed by your guards. I have much to discuss, and not many hours until the sun rises."

Jade had begun to calm down slightly. She was on her back on the bed with her legs dangling over the edge of the mattress. Lyon sat with his legs folded beneath him, the deadly dagger held at the ready in his hand, though he no longer kept it at her throat. It was when Jade watched Lyon's gaze drift briefly from her face down to her scantily concealed bosom, then back to her face again, that her momentary calm was shattered. She tried to sit up, but a strong hand on her shoulder prevented this.

"You can talk just as well from that position, and you present much less a threat," Lyon said, the warm twinkle in his eyes giving him a boyishness that had not been there before. In his mind, he knew that Princess Jade presented the greatest threat of all if she remained on her back, her lushly rounded breasts rising and falling with her shallow, frightened breathing; the thin silk of her nightgown covering her form but not in any way hiding the enticing figure beneath.

"What do you want to talk about?" Jade asked, her voice not sounding as calm as she wanted it to.

This conversation, she thought, was nothing but an

34

imitation of polite discussion. While looking into Lyon's eyes, she crossed her arms over her bosom to hide herself, and the brief, flickering smile she received from the knight told her that he understood why she had placed her arms so.

"Taxes, mostly," Lyon replied. "Taxes, and the way you've been treating your serfs since the death of Prince William."

He thought of mentioning the attacks upon villages within von Mueller's enfeoffment, then discarded it. First she would answer for transgression upon her own people; there was time to add to the charges against her later.

"Treating the serfs? I've treated them the same as always. Everyone knows that I come from humble parentage," Jade said, her tone pure and honest, her eyes showing the confusion she felt at the accusation. There was also a touch of pride in her declaration of coming from common stock. "It is the villeins who have treated me differently since the death of my husband."

Lyon chuckled softly, shaking his head. He clearly did not believe her, and she sensed that if he had been impudent toward her before, he was openly scornful of her now.

"How *they* treat you? Ha! And I suppose it is the serfs who have raised taxes levied against *you* that *you* cannot possibly afford to pay? I suppose you want me to believe that it is the serfs who have sent men riding into your home in the dead of the night to terrorize and intimidate you, drag you away, never to be heard from again? The *serfs* haven't done that to you, m'lady, but *you* have done that to *them!*"

Jade's discomfort at her indecent wardrobe vanished. She was now listening to Lyon intently, hearing the confusing accusations he was making. Could this knight possibly believe that she was responsible for such things?

"Knight Beauchane, I assure you, I have never ordered anyone to be taken from their home in the night," she said quietly.

She wanted to sit up, but rather than trying a second time, she thought asking would please the intruder more. In the back of her mind, though, Jade promised herself that someday she would make Lyon pay for intimidating her so outrageously. It wasn't merely a desire for revenge that motivated her; Jade just didn't want any other woman to suffer the indignities that she now had to endure.

"May I please sit up?"

Lyon nodded. When Princess Jade sat upright at the edge of the bed, he watched the movement of her breasts beneath the silk, and a sudden burst of desire exploded in his chest. With a sweep of his hand, he indicated that he wanted Jade to sit in the middle of the bed. She shot him a suspicious look, thinking the worst.

"I will not accost you, m'lady," he said with a strained smile curling his sensual mouth.

"Again, you mean."

She saw the glint of anger spark in his blue eyes, and it pleased Jade that she had been able to touch him inside with her words. It was a dangerous game to taunt and tease this dagger-wielding intruder whenever the opportunity presented itself. But to do otherwise, to accept her fate passively and meekly, was something too contradictory to Jade's nature to even consider.

"If you were assaulted, then, if you can prove your innocence of other charges, I will throw myself upon your feet and ask for your mercy," Lyon said, his words striking Jade like tiny chips of ice thrown in her face. "If you are guilty of the crimes you have been accused, then, you will not be alive long enough to accuse me of any wrongdoing before a tribunal."

Jade looked away. She could not continue to look into Lyon's eyes. She had known many hard men who had fought battles and who knew the horrors and senseless slaughter of war, but she had never before met a man who so succinctly represented danger.

She had heard men brag of their conquests and victories on the field of battle. Her husband had been among the worst of the braggarts, and she had learned that the stories were empty tales that lacked any substance. It was hearing Sir Lyon's voice and looking deep into his icy blue eyes that convinced Jade that this knight did not boast of his victories because he had no need to lie. So when he made a threat, it carried great substance, and Jade believed the threat as though her life depended upon it.

She curled her knees beneath herself, folding her hands in her lap after pulling her nightgown well over her knees.

"What do you want of me?" she whispered, not looking up.

The anger that had blazed in Lyon only a second earlier vanished instantly. When Jade had pulled her nightgown down over her knees, the silk was pulled low and tight across her bosom. Now, in the dim moonlight, he was able to see the velvety inner swells of her breasts in the cut of the neckline.

His mouth went dry. The continuing mood changes that he was going through perplexed him.

"Princess Jade," Lyon said, pausing to moisten his lips. "I would be most happy if you would choose your words more carefully."

Jade's cheeks colored at the sexual innuendo, and for only an instant she squeezed her eyes tightly shut. Why did this have to happen to her?

"I will do what I can," she said icily.

Jade looked up into Lyon's face, and she saw the direction of his gaze. Her first reaction was to cover her bosom with her arms again, but a wiser part of her resisted it. If how she looked and what she wore distracted this intruder enough so that she might escape, then she would let him look at her however long he wanted.

This awareness that her beauty gave her some power over her male adversary filled Princess Jade with condescension toward Lyon Beauchane in particular, and all men in general. Such fools they all were to be so incensed and made stupid by feminine charms!

She gave Lyon the faintest suggestion of a smile then. It was only a matter of time, she told herself, before Lyon did something foolish that would allow her to escape. For now, he had positioned himself between her and the door. That fact, Jade believed, was only a temporary inconvenience. She was certain she could maneuver him to suit her wishes.

"Tell me now of your accusations," Jade said in a conversational tone, as though she were sitting upon her ornate receiving throne, the one in the grand ballroom she sat in when she accepted travelling dignitaries, or when she listened to disputes among the serfs. "Tell me all of them, and I will tell you the truth."

"You say that in such a way as to accuse me of lying."

"I say that in such a way as to indicate that you have heard things which may not be true. I alone know my own truth. And since you have come seeking that truth . . . and since you hold a dagger in your hand . . . then truth is what I will give you." Her eyes locked onto Lyon's, and when she spoke again, there was no mistaking the challenge in her voice or the strength in her spirit. "And when you have finished, Knight Beauchane, there have been a number of tales that I have heard which require clarification."

Jade listened to Lyon tell her what he had heard, and the stories appalled her. Murder. Intimidation. Rape. Burning homes. Extortion and taxes so high no serf could possibly hope to pay them. And all of it was being blamed on Princess Jade Crosse, and her sudden quest for massive wealth and power now that she was a widow and in complete control of Prince William Crosse's fields and fortune.

"It is a lie! All of it!" Jade said at last. "I have not done any of those horrible crimes that you accuse me of. It is the serfs who have turned upon me, good sir! Why, upon Bishop Fields's request, I even had to move my bedchamber to the seaward side of the castle so that I would be protected! The bishop was afraid that an archer could reach my bedchamber window with an arrow."

Lyon snorted in disgust, looking away. It wasn't easy blocking out the exquisite, beguiling sensuality that Jade exuded. He needed to concentrade on her words, but that was very difficult, especially when every instinct in him was screaming to take her into his arms and shower her with kisses.

Concentrate! She's had poor peasants killed for no greater offense than voicing their disapproval for having their taxes raised! Lyon silently told himself.

"If you are receiving advice from Bishop Nathan Fields, then you are being guided by a treacherous man with no loyalties to anyone but himself," Lyon said sharply, angry with himself and with Jade for making clear thought so difficult to maintain.

"Bishop Fields is a man of the cloth," Jade shot back defensively. Even though she had begun to have some grave doubts concerning the bishop's fealty to his faith, and to silently question his advice, she felt morally obligated to defend him.

"Bishop Nathan Fields," Lyon said slowly, biting the words out between clenched teeth, "is a man for himself."

Jade glared at Lyon. She had heard the stories of what kind of man Lyon was. You couldn't be a part of her fiefdom, nor live in or near Castle Crosse, without hearing the almost legendary stories of the prowess of Knight Lyon Beauchane, with both women and weapons.

She glanced at him, thinking that she could understand why maidens had fallen prey to his seductive charms. There was something about Lyon that touched a woman deep inside, in a special place that usually never made itself known.

"You speak the truth when you tell tales of night raids?" Jade asked quietly, after a long silence between herself and the intruder.

"Aye, m'lady, I speak the truth. Though I have been

away at war, I have been given the tale by men of unquestionable integrity. If they say it is so, then it is so."

"And who might these examples of virtue be?" Jade asked with just a hint of condescension in her voice.

"Concerned men. Good men. That is all you need know."

Jade made a sound in the back of her throat and looked away, momentarily dismissing Lyon. She felt his anger and felt his eyes upon her. Surprisingly, she was not nearly as offended as she felt she should be at his intrusion into her private world.

"You have more questions than answers, Knight Beauchane," Jade said. "Perhaps you'd like to hear what has been said about you?"

Lyon's eyes narrowed. "And perhaps you'd like to tell me."

Jade then told of what she had heard. They were ridiculous tales that no one who really knew Lyon believed, but the fact that a good percentage of the stories were being circulated by Bishop Fields lent them at least some semblance of credibility. While Jade told of how she had heard that Lyon, during his battles abroad in the name of Prince William, had ordered the slaughter of a small village of women and children, she saw a muscle twitch in his jaw, and saw the seething anger glinting in his blue eyes.

"I would never slaughter women and children," Lyon said. The brittleness in his tone was the most noticeable sign that the vile accusations of barbarism bothered him deeply. "Ask any man who has ever served with me and you will know that I would never command or allow my troops to do such things."

41

Jade nodded and pushed a thick strand of blond hair behind her ear to keep it away from her face. "True or not," she said, "it is being spoken. Many people believe lies as readily as they believe the truth."

"Especially if those lies are being told by a princess?"

The moment that Jade was to answer, the knock at her bedchamber door silenced her. Suddenly, the reality of her predicament came back to her and she again realized the danger that she was in, especially when Lyon moved soundlessly off the bed and crouched low, holding the dagger at his side, in position to strike with immediate, deadly certainty if the need presented itself.

"M'lady Jade, are you all right in there?" came the female voice through the door.

Chapter 4

Lyon looked at Jade questioningly. He touched a forefinger to his lips, indicating he wanted her to keep her voice low while still answering his unspoken questions.

"It is my servant," Jade whispered, still sitting in the middle of her bed, her eyes wide with fear.

Lyon looked from Jade to the door, then back again, torn between what he should do. He had not expected her to be disturbed at this late hour.

"M'lady Jade, are you not feeling well?" Mary Ellen asked, her voice louder than before. "Is there anything you'd like me to get for you?"

Jade tried to speak, but her throat was constricted with fear.

"Answer her, woman!" Lyon whispered. He could hear the impatience in the servant's tone, though it surprised him more than just a little that the servant hardly sounded at all humbled toward the princess.

Mary Ellen knocked on the thick door to Princess Jade's bedchamber once more and asked, "Must I come in, m'lady?"

Under his breath, Lyon cursed all the gods on Earth and in Heaven. Why wasn't Princess Jade saying anything? Her silence would force the servant to enter the bedchamber, and once she'd done that, there was no hope for him to escape. He was four floors from the main floor of Castle Crosse, making it impossible for him to fight his way out.

Hasty flight through the balcony and scaling down the castle wall was beyond the realm of possibility, especially with the moon occasionally hidden behind clouds.

In a single, horrifying second, Lyon pictured himself trying to fight his way past the guards, moving down long, winding corridors, watching as more soldiers came forward into the fray. He saw himself falling beneath their swords.

"M'lady, if you don't answer me now, you'll leave me no choice but to enter!" Mary Ellen said sharply.

Lyon almost tossed himself onto the bed then. He grabbed Jade's ankle and dragged her off the bed, heedless of her nightgown which was pushed up to her waist once again. As he pushed her toward the bedchamber door, he kept his left hand tight around her wrist. He touched the tip of his dagger to her back, just beneath her ribs.

"Betray me, m'lady, and I will be the last of your servants you betray."

Jade felt the dagger at her back, and it turned the blood to ice in her veins. As she reached for the door, it was suddenly opened from the outside. Jade placed her bare foot in the way of the door to keep it from being opened more than just a few inches. She had to bite her

44

lip to keep from crying out in pain when the heavy door scraped against her bare toes.

She stuck her face into the opening and attempted a smile for her servant's benefit. "What's the matter, Mary Ellen?"

The look she received told Jade that her servant could not be trusted. Mary Ellen looked sleepy, suspicious, and angry at having been disturbed. She clearly was not at all concerned with Jade's welfare.

"The guard woke me," Mary Ellen said, pushing a bit at the bedchamber door, trying to open it more so that she could see inside. She was unable to move it past Jade's foot. "He said he was hearing voices from your chambers." Mary Ellen's narrow eyes inspected Jade's face critically. "A *man's* voice."

Jade's hands were trembling and she held tightly onto the door. Only the thickness of the door separated her servant from her captor, and though she had no love for nor trust in Lyon Beauchane, she also had no trust in Mary Ellen, who was becoming less servile with each passing day.

"Is that so?" Jade raised her eyebrows and tried to laugh, but she failed miserably. The odd, strained sound that came from between her lips was foreign to her own ears. "Perhaps we should check to see what the guard had put into his stomach, and then we'll find out why these silly things have come into his head?"

Mary Ellen did not smile at all. She pushed at the door again, harder than before. Her eyes bore into Jade's challengingly. "You're sure you're alone in there?"

"Are you doubting the word of your princess?" Jade asked, struggling for but not quite reaching the imperious tone she wanted. "Are you questioning whether I have a man in my bed?"

Jade had expected the servant to be cowed by the threats and accusations, but she wasn't. Mary Ellen, instead of backing down under Jade's implicit threat, just squared her shoulders a little more, and appeared even more annoyed and suspicious. Never before, since becoming Prince William's bride, had Jade been treated in such an openly contemptible manner, and she could only wonder what power was behind Mary Ellen to give her the courage to behave so brazenly.

"I'm only concerned for you, m'lady," Mary Ellen explained with little conviction in her tone.

"Fine," Jade replied, thinking that surely Mary Ellen would sense Lyon's presence just on the other side of the door. If that happened, then Jade was certain that the dagger now merely touching her ribs would draw blood. "Then I'll thank you for your concern, and excuse you now, since I would like to return to my bed."

"The voices, m'lady . . . even I heard voices," Mary Ellen continued, her palm flat against the door as she pushed against it once more. "I had my ear to the door, and I know what I heard."

Jade could feel panic rise slowly and inexorably within her.

"You heard me talking in my sleep, if you really must know. It is embarrassing to have to admit that, so I'll thank you to keep that information to yourself." Jade felt Lyon's fingers tighten around her left wrist, which was hidden from Mary Ellen's view. She knew what the additional pressure indicated. "Go to bed now, Mary Ellen, and I'll do the same."

"Yes, m'lady," Mary Ellen said. She took her hand off the door, and the final look she gave Jade was filled with more than mere suspicion, it carried contempt, and something more.

Jade looked over Mary Ellen's shoulder and saw that a guard was standing in the shadows, watching her with large eyes, looking at her with lustful intentions as she stood partially revealed in the doorway wearing the thin nightgown.

Jade shut the door, then closed her eyes, leaning forward so that her forehead was against the smooth, hard wooden surface.

"Very good, m'lady," Lyon whispered.

His lips were so close to Jade's ear that she felt the warmth of his breath, as well as the heat of his body passing through her silk nightgown. His hands were at her shoulders, his dagger already sheathed.

"You're a skilled liar. It is a skill that does not particularly surprise me to discover you possess, though I am thankful for it nonetheless."

He took a quarter step closer to Jade, his long, lean body touching her now along the full length of her. She felt the heat of him, and sensed his vitality and his virility.

"I've done as you asked," she replied in a whisper that was so soft Lyon was forced to lean over her to hear. She was deathly afraid of Mary Ellen's return. "Can't you leave now? I promise, I'll never tell a soul that you were in here. It'll be our secret."

Jade kept her eyes shut as she waited for Lyon's response. She could feel all the places along her body where he touched her. Perhaps under other circumstances, she would have been excited at the warmth of

47

so virile and handsome a man touching her, especially since she had been so lonely. But as it was, her mind kept going back to the talk she'd had with Mary Ellen.

There could be no doubting that Mary Ellen held allegiance to someone other than Princess Jade. Her thinly disguised undercurrent of scorn had been there for some time, and tonight it had been revealed in all its naked, appalling existence. She did not trust Lyon, or believe the horrifying stories that he had told her. But she could not trust her servant either, since Mary Ellen had openly admitted that she had her "ear to the door."

Had the vile stories of Lyon's sexual excesses and war atrocities all been a lie by Bishop Fields? If those stories weren't lies, then why hadn't Lyon returned straight away to Castle Crosse to present himself to his princess, as would be expected of a knight upon his return from battles abroad?

"Come, Jade, we must speak further," Lyon whispered, his hands resting lightly on her shoulders. He could feel her body tremble softly and sensed accurately how frightened and confused she was. "When the sun rises, there can be no confusion over which of us speaks the truth and which of us believes in rumors and lies."

"I'm so confused," Jade whispered truthfully. "I . . . I'm tired of thinking . . . tired of worrying all the time about what is happening."

His hands moved in a kneading motion, first at her shoulders, then moving higher to the nape of her neck. Jade sighed softly as the handsome knight's long, strong, skilled fingers worked loose the tension-knotted muscles in her neck.

"My friends . . ." Jade began, then her words trailed off as the soothing relief of Lyon's ministrations crept through her. The tip of her pink tongue stole slowly around her mouth to moisten her lips before she tried again to speak. "The girls that I grew up with, they all think that I've led such a magic existence." She made a short laughing sound of derision. "If they only knew the truth."

She felt Lyon turning her so that she had her back to the door and faced him. She did not have the strength or the desire to argue with him, to deny him. When he moved her just one step to the side to look for the bolt to lock the door, she smiled a sleepy, disillusioned smile.

"It's gone," she whispered in answer. "I asked Bishop Fields about it, but he said that as the mistress of Castle Crosse, there was no need for me to bolt my bedchamber door. Nobody, he said, would dare step foot in my room without my permission." She issued another short, bitter laugh. "Clearly, he was mistaken."

"Perhaps he was not mistaken at all . . . in his intent," Lyon replied, also in a whisper, aware that Mary Ellen had her ear to the door before and might again.

To hear the defeat in Jade's tone tore little holes in Lyon's soul. Though he still suspected her of the worst crimes against the serfs in her fiefdom, it was now apparent that she was entirely acting on her own, and that she was not completely happy about the changes that had occurred in her life since the death of her husband. As much as anything else, it was the servant's attitude and the fact that the bedchamber bolt had been removed that proved to Lyon that Jade was not all-

49

powerful within the heavily fortified walls of her own castle.

Jade leaned back against the door, her face turned away from Lyon. He had never before stood quite so close to her while she faced him, and the impact upon his senses was intoxicating. A full foot taller than she, he looked down at her, his gaze taking in all of her, drinking in her beauty slowly as a connoisseur would savor a vintage wine.

She was a study of contrasts that beguiled his senses and tantalized his curiosity. He knew that she possessed great wealth, yet she wore a shapeless old nightgown that had seen many better days. The nightgown was of the finest quality silk, yet was unembroidered with anything extra to lend it feminine grace.

"My lady . . . if we are to speak, as we must, then we must . . . move from the . . ."

Lyon paused, unable to speak more, his throat constricted by a whirling flame of raw desire that burned through his veins.

His hands, large and strong, rested lightly on Jade's slender shoulders, the tips of his fingers an inch from the collar of the filmy nightgown. All he would need to do was curl his fingers into the neckline, and with just a fraction of his strength rent it apart. He would shred the nightgown and reveal at last the naked splendor of his princess.

Hardly had the thought entered his head when self-revulsion gripped Lyon by the throat. Perhaps other men would resort to violence to satisfy their carnal hungers, but he did not.

She turned her face toward him then, her eyes large,

50

round, softly amber, full of confusion and hurt. "Move?" she asked softly. "Move where? I cannot take a step without someone following me. It is all for my own protection, I am told . . . but sometimes I wonder."

On only a few occasions in Lyon's life did he feel truly protective toward a woman, but that was how he felt now. He realized that Princess Jade needed his help, and he felt so guilty for wanting to take her into his arms, to remove that old nightgown from her with tender ease, and to make sweetly passionate love to her for days on end.

"The balcony," Lyon whispered, bending down to speak directly into her ear. When he did so, he was able to catch the aroma of her body, the smell of her hair, and to spy a brief, moonlit glimpse of pale and smooth flesh, beneath her neckline.

He looked away instantly, as though burned by a flame much too dangerous to toy with.

He took Jade's small hand into his own and guided her through the bedchamber out past the heavy curtain and onto the balcony. A warm breeze played with Jade's long, wavy tresses and molded the silk nightgown more snugly to her form. The moonlight cast directly down upon her, and to Lyon's chagrin, he discovered that her beauty was even more undeniable on the balcony than in the dark bedchamber.

Lyon positioned himself so that he could still see the bedchamber door. Should Mary Ellen return, he could hide behind the wall, or perhaps in the curtains. He continued to hold Jade's hand in his, and he played the pad of his thumb softly back and forth across her knuckles.

"I have been gone many years," Lyon said, speaking

51

at least in a nearly normal tone now that he was well away from the door. "In the time that I have been gone, you have changed from a child bride full of promise to a woman who has honored that promise."

A vaguely defeated smile pulled at Jade's ripe, full-lipped mouth. "A woman who suddenly feels much older than she ever dreamed she would be."

Jade was aware of the touch of Lyon's thumb, of his holding her hand, and of the way his eyes occasionally strayed from her face down to her bosom. She no longer felt like fighting him. She didn't feel like fighting anybody. No cause was great enough for that. She had tried so hard to remain happy in these troubling days since Prince William's demise.

I'm tired of fighting, Jade thought. I'm tired of wondering who is really my friend, and who is my enemy. I'm tired of looking into people's eyes and wondering what their motives really are.

She saw Lyon's hand come into view, and only then realized that she had been looking down while she thought, staring at the toes of Lyon's boots. He touched her chin with a fingertip, tilting her head up so their eyes met.

"If you are as innocent as I now believe you are, then you will act immediately to correct some of the injustices that have been perpetrated upon your people in your name," Lyon said as he looked down at her.

His fingertips trailed lightly from her chin, down the velvety expanse of her throat to her shoulder.

Was there another woman in the whole world with skin so soft? Repressing the urge to taste that skin and to kiss her mouth, throat, and shoulder was profoundly disturbing to a man of Lyon Beauchane's hotly passionate nature.

"When I left to fight your husband's battles for the Crown, you were respected by your people. They loved you and considered you one of their own. They don't feel that way about you now, but they will again if you will only do what you can to prove to them that you're not the—" The word "wench" came to mind, but Lyon bit it off before it escaped. "The cruel tyrant they believe you have become."

As she listened to him speak, the spirit fluttered slowly back to life in Jade's heart. She pushed Lyon's hands from her shoulders and took another step backward to put more distance between herself and the knight. She felt the marble railing surrounding the balcony against her buttocks, and the coolness of the marble reminded her of how little she wore.

"This evening has turned into a nightmare, Knight Beauchane," Jade said, keeping her voice a bit more quiet than a normal conversational tone, but still angry. "And you have been an integral part of that nightmare! Yes, it is true that apparently some things have been happening within the fiefdom that I have been unaware of. This does not mean that people I count on to give me advice are responsible, nor does it mean that everything *you* have heard must be accepted as undeniable truths!"

Jade's anger was rising, and she embraced it. The depression and helplessness she had felt just moments earlier vanished like smoke, replaced by her natural combativeness.

"If you are all that you say you are, if you are as concerned about your duty as you would like me to believe, then why haven't you come to me, your princess, upon your return from the wars? How is it you, who has sworn an oath of loyalty to my husband and myself, has not asked me what has been happening within my borders, but has chosen instead to *accuse* me of atrocities of the worst kind?"

Though it was clear that Princess Jade was getting angrier by the second, Lyon could not keep the fragment of a smile from playing across his mouth. He much preferred to see her angry and defiant rather than looking wounded by circumstances and a life that she really had not chosen for herself.

Seeing his smile heightened Jade's annoyance. She pushed her unbound hair away from her face, oblivious of how her breasts moved beneath the nightgown as she moved, and stepped closer to Lyon.

"You find all this humorous, Knight Beauchane? Might I remind you that if I am the monster that you accuse me of being, I would have you flogged in the public square on the morrow!"

"There is an element of humor in all of this now, but I assure you that it has nothing to do with public floggings." The smile vanished from his face, and the amused brightness in his eyes disappeared behind an icy mask of scorn. "But your threats do prove that the years, and the power you wield over people, has changed you, m'lady."

Jade watched as Lyon's eyes went up and down over her. To her surprise, when their gazes met again, he issued a dismissive sneer, indicating that he did not hold a favorable opinion of what he saw. Jade again crossed her arms over her bosom, but pride prevented her from taking even a single step backward.

"The last time I saw you, Princess Jade, you beckoned me and my men to ride victoriously into battle. We were, you said so many years ago, the pride of Castle Crosse. And now, after fighting so many battles and killing so many men at the behest of you, your husband, and the bloody crown, you tell me I should be flogged at the square on the morrow."

Lyon sneered derisively at Jade, and for only a moment she suspected that if he did not have such powerful self-control, he would strike her. She realized that all she need do was scream for the guard and Lyon would be tossed over the balcony and shattered on the rocks below.

I am not a murderess, and I will not be intimidated by a knight . . . no matter how handsome or deadly he looks, Jade thought, squaring her shoulders and tilting her jaw slightly upward defiantly.

In a clear, even, faintly imperious voice, Jade replied, "I in no way intended to insult or deny your achievements in the past. I merely refer to the simple and undeniable fact that you have broken into my bedchamber and accosted me in my own bed. You can hardly deny, after putting your dagger to my throat, that you tried to kill me."

Lyon moved very quickly. His long, black cape trailed behind him, flapping softly like ebony wings. He took Jade by the upper arms and shook her hard.

"Accost you? Tried to kill you? My dear lady, if my intention had been to kill you, you would not be complaining to me of it now. Those people I intend to kill never complain to anyone again."

Jade stepped backward, shocked at the sudden and mercurial mood change that this traitorous knight was

55

capable of. Only the marble, waist-high railing halted her retreat as her mind rapidly calculated the odds of her being able to escape back into her bedchamber to call the guards, before Lyon Beauchane bodily tossed her over the railing and into the blackness of the night beyond.

"I went to war," Lyon continued slowly, looking at Jade now in a way that made his throughts unreadable. "I fought for your honor, and the honor of my country. And now you look at me as though it shocks you to discover that I know how to kill. If killing is something I've learned then kindly remember that it's a skill I acquired for your benefit, because you and people like you have found it profitable or politically prudent to have me kill."

"T-that's not true!" Jade replied, stammering in her haste to utter the denial. "I abhor violence! Everyone knows how I detest violence!"

"Perhaps you should tell your serfs how you detest violence. In Richland, a mother still cries because her young son was killed by riders in the night."

"Riders? What riders? What colors did they wear?" Jade demanded.

"They wore no silks. But their armor was shiny and polished, of the finest quality, like the armor of the knights under your command, m'lady. And if you request them to remove their silks and plumes and ride without blazon, then how would these men ever be recognized behind their face shields?" Lyon slipped the dagger from its sheath at his left hip. He touched the point to his fingertip, testing its sharpness in a threatening manner. "It seems her son, not yet fourteen, voiced his opposition to being forced into being a stable boy for none other than Princess Jade's mounted soldiers."

The blood drained from Jade's face. She knew the village of Richland, knew many of the serfs who lived there. When she asked Lyon for the name of the boy, he refused to give it to her, suspiciously questioning if she would have the boy's mother murdered as well.

She wondered if everything he was proclaiming was a lie. Might there not be more than just a grain of truth in the awful tales he told? And if Lyon Beauchane did tell the truth, then men in her castle were not merely lying to her, but were murdering villagers as well, and turning those villagers against her!

"What can I do to convince you that I am not guilty of these awful crimes?" Jade asked, her voice quivering slightly.

She could imagine what the villagers of Richland must think of their princess if they believed she ordered a young boy to be murdered before his own mother's eyes. Tears glistened in her eyes as she thought about the horror the boy's loving mother must have experienced.

Her gaze became distant as she recalled how she had visited Richland during the planting season two years ago. The villagers lined the streets and cheered for her enthusiastically. In that tiny village, two girls, born that year, had been named Jade in honor of Princess Jade Crosse.

Crystal tears spilled from her eyes.

"Do your tears speak the truth of your heart?"

Jade blinked, and more tears slid slowly down her cheeks. Lyon's boots came into view as he stepped closer. She realized in an oddly disconnected way that they were Italian boots, and she wondered how far this roguish knight had travelled, and what adventures he had known.

The news of the boy's murder in the hamlet of Richland reminded Jade of how little she had travelled, and how wonderful it would be now travel far away to a land where nobody called her "Princess," and she could believe the words that people told her.

"You vex me, m'lady," Lyon said softly, the timbre of his voice deeply resonant and not just a little seductive. "One minute you're threatening me with public flogging, and the next minute you're crying over the death of a boy you did not even know."

"I might have known him." Jade said defensively, not sure if Lyon was still belittling her. "You wouldn't tell me his name."

"For the mother's protection," Lyon repeated.

Jade searched Lyon's face, looking deep into his eyes for compassion. If he had come to taunt her, then he was succeeding brilliantly. If he had come searching for knowledge, for the truth, then surely he had to see that she was not the kind of woman whose heart was icy enough to demand the murder of a child for a minor offense against her authority.

"You must believe me," she said in hushed tones. She approached Lyon, placing her palms lightly against the leather vest he wore over the white silk shirt. She turned a tear-streaked face up to his. "Please, you must believe me! If the people . . . if they turn against me . . . I have so little left. You don't realize this, but I never really did have much. My marriage to William, it wasn't . . . he couldn't . . . and money . . . money never mattered to me. I just wanted to be happy. It was

58

William who thought buying me gifts would take the place of the life we didn't really have . . ."

Looking down into her eyes, seeing the sincerity and honesty there, the last of Lyon's doubts vanished so completely it was as though he'd never had them at all. He cupped Jade's face lightly in his large hands, and with his thumbs wiped the tears away from her cheeks.

"Hush, Jade, don't cry."

He looked down at her, aching, suddenly, for a taste of her lips. Gone was the imperious bluster of a young princess who held complete power of life and death of all the subjects in her fiefdom within her small jeweled hands. Now there stood before Lyon just an exquisitely beautiful young woman, clad only in a clingy silk nightgown, with dishevelled hair that flowed over her shoulders and down her back in satiny waves of golden blond. A young woman who was frightened and perplexed by the world around her, a world that she no longer understood and was filled with faceless threats that lurked within the shadows of her nightmares.

"Please believe me. I'm not a bad person. I'm really not a bad person."

"I do believe you," Lyon replied in a passion-choked tone. "And you must never, ever think yourself a bad person. M'lady, you are a princess. You are *my* princess!" he concluded with a strangely possessive tone that had never been in his voice before.

She watched his face come down slowly toward her, his lips moist and inviting.

Chapter 5

Jade thought she should say something to prevent the kiss. She was a widow, after all, and though she was really no longer in public mourning, it was still terribly improper to allow a man like Sir Lyon Beauchane, whose reputation for having only transitory relationships with women was unequalled on the island called England, to kiss her.

It all seemed to happen so slowly. When Lyon's mouth was just a fraction of an inch from hers, he paused and whispered, "You mustn't cry, m'lady. It tears my heart in two to see you cry."

And then his lips were lightly touching her own, kissing away the moist, salty tears that had sprung unbidden from her eyes and trickled down her cheeks. She trembled softly, standing barefoot outside on the balcony, her hands at her sides. Lyon Beauchane kissed slowly from one side of her mouth to the other, kissing the tears from her lips. He held her face gently in his hands, tilting her head just slightly to one side for the most favorable angle for his pleasure.

This is madness, Jade thought with that corner of her mind that functioned perfectly, despite the despair in her heart, or the pleasure she felt at receiving Lyon's gentle kisses. This man is a knight, a man of violence, and I must have nothing to do with him. I should not let him near me, much less let him kiss me.

His mouth touched hers so softly, so gently, that Jade was barely able to feel the contact. But then, when the tears had been kissed away, she felt the tip of Lyon's tongue against her lips, tracing the outline of her mouth. His right hand slipped from the side of her face, moving around her neck, his fingers entwining themselves in the luxuriant mane of hair that trailed down her back. His left hand, too, moved away from her face, sliding down the smooth, taut length of her throat, and down further still to her shoulder, pushing aside the silk nightgown so that there would be nothing separating them.

The kiss deepened. Jade stood upon trembling legs, feeling a strange heat flame to life within her. Lyon's mouth slanted down over hers, pressing against her more firmly now; the seal perfect, taking her breath away. A low, throaty moan registered in Jade's ears, and it took a moment for her to realize that she had uttered the moan of passion herself.

"Never cry, Princess," Lade whispered, his lips nuzzling against Jade's as he spoke the few words.

She tried to tell him that she did not want to cry. All she really wanted from this world was to be happy, and to make the people in her life happy, but circumstances had conspired to make that impossible. She wanted to tell Lyon so many things, but all of those words seemed to get lost in the hazy fog that had been produced by his sweetly devastating kisses.

When the tip of his tongue again touched her lips, slipping gently between them, Jade opened her mouth just a little, very hesitantly. A moment later, Lyon kissed her more deeply, pulling her closer to him so that the hard, rough surface of his leather-vested chest was crushed against her breasts. He forced her mouth open wider, and Jade was not even aware of being forced until after the deed had been done. To Jade's extraordinary surprise, she curled her tongue around his, tasting him, touching him, shivering as a deep, moist warmth curled through her from head to toe.

"Princess, you are . . ." Lyon whispered, then was able to say no more. He caught Jade's full, lower lip between his teeth and bit softly. She gasped with pleasure, inciting the passion to burn even hotter in the knight's veins.

I must push him away, she silently vowed.

It was an annoying little voice within Jade's mind that whispered such impossibilities. She heard the voice and immediately discounted it.

Even if she wanted to, she could not possibly push away a man as tall, broad-shouldered, and powerfully built as Lyon Beauchane. That was the excuse she told herself, and she accepted the self-delusion heartily. It was less damning to her than to admit that the taste and feel of Lyon's mouth against her own had incited a passionate insanity that she had not even known was possible.

She felt his fingertips rubbing against the nape of her

neck, right at the base of her skull, and it seemed to make her entire scalp tingle. A low, rumbling purr of contentment worked its way up through Jade, finally reverberating from between her moist lips as Lyon kissed them.

She had never before known kisses could affect her senses so strongly. Her amorous occasions with her husband had been few and far between, and she had been very young. Too young, she often thought. But she was no longer too young, and her body, now ripely voluptuous and long neglected, was responding to the caresses of this battle-scarred knight with the gentle hands.

Lyon's other hand moved slowly around her shoulder, the palm dragging at her nightgown briefly before sliding around to the small of her back to pull her in tighter against his unyielding body. When her pelvis pressed against him, Jade felt the hard, prominent swell of his arousal straining to be freed from the confines of his garments. This awareness of his passion for her added a new element that she did not welcome.

"Wait!" Jade gasped, turning her face aside to break the devastating kisses that stole her breath away and made clear thinking absolutely impossible. "Wait! Knight Beauchane, this has got to stop! This has gone too far!"

The sound of her own voice sounded foreign to her ears, and, under these intimate circumstances, referring to Lyon in the formal manner sounded comical. Still, Jade raised her hands to his chest and tried to push away.

"Jade, don't," Lyon replied. Though he and Jade were saying very nearly the same words, their intent was at odds with each other.

"We can't!"

She pushed against his chest; his arm, still around her waist, prevented her from doing any more than breaking the contact of their upper bodies.

Jade's breasts felt very full and tight in a way that she had not experienced before, and she was pleased they were no longer in contact with the raspy surface of Lyon's chest and his leather vest. But by bending backward, her lower body was in even firmer contact with Lyon than before. There seemed to be no way to completely disentangle herself from sensations that threatened to strip away her sanity.

He had always seen himself as a gentleman. Perhaps Lyon had loved a bit loosely and recklessly, but he had never loved deceptively or destructively. But as he held Jade's thrashing body in his arms while she pushed against him, he could see the motion of her breasts beneath the nightgown, saw the nipples that had hardened and become elongated. Was it by fear or by passion? He could feel his own self-control straining and fraying, like the individual threads in a rope.

Jade's gaze met Lyon's, questioning, passionate, unsure amber eyes meeting fierce, confident blue ones.

Slowly, Jade relaxed the muscles in her arms, allowing Lyon to pull her against him again. The feel of him, the scent of him, the awesome awareness of his strength and virility became Jade's undoing, and made her sigh with joyous acceptance, tilting her head back and parting her lips to receive yet another deeply probing, enticing kiss from the too handsome and much too bold knight.

Jade's hands were still at Lyon's chest, though she no longer pushed against him trying to escape. Her body was suddenly aware of the possibilities of pleasure and sensuality; of the unspoken, instinctive reaction that happens when a man and a woman, destined for each other, at last are holding each other.

Hungry for all the sensations that she had been denied, Jade twisted her arms around Lyon's neck, rubbing her aching breasts against him as she rose on tiptoes. Boldly this time, she thrust her tongue into his mouth, and she felt him react to her boldness; first with momentary shock, then hungry acceptance of her forcefulness.

For Jade, it was as though she was someone else, because Princess Jade Crosse was simply not the kind of wanton woman who would behave so brazenly. Jade Crosse was not the type of woman to stand out on her own bedchamber balcony with a knight, kissing him deeply and moving her shoulders from side to side intentionally to rub her passion-hardened nipples against his chest!

But if it wasn't her on the balcony in Lyon's arms, then who was it? Or was it *really* her? Was this the *true* Jade Crosse, who had been denied and repressed for so long, who had just now come to life under Lyon's kisses and erotic caresses?

Jade pushed the unsettling thoughts away because she did not want to think. All she wanted to do was feel, and thinking got in the way of feeling.

She felt Lyon's hand slide downward from the small

of her back, his palm warm through the thin barrier of silk that separated them. When he cupped her buttocks in his strong hand and pulled her tighter against him, a fresh, new, pulsing heat seeped through her.

A hungry, empty, ravenous need for Lyon swept through her. The propriety of what she was doing no longer had any bearing upon her life. The code of her behavior was inconsequential, because she could not control or deny her needs. Lyon's powerful hand cupping and squeezing her bottom, pulling her in so that she pressed intimately against him, had acted as a catalyst to strip away the last of Jade's hesitation.

"You're a heady wine, m'lady," Lyon whispered.

Her eyes remained closed, her lips slightly parted and moist from Lyon's kisses.

Jade did not want to hear Lyon speak. His glorious lips were much better suited for kissing her. Without opening her eyes, she pulled at him, bringing him down once again. When his mouth slanted over hers, she parted her lips in sultry invitation, and she was not disappointed.

Jade felt Lyon moving her, turning her so that she leaned back against the marble railing that surrounded the balcony. Next she felt his hands at her wrists, pulling her hands away from his neck.

For only an instant, Jade thought that Lyon was going to stop kissing her. To her absolute surprise, she discovered that she was ready to protest.

At first she had not wanted Lyon to start. Now she was ready to do whatever was necessary to make sure he did not stop!

He lowered her hands to her hips while continuing

to kiss her. Then, with startling speed, he tugged at the shoulder of Jade's nightgown, pulling it down on one side, stretching the gaping neckline just enough to expose one plump, aroused breast.

"Oh!" Jade gasped, looking down, surprised to see her own breast glowing eerily, erotically in the moonlight.

She looked up into Lyon's face and thought once again that Lyon Beauchane was too handsome, too confident, to perfectly proportioned and well-muscled, for any woman to deny him long.

"You respond so sweetly," he said quietly, his gaze boring into Jade's.

She was unable to drag her eyes away from Lyon's. She watched him, confused and aroused, as he brought his thumb and forefinger to his mouth and moistened them.

"Watch," he instructed.

She was powerless to do anything but what he commanded. Her eyes, as though she had no will of her own, followed his hand to her breast. She watched the moist forefinger and thumb capture her nipple and pinch it softly, using just the right amount of pressure to draw the maximum amount of pleasure from her. Jade's legs began trembling, and she was certain that if she did not have the railing to lean back against, she would not be able to remain standing long.

"Such a passionate nature," Lyon said.

Passionate nature?

The words rang in Jade's ears. She had never before considered herself at all passionate. But then she had never been alone with Lyon Beauchane before. She had never enjoyed kissing a man before Lyon had taught her what it could really be like. Her body had never before felt like it was melting inside, as if she was ravenously hungry for something she did not entirely comprehend.

"Watch," Lyon commanded.

He cupped her breast from the underside to raise it, leaving the passion-darkened crest exposed. Jade watched herself physically respond as he rubbed his thumb over the tip, sending flames soaring through her. Then he bent down, and she saw his handsome face come into view.

He's going to kiss me there!

It had happened to her before, of course, with her husband long ago. But when it happened back then, in the ebony darkness of their bedchamber, it had only made her feel clammy. To be kissed there was just part and parcel of an unpleasant experience that she figured she was supposed to endure now that she was a married woman.

She watched his pink tongue flick out and graze against the tip. Being struck by lightning would have had a lesser impact upon her senses. A moment later, when through glassy eyes she watched Lyon's mouth open to take her breast between his lips, she instantly pushed her fingers through his long blond hair and hugged him to her breast.

Her knees trembled powerfully then, and though she tried to continue watching, her eyes drifted shut as the heat of Lyon's moist mouth suffused her senses, travelling completely through her. He heightened everything that she felt and changed forever her perception of what pleasure really could be.

She was still hugging Lyon, wanting to keep his mouth on her breast, when he suddenly stood upright and pushed Jade's hands from him.

"What have I done wrong?" she asked, not wanting anything to stop.

Lyon didn't say a word. He just turned away from Jade and leaped over the railing into the ebony darkness beyond!

Chapter 6

Jade's eyes rolled back in her head, and her knees finally did give out as she stared into the emptiness where Lyon had stood before hurling himself off the balcony. She slumped to her knees, oblivious to how hard her knees struck the balcony floor, or to how her elbow collided painfully with the railing as she went down.

Why would he suddenly leap to his death?

"M'lady, what's happened to you?" exclaimed Mary Ellen as she stepped onto the balcony.

Jade, numbed by the strange event that had just happened, turned dazed eyes up to her servant. The angry, condescending look she received from Mary Ellen let her know that there was still no love lost between them. Then she saw the tall guard looking down at her over Mary Ellen's shoulder, and she realized that her nightgown was still pulled down, exposing her breast.

None too gently, Mary Ellen adjusted the bodice to cover her mistress, then grabbed her by the elbow and hoisted her to her feet.

"You can leave," Mary Ellen said angrily to the guard, who was staring at Princess Jade with hungry eyes. "Get out now. She doesn't have anyone in here with her, she's just gone dithers! Go, curse you!"

The guard was grinning, still staring at Jade. From deep within herself she found a pocket of strength and stability, and she straightened her shoulders, shrugging Mary Ellen's hand off her elbow.

"Leave!" Jade commanded, raising her hand, pointing a finger toward the bedchamber. She looked at the guard as though she would have him flogged and beheaded, unless he did exactly as she said.

The guard's grin vanished, and he left the royal bedchamber nearly at a run.

Jade then turned to Mary Ellen, looking into her eyes, hoping to see some concern there, some sense of loyalty or duty in their depths. When she didn't, she wasn't surprised.

"And you may leave as well," Jade said with quiet resolve. "And on the morrow, even if Bishop Fields objects, there will be a bolt upon my bedchamber door so that this sort of invasion into my life will *not* happen again!"

Mary Ellen was not entirely cowed by Jade's anger. "I heard voices, m'lady. I heard you talking to someone. I had to see that you were not possessed of demons."

"Heard voices? You're hearing voices and yet you have the temerity to tell that guard that *I* am mad? I'm not mad, I'm furious!" Jade again pointed to her bedchamber door. "Leave, Mary Ellen, and in the future, you will show me respect in every word you speak and every action you take, or I will show you how far apart our stations in life truly are."

Mary Ellen glared openly at Jade. "Yes, m'lady," she said with very little respect in her tone.

Jade stood firmly in place until she was again alone in her bedchamber. Then she rushed out to the balcony to the spot where Lyon had leapt over.

A great elation swept over Jade when she saw Lyon's pale face, showing strain yet smiling, glowing in the moonlight. He was clutching onto the side of the castle wall, his body pressed flat against the jagged surface.

Jade realized then how he had gotten into her bedchamber, though it still surprised her that he could leap over the railing and still find sufficient handholds to stop his deadly plunge to the sea below.

"You nearly scared me to death," Jade whispered, leaning over the balcony, extending a hand toward Lyon.

He pulled himself up, and only when he was securely on the balcony did he take Jade's hand. He pulled her close, sliding his arms around her waist, and received a frosty look for his efforts.

"Stop now!" Jade hissed angrily through clenched teeth. "She's probably still got her ear to the door."

"Then we must make a point of being very quiet, mustn't we? Oh, well, that really isn't that much of a disadvantage, actually."

Lyon tried to kiss Jade, raising a hand to squeeze her breast through her nightgown at the same time. She pushed away from him, grimacing as he tried to kiss her, slapping his hand away with much greater strength than was necessary.

"Get away from me," she whispered, vastly angry

with herself for the things she had allowed to happen.

The relief that she had felt when she discovered that he had not, as she'd feared, had his beautiful body shattered on the rocks below was a two-edged emotion; Jade really didn't want to be *that* happy that he was still alive.

She looked over the balcony railing and her heart skipped a beat. Could he really climb the castle wall? It seemed a godlike feat, but Jade had already learned to accept the fact that Lyon was no ordinary man.

"Princess Jade . . . you have a very short memory," Lyon said, the timbre of his voice soft, intimate, and very seductive.

"And you've forgotten that *I* am Princess Jade Crosse, and *you* are my servant!"

He smiled more broadly then, and Jade wanted desperately to slap the smile from his face. He was so sure of himself, so confident in his charm and his seductive ways. Jade wished that he would be just a little insecure, like she was, perhaps even a little perplexed over the extraordinary reaction that had taken place between them minutes earlier.

He accepted a woman's unbridled response as commonplace, and this bothered Jade.

All she had to do was look into his smiling blue eyes to know that he was a man who had experienced the passion of many young women; so many that he was no longer surprised when even the most resistant women succumbed to his passion.

"You've gotten what you came for," Jade said, ending the silence that had sprung between them. She was suddenly aware that her words could be taken several ways, and when Lyon's smile broadened even

73

further, she knew that he was most definitely taking her words the *wrong* way. "You came for answers, and that's what you've gotten from me."

"I've gotten *your* side of the story. Nothing more. Whether you speak the truth has yet to be determined."

Jade was happy to see the smile slip from Lyon's face because it was infinitely easier to think logically when he wasn't smiling, when his damnable dimples weren't dancing in his cheeks.

"I can do no more than tell you the truth," she said. "I can't make you believe anything."

"You can prove to me you're truthful," Lyon said then. He paused, looking eastward. The sky held the faintest hint of pink. "It'll be morning soon. I'll leave, but I'll return tomorrow night. If you're here, and you're alone, then I'll know that you've been honest with me. If you're not here, or if there is a trap set for me, then the men who are most concerned with your behavior of late will know why I have not returned to them."

Jade was of two emotions when she heard that Lyon intended to see her again alone in her bedchamber the following evening. Propriety dictated that she say something against this plan, but she couldn't find sufficient desire to deny Lyon.

"I truly hope you have told me the truth," Lyon said, obviously concluding the conversation. He kicked a foot over the balcony railing, causing Jade to gasp with fear. "I'll be back tomorrow night. At midnight."

He disappeared. Jade went to the railing to watch him climb down, but she couldn't watch long. It was too frightening. She went back to her bedchamber and crawled between the blankets of her bed. She closed her

74

eyes, even though she knew that sleep was a long way off.

What had happened? Why had she responded to Lyon the way she had? Why hadn't she alerted the guards to his presence? Would she be waiting alone for him to return tomorrow evening at midnight, or would she set a trap and have the presumptuous knight arrested and thrown into the dungeon?

Jade tried not to think about Lyon's powerful sensuality, and just concentrate on the things that he had told her. Were villagers really being murdered? Was she really being blamed as the cause of those murders? Were villagers really being taxed and taxed again until they hadn't even enough money to feed their own families?

The sun had risen before fatigue at last claimed Jade, and she was able to drift into a shallow, disturbed sleep.

Chapter 7

"Are you hale, m'lady?"

Jade shot Mary Ellen a withering look that had little effect. "What makes you ask?" she replied, doing nothing to hide the anger she still felt toward her maid's churlish behavior the previous evening.

"You seem flushed and nervous. Is anything wrong?"

"Nothing is wrong."

"But last night—"

"I don't want to hear about last night!" Jade cut in crossly. "Not another word. Do you understand?"

Jade glared at the young maid, and the look Mary Ellen returned wasn't in the least bit abashed or frightened, although she did seem a little shocked at the forcefulness of the threat. Someone was behind this woman, paying her to spy, Jade decided. How else could a simple maid have such courage, such temerity? Blast! Maybe she was just imagining all of this, letting Lyon Beauchane's traitorous words distort reality so that she saw enemies where there were none.

"I don't wish to be disturbed just now," Jade said in a

slightly softer tone, no longer entirely sure of herself or her own emotions. The only things she was absolutely certain of was that she did not want Mary Ellen nearby. Not while she needed to think clearly. Mary Ellen distracted her by reminding her of a frightening episode in her life, one where Jade had behaved in ways she had not thought possible.

"But m'lady, you're late for your morning meal," Mary Ellen said. Loyal or not, she knew Jade's schedule, and it seldom varied. "You've got to eat to keep your strength up . . . especially after last night."

Amber flames shot from Jade's eyes, but she kept the angry words to herself. It would do no good antagonizing Mary Ellen. If she was, in fact, a spy for someone, then making her angry would accomplish nothing; if she wasn't a spy sent to keep an eye and ear on Jade, then making her angry would be entirely unwarranted.

"I told you that I didn't want to hear about last night."

Jade turned toward the balcony, smoothing her hair. She felt like walking out onto the balcony, but doing that meant standing too near the place where so many of her chaotic memories had originated. She balled her hands into small, futile fists and tapped them against her hips.

"Last night . . . was a nightmare. I had a nightmare and it scared me." Jade turned slowly toward her maid. "It scared me more than I care to admit. I guess that must be why I behaved so . . . strangely."

"Yes . . . of course," Mary Ellen replied unsympathetically. Mary Ellen moved a little closer to Jade, studying her intently. "Would you care to see someone

77

else, m'lady? You look a bit peeked? Pale and tired and all."

"I didn't sleep well last night; you are aware of that."

Mary Ellen was not easy to dismiss, but Jade at last managed to have the bedchamber to herself. She looked into the brightly polished mirror and, to her horror, saw dark smudges of fatigue beneath her eyes. She still hadn't brushed her hair, which was usually the first thing she did upon rising. But then, she usually didn't wait until nearly ten o'clock to rise.

Jade heard a short rap of knuckles upon her bedchamber door. Before she could call out that she did not want to be disturbed, the door opened and Bishop Nathan Fields, tall, angular, ebony-eyed, strode in purposefully.

"Jade, have you taken ill?" the bishop asked, moving close, taking her hand in his. Jade tried to pull her hand away, but the bishop refused to release her. "Don't fight me, child. I am only concerned for your happiness and good health."

Jade wanted desperately to believe him. She needed to believe someone was concerned for her happiness without having any ulterior motives. She longed to trust Bishop Fields, but his eyes were too dark and fathomless for her to read his mind.

He never seemed to be quite relaxed. He was like a hunted animal, ready to pounce. Jade couldn't completely trust him, even though he continually reminded her that he was a servant of God put on Earth to spread His word and do His good deeds.

To add to her annoyance, Jade was still only wearing the simple nightgown that she had slept in. She was getting very tired of people who were supposed to be her servants looking at her while she was less than decently attired.

"Speak to me," Bishop Fields said. He had turned Jade so that she was facing the center of the room, and was guiding her back to the bed. "I cannot help you until you tell me what ails you!"

"I'm well. Really."

Bishop Fields made a huffing sound, making Jade feel like he was thoroughly patronizing her. She could accept open scorn and contempt easier than she could the insult of being patronized.

She jerked her hand out of the bishop's and deftly twisted away when he tried to put his arm around her waist. She grabbed a modest green wrapper from the foot of her bed, and pulled it on, knotting the sash tightly around her waist.

"You needn't be embarrassed with me," Bishop Fields said quietly. "I'm like an uncle. I'm almost family to you. And I am, might I remind you, a man of God."

"Yes, of course," Jade replied.

Under the bishop's steady, unwavering gaze, Jade did begin to wonder whether she shouldn't simply give her complete, unreserved trust to Bishop Fields. Through all the grief that she had gone through, it was Bishop Fields who had remained beside Jade. He would tell her, even when times looked their bleakest, that she would be happy some day, and that God would provide if only she would believe in Him and, by holy extension, in Bishop Nathan Fields.

"Tell me now what is troubling you, child."

It was a command, not a request, and it bothered Jade, though she could not really voice her feelings.

Bishop Fields forced her to sit at the edge of the bed.

"Nothing is troubling me."

"You haven't been sleeping well. I can see that in you. You haven't slept well since William rode off to fight his wars."

Jade thought, I hadn't slept well long before that.

Bishop Fields stood and looked down at the lovely young blonde, putting his hands on his hips in the way he did whenever he was about to make some elaborate statement.

"Is it loneliness that is disturbing you, Jade?"

"I have been lonely," Jade agreed.

It was hardly much of a confession. Anyone who knew her vouched that she was the type of woman who enjoyed the companionship of others. Since her bedchamber had been moved, she was even more isolated from the people who gave her comfort.

"Is it more than loneliness?"

There was something in the bishop's tone that made Jade look up. It was disturbing to have him standing so close to where she sat, because it put his waist at her eye level.

"Is it . . . desire? Unrequited desire?"

Bishop Fields stepped even closer and reached down to place a hand on Jade's shoulder. From his vantage point, despite the wrapper she'd put on, he could look down her bodice and see more than a glimpse of firm, satiny breast. He cursed Jade inwardly for being so prudish she felt that the wrapper was necessary.

"You haven't been with a man since your husband died. Is that what has been bothering you?"

At first, Jade was unable to respond. She did not want to talk about what William always boorishly referred to as "a husband's prerogative," and she didn't want to think about her own wicked behavior when she had been in Lyon's embrace.

For the first time since she had known Bishop Fields, Jade wondered whether he had impure thoughts about her. It wasn't anying in particular that she could point her finger at, not the glaringly obvious and lustful leer of other men, but just the same, his dark-eyed, unblinking stare made her feel distinctly uncomfortable.

She could not help but wonder what passions lurked beneath his pious exterior.

"Exactly what are you asking me?" Jade challenged.

She saw his expression change at the hard-edged tone she'd used. She knew then that Bishop Fields, despite his chosen vocation, was nevertheless a man. Though he tried to mask and sublimate his passions, they burned within him just as brightly as within any man.

"I am inquiring on how well you feel. Nothing more than that, Princess." Bishop Fields cupped his hands and smiled benevolently, his expression one of absolute innocence and selfless concern.

Jade sensed that for once she had the bishop at a disadvantage, and she was determined to make the most of it. Lyon's accusations still rang hauntingly in her ears, and she was determined to find out if there was any truth to them.

"There is something that I would like to do today," she said as Bishop Fields turned slightly and moved several steps away.

"Speak your wish, m'lady, and I will make it so!" he said with a flourish, pointing a finger toward the ceiling in a gesture he sometimes used at the pulpit when stressing a moral law to his congregation.

"I would like to ride to the village of Richland. I haven't been there in far too long. I miss seeing the people."

For a moment Bishop Fields's eyes narrowed suspiciously, then opened wide with incredulity. He shook his head slowly.

"I'm afraid that cannot be so, m'lady. As I have explained to you before, the peasants have taken to an ugly frame of mind. It wouldn't be safe for you to go to the village."

"It was once safe for me to be among my people. What has changed, bonsier, to make the people change?"

Jade avoided using the word peasant, though it and many even more derogatory words were often used by the bishop and others of his coterie.

"Times have changed. The peasants have become agitated since the untimely death of Prince William. Since that time they have become so rebellious, so violent." He spoke the words slowly, enunciating them carefully, as though they did not taste good to his tongue and he feared having to repeat them if he erred the first time through. "I understand your desire to be among the people, but I simply cannot allow it. Especially not riding, m'lady. The least you must take is a carriage, and then with a full complement of your most loyal and well-trained knights to guard you."

"I don't need a carriage. I am, as you well know, excellent on horseback."

"Of course, m'lady, but it is so . . ."

Bishop Fields let the words die away, and he blushed

82

slightly with feigned embarrassment. Princess Jade had grown up a peasant and, though it was entirely unladylike, she rode astride her mount, not sidesaddle, as fashion dictated women must.

Jade scowled at the reminder of her inappropriate riding style. The only time she had ever tried to ride sidesaddle, she had fallen off, and it caused an uproar at Castle Crosse. Prince William, from that point forward, forbid Jade to ride.

Though anger heated her blood, Jade squared her shoulders and looked straight into the clergyman's intimidating black eyes. "I insist upon visiting the village of Richland," she said defiantly. "If you feel it is necessary to put me in a carriage, then that is the way I must travel, but do not assume now nor ever that I must be *allowed*"—she drawled the word out slowly, imperiously—"the privilege of seeing my people. That is something that I will do *whenever* and *wherever* I choose. Is that clear, Bishop Fields?"

He stood looking at her as though he looked upon a stranger. Never before had she stood up to him in so forceful a manner. Bishop Nathan Fields did not at all like this change in the princess's behavior, but as her subordinate he had little power to force a change, at least overtly.

"If you insist, m'lady, then I will relent to your wishes, of course. But you must grant me one wish."

Belying her brave exterior, Jade was quaking inside. She had her own suspicions of what happened to people who defied the bishop, and she was actually quite surprised that he had acquiesced to her desires. So when the bishop asked for one wish, Jade gave her word that it would be granted.

"Postpone your visitation to Richland until tomorrow."

"But I wanted to see the village today."

Jade sensed deception, though she couldn't say why. Lyon had said a young boy from Richland had been murdered under Jade's orders. She was certain that if she could go to the village, she would learn who was behind the murder as well as convince the villagers of her innocence.

"Yes, m'lady, but even a princess must sometimes agree that there is a difference between what we want and what we can have. And you did, after all, give your word."

He smiled then, flashing that avuncular smile that pulled his thin lips back away from the small rows of his fine white, catlike teeth. He stepped up to Jade and took her by the arms, bringing her up to her feet. His arms went around her, and he hugged her tightly.

"I see it in your eyes that I have made you angry again," he said. "It seems I am always making you angry these days."

Standing with her hands hanging at her sides, a faint grimace on her lips, Jade replied, "Only when you speak to me as if I am a helpless little girl."

"But you must remember that when I met you, you were just a little girl."

Not so much a little girl that you didn't make sure I had no choice but to marry William, she thought, surprising herself since she believed that that particular resentment had long since died away.

"It is agreed then," the bishop said, stroking Jade's hair softly, running his hand down her back. "On the morrow you will take a carriage to the village of

84

Richland, and then you will return to Castle Crosse. Agreed?"

"Agreed."

A moment later Jade was alone in her bedchamber, wondering whether she would soon know if Lyon was a lair or a messenger of truth. Either way, she would learn more at midnight, when he would return to her bedchamber, entering again like a cloaked thief in the night.

The thought of it made Jade sigh softly, though she wasn't certain whether apprehension or excitement had caused her intake of breath.

Lyon shifted positions slightly, but he remained squatting in the bushes a hundred yards beyond the exterior walls of the grounds of Castle Crosse. His thighs ached a little from remaining in one position for so long, but he accepted the pain, realizing that the self-discipline was good for him mentally and physically.

He had been outside the village brick walls, watching the comings and goings of knights, soldiers, peasants, and shopkeepers, looking for a sign that Jade had spoken to someone about his entrance into her bedchamber in the night. If she told anyone, then the movements of the people, especially among the knights, would deviate from the normal.

It was past two o'clock when fatigue pulled hard at Lyon's eyes. He had been awake for over thirty hours, when he decided that Jade had probably not warned anyone of his actions the previous night. He moved deeper into the forest that surrounded the castle, letting the shadows and the foliage envelope him. Not even the years that he had spent away in wars could diminish his knowledge of this forest. He knew it, with all its winding pathways, animal trails, and hidden dangers, as well as any animal that hunted in the night.

Bishop Nathan Fields, Sheriff Sean Dunne, and Sir Garth Rawlings sat at the small, oblong table, drinking mead and eating cheese; speaking openly and casually about how much longer they needed to tolerate Princess Jade Crosse's continual presence.

"We've got to wait until all the peasants loathe the sound of her name," Sheriff Dunne said, his cheek puffed out with cheese as he spoke. "Then we can behead her if we want to and they won't make a peep."

Bishop Fields shook his head. "No! No matter how badly the peasants end up hating her, we mustn't let the Crown believe that we are responsible for her death. It shouldn't be difficult at all to murder her, and place the blame upon the peasants."

Garth Rawlings chuckled. "And which of one of us gets the job of killing her, eh?"

As the only trained soldier among them, he was the one who performed most of the violent acts upon the villagers. Since the death of Prince William, Garth had been given a free hand in dispensing violence whenever he wanted, and the spilling of blood was something he cherished.

No one at the table doubted that Garth wanted the task of murdering Princess Jade.

Sheriff Dunne, bright and devious of mind, closed his eyes as he thought about what would happen when King Henry learned that Princess Jade Crosse had been murdered. He was by nature a skeptical man who believed in very little.

"Sure the news of Princess Jade's disrepute among the lower classes is not unknown to the Crown." He sipped his mead carefully. He had murdered enough men while they were drunk to know the inherent danger in letting one's reflexes become dulled with spirits. "The worst that can happen is King Henry will send men here to investigate. We don't want that to happen."

"Don't be a woman about this," Bishop Fields sneered contemptuously. "When I tell you that I've thought of everything, then I've thought of everything. London is concerned with maintaining life the way it is. All we have to do is convince the Crown that the peasants here are no different than the peasants anywhere, that they can't be trusted, and that Princess Jade was nothing more than the unfortunate victim of the violent nature of the lower life forms." Bishop Fields chuckled. "Once that is done, then I should have no trouble convincing the London politicians that if I am placed in charge of Castle Crosse, the taxes to London will continue on without interruption, I will hold all the power within my hands."

He held out his hands, fingers spread and palms facing upward. It was the same gesture he used when he asked for offerings from his congregation after a sermon.

"What if the Crown sends someone here before the princess is killed?" Garth asked.

Bishop Fields shot him an angry look. They all knew that the early arrival of agents from London could well prove disastrous to their plan.

87

"It is your task to make certain that I know well in advance of any spies sent by King Henry," the bishop said quietly, threateningly.

Sheriff Dunne, sensing the barbed animosity between Fields and Garth, said, "I have spies all through London. If the Crown makes a move, we'll know of it."

Bishop Fields nodded his approval, but his anger toward Garth was unstaunched.

"I've spent years planning the perfect strategy," the bishop said softly, his tone distant as he thought back over the decade that he had spent plotting and waiting to take control of Prince William Crosse's fiefdom. "I've thought of everything, planned each move to minute detail. All we need yet to do is convince the peasants that the princess is behind all their misery, then convince the Crown that it was the peasants who murdered Jade. Blame will be aimed in every direction except ours. If we follow my plan, gentlemen, we will all be very, very wealthy."

Sheriff Dunne did not resist the temptation to bring up another troubling possibility. "And what of Sir Lyon Beauchane and his men? I have heard that they are on their way back here, recalled from duty since Prince William has been killed. What can we do if he returns?"

Garth spat on the floor, then bolted to his feet. "I for one look forward to facing that swine again! You don't have to worry about Lyon, Sheriff, because when I see him, I'll cut his heart out and hand it to you myself."

"Brave words," Sheriff Dunne replied coolly.

Everyone knew that Garth was a skilled knight, the most talented warrior in the fiefdom. They also knew that he had trained with Lyon, and that Lyon had bested him at nearly every turn. It was only after Lyon Beauchane had been sent off to war that Garth was able to ascend to the top rank among the fighting men at Castle Crosse.

The three fell silent as they contemplated Lyon Beauchane's return to Castle Crosse. Though they were all given to bragging in their own way, none of them truly cherished the thought of making an enemy of Lyon. Until Jade was killed and Bishop Fields was accepted by the Crown as the man rightly in control of Castle Crosse, and all the lands once owned by Prince William Crosse, they needed to remain united, each serving an indispensable function to the others.

"Lyon must be killed when this is all done," Sheriff Dunne said, breaking the silence. "Killing him is the smart move to make."

"Perhaps. Although he's made himself a hero with the Crown, his heroic exploits over the enemy are the makings of legend," Bishop Fields commented.

Garth was silent, hating such talk of his detested rival. He would rather his partners in crime simply accept the fact that he would best Lyon in battle, but they continued with their plotting.

"If he returns, he must be slain immediately," Dunne said, amending his original assessment of the threat Lyon represented.

Bishop Fields, the superior strategist of the three, said, "No, not so quickly. First we must destroy his reputation, which should prove considerably easier than destroying Jade's. We'll simply convince the peasants that Lyon is behind a murder or two. We'll let them think that fighting is all he lives for now that he's back in England. The peasants haven't seen his face in years."

Garth smiled, enjoying this new line of thinking. His mind conjured wicked pleasures, all in the name of destroying Sir Lyon's reputation. "Perhaps a sweet young maiden or two could be raped ... young enough to have no accurate memory of what Lyon looks like?"

Bishop Fields grinned wickedly, showing his small, catlike teeth. "Garth, occasionally your brilliance impresses me."

And after that, all animosity between the three vanished, and each was left to contemplate his own responsibilities in what must be done.

Chapter 8

"But m'lady, it's late and you haven't been sleeping well," Mary Ellen said, holding Jade's plain nightgown in her hands. "You've got to get ready for bed now. Bishop Fields says so."

Jade did not want to put on the nightgown. In a few hours, Lyon would arrive at her bedchamber balcony, and she did not want to be as indecently or as plainly dressed as she had been the previous night.

"I'm not tired," Jade said finally, ignoring the stern look her maid shot her. "Besides, I'm becoming weary of that old nightgown."

"Then let me get you another one. You've got some you haven't even worn."

There was a slight undercurrent of jealousy in Mary Ellen's last sentence, and Jade wondered whether her maid was dissatisfied with her station in life. Jade smiled, trying to soften the impact of her denial of Mary Ellen's wishes, but the maid would not be discouraged.

"You've been acting strangely, m'lady," Mary Ellen

said in a voice just above a whisper. "Is there some reason that you don't want to go to bed?"

Afraid that Mary Ellen might become even more suspicious, Jade relented with an exasperated nod. A moment later Mary Ellen disappeared into the clothes anteroom off Jade's bedchamber. She returned with a white silk nightgown that Jade had never worn.

"Let me help you with this, then you go to bed."

Jade's first reaction was to protest her selection. This nightgown was made of very fine silk, the decolletage trimmed in exquisite Italian lace, the neckline plunging deeply. It was the immodesty of the neckline that prevented Jade from wearing it before.

One look into Mary Ellen's eyes warned Jade that to protest now would be to risk heightening her suspicions even further.

"I can dress myself," Jade explained tersely, wanting to be alone. She idly wondered what Lyon would think if he saw her in the revealing nightgown, then cursed herself. As a widow still in mourning theoretically, such wicked thoughts were absolutely forbidden.

Mary Ellen laid the sheer nightgown down carefully on the bed. "I'll be back later to see if you need anything."

"You needn't trouble yourself."

"It's no trouble, m'lady."

She dared not protest further. Smiling a false smile, Jade nodded and waited until she was alone in her bedchamber before she hastily undressed, and pulled the nightgown over her head.

She went to the looking glass and inspected her appearance. In that instant, as she looked at herself, Jade felt exactly as she did years earlier, when she was a virgin child bride preparing for her wedding night. A flush of warmth washed through her, embarrassing her even though she was alone. She may feel like she had felt so many years ago, but she certainly did not look like she did back then. The nightgown she'd worn on her wedding night did not exactly hang upon her body, but she certainly had not filled it out then the way she filled out the beautiful silk nightgown now.

Jade turned away from the looking glass. She put her hands to her cheeks. They felt warm. She felt warm all over.

I'm not going to see him wearing this, thought Jade, but she was deluding herself, since she knew she would not put her old gown back on to wait for Lyon's arrival, despite a nagging voice that told her she should.

In her heart, Jade knew that she wanted to see the appreciation in Lyon's eyes when he first saw her. She wanted to feel beautiful deep inside, to see his open approval.

By the time Mary Ellen returned, Jade had also donned her modest wrapper, and was sitting in the chair by her bed, a single candle illuminating her. The curtains to the balcony had been left open, undrawn.

"Good night, Mary Ellen. Sleep well."

"You sleep well, too, m'lady." Mary Ellen stopped at the doorway. "Don't tarry too late thinking. Even if you can't sleep, it'll do you good to be in bed."

Jade just smiled in reply. She would not be caught by Lyon in bed again. All she had to do now was wait for him to arrive. When she talked to him and looked into his eyes, she would know if he spoke the truth or told her damning lies.

*　　*　　*

She awoke with a start, arms and legs jerking outward, eyes bursting open. For a second, Jade could not remember where she was. The confines of her new bedchamber were not yet entirely familiar to her. Then she remembered how she had been determined to stay awake until Lyon arrived, but she had fallen asleep in the chair beside her bed. It was the candle, sputtering in the final moments before it burned itself out, that had woken her.

With a groan, Jade rubbed her neck, stiff from sleeping with her head hanging down, cocked slightly to the side. She rose unsteadily and walked out to the balcony. It was a warm evening, and from all that she could tell, there was no worthwhile reason for Lyon not to have followed through with his promise to once again climb the outside sea wall of Castle Crosse to see her.

Why should it surprise me that he lied? Jade mused angrily, hugging her arms about herself, staring into the thick darkness.

She could hear the sea crashing on the rocks below, but she did not look down. Part of her was afraid that she might see Lyon far below, his corpse at twisted angles, arms and legs askew.

No, she thought, Lyon wouldn't make that kind of mistake. A jealous husband will kill him, not a mere slip from the castle walls.

She turned back into her bedchamber, her heart heavy, her chest feeling tight. She shouldn't be disappointed, she told herself, but her heart didn't

94

listen to logic concerning the subject of an enigmatic knight named Sir Lyon Beauchane.

It was a small boat, one that would not draw any attention from the guards stationed in and around Castle Crosse. The single man inside was hunched over his oars, holding onto the slender fishing line. His clothes were nearly in rags, bespeaking of his poverty and his desperation to catch a meal for the evening to feed himself and his family.

The guards at Castle Crosse, who had always been well-fed, had been paid even more since Prince William's death because now they were expected to harass and intimidate people occasionally that they previously were to protect. If they paid any attention to the fisherman, it was only in passing, and to perhaps thank the Fates that they were not that impoverished.

But the poorly dressed man in the boat was not nearly as old as he appeared, nor was he bent over from years of desperate labor. Beneath the frayed hood of his cloak, brilliant blue eyes were trained upon the room in Castle Crosse, the one that so few people knew was now the bedchamber for Princess Jade Crosse.

The dull, eerie glow from inside the bedchamber had continued unabated for hours. Lyon had watched the deeply recessed windows of the castle darken as the people inside retired for the evening.

It was late, at least two hours from the time that Lyon had told Jade he would return to speak with her, that the light from her bedchamber wavered briefly and finally died away. It was the flickering light of a candle that had burned itself out, not the quick end of a flame that had been intentionally extinguished. It brought a smile to Lyon's wide, sensual mouth. In all the time that he had watched the castle, he had not seen one thing that would make him suspect that Jade had told anyone of his return to her lands, or his surreptitious entrance into her private bedchamber.

He was tossing the fishing line over the edge of the boat when a flowing vision of white robes stepped onto the balcony, glowing gloriously and ghostly in the moonlight.

"My God," Lyon whispered, even though he was far away from anyone and could not possibly be heard.

The sound of his own voice rang hollowly in his ears. Not even the great distance that separated them could mask the fact that it was Jade Crosse standing on the balcony.

Gone were the straight lines of the simple nightgown that Lyon had seen her wear the night before. Simplicity had been usurped by elegance, by glowing gowns that danced gracefully around her legs in the music of the night breeze. She looked like a dove landing after flight, gently placing her wings in proper place.

Not ghostly, Lyon thought, amending his initial assessment. Angelic. She looks like an angel.

She didn't stay out on the balcony for more than a minute before returning to her dark bedchamber, but in that time, she powerfully altered Lyon's mood.

He knew now that he trusted her *more* than he had before, and he knew, too, that she trusted him *less* than she had before. He had intentionally missed meeting her when he said he would just to check her reaction. Jade had passed that test, but Lyon could only wonder how angry she would be when she saw him again.

He had witnessed small doses of her anger before. Her temper was a fiery and not entirely displeasing force of her great passion.

With a smile on his lips, he began rowing to shore, keeping far away from the base of Castle Crosse. Jade would be angry, but he could talk away her anger and make her smile again.

Lyon Beauchane was confident in his charm, but then, he really didn't know Princess Jade Crosse as well as he thought he did.

Some time later, after snatching a few hours sleep, he dressed and stepped into the eating hall at Castle Frederick, where Lord Charles and Baron von Mueller were drinking strong, hot tea, and eating freshly baked biscuits slathered with rich butter.

"It's high time you arose," Lord Charles said through a broad smile, his bearded countenance showing his pleasure in seeing the young knight. "I'd begun to wonder whether you were going to sleep your life away."

Lyon just grinned. Baron von Mueller laughed, since everyone at Castle Frederick had been told that there would be hell to pay if anyone made a sound that awoke Sir Lyon Beauchane while he slept. The fact that he had slept so few hours had surprised everyone.

Without rising, von Mueller kicked a chair out at the table for Lyon. It was a casual gesture, but it had great meaning. Though he was a knight of high standing, he did not rank among the nobility, and yet Lord Charles and Baron von Mueller were casually inviting him to sit and dine with them. It was a sign of acceptance that surprised Lyon.

Lord Charles clapped his hands and a young scullery maid entered the hall, carrying a tray laden with a steaming pile of sliced goosemeat and various fruits. The slender, attractive young woman strained beneath the weight. There was enough food there to feed several people.

"Men of herioc deeds tend to have great appetites as well," Lord Charles said, explaining the huge amount of food. He patted his well-rounded stomach and smiled. "I am a shining example of that, I wager!"

All three men laughed then, and Lyon tore into the food because he truly was hungry, though there was more food than he could ever possibly eat. The young scullery maid remained a few moments at his side.

Lyon looked up at her and smiled, and she blushed.

"If you need me for anything, you just ask and I will provide," she said. Her eyes said that Lyon could ask for everything, and she would be only too happy to oblige him.

The men were silent while Lyon ate. Then, after he'd pushed his chair back from the table to indicate he'd finished, Lord Charles and the baron turned questioning eyes upon the young knight.

"Tonight, I will speak with Princess Cross again," Lyon said, choosing his words carefully because he was dealing with careful men. "I can't say yet that she is innocent of all that she has been accused, but I can say with confidence the facts do not necessarily add up to her guilt."

With a touch of impatience, Baron von Mueller replied in a growl, "That's not saying much of anything."

"Precisely. It's because I don't know very much yet." The two men met gazes that held. "Answers do not come as quickly as questions, *bonsier.*"

Baron von Mueller nodded his understanding. To show that he was impatient for results, but not displeased with the work performed so far, he poured a cup of tea for Lyon. A man of his station did not serve a knight unless it was meant as a gesture, and again, it was not missed by the three men long accustomed to the arcane rituals of power.

"If I do not return to you on the morning of the morrow, then it is not necessarily proof of Princess Jade's guilt. It is only proof that I have died."

Neither Baron von Mueller nor Lord Charles reacted with surprise at Lyon's casual acceptance of the possibility of his own death. The three had lived with high expectations of themselves and others, and they knew the price that sometimes needed to be paid if great deeds were to be accomplished.

"And how will she be able to prove to you that other forces are responsible for the villainy within Castle Crosse?" Lord Charles inquired.

"I have a series of tests designed for her."

"And what makes you think she'll agree to do these tests?" Baron von Mueller asked.

"I will explain that if she refuses, then she will appear to be guilty. If that is the case, then I will be duty bound to end the villainy that has made life in her enfeoffment a living hell."

"In other words, you'll threaten to kill her?"

Lyon's mouth pulled up on the right side in a small grimace as he looked at the baron. "Not in other words. Those will do."

Lord Charles asked, "What are these tests?"

"Under the circumstances, it is best that you not know. If you wish to remain unknown in this endeavor, there are certain requirements."

Lord Charles grinned then. There weren't many people in the world who would look him straight in the eye, then refuse to answer his question. He took this as a mark of Lyon's courage and wisdom.

"God's speed, my son," Lord Charles said then. "My prayers go with you."

"And mine," Baron von Mueller said.

Much more reticent than his English friend, the German's words shocked Lyon. He smiled his approval and walked out of the great hall.

The scullery maid was waiting for him outside the door. She smiled shyly, doing all she could to let him know that she wouldn't mind his advances without being whorish about it. Lyon smiled at her and gently touched her soft cheek. Though she was an attractive young woman, she paled in comparison to Jade's beauty. Since he had held the princess in his arms and kissed her lips, she was all he could think of.

It was almost midnight. Jade was so angry that it was foolish to even think about getting sleep. She had been forced to cope with too much mendacity since the day began.

Her hopes had been high when Bishop Fields informed her that everything was ready for her to take the carriage ride through the village of Richland. Jade had been convinced that she would be able to tell from talking with the villagers what they had been through, and whether they blamed her for any of their misfortunes.

But Jade should have paid closer attention to exactly what Bishop Fields had said. Riding *through* the village of Richland was exactly what Sir Garth Rawlings and his knights allowed her to do.

All the townspeople had apparently been told to stand at the edges of the road that twisted through the village. Jade's carriage did not stop, nor even slow down. Before she had sped completely through the small village, she was screaming for the coachman to stop the carriage.

It was a mockery of satisfying her wishes, and Jade knew it. All she had been able to see was a collection of hard working people being forced to stand beside the road, waving at their princess with forced smiles upon their faces.

Upon her return to Castle Crosse, Jade openly castigated Garth Rawlings, then sought out Bishop Fields. The bishop would also taste her wrath for deceiving her.

But Bishop Fields was nowhere to be found. Not for several hours, anyway. He eventually arrived at her sun room with a benevolent smile upon his face, knowing full well that Jade had not had the pleasant visit with the villagers that she had requested and he promised.

Jade accused the bishop of deception. The bishop accused Jade of naivete, since she had to realize that it was much too dangerous to be walking around amidst the villagers. There were insurrectionists in the fiefdom now, and well-known traitorous murderers who would just as soon cut Jade's throat as look at her. Rebels like Sir Lyon Beauchane.

"Lyon?" The single word escaped Jade's lips before she had the chance to stop it. Bishop Fields looked at her critically.

"You know him, of course," he said, but he studied her as though to discern more answers than just that one.

Jade shrugged her slender shoulders, and instantly her anger at the bishop vainished, supplanted by new concerns. Was Lyon now considered a rebellious knight, a ruthless murderer? It seemed so very unlikely. She knew the tenderness that could be in his touch, but in his touch and in his kiss there was also deception. Jade was only too well-versed in that.

Smiling dismissively, Jade waved a hand. "I believe I met him years ago. It was the name that caught me by surprise. Such an unusual name."

"Such a fitting name. The name of a killer."

The king of beasts, Jade thought with mixed emotions.

They argued for a while longer, but Jade's heart was no longer determined to force Bishop Fields in to admitting that he had deceived her. He had complied with the literal spirit of her request, and he was far better at turning and twisting words than she was.

She spent the rest of the day thinking about Lyon. He was a rogue. Of that she hadn't the slightest doubt. But a murderer? No, she doubted that. At least she would need more proof than just Bishop Fields's accusation to convince her.

But he hadn't returned, as he had promised he would. Had he been too busy to come back to her? Had he spent the time in the arms of another woman? An unwilling woman, as Bishop Fields had suggested Lyon was given to doing?

Jade removed her wrapper and spread it out carefully on the foot of the bed. Once again, she had chosen to wear the plunging neckline nightgown that Mary Ellen had selected for her. A wry, sardonic smile pulled at her mouth when she turned away from her bed and caught her own reflection in the looking glass.

She had been afraid that the nightgown would incite Lyon's passions when he saw her in it. But as it turned out, he never returned last evening, as he had promised. It mirrored the way her husband would insist that she dress in her finest, then not show up at his own bedchamber because he was too busy talking and bragging with his male friends.

The irony was laughable.

From the tray of meats and cheeses beside her bed, Jade took a square of cheese and popped it into her mouth. She had been too angry to eat earlier, and Bishop Fields had instructed Mary Ellen to prepare the tray for her. There was even a pitcher of wine, though Jade had never really acquired a taste for intoxicating spirits of any kind.

She wished she had never met Lyon Beauchane. A

person does not miss what she has never known. Until she found herself in Lyon's arms, she had never believed that touching and being touched could elicit sensations that went far beyond just those areas where hands and body met.

"Lyon . . . what kind of man are you?" she murmured.

"That depends upon whom you ask."

Chapter 9

Her heart nearly stopped!

She wheeled to find Lyon standing calmly at the doorway to the balcony; hands on his hips, his ebony cape pulled over his shoulders to make him one with the night.

"You scared the devil out of me!" Jade said, a hand to her heart.

Lyon smiled crookedly, stepping into the bedchamber. He had been standing in the shadows long enough to be assured that Jade was alone, and that no trap was set for him. His piercing blue gaze roamed over Jade, appreciating what he saw, making the desire burn in his veins.

"I'm inclined to doubt that, m'lady. One look into your eyes tells me that the devil is still there."

Her eyes narrowed. She put her hands angrily on her hips, momentarily forgetting the deep scoop of her neckline, and the pale, taut flesh that was exposed above the delicate lace trim.

"Are you saying that I'm a hellish woman?"

Lyon stepped withing arm's reach. He dared not get any closer to Jade, or surely he could not keep his hands to himself. She was much too enticing, especially when she was looking at him with such fire in the depths of her amber eyes.

"No, Jade, I am not saying that at all," Lyon replied, the hoarseness in his voice proof that her allure was more enticing than ever.

"Then, mayhap, you'll tell me what you *are* saying?" Jade asked.

She suspected that she should not continue this line of conversation with Lyon, but she could not help herself. He looked especially handsome in his shirt of navy blue, over which he wore a black coat, and his exquisite black cape. His boots were knee-high and brightly polished, though the toes had been scuffed during the long, slow, dangerous climb up the wall of the castle to her bedchamber balcony.

"I am saying that you have the devil in you, it is true, but you also have an equal amount of the angel in you." His tone dropped lower as he moved closer, close enough now so that he could practically feel the heat of her body reaching forward through his clothes, heating his blood. "There are times, Jade, when being with you is positively . . . heavenly."

Her anger evaporated, though Jade tried to hold on to it. The intensity of Lyon's gaze seemed to burn straight through her. When she noticed that his gaze dipped down for a second before coming back to meet her eyes again, she felt embarrassed and vulnerable.

"You . . ." Her voice was just a croak. Jade cleared her throat, then started over again, determined that she would not take a single step backward for this man who thought he could come and go in her life whenever and however he chose. "You said you would be here last night, not tonight. I assume you have a good explanation."

"I was testing you."

"That means you were lying to me."

"In a way, I suppose, but it wasn't meant to be a lie."

"Liars never mean to lie, it's just what they do." Jade saw that her words had cut him, and she was happy for it. "As long as we've come to an agreement on what you are, shall we discuss some of the other accusations you made concerning me and how I have been running Castle Crosse?"

Lyon's ardor cooled under Jade's insults. He turned away from her and went to the small table, where the tray of meats, cheeses, and wine was waiting. He poured a goblet of the hearty red wine and began to eat a morsel of meat.

"Thank you," he said, knowing his comments would infuriate her. "I appreciate your thoughtfulness."

"I didn't have that sent here for you," Jade snapped.

Lyon smiled and said, "Of course you didn't." Then he laughed softly, apparently used to women doing things for him and then denying that their intention was to please him. "Just like you didn't mean to make a charade of inspecting Richland village this afternoon, either." He laughed bitterly. "No doubt, as you sped through, you saw the handiwork of Garth and his men."

"Handiwork?"

"The villagers were under orders to smile and wave. If any of them said a word directly to you, or if they did not smile with appropriate enthusiasm, Garth promised that a night visit was in order. Isn't that a chillingly pleasant way of describing murder and mayhem? Garth told the villagers that you wanted to see them paying their emotional tribute to you, and that you would be furious if they displeased you in any way."

"Perhaps that's what Sir Garth Rawlings told the villagers, but it wasn't what I asked for."

"So you say. It is not what the villagers heard."

"And I heard that you rape women. That you're a murderer."

Jade turned away so that she wouldn't have to look at him. Her blood felt heated, and though she should modestly put on her wrapper, it seemed much too warm for that. She walked to the edge of the balcony, where the breeze always came in off the ocean.

"We've been through this verbal duel before," she said softly. "We are no closer to finding out whether I am a tyrant or you are a murderer than we ever were. How do you propose we change that?"

Lyon leaned against the thick poster of the bed, studying Jade. Aside from the glaringly obvious fact that she was without any doubt the most erotically beautiful woman he'd ever seen, she had also learned to put a commanding and authoritative quality in her tone when she needed to be taken seriously. It was this competence that most surprised Lyon.

"What about you taking another ride to the village of Richland?" Lyon asked, thinking aloud. "Only this time, don't go with Garth's men there to insulate you. Go alone so that you can talk to the villagers, and they can talk to you. After all, it is the villagers that you must really convince, not me. And the villagers will convince you that I am no murderer, and certainly no rapist."

"I tried that once. Bishop Fields twisted my words and made a fool of me."

"You are the mistress of Castle Crosse. Don't ask him to allow you to go, tell him what you are going to do. Or, better still, simply do it without telling anyone what you intend to do."

"But the people? Bishop Fields says there are many who would kill me if they had the chance."

"Nathan Fields would tell a lie rather than the truth if for no other reason that that he is more comfortable with lies. I wouldn't believe anything that cur says."

Jade thought about Lyon's suggestion. If she could get to Richland and truly spend some time talking with the people, she felt certain she could convince them that she had not forgotten that she had once been a common villager like them. She could make them believe that if the taxes had been raised and were being collected in a brutish and violent manner, it was an illegal tax, and not one imposed upon the people by her. And she could also talk to people who apparently knew Lyon without being frightened of him. If he was the murdering fiend that Bishop Fields had made him out to be, then they would tell her of it.

"As much as I hate to admit it, I think that perhaps you have come up with a solution to our mutual distrust of each other. If the villag of Richland is where the young boy was murdered—alledgedly under my orders—then that is where we must begin."

The breeze came through the window slowly but steadily, cooling Jade slightly. It molded the nightgown to her legs and rounded hips; whispered through her hair and over her shoulders and down her back; touched her own skin softly, not unlike a caress.

She continued looking out to sea, seeing nothing in the darkness. But in her mind's eye, she could see Lyon looking at her. Now that they had come to an agreement of sorts, her anger had cooled and she was again aware of the strange, vaguely intoxicating pull of his sensuality, and of a whispering in her own blood that she could not deny.

Turning, she had intended on going to her bed to retrieve her wrapper, but the look in Lyon's eyes froze her in midstep. He stood, tall and regal, hands on his hips. His cape flowed in shimmering ebony folds over his shoulders and arms, dropping nearly to his ankles. His eyes were like pieces of blue diamonds illuminated by a burning inner fire ignited by Jade's beauty.

"M'lady . . . might I say that I approve of your evening attire." He took another step closer to Jade, unwilling to take his eyes from her, unable to resist her magnetism. "It suits your extravagant beauty so much better than your other nightgown." He stepped closer still. Jade turned so that she faced him. He watched her throat work as she swallowed dryly. "You have the type of beauty that should be embraced by only the finest accouterments." He stood very close to Jade now. The tip of his tongue went around his mouth to moisten his lips, his throat felt constricted. "Dressing you in a plain nightgown is akin to framing a masterpiece of art in a cheap and shabby frame."

Jade raised her hands, intent on striking them against Lyon's broad chest. He caught her wrists, bringing her hands to his mouth.

"Beautiful hands. All of you is so beautiful," he said

softly, his breath warm against the sensitive tips of her fingers.

Jade watched, both fascinated and frightened, as Lyon kissed the tips of her fingers, paying great attention to each one. Then he kissed her palms, and she felt his tongue moisten her hand.

It was, she thought, a strange thing to do; she found it incredibly exciting and deeply intimate.

The insistent little voice that always cried out whenever she was with Lyon whispered that she should pull her hands away from him. She ought to shout immediately for the guards to come and rescue her before she did something that she would surely regret.

But just like before, Jade ignored the inner voice of reason and decorum. Lyon was dangerous, and he was unreasonable. Tonight—for just this one night—Jade had no intention of being reasonable.

"You are . . . aren't supposed to be here," she stammered.

"There are a lot of things that I'm not supposed to do. But I do them, m'lady. In fact, I do them exquisitely well."

He's so arrogant, Jade thought.

She wanted to tell him as much, but when she looked into his eyes, words suddenly failed her. She watched as Lyon's tongue curled around the tip of her forefinger. The soft sigh that escaped her lips was born of shock more than pleasure, but it nevertheless drew a smile from the roguish knight.

He twisted her hands within his grasp, exposing her palms. Jade felt the sleeves of her nightgown slide up her forearms; the touch of the silk against her skin was exhilarating. Lyon's nearness had a strange way of heightening her every sense.

He kissed her wrist, and again his tongue explored her flesh. Jade felt as though he was kissing her soul, and touching her somewhere deep within herself, a place that she had not known existed until she met Lyon Beauchane. Can he really feel my heartbeat with his tongue? she wondered, then cursed herself because it wasn't a question worth pondering.

"Tell me," Lyon continued, kissing Jade's forearm. He tasted her flesh with the tip of his tongue. "Tell me that you want me." It was that capitulation from Princess Jade Crosse, the verbal acceptance that she wanted the pleasure and sensual satisfaction that Lyon alone was cabable of dispensing, that he wanted most.

Jade tried to speak and found she couldn't. She watched as Lyon's tongue fluttered lightly in the curve of her elbow. Never had she thought that the inside of the elbow was a place where a woman could realize sensual excitement, but as Lyon's gently rasping tongue worked its way from side to side, Jade concluded that her elbows were much more sensitive than she had ever dreamed possible.

"My maid . . . Mary Ellen . . . she might come in again," Jade finally managed to say.

"Not tonight. We have both been very careful to keep our voices down. She couldn't possibly hear anything."

Lyon released Jade's left hand so that he could hold her right in both of his. While holding onto her wrist, he pushed the sleeve of her nightgown high on her arm, exposing her biceps. He had to bend down to kiss her upper arm, but his gaze never left Jade's, and the confident smile in his eyes was as seductive to the princess's senses as it was infuriating to her better judgement.

"You're wicked," Jade said, her gaze transfixed upon Lyon's as his tongue trailed a small, tender circle on her upper arm.

"You're willing."

"You're lying."

He just smiled a little more, then stepped even closer to Jade.

"Don't . . . don't kiss me," Jade said.

It was a last desperate hope that she could somehow convince Lyon of something that really wasn't true. In the chaotic rambling of her passion-addled mind, she thought that if she could convince Lyon that she did not want him, then maybe he would leave her alone. It had already become abundantly clear to Jade that she lacked the strength of will to deny herself, so she hoped with fervent desire that Lyon's willpower was such that he could walk away from her.

Jade's wish was resoundingly denied. Lyon Beauchane was a man known for many things, but self-denial had never been one of them, especially when an attractive woman somehow played a role in that sacrifice.

"Please don't," Jade whispered tremulously, her soft amber gaze locked onto Lyon's mouth as it descended closer and closer to her own. "Kiss me," she said, and neither she nor Lyon could be sure if it was the conclusion of one sentence, or the beginning of a new one.

Chapter 10

This is madness, Jade thought. A more exquisite madness she could not comprehend. Such a sweet madness!

Lyon's mouth sealed over hers, slanting down, stifling the soft sound of protest she felt inclined to make. His lips moved gently and erotically against her, and whatever reservations Jade harbored vanished into the misty irrelevance of the notion of rights and wrongs dictated by other people.

Jade twisted her arms around Lyon's neck, pulling his powerful body down as the deepening kiss warmed her blood. She parted her lips, and Lyon's tongue immediately entered her mouth.

She knew now what this was all about, and she knew she never wanted it to end. This was not the first time she had been in Lyon's muscled embrace, not the first time she had felt the strength of his tall, lean body pressing tightly against her own. She knew what was happening, and what she would feel. She wanted to know those feelings again!

"Lyon . . . oh, Lyon!" Jade gasped when the kiss ended briefly.

The sound of her own voice shocked her, the almost pleading hunger she heard in her own tone. She pushed her fingers through his shoulder-length hair, enjoying the feel of its silken luxuriance. She played her tongue against his, trembling at the texture of tongue against tongue.

Because he was so much taller than she, Jade was forced to arch backward in order to press against Lyon while he kissed her. If this caused her any discomfort, she was unaware of it. Nothing mattered to her, as she feasted upon his mouth, but the continuation of this single, rapturous moment.

She felt everything with startling clarity, as though there were two of her. One was able to delight in Lyon's kisses and caresses and feel mindlessly all the magnificent sensations he was igniting; one of her was able to stand aside, somehow detached, able to coldly and logically understand and intellectualize what it was he was doing to her, and why it felt so good.

Lyon lifted his head, squaring his shoulders to look down into Jade's wide, soft amber eyes. Before he spoke, Jade touched his mouth with the tips of her fingers. She sensed that he was going to ask her whether she really wanted this to happen, and though that was indeed the gentlemanly thing to do, she did not want him to be gentlemanly. For too long she had lived a lonely life, a life without any great highs or lows. And then Lyon burst into her life one night, and though he nearly scared her to death, he also brought an excitement into her life that she had never experienced.

As she looked into Lyon's fierce blue gaze, the questions that he silently asked were answered with the slightest nod of her head.

"M'lady . . . my Jade . . ."

Lyon lifted her in his arms and carried her to the big bed that dominated one side of the large bedchamber.

Holding her easily in his arms, Lyon placed a knee on the bed, leaning far forward to gently place Princess Jade down upon the center of the mattress. Her hair, honey blond and falling in loose rings well over her shoulders, spread out upon the soft comforter to form a halo around her.

Jade reached for Lyon, but he leaned back. He wanted to take just a moment to look down at her, to take in all her glorious beauty with the detachment that was only possible when he wasn't being intoxicated with her kisses, when he wasn't touching her golden flesh, feeling her awakening passions.

"When I left for the wars . . . you were such a young girl," Lyon said in a passion-hoarse whisper.

His gaze trailed slowly over Jade as she lay on the bed, turned just slightly away from him. He had seen so much ugliness during his battles that it heightened Jade's beauty and made him appreciate her that much more.

"Look at you now. You're a woman in full bloom at the absolute height of your magnificence!"

Jade had looked away, unable to watch Lyon's eyes as they touched her. She rolled just a bit more away from him, self-conscious of flaws in her beauty that were imaginary to everyone but herself.

"I feel uncomfortable when you look at me that way," she whispered.

She heard him laugh quietly, and it touched an open nerve within her. Why did he have to be so sure of himself? She wished such a question would not insinuate itself into her thoughts at a time like this.

"You shouldn't feel uncomfortable, m'lady," Lyon replied. "Turn so that I can see you. All of you."

She felt her bed move, and knew that he was standing. Was he leaving her because she wouldn't turn toward him?

Against her will, she turned on the mattress, rolling toward Lyon. She saw him standing there calmly, his booted feet spread to shoulder's width, hands on his hips.

He unbuttoned the neck clasp on his cape and removed it with a certain flourish, tossing the cape to the foot of the bed. Next he cast aside his jacket with a disdainful shrug of his shoulders. Lastly he opened his shirt nearly to the navel, exposing an expanse of finely muscled chest, covered lightly with curly brown hair.

Jade sighed softly as she looked at Lyon's chest. She hadn't thought it possible for a woman to enjoy so thoroughly looking at a man's body. As she watched Lyon slowly pulling the tails of his shirt from his breeches, watching the muscles in his pectorals moving sinuously beneath the surface of his skin, she felt herself being touched by an invisible hand, caressing her in an imaginary way that triggered a very real response in her body.

When his shirt had been pulled completely free of his

117

breeches and opened, showing his chest and the rippled, corded muscles of his stomach, Jade could remain still no longer. She rolled onto her knees, rising as she reached for the young knight. He came to her then, taking her shoulders into his hands. Jade saw the long, jagged scar snaking white across Lyon's ribs. She knew it was an old scar from a battle long ago, but it bothered her that Lyon's body should have been violated by weapons in some needless battle, part of some needless war.

He pushed her backward onto the bed, forcing her to conform to his will, and Jade did not mind. Her legs were bent beneath her, but that, too, was inconsequential when Lyon's arm went beneath her head and his other hand cupped the side of her face.

"Jade," he said, saying her name with the reverence of a prayer.

He kissed her then, and she kissed him back with great need and hunger. With his naked chest pressing against her, compressing her breasts within the bodice of her nightgown, Jade could feel the heat of his body radiating through her, as if nothing separated them. Her nipples had become erect and extremely sensitive, made even more responsive by the hard wall of muscle that constituted Lyon's chest.

Lyon pulled Jade toward him, moving her so that her legs were no longer bent beneath her. Then he rolled toward her, forcing her thighs apart with his own knee. His desire for her was so overwhelming that his famous self-control was shattered.

With a groan of primal need, he curled his fingers into the neckline of Jade's immaculate nightgown and pulled down harshly. A single breast, full and round, its crest darkened and peaked with passion, sprang free. Lyon descended upon the breast with ravenous desire, catching the peak between his lips, sweeping his tongue across the tip.

Jade's strangled cry of ecstasy told Lyon that she was burning with a passion as hot and consuming as his own.

Jade opened her eyes, and through the dimness of her bedchamber, awash in shadows and golden light from the candles that burned, she saw Lyon's handsome countenance as he kissed her breast.

"When you k-k-kiss me like that . . ." Jade gasped, hugging Lyon's face to her breast. She tried to say more, but passion made coherent words impossible.

With greater courage than she thought she possessed, Jade thrust her hand into Lyon's opened shirt to feel his flesh without the restriction of clothing separating her. The hair of his chest was suprisingly soft, not bristly like the hair on a man's face. With this single revelation, she realized that she knew very little about men.

She felt the leathery muscles of Lyon's chest. When she scraped her thumbnail over his nipple, he groaned his approval, but did not lift his mouth from the crest of her breast.

She could wait no longer. Her body felt like it was burning, being consumed by the sensual inferno of Lyon Beauchane. Jade pulled at Lyon's shirt, frantic to remove it completely. Only then, when she clumsily pulled at the cloth, did Lyon raise his head from her breast.

There was no longer a faintly taunting smile curling his lips, no vague arrogance that suggested this encounter meant much more to Jade than it did to him. His eyes glowed bright blue with a fierce, primal need that matched Jade's own.

With strong, demanding hands, Lyon grabbed Jade and quickly, artlessly, removed her nightgown. Then, frantic to return to her on the bed, he stripped out of his own clothes. He refused to look at her in all her naked splendor, knowing that if he did he would never have the patience necessary to take off his knee-high boots and the rest of his clothing. One glance at Princess Jade's extraordinary body, at her creamy skin and her voluptuous curves, and Lyon would merely bare his manhood and couple with her frantically in a manner more befitting an act of violence than an act of passion.

"Oh!" Jade gsped when Lyon at last turned toward her again.

He was completely naked and fully aroused, and he seemed much larger than ever before, though he was mostly shrouded in shadows. In the flickering candlelight, as Lyon put a knee on the bed to move closer to her, she saw that his body was even more sculpted, more muscled, than she had suspected. Even the scar on his chest, and the scar on his cheek which he so often tried to hide, did not mar his masculine, virile beauty. Indeed, the scars made Jade think of Lyon as a young lion, in his prime, scarred from battles that had been fought and won.

He slipped into her arms, and as before, separated her knees with one of his own. Lyon raised his knee, his leg sliding intimately between Jade's until at last she felt his thickly muscled thigh pressing tight against her femininity.

There was no friction in the contact, just pressure, hard muscle pressing against the sensitive, moist petals of Jade's femininity. But that pressure ignited sensations that caused Jade to toss her head back, sending her mane of honey blond hair cascading across the bed. She opened her mouth to cry out in pleasure, but the scream was silenced by Lyon before it could arouse the suspicions of the guards who surely stood just outside the bedchamber door. Lyon kissed her hard, his lips firm against Jade's as she shivered in naked abandon on the bed, trembling under the onslaught of new, incredibly powerful feelings.

Her hips jerked violently upward, as though jolted by some strange force. For a brief moment, Jade contemplated exactly what was happening, whether she should allow it to happen, if she wanted it to stop, and whether she could get Lyon to stop. The thoughts, born of insecurities of her own sexuality, did not last long, though Lyon sensed her momentary lapse in concentration.

"Don't worry," he said, pushing his fingers through her long, luxurious mane of golden hair. His face was close to hers as he looked deep into her eyes, the length of his sculpted body pressing down upon her, heating her flesh. "It will be perfection, I promise!" He kissed Jade between words, as though sealing the promise on a contract with an invisible bond that would never be broken. "It is what is meant to be. This is what we were meant for!"

Jade looked away. It was impossible to look deep

121

into Lyon's eyes and remain intellectually calm, able to think problems through rationally. But before she could spend much time thinking of the things that she should do, Lyon forced her face toward his again, and he was kissing her with gentle whispering lips that danced from one corner of her mouth to the other.

"Touch me, Jade," Lyon whispered.

He caught her bottom lip between his teeth for a moment, biting softly, preventing her from speaking even if she wanted to. Though he ached to feel himself buried deeply in her receptive body, he was still looking for her total surrender to the senses. Though he would never admit it to himself and certainly not to anyone else, Lyon wanted Jade to not merely surrender to his seduction, but to be an active and ardent participant in the conquest.

He forcefully turned her head, and bit her slender throat, his teeth sharp against her tender flesh. Jade flinched. A moment later, when Lyon smoothed over the area that he had just bitten with the moist tip of his tongue, Jade sighed with pleasure. Her arms wrapped tightly around the knight's body, her knees squeezed tightly together to keep Lyon's warm, muscular thigh pressing firmly against the juncture of her thighs.

Why has he stopped?

The question rang hollowly in Jade's mind. She was nearly delirious with passion, and yet she sensed that Lyon was holding something back. She could hear him speaking and feel the heat of his magnificent body, but his words seemed distant. Only his kisses and his wonderfully experienced caresses mattered to Princess Jade Crosse.

122

"Touch me," Lyon repeated.

Her lashes fluttered against her cheeks, then she opened her eyes, conscious at last of what Lyon had said. Wasn't she touching him? She had every part of her body pressed against him!

"But Lyon . . ." she said, about to question him when awareness dawned on her.

She looked into his eyes, and it suddenly occurred to Jade that, though she was a widow, she was still thoroughly inexperienced in the realm of sensuality. But then, she mused, every woman would have to be considered inexperienced until she had known the pleasures that were to be awakened by Lyon's skills.

Jade ran her trembling fingertips down from the small of Lyon's back to his hip. She shifted positions slightly beneath him, and his masculinity, no longer trapped between them, seemed to spring free. The heat of it seared Jade's stomach.

"Touch me," Lyon repeated, raising his knee once again to press his thigh against Jade intimately. There was the touch of command in his tone this time, and she found his tone surprisingly appealing.

She was afraid to touch him, afraid that she would do something wrong that would destroy the magic of this golden moment. But drawing on her inner courage, she reached between their bodies. Her long, slender fingers curled around him, and his deep, rumbling sigh of pleasure was all the confirmation Jade needed to know that she had done what he wanted.

She squeezed him tightly and, in the back of her mind, thought, He's too big for me. It'll hurt. It'll hurt terribly.

123

She was thankful, too, that Lyon had closed his eyes, since she did not want him aware of her trepidation. For good or bad, for pleasure or pain, Jade could not stop herself from continuing along this sensual path, much less stop Lyon now that she had driven him mad with passion.

As she moved her hand, she studied Lyon's face, pleased to see the changing tapestry of passion flicker and flash over his countenance.

"Help me," Lyon whispered, moving upon the bed, rolling so that more of his weight was upon Jade.

You could never need help, Jade thought.

Looking into her eyes, Lyon read the unspoken question there. "Show me the way," he said in a breathy whisper.

The soft, sensual purr that came from Jade surprised her. She had not even thought that she was capable of such a sound, or of the emotion that produced it. When Lyon shifted, she moved upon the bed, too, parting her knees wide to accommodate his lean hips. He supported his upper body, keeping his weight off her. As their gazes held each other's Jade reached between them with both hands.

"Slowly," she whispered, bringing the throbbing tip of Lyon's manhood to her moist entrance. "You're too big."

"I will teach you that I am not," Lyon replied.

The pain that Jade had envisioned never really materialized. When she felt the pressure building, she bit her lip, afraid that she would cry out in pain when Lyon finally entered her. She had not cried out, and even if she had, it would not have been a sound of pain.

She opened to him as a flower blossoms to the sun, trembling with desire. Each slow, measured thrust was just a little deeper than the one before. Jade felt herself teetering upon the brink of an abyss that was awesome in its intensity and utterly irresistible in its allure.

With a groan of pleasure, Lyon at last buried all of himself into Jade, and he lowered his chest to feel the plush mounds of her breasts, firm and naked, against him.

He tried to kiss Jade, but when he did, she tore her mouth away. She could not kiss him—not when she could feel him pulsing with virility, with life itself, deep within her very being. This awareness was pushing her relentlessly into a blazing inferno of emotion.

"Lyon!" she gasped suddenly as she tightened around the driving, thrusting manhood that filled her.

Lyon kissed her before she could make any more noise, and he smiled to himself as she thrashed beneath him, lost in the throes of an orgasm that obviously had surprised her both in the swiftness of its arrival and in its intensity. He continued on, loving Jade with a certain amount of emotional detachment, determined to please her as he had never pleased a woman before.

It took some time for Jade to recover her senses. When at last her breathing had returned to some semblance of normality and her vision had cleared, she looked up into Lyon's handsome face. It was mildly disconcerting to her that he was smiling confidently, as though driving young women insane with desire was nothing new to him. She reached up to hold his face in her hands, running the pad of her thumb over his lips.

125

Words failed Jade. She wanted Lyon to know exactly how magnificent it felt to be with him, to be one with him, but she could think of no words that would do this lovemaking justice. When Lyon thrust deeply into her again, passion constricted Jade's throat, making it impossible for her to even attempt mere talking.

Though not much time had passed since she had been blinded by the consummation of passion, Jade again felt herself becoming pulled along by the current of desire. It pushed her toward something that was still a little frightening, but no longer unknown. Through the thick, dark curl of her lashes, she saw passion constrict Lyon's sculpted features, and felt the ardency of his actions increase.

"Love m-me," Jade stammered, giving herself fully to the feelings that consumed her, surrendering to the man who had introduced her to a new world of sensation. "Love me, Lyon!"

She felt his hands all over her, touching her bottom, her breasts, her thighs, caressing her sometimes with light touches that tantalized, sometimes with strong touches that demanded she respond.

He repositioned her, placing her calves upon his shoulders, tilting her pelvis to elicit yet new sensations, both for herself and for him. When he thrust into her again, she felt him filling her with his heat, with his strength. She felt his taut, lean hips colliding with her buttocks, felt his desire for her, his ravenous hunger.

"Lyon!" Jade cried out again as she tumbled headlong into the world of sensual abyss where the only reality was the release of pure emotion, and the only way she could know that reality was through Lyon.

She was still writhing beneath him, her voluptuous body shaking through the waves of ecstasy that had again claimed her, when Jade heard the groan of pleasure that rumbled forth from his chest. She felt the reverberations rumble through him, seemingly moving straight into her own body through the sensitized tips of her breasts.

He bore into Jade deeply, fiercely, and released the passion he had held back for so long.

Chapter 11

Later, with Lyon's head upon her shoulder, Jade stroked his hair and shoulders as he slowly descended from the heights of his passion. He eased himself from her, and Jade sighed softly with displeasure. She suddenly felt very empty and alone without the weight of him pressing her into the mattress; his powerful, athletic body reassuring her without words that she was safe, and that he would not allow anything bad to happen to her ever again.

It was the knock on the bedchamber door that brought the outside world charging back into Jade's life, jarring her newfound serenity.

In a series of seamless moves that were hurried yet smooth as the surface of a tranquil pond, Lyon rolled off the bed, scooped up his clothes in one hand and drew his dagger in the other, then headed, naked, for the balcony. He dropped his clothes behind the curtain, tossed the cape around his shoulders, then motioned for Jade to open the bedchamber door. She was still reeling from what she had been doing with Lyon, and it took a few seconds for Jade to gather her wits.

When Lyon wrapped the cape around himself and stepped into the shadows of the balcony, he practically disappeared right before Jade's eyes. She then realized why he always wore the black cape, even when it was warm out.

The third knock on the door was followed by Mary Ellen's warning that she would enter bringing the guards with her unless the door was opened instantly.

Frantically, Jade pulled her nightgown over her head and managed to get to the door a moment before it was opened. She knew her hair was a mess, and her heart was racing in her bosom. Did she look like a woman well-loved?

"What do you want?" Jade demanded in her most imperious tone, deciding it was best to bring the attack to her spying maid rather than let it be brought to her. She threw open the bedchamber door, wearing only her nightgown, her eyes spitting angry flames of amber. "What do you think you're doing disturbing my sleep once again?"

Jade drew the reactions that she was looking for. The two guards were speechless and their eyes bulged, staring at Jade in the shimmering silk nightgown with the low, lace-trimmed bodice. Mary Ellen was rendered dumb by the vehemence of Jade's attack.

She pushed past Mary Ellen to look up at the guards. With much more confidence in her tone than she felt in her heart, Jade said with deadly intensity, "If you insist upon looking at me that way, then I will insist upon taking measures which will ensure that your minds do not stray toward impure thoughts." She saw that the guards did not understand her subtle threat, so she added, "Once you've been made eunuchs, I'm sure you won't look upon me quite that way again." The blood drained from the guards' faces. "Leave me."

The guards left at a dead run, understanding fully the price they might have to pay for having looked at Princess Jade Crosse while she wore only her nightgown.

"You shouldn't have done that," Mary Ellen said.

The maid she did not like one-to-one confrontations with the princess, and she especially did not like this sudden change, this display of courage and conficence that had not been there before. "They are to ensure security."

"Whose security? Yours or mine?" Jade shot back, still standing in the doorway to her bedchamber, blocking Mary Ellen's entrance. "Now I asked you a question and still haven't received and answer. What are you doing here at this hour?"

Mary Ellen made no effort to hide the fact that she was looking over Princess Jade's shoulder into the bedchamber. "I heard noises."

"Noises?"

"Yes, noises. And I heard you cry out." Mary Ellen looked at the bed and saw that it was extremely rumpled. She pushed past Jade, forcibly entering the bedchamber, all her suspicious instincts tingling, hoping to catch the princess doing something wrong. "You called out 'lion,' I believe."

Jade's heart sank. Why couldn't she keep her passion silent? She watched as Mary Ellen walked slowly around the dishevelled bed. Could she tell that the bed had been a shrine of passion only moments before?

"What happened?" Mary Ellen asked.

She came to a halt on the far side of the bed, less than fifteen feet from the balcony where Lyon stood hiding in the shadows, a lethal dagger in his hand. Jade knew she had to think of something quick or her maid would die.

"I had a . . . nightmare," Jade said softly, fighting to control her fear, struggling for the confidence she had felt only moments earlier. "It was a bad nightmare. I dreamed that I was being attacked . . . eaten alive, devoured by a lion."

"A lion?"

"Yes, a lion."

The maid made a cursory inspection of the balcony, saw nothing, then left the bedchamber, suggesting that Princess Jade drink lots of wine and get back to sleep.

When Jade closed the door behind Mary Ellen, her heart at last resumed beating, and she slumped against the door.

My nerves can't withstand this, Jade thought as she leaned against the heavy wooden panel.

As though materializing from the night air, Lyon stepped out of the shadows and dropped his cape, standing completely naked and unembarrassed, holding the deadly dagger loosely in his hand. He crossed the bedchamber to Jade, a faint smile playing with his mouth as it so often did.

"You think everything is funny, don't you?" Jade whispered accusingly when he reached her.

Lyon gave her a boyishly innocent look, which brought a smile to Jade, even though she didn't want it to. He took her hand in his and began leading her toward the balcony. Though Jade knew she shouldn't follow him, she did, watching the taut movement of his naked buttocks as he walked.

Outside, Lyon turned toward Jade and tried to kiss her, but she twisted away from him.

"Don't you think you should put something on?" she asked, not finding his lack of embarrassement at all amusing. Or so she tried to tell herself.

"Why?"

"Because you should. Isn't that reason enough?"

"For some, I suppose."

Lyon wasn't inclined to dress. While it was true that he had brought Jade to the summit of passion twice, he himself had only been there once that night. He could not be satisfied with that; not when he had been consumed for days with the thought of what it would be like to feel the passion of the extraordinary Princess Jade Crosse.

She turned her back to him. Lyon put his hands on her shoulders, and the look that Jade gave him over her shoulder was unyielding. He took his hands from her, realizing that it really would do no good to fight her on this. He'd seen this reaction before from women unaccustomed to discovering their own passion. Once the desire had cooled, they didn't know what they were supposed to say or do or how to react. Since they invariably felt betrayed, both by Lyon and by their own bodies, they became angry.

He padded silently back into the bedchamber, and in moments had his clothes back on. He fixed the cape over his shoulders, and lastly replaced the slender, lethal dagger to the sheath at his left hip.

When he went back out to the balcony, Jade was looking out to sea, the breeze fluffing her blond hair over her shoulders and down her back. Lyon moved to

132

the left to look at her in profile, and the vision of flawless femininity gripped him with physical force.

She folded her arms together beneath her breasts. It was a defensive posture, one of a young woman thinking deeply about what she had just done. What Jade did not realize was that by positioning her arms so, she was lifting her heavy, round breasts just slightly, causing them to stretch and strain against the deep neckline of her nightgown.

Lyon moved to her side, gently sliding an arm around her waist. He leaned over to kiss her hair.

"You are so beautiful," he said quietly.

He knew she needed words of comfort, but he did not know what to say. What words should he use? He had never been skilled at such comforting, and it somewhat annoyed him that Jade appeared to require it now.

Jade stepped to the side, spinning slowly as she did, shrugging Lyon's hand off.

Still looking out at the moonlight shimmering upon the sea, Jade said, "Is it agreed then that we will meet at the village of Richland on the morrow?"

She wants to pretend nothing happened between us, Lyon thought.

Her apparent nonchalance rankled him. For one of the few times in his life, he did not want the loving to be quickly forgotten.

"Well?" she asked, an edge to her tone.

"Let's make it the village of Hogarth on the day after the morrow," Lyon finally answered. "And this time I promise it's not a test."

Jade uncrossed her arms. She leaned against the marble railing that surrounded the balcony and breathed deeply. Since she had a slight fear of heights that she tried to pretend did not exist, she had never really looked down at the rocks before. Not for long anyway, and never when she did not have to. But she wanted to be afraid now. She wanted to know an emotion that kept her mind far away from thoughts and memories of what she had just experienced with Lyon in her bed.

When she looked down, she saw the moonlight shimmering upon the crashing waves that exploded against the rocks, and she breathed again deeply. Her fingers tightened around the top railing, and though instinct tried to push her away from the balcony and into her bedchamber, Jade continued to stare down the chasm of three hundred feet to the water below.

She wanted to frighten herself, and she was succeeding admirably.

"Is that acceptable to you?" Lyon asked. His words sounded like a terse negotiation, and he didn't like the tone of it, not while speaking with Jade. "The village of Hogarth in two days?"

Jade nodded, but did not speak. She could feel Lyon's presence so close to her. Though he did not touch her, her skin tingled from head to foot, as though his eyes had once again ignited a fire deep within her. It was a fire that Jade had experienced before; one that she was trying hard to pretend she had extinguished so thoroughly it would never again flame to life.

"What we did, my lady, was destined," Lyon said softly, moving closer to Jade, standing directly behind her.

He could tell that she was frightened, and that looking down into the sea was something she was forcing herself to do. Why she was doing it baffled him completely. Though the gentleman in him suggested he find out so that he might comfort her, the man in him suggested in a much louder voice that he pleasure himself with Princess Jade's voluptuous body once more before answering the dictates of duty.

She shook her head, sending her long, silken tresses swirling over her shoulders and down her back. Lyon moved so close that his groin pressed against her buttocks. He pushed her hair away from the nape of her neck and kissed her at that velvet point, her head to one side.

Jade sighed, but it wasn't a sigh entirely of pleasure. There was also reservation in the sound, a thread of sadness weaving through it. Lyon's pride made him resolve to change the sound of her sigh to a sound of unabashed and uncontrollable ecstasy before he left her.

"You've denied yourself for too long, Jade," Lyon whispered. He stretched his arms out to grip the top railing, encircling Jade with his muscled frame. His cape flowed over his shoulders, dark against the white of her nightgown. "You don't need to deny yourself when you are with me."

These were not the words that Jade wanted to hear. Deny herself? That was how Lyon saw the act of making love. Something physical that's done simply with the bodies. The minds and hearts of the participants were not important in his view.

He moved slightly behind her, and she felt him, thick and swollen once again. Instantly, a thousand recent unbidden memories of what it had been like to feel his great heart beating next to her own flooded her mind.

135

"Don't do this, Lyon," Jade said, her knuckles now white as she gripped the marble railing. "It isn't right. Not proper." And it means nothing to you! she thought with a burst of sudden anger and sadness. Confront him with what you know!

But the words would not pass from between her slightly parted lips. When Lyon pressed himself against her, even through the combined layers of his breeches and her nightgown, she was able to feel the heat and excitement of this virile man.

"Jade . . . Princess Jade . . ."

His hands moved from the top of the railing over to her wrists. He tried to pull her hands from the marble railing so that he could turn her to face him, but Jade held on tightly. She foolishly believed that if she did not face Lyon Beauchane, then she would not succumb again to his devastatingly seductive charm.

He leaned against her, pressing his chest against her back. The heat of their bodies, the passion that beat between them with an ancient pulse, could not be concealed by their clothing.

With just a slight twist of his hips, Lyon felt himself become nestled tightly against Jade, snug and secure in an erotic valley. When she pushed back against him, making the fit a bit tighter, Lyon could not be sure whether she was becoming aroused, whether she was trying to avoid him and get away, or if he was simply imagining a response from her at all.

"Look at me," Lyon whispered, his face pressed into the velvety curls of her hair, his lips brushing her ear as he spoke. "Turn to me . . . let me kiss you . . . let me take you there again."

Jade shook her head. She had succumbed to his

desires before, but she would not again. Didn't he realize that Mary Ellen already suspected that she wasn't alone in her bedchamber? Didn't he have any fear at all? Any sense of decency? Didn't he realize that she was a lonely woman, vulnerable and scared? If he was any kind of gentleman, he wouldn't take advantage of the circumstances.

His hands released their tight hold on Jade's wrists, but they did not leave her. Instead, very slowly, his hands went up Jade's arms, touching her lightly, at first pushing the sleeves of her nightgown up, and then, at the elbows, touching her through the fine garment.

Jade watched, her heartbeat quickening, as the hands of the passionate knight slipped over her biceps, moved inward, then cupped her breasts through the silk. Against her will, her nipples instantly hardened beneath Lyon's touch. When he caught the twin peaks between his forefingers and thumbs, Jade sighed, and this time the sound held only passion.

"So firm," Lyon purred.

He caught Jade's earlobe between his teeth and bit softly as he manipulated her nipples. His manhood strained against the front of his breeches. If he did not do something to free himself quickly, he would surely go mad with want.

He filled his hands with her breasts. Looking over Jade's shoulder, he saw that her forearms were quivering because she was gripping the marble balcony railing so tightly.

Despite the burning hunger that set the blood boiling in his veins, Lyon smiled to himself. Jade had succumbed to his desires earlier in bed, and she had done everything that Lyon had asked of her. But out here on the balcony with a warm seabreeze playing over them, he would need to take every initiative if they were to make love again. His stubborn princess wasn't going to assist or deny him in any way. In a strange fashion, Lyon found Jade's attitude of indifference wildly challenging and exciting.

He released her breasts, then reached down and grabbed the bottom hem of the white nightgown. Without haste, he raised it slowly, inch by inch, stepping back to watch as she was revealed to him.

Chapter 12

"Ohhh!" Jade moaned as she felt her nightgown being lifted.

She felt heated, wet, a little sore. He can't want me again, she thought, but everything else she knew about Lyon told her he did.

I can't make love to him again was her next thought, but she knew that that wasn't true. There was something magical about Lyon that made her melt inside. She knew, though she really had very little experience in such matters, that she would always be able to make love to Lyon. He would, in his unique and exhilarating way, make lovemaking different each time, with the only commonality being the heights of pleasure that he would take her to.

"I'll never get enough of you," Lyon growled passionately.

There was a certain truth to his words that shocked him, and he paused for just a moment to ponder it. Then, spreading his hands together beneath the nightgown, he raised the silk above Jade's hips, splaying his hands over her taut buttocks.

"Perfection," he whispered.

Being guided by Lyon's all-knowing hands, Jade took a half-step backward, but continued holding tightly onto the top edge of the railing. She leaned forward a bit, feeling the strong commanding hands touching her, stroking the glowing embers of a passion that would soon burst anew to full flame.

With spread legs, Lyon opened his breeches and his manhood leaped out gratefully, fully engorged. His desire for Jade was something more than just the lust of a virile knight for a beautiful and willing woman. It was much more than that. Did the inferno burn in his soul because she was his princess, and she had the power to command his execution? A man did not become a knight without having a taste for danger, and a man who was a leader of knights and an accomplished warrior in battle needed a positive thirst for it. But even this craving for danger and excitement did not quite explain the hunger, the ravenous need for possession, that now gripped Lyon with invisible, intractable tentacles.

This was not the time to ponder such matters, he told himself crossly. But in the back of his mind, he knew that Jade was different from all the other women he had known intimately. She had sparked something within him that was more than mere physical excitement.

With a certain sense of anger at himself and at Jade for making him hunger for her as he did, Lyon braced himself behind her, bending his knees to be at the proper angle. When he touched her, feeling her moisture and knowing how ready she was, a grim, determined smile pressed his lips into a thin line.

"Tell me to stop and I will," he said, no longer whispering.

Jade squeezed her eyes shut. She felt the heat of Lyon's masculinity touching her. She knew the next sensation of being pierced by him would be meltingly satisfying.

She could not tell him to stop when her knees were shaking as hard as they were, and all her thoughts and senses were tuned toward the thousand different feelings that went through her when he first entered her. He filled her so completely that she had no room for reality, for fear, for worry, for thoughts of anything but Lyon Beauchane.

With a slow, steady, powerful thrust, Lyon entered her. Jade's eyes burst open, and with glazed vision she realized that she was looking down at the surf far below as it exploded against the rocks.

She could not see Lyon, but she could feel him, and she could sense him, and that was the important thing. He was not merely inside her, and he was not merely touching her. He was all around her, suffusing her with his being, protecting her with his strength. He was surrounding and feeling and completing her with his mind and body and soul.

She felt everything distinctly, her passion mounting with startling swiftness, rushing furiously toward the summit of ecstasy as the waves crashed ceaselessly upon the rocks below. And yet, through this blinding passion, she was able to see in her mind's eye and appreciate logically all the subtle and exhilarating things that Lyon was doing to her. She was able to see each individual brush stroke in the vast mural of eroticism that the enigmatic knight was painting for her.

The marble railing was cool against her stomach as she leaned over it further, wanting to feel him thrust even deeper into her. She watched her own hair, blowing gently in the evening seabreeze. She felt her breasts rocking gently inside the bodice of her nightgown, moving gently as she responded to the soft collision of flesh to flesh. She heard the waves crashing on the rocks far below, and she heard the slap of taut hips striking against hers as Lyon drove himself deep into her with increasing fury.

It was almost as though Jade were drugged or in a trance. She had not really intended for this to happen, and she had been unable to summon the strength of will necessary to prevent the relentless lovemaking.

She had not thought it possible for a woman to become so enraptured with the act of making love. No one had ever told her such a thing could happen. On the night before her wedding so many years ago, Jade's mother had told her to keep her eyes squeezed tightly shut, and that "it isn't so horrid after a while."

Sleepily, Jade smiled, her eyes closed, her body rocking gently to and fro. Horrid? Such a strange word it seemed now to describe lovemaking. But while she was married to Prince William, Jade would not have used any superlative, either good or bad, to describe the marital experience.

Lyon held Jade's hips tightly in his large hands, pulling her backward to meet his thrusts. Perhaps in other circumstances, the strength that Lyon used would have been too great for Jade's pale flesh, and would have bruised and hurt her. But with the passion singing in her veins, all she felt was satisfaction, and the unusual yet thoroughly exciting sensation of being consumed by a strong man's desire for her.

She felt his hand against her thigh, sliding around, then experienced fingertips touching her where their bodies were joined.

Her body was wracked with a series of hard, jolting spasms that shot through her, convulsions of the release of emotion.

Jade tossed her head up, her hair flying to stream down her back. If Lyon had not held onto her so tightly, she surely would have fallen to her knees as her climax subsided, and all strength and energy suddenly left her.

She was still twitching through the last of her culmination when Lyon issued a mighty roar and he, too, was pitched forward into the abyss of ultimate pleasure.

It was later, after Jade had caught her breath and Lyon had properly rearranged his clothing, that they stood in the darkness, leaning against each other. Lyon's midnight black cape surrounded both of them, hiding them from a world that held mysteries and conspiracies that neither understood and both had reason to fear.

"I will see you again in two days," Lyon said quietly, holding Jade in his arms. He stroked her hair, running his hand down her back. "Until then, my precious lady."

"Until then," Jade replied.

She did not want to let him go. He still had the climb down the side of the castle before he could escape. Though he had already managed to do that several times, Jade now feared for his safety. Had she weakened him with their lovemaking to such an extent that he would make a mistake? Just one misstep would send him hurtling to his death on the rocks below.

Silently, Lyon extricated himself from Jade's arms, kissing her one last time, then disappeared over the balcony railing.

Chapter 13

"You really want us to believe that she doesn't know who is making the decision in her own fiefdom?" Lord Charles Frederick asked, his round, bearded face twisted into a scowl of disbelief.

Lyon watched as Lord Charles and Baron von Mueller exchanged incredulous looks. It was inconceivable to them that Princess Jade Crosse couldn't be the one making the decisions in her fiefdom, and wasn't fully aware of all that was happening. In their own fiefdoms, they held total power in their hands, and anyone who had any doubts of that, or in any way presented a threat to that, soon discovered the error of their ways.

"That isn't what I said," Lyon replied.

Sometimes he found these cantankerous old men difficult to deal with. They were, individually and collectively, intelligent, resourceful, fair, wise, and resolute. They had run their various fiefdoms and business enterprises profitably, and those whose lives and livelihood they held in their hands benefited. But what was equaly true was that they had absolutely no patience whatsoever for anyone less competent than themselves. They were impatient when it came to getting answers. They wanted to know *now* why Jade Crosse was behaving the way she was, and getting the peasants all riled up in the process.

"Then perhaps you'd like to explain exactly what you did say," Baron von Mueller replied, leaning back in the huge chair that accentuated his short stature. He fixed a steely stare upon Lyon, who met his gaze.

"I said that at present I cannot say for certain whether Jade Crosse is in control of her own fiefdom. If she is, then she is responsible for murders and extortion and all the other crimes that we have heard about. If, however, she is not in control, if there are forces working to prevent and subvert her control and authority, then it would be foolish to hold her accountable for the actions of men who may well be supplanting her power."

Lyon rose swiftly. He didn't like having to explain himself. With Prince William, he had been held in such high esteem that no one, not even Prince William, had ever questioned his word or his opinion on anything.

Lord Charles and Baron von Mueller weren't so easily impressed.

Pacing the room, Lyon continued, trying to keep the memory of his lovemaking with Jade out of his thoughts. They were too perceptive for him to assume that they wouldn't deduce what had happened between himself and Princess Jade.

"A meeting has been scheduled at the village of Hogarth. I believe that if I can speak with . . ." he paused just a moment, nearly tripping over the strange formality of the proper noun, "Princess Crosse, alone and for a protracted period of time, than I believe that I can find out once and for all the truth that has thus far eluded us."

Lord Charles made a growling sound, not liking the fact that he would have to wait at least one more day, and possibly two, before he could get the answers that had vexed him since the death of his neighbor, Prince William Crosse.

"Find out about taxing the peasants at Millbury," Lord Charles commanded. "I heard a particularly vile story about a murder at night. Soldiers came later and buried the body, then charged the victim's family a tax to bury him." His face was twisted into a bearded scowl of utter contempt. "Several of the young men from Millbury vowed to get revenge, and they looked to other young men in North Hexsum to enlist in their ranks."

"But North Hexsum is in your fiefdom, good sir," Lyon said.

"Percisely. Because of that widow's greedy madness, three young men from fine families are now outlaws! Men with a price on their heads!"

Baron von Mueller cursed in German, shaking his head as Lord Charles paused briefly.

"This is exactly what we did not want to have happen," the baron said. "When young men get the fever in their blood, anything can happen. We do not need Princess Jade's peasants turning everyone against the landowners. It won't do us any good. It won't do anyone any good."

Lyon finished the last of his wine, then set his goblet

147

down. Whatever problems he might have with the personalities of Lord Charles Frederick and Baron von Mueller, he had none with their philosophy of leadership, or in how they treated the peasants living on their land.

"Give me a few more days," Lyon said, tossing his ebony cape over his shoulders. "Just a few more days and then I'll have all the information that any of us will need." He stood, tall and commanding, in the center of the library, fastening the buckle of the belt that held his sword. "But gentlemen, if Princess Jade Crosse is the monster that rumor makes her out to be, then you'll need to find another man to solve your problem. I'm a knight, a warrior. I'm not an executioner to satisfy this kind of political convenience."

Lyon Beauchane left the room. Lord Charles turned to his companion and said, "For my money, that young man has become smitten with Princess Jade."

The baron shook his head. "I've heard his heart is not in any way attached to what he carries in his breeches. Don't worry, Sir Lyon will do what must be done."

"Perhaps . . . perhaps." He sat down heavily. "Let us hope."

Garth Rawlings did not like being summoned to Bishop Nathan Field's living quarters in Castle Crosse. In theory, the bishop had little power over Garth, who commanded the knights in Princess Jade's control. Bishop Fields, as a man of religion, was to offer emotional and spiritual guidance to Princess Jade, and help her decide what wars should be fought, chiefly in the name of the Lord. Beyond that, it wasn't any of the bishop's business what Garth did.

But it wasn't that way in real life, and since Garth was secretly intimidated by Bishop Fields, he despised the man.

He walked up the stairway, his boots crunching softly against the stone underfoot, the tip of his sword's sheath tapped against the steps, trailing a steady metallic ringing down the narrow, winding stairway.

"I thought it would be you, m'lord."

Garth looked up, shocked at the feminine voice that had interrupted his thoughts of Bishop Fields. It was Mary Ellen, the spy under the bishop's employ.

"How did you know it was me?" Sir Garth asked, but what he was really wondering was whether Mary Ellen had just been warming the bishop's bed and body.

"You wear you sword so low it always hits the ground when you walk."

Mary Ellen smiled as she took another two steps down the stairway toward Garth, pleased that she had surprised him. He was not an ugly man, she concluded, and there was an earthly, animal savagery to him that appealed to her own sense of primitive desire. Also, she was much more intelligent than he was, and that appealed to her, too, since she enjoyed feeling superior to the men she spread her legs for.

She smiled flirtatiously at Garth and asked, "Is there anything *else* you wear that hangs so low?"

The openness of the statement caught Garth by surprise, and for a moment he couldn't think of anything to say in response. Before he could say a word, Mary Ellen laughed softly and continued on her way down the stairs.

"Think about what you want to say the next time we see each other," the spy said with a tinkling laugh as she descended the winding stone stairway.

The idea of stealing a woman from Bishop Fields excited Garth to the core of his soul, and he rushed up the stairs with a new lightness to his step.

In the bishop's quarters, Garth was escorted in by an attractive young maiden he hadn't seen before; Garth was promptly ignored while the bishop continued to read some papers on his desk. Only after a sufficiently humbling time did Bishop Fields finally raise his gaze upward to fix it, cold and black, upon Garth.

"Princess Jade has been asking impertinent questions lately," Bishop Fields said, pushing his chair away from the desk. "She's been demanding to see the peasants in the villages. For obvious reasons, we don't want that to happen."

Garth got the distinct feeling that Nathan Fields was actually just talking to himself. He felt like he was listening in on a conversation that really didn't involve him. Along with so many other things, this heightened his distrust and contempt for the bishop.

"She has demanded—good Lord, I couldn't believe she actually had the courage to make a demand of *me*—that she be allowed to ride alone to the village of Hogarth."

At last Fields turned to fix his gaze directly upon the knight. "I want you and your men to go to Hogarth ahead of her and make sure that they hate her. Do whatever you think is necessary, use whatever means you feel is best, but I want Princess Crosse's name to be a curse upon the tongue of every man, woman, and child in that village."

Garth suppressed the smile that tugged at his mouth. This was the kind of assignment he appreciated most, what he was best at. Hadn't the bishop said before that there wasn't a man in all the fiefdom more adept at spreading terror among the villagers than he?

He puffed his chest out a bit, containing his pleasure and excitement. "Rest easy knowing that I will handle everything to your satisfaction."

Fields turned his attention away from Garth, back to the papers on his desk. "I had better be satisfied. Your value to me hinges upon it. Leave now."

Garth's proud stance held fast, but he felt as though a dagger had been thrust between his ribs. Bishop Fields saw him as nothing more than a hired sword, a mercenary, a killer. A useful and skilled killer, perhaps, but just a man for hire.

Sir Garth Rawlings had no doubt that should the time come when he was not useful to the bishop, a man would be paid to execute him. Even before he had left Bishop Fields's private quarters in Castle Crosse, Garth promised himself that he would take steps to ensure his own safety. If necessary, that included the murder of Bishop Fields.

Garth pulled back lightly on the reins and his destrier came uneasily to a stop. He patted the gelding's neck as the horse pranced in place, eager to get into the fray, sensing that a fight was near at hand.

Behind Garth, seven of his finest and most bloodthirsty knights, along with Sheriff Sean Dunne and several of his men, also pulled their mounts to stop. Their weapons gleamed silver in the moonlight on the tree-lined road that led to the village of Hogarth. Sheriff Dunne reined over to Garth.

"Your men won't carry it too far?"

Garth shook his head. He and his men had been through similar raids of terror before, and he knew he could trust his men to do exactly what they were ordered to do, and nothing more. Perhaps one or two more peasants would be killed than was planned, but Garth had always considered that an inconsequential figure, something of little importance.

"They talk of blood and death. They like this kind of war?"

Garth's eyebrows raised. He pushed the leather and metal helmet back slightly upon his forehead, smiling wickedly. "War, Sheriff? Who told you we were at war?"

"We're at war with Princess Crosse's reputation, and if you don't think that's true, then you've learned nothing at all from your association with the good Bishop Fields."

The two men did not trust each other, but they both had much to gain from the bishop's ascension to power, so they remained uneasy allies.

In the distance, a wolf bayed at the moon, as though issuing a warning to the peasants in Hogarth . . . a warning they did not hear.

Sean Dunne motioned one of his men over. The man was in his twenties, tall and broad-shouldered, with shoulder-length blond hair. His nose had been broken at least once and angled sharply to the right, and a front tooth had been chipped in a fight long ago. The man's savagery was readily apparent, easily visible to the experienced eye of Garth Rawlings, who appreciated such traits.

"This is Edward," Sean Dunne explained. "He's

going to be our Lyon tonight."

Garth looked at the man. He was approximately the same height as Lyon Beauchane, though any real similarity ended there.

"I suppose he'll have to do," Garth said, making no effort to disguise his distrust of the man and displeasure with the masquerade. "He can do what it is we want him to?"

Edward growled at the question, but kept his comments to himself. He had fought many battles, winning and losing his share. He knew that if he crossed swords with Garth, there was a very real chance he would not see another sunrise. He let the insult pass, knowing that soon he would be enjoying the kind of entertainment that pleased him most. The fact that he looked like Lyon Beauchane in some minor way, and that he would soon be responsible for destroying a great man's reputation, was reward enough for him to allow the insults and questions to pass.

Twenty minutes later they rode into the small, sleeping village of Hogarth. The men fanned out, moving in the way they had planned while in the knight's quarters at Castle Crosse.

Garth and Sean, leaders of the men, reined their destriers to the crossroads where the village's only two roads intersected. It was from there they could see the work of their men and issue commands accordingly.

The first sounds that came from within the small, tidy huts and homes were of confusion. Then there were the shouts of fathers and older sons who felt it was their responsibility to protect the women and children from attack, even against much greater numbers and

153

strength. And lastly came the high, shrieking screams of women, frightened to the core of their soul. They knew that whenever men are riding at night, leaving destruction in their wake, it is the women who invariably suffer the most, who pay the cruelest price for male aggression and violence.

For five minutes there was general assult, as Garth's knights, working in teams, systematically brutalized several of the villagers, striking them down with the heavy hafts of their broadswords, then using their boots on the fallen men. They beat the men and boys brutally, but with a stratagem. The intention was to leave bruises behind that would be remembered, not broken bones, and not a corpse.

From astride his powerful war horse, Garth watched as the ghostly image of a woman in a flowing nightgown crossed the dusty street, hands stretched out in front of her. She ran as though reaching for something that would save her from the tall man who was close at her heels. The girl had nearly reached the comparative safety of another hut when she was tackled to the ground by her pursuer. She was so frightened that she didn't even scream as his heavy body came down hard upon her, his calloused and dirty fingers entwining in her long hair.

"Edward?" Garth asked the sheriff calmly. It was difficult to see clearly in the moonlight, and the riders had not brought torches with them.

"Yes." Sean Dunne smiled, pleased with his choice of men for the dirty task of rape. "He was told to choose a woman young enough so that she wouldn't have a precise knowledge of what Lyon Beauchane looks like."

The woman was hoisted onto Edward's shoulder, and he carried her away from the village, into the shrubs and shadows. The girl screamed and pounded Edward's back with her tiny fists. Edward just laughed, his blood so hot that he couldn't even feel her fists striking him.

A man, perhaps the woman's brother or father, chased after Edward. Before he could even cross the street, he was struck down by heavy axe blows from two of Garth's knights.

The screaming continued as Edward and the girl disappeared into the shadows. Then, abruptly, the screaming ended.

Garth turned again to Sean Dunne and asked seriously, "He won't kill her, will he?"

"No. It would do us no good whatsoever if she dies without telling everyone that it was Lyon Beauchane that raped her."

Sean tugged at his lower lip in an effort to keep from smiling. The idea to have a girl raped, and then be told that it was Lyon Beauchane who had raped her, had been his idea, and he was particularly proud of it. He just hoped that Bishop Fields would be equally as proud of it, and would reward him accordingly.

Eventually, after the carnage and terror had reigned for ten minutes, an old man with long hair the color of snow was dragged across the square to where Sheriff Dunne and Garth Rawlings sat astride their mounts. Two knights held the old man by the arms, keeping him standing. The peasant was bleeding from the mouth and had been struck repeatedly in the head.

"Gather them," Garth said to one of his men. Peasants were quickly gathered, forced to stand

155

barefooted in the dirt, trembling with fear and indigantion.

When the audience was in place, Sean stood in the stirrups to be seen more easily, and to heighten his air of authority.

"This man before you has voiced his opposition to Princess Jade Crosse. And this is what happens to men foolish enough to do that!"

Sheriff Sean Dunne raised his fist high over his head. He then brought his fist down, and while all eyes were upon him, Garth drew his sword and thrust it into the old man.

A gasp went through the villagers as they watched the old man's body slump lifeless to the ground.

There was madness in Garth's eyes as he sheathed his sword, and everyone there knew that he longed to kill again.

Sheriff Sean Dunne walked his horse closer to the crowd. His destrier pranced beneath him, nostrils wide, smelling the blood.

"This has been a legal execution for treason," the sheriff explained. "Princess Jade Crosse has spared the rest of you. If she was not so kind hearted, she would have commanded this entire village be burned to the ground, and everyone here legally executed on this very night. That is the punishment for opposing her will! But she is a kind woman, and she has chosen only to remove this treasonous troublemakeer."

He raised his hand then, and the soldiers all quickly remounted. Edward came stumbling forward out of the shadows, a sadistically triumphant smile on his lips. A moment later the men rode out of Hogarth, leaving behind one frightened woman in a tattered nightgown who believed with all her heart and soul that she had just been raped by Lyon Beauchane. They left in their wake a village of peasants who had no reason to doubt that Princess Jade Crosse had just ordered the execution of an old man who had done nothing more than complain that she had yet again raised his taxes.

Chapter 14

Lyon knelt near the young woman. Her eyes were glazed. Though it was warm, she clutched blankets up to her chin.

"Look at me," Lyon said, his voice barely above a whisper. "Have you ever seen me before?"

It took several seconds, but the woman finally turned her eyes away from the wall and toward Lyon. After several more seconds, she finally shook her head. The sight of any man seemed to frighten her greatly.

"My name is Sir Lyon Beauchane."

The young woman gasped and pushed herself against the wall, trembling with fear upon her small, thin mattress. She stared with primal horror at Lyon, and then her expression changed slowly to one of confusion.

"What happened to you . . . it wasn't me," Lyon continued, speaking very slowly and softly.

He wanted to take the woman's hand to comfort her, but he sensed that she would not appreciate it. If she never again wanted a man to touch her, he wouldn't blame her at all.

"He said he was me, but he wasn't. He was someone else. He was lying to you. And do you want to know something else? I'm going to find that man, and I'm going to punish him for you."

That brought a spark to the woman's eyes. It was the first real sign that she understood what he was saying.

"When . . . when you find him . . ." she pleaded softly.

Lyon had to lean down further, putting his ear very close to her mouth to hear her. "What do you want me to do when I find him?" Lyon asked.

"Geld him," the woman replied.

Lyon leaned back. He could not promise to geld the rapist who had done this awful thing to this woman, and who had claimed that he was Lyon after doing it. But what Lyon could do was make sure that the man never again harmed another woman. He wouldn't take away his manhood . . . but he would take the rapist's life.

"When I find him, he will suffer mightily," Lyon said, and the quiver in his voice spoke of his inner rage. "He will suffer, and he will die, and no woman will ever again be afraid of him."

Lyon knew that getting his revenge would not take away the suffering that this woman had undergone, but killing the guilty man would at least prevent more victims from enduring the same fate.

With his jaw clenched in rage, with blue fire spitting from his eyes, Lyon left the small hut in Hogarth, leaving the frightened young woman to be cared for by friends and relatives.

Outside, the men were sitting in a circle around a

small fire made near the spot where the old man had been slain by Garth. Lyon approached them, and when they turned to watch him, he could see that they were looking for revenge against the person they felt was really responsible for the execution—Princess Jade Crosse.

Lyon sat upon a wood stump that served as a chair at the gathering spot.

"She's strong here," Lyon said, tapping his heart, referring to the woman he'd just left. "It may take a while, but she'll recover."

The men, the leaders of the village of Hogarth, remained silent. Some of them had known Lyon prior to his leaving to fight the war years earlier. Others had simply heard of his reputation as a knight of honor and valor, and a leader of men. When the woman had first claimed that it was Sir Lyon Beauchane who had raped her, there were some who did not want to believe her; others nodded in agreement, knowing that wars have a way of twisting men's minds and bending their character. All the men of Hogarth were glad now that they did not have the real Lyon Beauchane to worry about. They had enough enemies without adding such a formidable warrior to the list.

"That murderous wench," a man said, staring into the flames of the fire, whick heated water for tea. "I remember when she married Prince William. Remember how happy we all were that our princess had been common folk, just like us? Remember how easy we all thought our life would be? Now she sends those killers, Rawlings and Dunne, to murder silly old men who talk too much."

Lyon said nothing. It was nearly noon, and he had

arrived shortly after dawn, just minutes after the men had finished burying the old man's corpse. He stared into the flames, letting his mind drift, separating himself from the words of the men.

The story wasn't complete. If Jade had commanded Sheriff Dunne to commit the midnight execution of the man complaining of his taxes, why would the men lie and say that Lyon was the one responsible for the rape? Any why had only one woman been raped by one man? Lyon's experience with such barbarism had been that when savage men congregated, there was nothing stopping them. If *one* man involved himself in the heinous violence of rape, they *all* did.

Was Jade responsible for some of the carnage that had occurred in the village of Hogarth a few hours earlier, or all of it?

It didn't seem like Jade to demand the execution of an old man just for complaining about the taxes that he had to pay, but then what possible reason would Sheriff Dunne have for killing the man if not under Princess Crosse's orders? Even if Jade was not aware of everything that was happening within the walls of Castle Crosse, could she be so oblivious to the world around her that men like Sheriff Dunne and Garth Rawlings could commit murder *in her name* and get away with it?

The questions went round and round in Lyon's mind until his head ached. Villagers asked Lyon if he would ride to Castle Crosse immediately to try to speak with Princess Jade, but he told them that was not possible. Not yet, at least.

"And don't any of you go to the castle," he warned. "If you do get past the drawbridge, like as not you'll never be seen again."

"Then what should we do when one of our own has been murdered, and another has been violated?" asked an old man, the strain of doing nothing showing plainly on his weathered face.

"For now, you try to comfort the women and children, and have faith that I will not rest until I have found the truth behind all the lies, and have brought to justice those who have violated the laws that govern decent men."

Lyon left the village shortly thereafter, his mind in a whirl. Could Jade really be the coldhearted murderess that the villagers believed she was? And if she was, could Lyon do what was necessary to put an end to her reign of terror?

On the following morning, Jade paced her bedchamber nervously. She had several different gowns strewn across her bed. Each had been tried on, inspected before the looking glass with an extremely critical eye, and then rejected.

One question dominated Jade's thoughts: What will Lyon think of me in this?

And then, as soon as the question became clear to her, she would reject the gown with anger. She was not going to completely rearrange her life, or her tastes in clothes, just to suit Lyon Beauchane's masculine tastes. She had been forced to do that with her husband, but that was when she was very young, and really had not known better.

Jade was twenty-four now, and she was much more confident than she had been in that life so long ago. She

162

would not become someone else just to suit Lyon Beauchane's tastes! And she was lying through her teeth when she thought such nonsense! She did want to please him.

She settled at last on a velvet dress of cobalt blue, trimmed with exquisite white lace from the south of France. The dress was formal enough to represent Jade's social position, but not so impressive that it would be more appropriate for evening wear. The U-shaped neckline came down from the puffed shoulders to show the crests of her creamy breasts in a fashion that would surely draw Lyon's attention, and yet stopped short of being as revealing as an evening gown. It was, Jade concluded, an attractive dress that would please Lyon without being absurdly fawning in trying to appeal to his masculine interests.

As Jade looked at herself one final time in the full-length bedchamber looking glass, tying her long honey-colored hair back with a blue ribbon, she realized that she was taking a certain amount of satisfaction in dressing to win Lyon's approval. His desire for her made her feel more attractive than she could ever remember feeling.

Jade plucked a fresh strawberry from a bowl and popped it into her mouth. She moaned softly at the taste, and marvelled how her senses appeared far more finely tuned since Lyon's unexpected intrusion into her life, her bedchamber, her arms . . . even into her very heart and soul!

A blush crept up Jade's throat to color her cheeks as memories flooded through her, reminding her of her abandonment to Lyon's sensuality. There was within her a secret someone—a woman of sheer, unbridled sensuality. Jade had not realized that that passionate woman existed until she had discovered such glory in Lyon's kisses. Jade wanted Lyon to embrace and revere *that woman*. In Lyon's arms, she thought of herself as an entirely different woman from Princess Jade Crosse who lived a lonely life in an upper room in Castle Crosse.

A smile came to Jade's lips. *That woman* had finally helped Jade to stand up to Bishop Fields, demanding that she be allowed to ride to the village of Hogarth. His denials only heightened her anger. And when Jade at last insisted that she would be the only person who would write the laws that govered her own life, not to mention her fiefdom, Bishop Fields at last relented.

The only lingering misgivings that Jade had concerned Lyon. What would he think when he saw her riding astride her horse instead of sidesaddle? It was so unladylike. But hopefully he could see past that, since she simply could not ride sidesaddle with any sense of confidence, and it was confidence that Jade was most enjoying now.

When she arrived at the stables, Jade had no doubt that Bishop Fields had warned the workers of her arrival that morning. Three of the most gentle and well-trained mares were already lined up, ready and waiting for Jade to select whichever one most appealed to her. She chose a well-muscled cream colored mare, which was quickly saddled with one of Prince William's old saddles. Once the stirrups were raised to accommodate Jade, she was ready to leave.

A young stable boy rushed forward with a footstool for Jade to use in mounting the horse, but her spirits soared back to the days of her youth, and she refused the assistance. Grabbing the pommel of the saddle, she kicked her slippered foot into the stirrup, then swept her leg over the mare's back. She heard the gasp as the men caught a glimpse of their princess's leg, but she was undeterred.

Nothing could stop her now. Nothing, and no one!

Sitting in the saddle, Jade suddenly realized that the dress was not made for riding; her legs were displayed almost to the knee. She adjusted the skirt of the dress as modestly as possible, then took the reins confidently in her hands.

"I will return later," Jade said to the eldest of the stable hands.

She intentionally kept the time of her return a secret. She did not want anyone knowing exactly what she was doing while she was away, and she wanted nothing to interfere with her time together with Lyon Beauchane, when she at last met up with him in Hogarth.

A tremor of excitement tickled Jade's spine as she tapped her heels against the mare's ribs. She rode through the gate and over the drawbridge, feeling freer and more alive than she had since a young peasant girl with the unusual name of Jade became Princess Crosse.

Lyon sat on a thick, horizontal limb of a tree, his back to the trunk, watching the slow approach of the single rider far off, making steady progress through the grassy valley.

As the rider got closer, Lyon's interest heightened.

165

Could that really be Jade (*his* Jade, as he privately thought of her) riding alone?

A devilish smile curled his lips. It shouldn't have surprised him that Jade would ride astride a beautiful cream colored horse, but it did.

She continued to surprise him in so many ways, and that was just part of what Lyon found so intriguing about Princess Jade Crosse. There was nothing conventional about her.

"What a woman," he murmured softly to himself. He shifted his position slightly on the limb that allowed him a perfect look-out position over the valley and the grain fields that surrounded the village of Hogarth.

She rode easily in the saddle, he noted. Perhaps she was a bit stiff-backed due to being out of practice, but her posture and demeanor still bespoke the skills of someone who, early in life, had spent many hours on horseback.

He was just about to leap from the tree to the ground ten feet below when he noticed movement at the far side of the valley. At first he couldn't be certain that it was human movement, but then what he saw made his teeth clench in lethal rage.

"That wench!" he hissed, repositioning himself on the limb.

He stared, squinting his eyes, not at Jade but at the moving shadows at the far side of the valley, right at the treeline. There were riders there, but he couldn't yet tell how many. The shadows yielded only fleeting glimpses of men, and an occasional glint of sunlight against armor, or perhaps against the polished and sharpened blade of a sword or dagger.

It was a trap. Following Jade were the soldiers that she had promised him she would not bring.

A cruel smile twisted Lyon's mouth into an ugly sneer. How he had believed her lies! Oh, how he had embraced the sweet words she'd spoken, too smitten with her charms, with the physical delights of Princess Jade to see beneath the gilded surface to the ugly, manipulating monster beneath!

How could he possibly have been so foolish as to believe her? Hadn't he spent many nights in bed with women that he hadn't loved, perhaps hadn't even liked very much? Didn't he know the difference between love and lust? It surprised him that Jade could be so mercenary about her loveplay. But wasn't she always surprising him in one way or another? Wasn't this just one more twist in the convoluted knot that was Princess Jade Crosse?

She was close now, less than a hundred yards away, and she looked as beautiful as ever. He would have found it so much easier to hate her, so much harder to believe her lies, if she wasn't so damnably beautiful.

If the soldiers hadn't hugged the treelines so closely, Lyon wouldn't have been able to spy them in advance. He realized how close he had come to making a fatal mistake, a lesson he would not forget.

He leaped lithely to the ground, a lion about to go on the hunt. He retrieved his bow and quiver full of arrows, and set off to gain revenge upon the woman who had destroyed his faith in royalty and the fiefdom. He would teach the soldiers who worked for the traitoress that they were making a fatal mistake in whom they placed their fealty.

167

It was time Princess Jade Crosse stopped being insulated from the violence that she commanded.

Lyon's lips curled back in a cruel sneer. He set out on the hunt, moving silently, driven by revenge and heavy with a sense of betrayal that he believed would never truly leave his heart.

Chapter 15

Jade rode out of Hogarth slowly. The sun would set in an hour or so, probably before she returned to Castle Crosse. She didn't care. Her heart felt heavy . . . and betrayed.

Lyon had not come, as he had promised, to meet her at Hogarth. Jade kept waiting for him, sure that any minute he would ride around the corner with that boyish grin on his face, a twinkle in his fierce blue eyes, and a deep, devilish dimple in his cheek. He would no doubt leap off his stallion while the horse was still pulling to a halt, and with a casual shrug would explain that he had been busy somewhere, doing something terribly important, and he would dismiss all Jade's worries with his carefree confidence and charm.

But it never happened. He never did ride into Hogarth. And the people hated her.

She saw it in their eyes, felt it thick as a morning mist in the air. The people of Hogarth spoke politely to her, but they did not smile unless she looked directly at them. When she spoke to a child, their answers were simple one-word responses; the parent hovering nearby, watching every move that was made, clearly frightened that the child would do something to displease Princess Jade.

On three or four occasions Jade took a peasant aside and tried to speak forthrightly, asking why the villagers were treating her with such fearful formality. Each time, she watched the blood drain from the person's face; then listened as the person explained that nothing was out of the ordinary. The villagers weren't treating Princess Jade any differently than they ever did, but if the great and honorable princess would like to be treated with less respect . . . then consider it done!

Jade realized that these people would do whatever she asked of them not because they loved her as the princess of their fiefdom, but because they were afraid of the power she held. This bothered Jade more than anything else.

Realizing that she would never receive honest replies, Jade finally asked that her mare be brought around. Clearly, the longer she stayed in Hogarth, the more frightened the peasants became of her.

It did no good to hope for any information concerning Lyon. Twice Jade asked if anyone had seen Sir Lyon lately. Twice she watched the villagers look away, then pretend that they either did not know the knight she spoke of, or claim they hadn't seen Lyon since he had left to fight on behalf of Prince William Crosse of Fitzpatrick some six years ago.

At least it felt good to ride again.

"Good girl," Jade said, patting her mare's neck.

The mare's golden coat shone in the waning sunlight, and though Jade was unaware of it, her tresses and the mare's mane were almost the same color.

Jade followed the path through the valley and into the forest that surrounded Castle Crosse. As she moved into the trees, going from the bright glare of the sun to the dim moss light of the canopied forest, she blinked, trying to adjust her vision to the sudden gloom.

It was at that moment that she felt the hand clamp down tightly over her mouth, and the touch of cold steel against her throat!

"Not a sound, my lady!" Lyon hissed as he pulled Jade from the saddle.

Jade's heart felt like it would burst from her chest. She recognized the deep timbre of Lyon's voice, but the hatred she heard in it was far greater than anything she had ever heard from him. She'd seen him angry before, and she'd seen him filled with distrust. But this time, his hand was much tighter over her mouth than it had to be. A blood-deep hatred in his tone made Jade believe he would kill her if he thought it necessary.

When she finally got her slippered feet beneath her, she clutched tightly onto Lyon's forearm, helping to right herself. The dagger never left her throat. Jade watched as her gentle golden mare bolted, racing across the valley, away from the deadly knight who had appeared out of thin air.

Jade could not blame her mare. Given the chance, she, too, would run as far and as fast from Lyon as her legs would carry her.

She felt his hand loosen slightly over her mouth. "Not a sound," he whispered in her ear. Then he removed his hand from her mouth. Jade gulped in air, realizing that she had been holding her breath since Lyon had pulled her from her horse.

"This way. Fight me and I'll slit your throat."

His hand wrapped tightly around her wrist. Jade felt certain that her skin was being bruised by his strong fingers.

What have I done? What have I done to make him hate me so? she thought.

Jade said nothing as Lyon led the way into the thick undergrowth of foliage. High overhead, the sunlight streamed through the canopy of leaves, and she felt the cushion of last year's dead foliage crunching softly beneath her slippered feet.

Lyon forged a rapid pace, causing Jade to run to keep up with him. She tried to intercept the low-hanging branches that seemed determined to swipe at her face with her free hand. On several occasions branches caught her golden tresses and pulled strands out. The slender strip of blue lace that she had used to tie her hair back became entangled with a branch, and Jade could only gasp as the ribbon was pulled painfully from her hair.

"Don't slow me down, woman!" Lyon hissed, glancing over his shoulder for only a second, never breaking stride as he dragged Jade further from the road, deeper into the forest that was his sanctuary.

A thousand different emotions raced through Jade in the minute or two that she was forced to follow Lyon. At first, painful memories of childhood came back; shameful, angry recollections of being taken behind the animal shed to have her backside spanked. But that emotion was immediatley replaced by a more realistic, mature one. Not only was she an adult, she was a princess, and this brutish man who was pulling her at a mad pace through the forest was her servant!

172

She did not appreciate and would not tolerate being manhandled by Lyon Beauchane, or any man!

"Stop!" Jade said at last.

She tried to pull her wrist out of Lyon's grasp. She might just as well have tried to pull the Excalibur out of the stone. Lyon's stride never even faltered.

In a more conciliatory tone she said. "Please, Lyon, can't we talk about this?"

He stopped then so quickly that he caught Jade by surprise, and her momentum sent her crashing into him. He looked at her with undisguised loathing. When his gaze dipped down to the cleavage that Jade showed, he sneered and turned away.

Jade's heart sank. She had worn the dress hoping to see the approval and pleasure in his eyes. Instead, he looked at her as though she was now ugly in his eyes. He could have spit upon her and she would not have felt more loathsome; he could have plunged his dagger deep into her bosom, and he would not have cut her as deeply.

He started off again, his fingers pressing into the white softness of Jade's wrist, his other hand holding tightly to the deadly dagger that had been at her throat too many times already.

As he strode, his long black cape billowing behind him, Jade was aware of his animal motion, of things real and unreal. Every move Lyon made was graceful, fluid, powerful. As Jade struggled to keep up with him, she thought if she were a man in combat that she would trust Lyon completely. He was a man of action, a well-tempered sword perfectly designed for battle. The easy world of politics which Jade had lived in when her husband had been alive and she sadly lived in now would never welcome a man such as Sir Lyon Beauchane. She suspected that suited him just fine.

Suddenly they came to a second halt. Lyon pulled Jade close, then twisted her sharply so that her back was against his chest. His big left hand was hard upon her shoulder, and though he did not touch the blade of his dagger to her throat, she was keenly aware of its presence.

She discovered that they had taken a half-moon course through the forest so that they now were again at its edge, looking out into the valley she had so recently crossed, yet far away from the opening in the trees where the road led to Castle Crosse.

Far across the valley, men on horseback were trying to calm and capture her mare. The horse was frightened and skittish, running aimlessly, the stirrups bouncing against her ribs to spur her on as she ran.

It was Jade's caring heart that made her worry first for the mare, and be concerned about the fear that must beat in the animal's noble heart. But then, once a soldier had caught the bridle and brought the mare to a stop, Jade paid closer attention to the men. In an instant she understood everything.

"Garth!" she whispered.

"Yes, Garth Rawlings," Lyon said behind her, looking over her head at the soldiers in the valley. "But he and his men won't be able to protect you now! The steel jaws of your trap are empty, and at long last you'll have to answer for your crimes!"

Jade tried to turn around so that she could look up at him. Surely the man who had taken her to such heights of ecstasy could not believe that she would intentionally lure him into some kind of murderous ambush.

Could he?

The hand at her shoulder tightened, making Jade wince in pain. She did not try to face Lyon again.

"I'd have killed most of them before they would have gotten me," Lyon said softly, his voice a growl of controlled rage. "And I would have killed you, too. You can believe that, Princess Jade. Believe it with all your heart."

"I do," Jade replied in a truthful whisper. "I fully believe you would have killed me, just as I believe you would have killed those men out there in the valley. I also believe that you are completely mistaken in what you are thinking."

Lyon's bitter, soft laugh dampened the small flame of hope in her heart.

"For now, I'm not interested in your lies. Just tell me, how many men did you assign to follow you? The least you can do is tell me how many murderers I must cross swords with."

"I didn't assign . . . I didn't even know that I was being followed."

Lyon's short, bitter laugh sent ice shivering through Jade's veins. She wondered how many men Lyon had interrogated in his days as a soldier and as a knight for Castle Crosse. She had no doubts that he always got whatever information he was seeking.

"They'll never find you," Lyon said, and though the words themselves did not sound overwhelmingly threatening, Jade sensed the warning. It made her shiver again. "Even if you called out to them now, they wouldn't catch me." He looked hard at Jade, challenging her to deny the truth of his words. "I own these woods. This is my forest, not yours. I know every twig and branch, every trail. I know every hiding place, every area where an archer can use his skills to the deadliest advantage." His hands on her shoulders tightened, and Jade grimaced in pain. "You think of that, m'lady, before you send men chasing me again."

Jade did not know what to say, what to do. All of Lyon's accusations seemed irrefutably true. She wasn't guilty, of course, but the appearance of guilt was so damning that, should their positions be reversed, she knew she would be just as bitterly distrustful of Lyon Beauchane.

Jade closed her eyes, weary and disheartened. She was a captive, she had always been a captive. First to her husband, who had desperately tried to recover his lost youth in the arms of a young wife; then to Castle Crosse, where she could not leave for fear of violence from the peasants that had once loved and respected her. And now she was the prisoner of Lyon Beauchane, who had accused her of foul crimes against the good people of her fiefdom, and who would kill her with his dagger unless she did everything he demanded.

The passion that they shared was dead, killed by mistrust and circumstances. The reality of this made Jade's heart tighten, and tears glisten in her soft amber eyes.

"That's a nice touch," Lyon said bitterly, seeing her brimming tears threaten to spill down her cheeks. "It won't work, but it is still a nice touch. Tell me, can you bring forth the tears with just a snap of your fingers, like you would call for a servant to refill your wine glass?"

The utter contempt she heard in Lyon's tone shredded her soul.

176

Garth and his men had by this time realized that the riderless horse was in fact Jade's mare, and there was a general melee of confusion as they looked to Garth for direction. The riders all stared into the forest, hoping vainly to see Jade, but they were looking a full three hundred yards from where she now stood, which drew a satisfied smile from Lyon.

"I took you right out from under Garth's nose," Lyon said softly, as much to himself as to Jade.

She said nothing in response. Lyon hated her, and her own advisors lied to her. She could not trust herself, because she knew all too well how her body betrayed her when she was in Lyon's arms.

"I know you don't trust me, but—"

"Quiet!" Lyon hissed, giving Jade a short, hard shake to emphasize the command. "Don't talk unless I give you leave."

Jade felt miserable, and completely alone. When Garth and his men rode out of the valley into the forest in search of her, Lyon chuckled, pleased with himself, then took her hand and led her deeper into the forest.

Jade didn't even bother asking where he was taking her.

He had his stallion tied nearby. The animal was huge, standing over eighteen hands high. He sniffed the air, his large nostrils dilating as Lyon approached. Jade had never before seen such an instant, unspoken rapport between man and beast.

Lyon released Jade, swung into the saddle, then reached down for her. For only a second, Jade hesitated. Was it possible, now, to escape?

"Don't even think about it," Lyon growled, reaching down further for Jade. "You'd never make it."

He pulled her onto his lap so she sat crosswise over his thighs. The big black stallion did not even respond to her additional weight. Lyon's right arm slipped tightly around her waist, pulling Jade in so that she was pressed tightly against him. But this time, instead of feeling the presence of his desire coursing through his veins where their bodies touched, she sensed the overwhelming extent of his contempt for her.

Never before had she been so close to anyone, and yet felt so very alone and misunderstood.

They rode slowly, walking the horse through the trails that Jade had not realized existed. Their path was a winding one, moving constantly away from the area where they had last seen Garth and his men, moving on a parallel course to Castle Crosse.

After several minutes had passed, Jade said guietly, "It isn't like what you're thinking."

"Stop. Don't say anything."

Their gazes met, their faces inches apart. Jade expected to see the fire of anger in his eyes. Or, perhaps, she thought wistfully, she might see suppressed desire, ignited by their closness.

She saw neither. When she looked into Lyon's eyes, she saw nothing at all. It was as though he had pulled down a veil. She could look *into* his eyes, but she could not look *past* them, not into Lyon's soul.

He had shut her out of his soul . . . out of his heart.

The painful reality of this bore down on Jade like a mighty weight, crushing the joy and hope for the future that not long ago had come to life within her bosom.

"Lyon . . . please . . . won't you listen?"

"I've listened to your lies already."

"But what if I'm not lying?"

178

He just looked at her, and the pull on the right side of his mouth might have looked like a smile to someone who did not know him as well as Jade did. She saw a ruthless, cynical sneer, an expression given to someone utterly without value.

Hot tears burned in her eyes. She kept her hands clasped together in her lap, sitting uneasily on Lyon's lap as the stallion moved gracefully down the circuitous path. The arm around her waist, holding her in position, might just as well have been a saddle harness for all the warmth and comfort it gave her.

She tried to hold her tears back. Lyon was being cold; cold and strong and completely insulated from any pain, and that is what Jade wanted for herself. She fought with herself, trying to be as heartless as Lyon Beauchane, but she could not. When the tears trickled slowly down her cheeks, Lyon cursed angrily, which didn't increase her comfort.

"Mayhaps you have spent too much time with soldiers to remember that such language is not acceptable in the company of a lady," Jade said at last. She would not allow Lyon to degrade her by behaving swinishly in her presence. Even *if* she *was* the monstrous, murdering despot that he accused her of, she had the right to *some* civility from him.

"You are right, m'lady," Lyon finally responded.

Jade couldn't be sure, but she thought there was the slightest softening of his demeanor as well as his tone. This give her a glimmer of hope that she might convince him that she had not set a trap to have him captured by Garth Rawlings, and the rest of his hideous band of hired mercenaries.

For a moment they looked at each other; looked

179

instead of glared. And then, just as Lyon was about to speak, Jade saw his expression regain its anger.

Before she could say a word, Lyon tossed her off his lap, throwing her to the ground from his tall stallion.

"What are you . . .?" she asked, landing on her feet but hitting so hard that she stumbled, falling to her hands and knees.

What followed took place in only a matter of seconds, but it would be repeated again and again in Jade's mind, achieving a life of its own.

Chapter 16

Three men, uniformed soldiers from Castle Crosse under Garth's command, rushed forward; two on foot, one on horseback. The foot soldiers were armed only with axes, the standard weapon for soldiers of their low ranking. The man on horseback, the commander, wielded a huge broadsword, which he clutched in both hands, raised high above his head, as he spurred his destrier toward Lyon.

They had caught Lyon by surprise, and for another man, that might have been all the disadvantage necessary to make a violent death a certainty. But Lyon Beauchane was a knight unlike any other. Even before the ground soldiers had reached him, he had his sword out and was whipping his stallion to the side. The nearest axe-bearer had pulled his weapon far behind, holding the handle tightly in both hands, prepared to swing the heavy, deadly blade forward when he was within striking distance of his target. The axe never came around. Before his reflexes could react to the fact that Lyon had attacked rather than retreated (which is what was expected of a man who is outnumbered three-to-one), the silver blade of Lyon's sword was whistling through the air.

Blade met flesh, and the axman fell lifeless to the ground.

The second axman, shocked at the suddenness of his friend's death, hesitated for only an instant in his attack. That hesitation was his death sentence. He was still in shock over the swiftness of Lyon's reactions when the blade arched in a deadly curve, slicing through body armor and the flesh beneath.

Lyon was still reacting to the second axman when the mounted swordsman rushed forward. He swung hard, holding his huge broadsword in both hands, aiming for a decapitating blow to Lyon's throat. It was Lyon's stallion that saved his life, lunging forward without being ordered to do so. The mercenary's broadsword cut through the air, close enough for Lyon to hear it whistle softly behind him.

Momentum carried the broadswordsman along so that, at least for the moment, he was safely separated from his adversary, who had already proven himself to be a greater threat than the commander had dreamed possible.

Lyon pulled hard on the reins, wheeling his destrier to face the next assault. For an instant, he looked at the man's face. Though the helmet he wore had a nose plate that came down almost to his upper lip to protect him, Lyon recognized the man as Ram Weston. He had been a low-priced mercenary, working for anyone and doing anything, for money.

It shouldn't have surprised Lyon that Weston had

risen in rank under Sir Garth Rawlings, but it did. The fact that the man held no moral conviction, yet had found not only employment but authority over other mercenaries, said a great deal about what was happening now at Castle Crosse.

Truly savage men are almost always cowardly at heart, and this man was no different. Now faced with an even fight against Lyon Beauchane, the mercenary wanted nothing more than the safety of flight. He turned his destrier, intending on fleeing from the tall blond knight who had already taken down two men, and appeared more than ready to make it a clean sweep.

Lyon's reactions were so fast that Jade could hardly believe her eyes. As Weston turned his horse and started to run away, Lyon dropped his sword. Even before the heavy blade reached the ground, he had pulled out his bow from a kidskin pouch affixed to the right side of the saddle. He withdrew an arrow from the quiver beneath his left thigh, the arrow was notched even before the mercenary's mount had reached a full gallop.

The arrow bridged ninety feet in the blink of an eye. The iron tip struck with deadly accuracy between Ram Weston's shoulder blades.

Gasping in horror, Jade looked away. She heard the body land heavily to earth, and knew beyond any doubt that there was no reason to check the mercenary for signs of life.

It had all happened so fast. Just a few seconds, really. But in the course of those few seconds, Jade was given a lesson in violence, and in violent men. Deep within her heart she knew a shadow of the horror the peasants had suffered through when riders came in the night.

"Quickly," Lyon said, reaching a hand down for Jade. He had dismounted from his stallion and now loomed over her. "That was a small patrol. If there is one, there is likely to be many."

Jade shook her head, not denying Lyon's request, but caught in her confusion over events which she felt were unexplainable.

"Hurry, blast you!" Lyon hissed. He grabbed Jade by the arms and hauled her briskly to her feet. He peered into her eyes, searching, assessing. "Were you hurt in the fall? I had no choice but to push you aside."

"No. I don't think so, anyway."

Though she tried not to, Jade could not prevent her eyes from continually straying to the bodies of the axman who had been cut down with blinding swiftness by Lyon and his mighty broadsword.

"Don't look at them," Lyon said as he put an arm around Jade's shoulders. He turned her face toward him, cupping her chin in his palm so that she could not look at the fallen killers. "They can't hurt anyone now. Pay them no mind at all, m'lady."

He began leading Jade to his stallion.

"So quickly," Jade said softly. "It happened so quickly. They were alive and now they're dead. You killed them. You killed all three of them, even when one tried to run away."

"Aye, I did. He was running away but he would come back later, perhaps with more of his friends than I could kill. Then *I* would be the one feeding the worms."

There wasn't the least bit of sympathy for the dead in

184

Lyon's voice, not a whit of regret, and that bothered Jade. Even if he had felt it was absolutely necessary to kill all three men, she thought it would show suitable knight-like valor and morality if he felt some remorse over what he had just done.

Lyon returned his weapons to their appropriate place, then slipped into the saddle, and reached down for Jade. She took his hand without protest, allowing him to seat her across his thighs once again.

"Who were those men?" she asked, her words coming out a bit unsteadily because the stallion was trotting now, not merely walking. "Why did they attack you?"

"You don't recognize them? They were wearing the colors of Castle Crosse."

Jade shook her head. The sun would soon set, and she suddenly felt terribly weary. All she wanted to do, at least for a few hours, was to not think, but she knew that Lyon wouldn't let her do that. In her heart, she resented him mightily for it.

"I don't have any call to see the garrison," Jade said finally, responding to Lyon's silent prompting. "Bishop Fields and Garth Rawlings see to that for me. And for civil matters, there is Sheriff Dunne. Those men take care of those matters for me."

Could it be that Jade really did not know the atrocities that were being committed in her name?

Once again Lyon gave the thought serious consideration. It seemed so very unlikely that she could head a fiefdom being run by corrupt underlings. But then, hadn't Lyon in his travels already seen a thousand unlikely things happen? Hadn't he seen strong men

185

felled by weak ones? Intelligent men outwitted by dullards? Hadn't he himself, by continuing to be alive, defied all the odds on earth and in heaven?

With a bitter edge to his voice, Lyon replied, "Mayhaps you would do well to seek new counsel, m'lady."

Lyon was furious. The attack had only added yet more questions to the riddle of who Princess Jade Crosse really was. It seemed as though each moment he spent with Jade prompted yet another question that demanded serious consideration. Answers were few, and even those that Lyon *did* hold fast in his mind's grasp, he no longer trusted completely.

The patrol that they had encountered, he knew, had nothing to do with Garth and his men. At least not directly, and not at this time. They were one of the wandering bands of mercenaries who roamed the feifdom searching chiefly for unescorted women and unprotected valuables. Lyon had heard about such patrols from Baron von Mueller, and at first Lyon could not believe that Jade could allow such a thing to happen within the boundries of her fiefdom.

But all he had to do was take a look at the axmen as they rushed toward him, and Lyon knew that they weren't really interested in him. All they had wanted to do was get Lyon out of the way so that Jade would no longer be protected.

They hadn't recognized Jade at first, not until it was too late, Lyon suspected. There had been that one shining moment when the commanding mercenary had

186

looked first at Lyon, then to Jade, then turned his mount to ride away. Then Lyon had seen recognition spread across his face.

But had he really.

The more Lyon thought about what happened, the more unsure he was of his initial analysis. Could the men really be a roving band of rapists and thieves who preyed upon the weak, the outnumbered, and the unarmed? Or were they a patrol sent out by Garth Rawlings and paid by Jade Crosse, roaming the forest in search for Lyon? Perhaps he even had a bounty on his head, with a sum of gold high enough to make even the most rational of men a bloodthirsty killer.

Lyon would have liked to travel all the way to Lord Charles's castle, where he would feel safe, and where he wouldn't have to watch over Princess Crosse every second. However, travelling that far was unwise, even at night. By now, the first rider from Garth's patrol would have returned to Castle Crosse with orders for every knight to mount up. And then there was the matter of the three-man patrol that had been killed. Even though they were not on an official patrol of the fiefdom, their presence would be missed, and men would be sent in search of them.

The only move to make was to hide somewhere and think things through. Lyon had been in enough battles, and played enough games of chess to know that hasty moves were often fatal moves both on the board and in full armor on the battlefield.

They followed a trail for a little over a mile. As the setting sun sent golden rays lancing through the thick tree leaves, Lyon followed the westward side of an embankment until he found the cave that he remembered from his youth.

The entrance was overgrown, and there wasn't sufficient room for him to bring his stallion into the cave, but it was a suitable place to hide for the evening. Lyon told Jade to stay put, and the look in his eyes warned her of the severe foolishness of trying to escape. He walked his destrier and tied him up where he could have plenty of rich green grass and cool water, far enouth away from the mouth of the cave to make discovery difficult should the horse be found.

When Lyon returned, Jade was sitting at the cave entrance, her face drawn and pale, hands folded lightly in her lap. For only a moment, Lyon's heart went out to her. He had to stop himself from taking her into his arms and whispering comforting words.

"It looks like we're going to be spending the night together," he said, but there wasn't even a hint of humor in his tone. "If we're very fortunate, we won't be found." Then, to press the unspoken point that she mustn't do anything to draw attention to them, he said, "I wouldn't want to kill any more men. At least, not tonight, and not without good reason."

Lyon entered the cave first, and after lighting a small candle, was able to see how the interior had changed. It was clear that the cave had not been frequented in quite some time, though years earlier young boys had used the cave as a meeting place, probably much the same as Lyon himself had twenty years earlier.

The first section of the cave was very narrow, moving straight into the hillside nearly thirty feet. Then it angled sharply to the right and ran parallel to the hillside for another forty or fifty feet. And finally, after a final right-angle turn to the left into the hillside, it widened to a circular area twenty feet across. The excellent ventilation was provided by a small opening on the far side of the hill.

The remnants of past fires were surrounded by a circle of rocks that had been placed in the center of the circle. When Lyon saw that the pile of straw placed near the far wall of the cave was only a few months old, arranged to serve as a mattress, he realized that the cave was still being used by young people . . . and still for romantic trysts of young lovers hiding from the rest of the world.

Jade, he knew, would hate the cave, but for Lyon, the old smells and sights triggered memories that brought him back to a time when all his problems seemed minor, and life and death decisions were shouldered by others.

He returned to the mouth of the cave to find Jade waiting for him. Whether she had stayed because she was legitimately afraid of his threat to track her down and punish her if she tried to flee, or because she truly felt she was guilty of no transgression, he could not say. For now, it really didn't matter.

"Come with me," he said, extending an open hand to her.

Jade looked at his hand but did not take it. Though there was definite sadness in her eyes, there was also a very faint spark of defiant anger, of thwarted passion, of self-righteous fury . . . all of it directed at Lyon.

"I haven't got time to argue with you," Lyon

snapped. He grabbed Jade by the upper arms and hauled her to her feet so fast that she nearly lost her balance.

He looked down into her eyes, and though his fighter's instincts were still heightened from the recent battles he had fought and won, he realized once again that he couldn't continue his anger at Jade for long. She was too beautiful, too defiant of his strength and superior fighting abilities, for him to maintain that destructive emotion.

During the course of his life, especially during the latter years when he had become the leader of fighting men, he had grown accustomed to having people heed his wishes, having people alter their plans to suit his own. But with Jade, that was different. Satisfying his wishes was not a priority for her, and though this was annoying, it was also intriguing.

"If we stay out here, we're likely to be discovered," Lyon said. He gingerly reached out to curl his fingers around her slender, white wrist. "Those men we left behind—"

"*We?* Don't you mean the corpses *you* left in the wake of your violence?"

"Call it what you will, m'lady. When the men who attacked us are missed, other men will come looking. Don't feel too sorry for them, though, because if I hadn't been there, they would have taken you." He paused a moment to let the black reality of his words sink in. "It wasn't me they wanted, it was you."

He watched as the anger faded from her face and a vague new fear replaced it. "But they attacked you?"

"They wanted me dead, but they wanted you alive.

At least until they'd had their fill of you."

Jade fell silent, contemplating his words and the disturbing meaning behind them. She had not recognized any of the three men, but she had recognized the colors they wore. Could it really be possible that she had men in her ranks who would do such a thing? Men so ill-informed they did not even recognize Princess Crosse when they saw her?

With her mind on other matters, Jade allowed Lyon to pull her into the cave. She had to duck her head to get through, and feel her way along the stony walls with her free hand, but she was not afraid. Lyon had clearly been here before, and no matter how angry he was with her, he would not torture her needlessly by bringing her into the cave unless there was a good reason.

They stopped. It was so dark that Jade bumped into Lyon, but she still couldn't see him. The single small candle gave very little light.

"Don't move," he said. "I'll light a fire, then it won't be so bad."

"You don't have to worry about me," Jade said tersely.

She felt his fingers leave her wrist. Though her eyes were open, she saw nothing at all. Only when she turned to look in the direction that she had come from did she see the barest illumination provided by the weak reflection of sunlight, pale and thin, bouncing off the dull gray, moss-grown rocks.

It didn't take Lyon long to light a small fire, first of straw, then of dried twigs, and finally of a few small logs. The fire quickly dried the dampness out of the air, which pleased Jade.

She surveyed their surroundings. Though the cave was a complete surprise to her, it was readily apparent that others knew it well. But how many others? Wouldn't this be a logical place to look for them?

"Relax," Lyon said casually, reading Jade's mind. He found a tattered, abandoned blanket and stretched it out over the mattress of straw. Then, with something of a flourish, he removed his ebony cape and placed it down over the blanket. "We've got a wait ahead of us. We might as well be comfortable."

Jade stood, one hand still against the rock wall of the cave, watching as Lyon sat cross-legged upon his cape, then removed his polished, knee-high boots and set them aside. Then he unfastened the harness of his sword-belt and placed that aside, too.

"So many weapons," Jade said quietly, breaking the silence. "Bow and arrows, a dagger, a sword."

"And I am proficient in all of them, m'lady," Lyon replied with pride. "Some say that I am the best." He smiled then, as though knowing he was stretching the truth. "The best archer, of that much I feel confident. There may be a man or two who, on a good day, might best me with a broadsword, but it would take a good day, m'lady. Of that I can assure you."

Jade made a face, not liking the swaggering tone Lyon used to describe his weapons of war, and his skill with them. "The Good Book would say that it is a high hope for a low heaven to possess such skills."

Lyon ran fingers through his long hair, pushing it back from his eyes as he leaned on his elbows. "It also says to be wise as the serpent and mild as the dove, does it not? And isn't it true that it was my skill with those

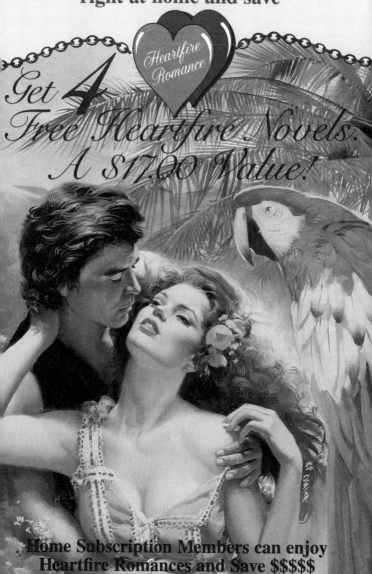

TO GET YOUR
4 FREE BOOKS
MAIL THE COUPON BELOW.

Heartfire Romance

FREE BOOK CERTIFICATE

GET 4 FREE BOOKS

Yes! I want to subscribe to Zebra's HEARTFIRE HOME SUBSCRIPTION SERVICE. Please send me my 4 FREE books. Then each month I'll receive the four newest Heartfire Romances as soon as they are published to preview Free for ten days. If I decide to keep them I'll pay the special discounted price of just $3.50 each; a total of $14.00. This is a savings of $3.00 off the regular publishers price. There are no shipping, handling or other hidden charges. There is no minimum number of books to buy and I may cancel this subscription at any time. In any case the 4 FREE Books are mine to keep regardless.

NAME

ADDRESS

CITY   STATE   ZIP

TELEPHONE

SIGNATURE

(If under 18 parent or guardian must sign)
Terms and prices subject to change.
Orders subject to acceptance.

HF 104

GET 4 FREE BOOKS

HEARTFIRE HOME SUBSCRIPTION
SERVICE
P.O. BOX 5214
120 BRIGHTON ROAD
CLIFTON, NEW JERSEY 07015

AFFIX
STAMP
HERE

weapons you so obviously detest that has kept your clothes upon your body, and your royal limbs unharmed, m'lady?"

"You don't know for certain that those men meant me harm."

"And you don't know for certain that they didn't."

Jade did not like the subject. It made her uncomfortable to even imagine that there were men capable of behaving like cannibals, preying upon their own kind without the slightest hint of human kindness or decency.

"How long do we have to stay down here?" she asked, crossing her arms over her chest. She wanted to sit, but the only comfortable place to sit was on the straw, and she didn't want to be that close to Lyon.

"A couple hours," Lyon replied. "By that time the darkness will be complete. Garth will send riders out looking for you, and they'll look in vain for an hour or two before realizing it would be best if they simply saved their energy and began anew in the morning when they can see what they're trying to do."

"And until then?"

"And until then, you and I are going to talk, and you're going to try to convince me that you really didn't set a trap with Garth Rawlings to capture me. If I'm convinced, then everything will be fine, m'lady, and I will guide you through the night back to your castle. Once there, there will be rejoicing because their beloved Princess Jade will have returned from her harrowing experience, hale and hearty."

Jade wanted to slap Lyon. She hated his sarcastic

tone, and all she had to do was look at him in the firelight to know that he did not truly believe she could convince him of her innocence.

She watched the flames, red and orange, licking hungrily at the dried wood. The smoke swirled at the ceiling of the cave, then followed a stream of air toward the far wall, when it disappeared through a small opening.

"A perfect air current," Lyon said, once again reading Jade's unspoken thoughts and questions. "The draft always comes from the mouth of the cave, where we came in, toward the back."

"What if someone sees the smoke? They could follow it to us."

"Not likely. The smoke comes out a long ways from where we are, and the opening is much too narrow for a man to crawl through."

"You know this area well, don't you?"

"I grew up here," Lyon said, staring into the fire. "It is in this forest that I learned what it was to be a man." He smiled, lost in some faraway, dusty memory. "When I was away fighting in Prince William's name, I used to dream at night of what it would be like when I returned. I could close my eyes and see every trail in this forest as though it were yesterday. I could close my eyes and once again I would be a young boy out hunting rabbits for the evening meal." He smiled to himself. "That was how I became so good with a bow. When you go hungry if your arrow misses its mark, you quickly learn not to miss."

"As the soldier riding away from you discovered," Jade said.

Lyon looked up from the flames, and there was a glint in his eyes. "He was not a soldier, he was a mercenary. He thought he could flee from my wrath, and he could not. That, m'lady, is a lesson you would do well to remember before you challenge me."

Jade regretted her comment. She was angry at being kidnapped by Lyon, but she had finally gotten him to speak about his past, of the days of his youth which had shaped the man that he was today. Her reproving comment had dammed the river of recollection, and she wondered if she would ever again get him to speak so freely and honestly of his youth.

Whether she simply became inured to the musty smell of the cave, or if the fire had taken the smell out, Jade couldn't be sure. Either way, her initial impression of the cave had changed so that she now found it warm and, should she be able to find something soft to sit on, comfortable.

"What can I do to convince you that I didn't know Garth and his men were following me?" Jade asked at last. She knelt, sitting on the backs of her heels, arranging the skirt of her dress beneath her knees to cushion them. "I thought I was alone. I suppose I should have known that Bishop Fields would lie to me."

"You should always assume that Bishop Fields is lying," Lyon replied. "The truth becomes foul on his tongue. He can't speak the truth."

"Then you believe me?" she asked softly. "You believe that I did not know I was being followed?"

Lyon rested his elbows upon his knees and looked at Jade over the flames of the fire. In his heart, he did not

195

want to believe her. *Not* believing her was the wise thing to do. It was better, or at least safer, to always assume another's guilt than believe inherently in another's innocence.

But he did believe her.

She believed too much in the goodness of people for him not to believe her. As he looked at her now, he tried to see her as Bishop Fields or Sir Garth Rawlings would see her . . . as a beautiful young widow suddenly holding enormous power in her hands, unable to realize the men she counted upon most for advice were, in fact, her worst and most pernicious enemies. Jade's enemies smiled at her and did everything they could to convince her that they wanted only the best of everything for her.

Princess Jade Crosse, with her gentle, fragile, loving heart, with her love of all humanity in general and her own people in particular, would be absurdly easy for someone of Biship Nathan Fields's intelligence and mendacity to manipulate, coerce, and befuddle.

"Yes," Lyon said at last. "I believe you. Against everything that I have seen, I still believe you."

Jade rose then, walking around the small fire to kneel upon the cape beside him.

"I don't know who to believe in anymore," she said softly.

Lyon slipped his muscled arm around her shoulders, pulling her against him. Jade put her head on his shoulder, closing her eyes as she did so.

"Believe in me, Jade," Lyon said in a raspy whisper. "Believe in me, and I will believe in you. Together, we will be unconquerable."

*   *   *

In the village of Willow's Crossing, two of the village elders sat on crude three-legged stools, passing a cup of strong ale back and forth, refilling it from a small cask at their feet. The men were not talking quietly away from other villagers because they wanted to become intoxicated in peace, and did not want to share their ale. Their meeting was much more important that that.

"You say it is so?" the elder of the two asked. His face was grave, the expression of a man who had heard news that shattered illusions dear to him.

"I say it is what I heard, nothing more and nothing less," the younger one replied.

"But Sir Lyon Beauchane?" the elder repeated incredulously. "A finer knight this land has never seen!"

"War can change a man," the younger said safely, as though he alone possessed this valuable insight. "War seldon changes men for the better."

"Still, it seems to me that a young man of Lyon's character wouldn't do such a thing."

"I'm not saying he did it, and I'm not saying he didn't do it. What I am saying is that there's a woman, not more than a girl, really, from what I've gathered, who says she was raped by Lyon Beauchane. He carried her out of her home and defiled her savagely. That's what I've heard."

The elder dipped the cup into the cask again. Lyon Beauchane raping a woman? As a village elder, he of course knew of Sir Lyon, had even watched competition among Prince William's knights in sword-play, jousting, and archery. Was it possible that a brave, proud, and strong knight such as Lyon Beauchane could turn into a raping half-man, half-monster?

In Harker village, three woman talked among themselves, speaking in soft whispers even though there was no one who might overhear them. They whispered because there were some topics that were too dastardly to be discussed in a normal tone of voice. One of those topics was rape, and that was the reason why the women whispered, though they were alone in a small, tidy hut.

"They said that he wanted a virgin," the eldest of the three whispered. She crossed herself and briefly turned her eyes heavenward, then turned her attention back to the other two women who sat closely with heads bowed to hear each softly spoken word. "Lyon Beauchane insisted that the village elders bring him a virgin! When they didn't, I hear tell he went from one hut to another until he found a poor lass. He dragged her into the village square and defiled her right there with everyone watching!"

The youngest of the three was the most skeptical. "Maggie, Maggie! You tell such stories! Why would Lyon Beauchane be such a rutting swine? I can think of four or five lasses who would gladly throw themselves at his feet, and have! Lyon Beauchane has no trouble finding women to warm his bed!"

"Aye, that's true, but I know what I heard, and sometimes a man wants what he can't have or hasn't got."

She crossed herself again reverently, just to make sure that the other women were certain of how terrible she thought the topic of conversation was. Maggie didn't want her friends to think for a second that she took any pleasure in gossiping about such hideous things.

She continued. "Sometimes men want to take, even when it can and would be given to them." She closed her eyes and shivered theatrically. "Men are beasts, ladies, and you'd be a silly lass if you didn't believe that was so!"

Chapter 17

"What am I going to do?" Jade asked quietly.

She had her head on Lyon's shoulder, and his arm was around her. They were sitting peacefully. It was one of the few times in all the hours that she had spent with Lyon that she felt suffused by a true peace. Being in the cave, so far away from everything that she had known or thought she knew, isolated her from the troubles of the world that existed *out there*.

For a long time, neither had said anything as they examined their own thoughts and emotions about what they now knew to be happening within Castle Crosse, and in the villages of her fiefdom. When Jade at last broke the silence with her question, Lyon flinched slightly, as though his nerves were lute-string tight. Then, relaxing immediately, he turned his head and kissed Jade's silken hair.

"The question should be: What are *we* going to do?"

Jade liked the sound of that. "So what are *we* going to do then?" she asked.

She had felt so very alone for so long, it was

heartening to know that she would have someone at her side to fight her battles with her. The fact that she was wildly aroused by that certain someone, and that she strongly suspected she was falling in love with him, only enhanced her pleasure.

"I don't know yet . . . but I'll think of something. Trust me, I'll think of a battle plan."

They lapsed into another silence, which didn't bother Jade. She did not like the sound of "battle plan," but the sound of Lyon's voice, the confidence and surety she heard there, pleased her enormously.

She wondered what exactly had Lyon meant with *we?* Was Lyon just being a typical military man, determined to keep morale high before the battle? Or did he really see himself and Jade as people on the same side of honor and justice, fighting a mutual battle against greed, savagery, and corruption?

Either explanation was likely to be true. Jade did not trust her emotions enough to ask for clarification from Lyon; she was too afraid of what his answer might be.

Logic told her that just because she had shared Lyon's passion, that did not necessarily mean she also shared his higher emotions. Her caresses had touched his body, but perhaps she had failed to touch his heart. But she could dream that it was so, and as she felt Lyon's fingertips tracing tiny circles against her arm just beneath the sleeve of her dress, she imagined that his thoughts were of her instead of the war that loomed ahead of them.

War was such an ugly word, an even uglier reality. She had seen, on a very small scale, the war that had raged between the three uniformed soldiers from Castle Crosse and Lyon. The sight of those men being hideously struck down continued to plague her thoughts, and yet that had been war on an extremely small scale. What would it be like with a hundred men on either side? Two hundred men? A thousand?

"What's wrong?" Lyon asked quietly. His arm tightened protectively around Jade.

"Nothing."

"Tell me."

There was a huskiness in his tone, a possessiveness, that soothed her ruffled nerves.

"If you don't tell me, how can I chase away your fears?"

Jade smiled. How long had it been since anyone had expressed the slightest interest in whether she was frightened or not?

"What makes you so sure that I am frightened?" she asked, snuggling in just a little closer to Lyon. She loved the smell of him, the beating of his heart beneath the shirt, and that patchwork of muscles that defined his chest with a sculptor's touch.

"You shuddered, despite the warmth of the fire. Your thoughts were far away. It is safe to assume that something frightened you."

"You are such a logical man."

Lyon turned his head to kiss Jade's hair one more. She felt his lips against her hair, heard him breathe deeply as he held her close. She resisted the impulse to turn her face up to his. If she did, then surely he would kiss her. Though she might take pleasure in the lovemaking that would follow, she would not be able to enjoy the quiet contentment she now felt in his arms.

Contentment was rarer than passionate excitement

when she was with Lyon, and it was its rarity that made it so precious.

"I try to be logical, but sometines it isn't logic that drives me."

"And what else drives you?" The words were out of her mouth before she could stop them. The tone of her voice held expectations and hope.

Lyon turned to look into Jade's eyes. For the first time since he had spotted her that day and believed that she had tried to trick him into a deadly trap, he saw her for who she really was, his vision undistorted by personal fury or any sense of betrayal.

He studied the delicate planes of her face; the small, straight nose, the narrow mouth with the full lips that seemed designed to be kissed. The flickering light of the small fire heightened Jade's beauty. In that instant, Lyon knew that he had never before seen a woman so equisitely beautiful, nor one who affected him so powerfully in so many different ways.

He tried to speak, but words failed him, like cowardly soldiers unwilling to face their inadequacy. Speaking from the heart was not something he had ever been good at, and certainly not something that he had ever made any effort to hone his skills at. He turned to face Jade, reaching out to take her shoulder, gently twisting her toward him.

"You are my madness," he said in a hoarse whisper, pulling her closer, his powerful arms encircling her. "You are a fire in my blood, a fire in my brain. When I saw Garth and his men following you—"

"Shhh!" Jade shushed, placing the tips of her fingers against his mouth to silence words she did not want to hear. "Don't speak his name. There's no need to

203

ever bring it up again."

But Lyon, once begun, had words that needed to be spoken. He moved her hands from his mouth and lay them over his heart.

"I thought the foulest things of you," he continued. "The rage I felt was so powerful because I had felt betrayed. Never before have I felt that way, and that is because never before have I felt this way about a woman."

Jade turned enough so that she faced Lyon directly, sitting on the backs of her heels. Her fingers splayed out, touching Lyon through his shirt. His words touched her like caresses, spreading sensations that went far deeper than just the surface of her skin. She watched as Lyon's eyes went from her face down to her breasts, which were held high and together, temptingly revealed in the bodice of the dress. Her bosom drew his attention exactly as she had hoped it would when she had chosen the dress that morning.

"I love . . ." she began, then stopped herself.

Was it wrong to use the word *love* with Lyon? Would it frighten him off, as she had been told it did to so many men? Jade pushed forward, determined to say words that before meeting Lyon she could never have admitted existed.

"I love the way you look at me. I can see in your eyes . . . the desire, the passion . . . the passion that's within you for me. That makes me feel . . ."

As she spoke, Jade's hand crept up from Lyon's chest until her fingers slipped beneath his thick, blond hair at the nape of his neck. Her other hand, trembling slightly and moving with a will and direction of its own, slipped into the bodice of her gown, pulling down slowly and steadily against the cloth.

Silently, Jade lifted her upper body while remaining on her knees. She pulled on her bodice until one breast, heavy and firm, the nipple erect with dormant passion, sprang free. She kissed Lyon's mouth quickly, briefly, then pulled him to her.

As Lyon laid claim to her breast, Jade emitted a harsh, shocking cry. The passion she heard in her own voice was unbridled, uninhibited. She knew definitely that a passionate woman existed deep within, deep beneath layers of guilt and shame and notions of ladylike conduct that she now questioned.

She could feel his tongue and his teeth against her nipple; sharp, tingling sensations raced through her blood. Jade shivered on her knees, holding Lyon's head tightly, fiercely to her breast, as though afraid to release him for fear he would leave, as though afraid her courage to initiate lovemaking would fail her.

Would he think less of her for being so bold as to expose her bosom, practically forcing him to kiss her naked breast?

Jade pushed the question aside. She would not think about anything now, worry about anything or anyone, except herself and Lyon Beauchane. They alone mattered, at least for this magnificent moment in time, despite the wirlwind political affairs, the sudden violence and the equally sudden passion that had become a part of Jade's life.

"Yesss!" she cried out. "Oh, yesss!"

She was not the same woman that Lyon had made love to days earlier. Then, she had not really understood passion, nor her own ability to experience it when she was with Lyon. Now, having made love to

205

him several times, she knew what was happening, and exactly what it was that she wanted.

She boldly pushed her fingers through Lyon's hair, then pulled his head back, tilting his face up to her own. She was aware that she was being very forceful but she did not care. She would allow nothing to stand in the way of the passion she felt for this tall, handsome knight who had captured her body and soul and desire and all her willpower in his powerful hands.

"I need you!" Jade gasped, looking fiercely into Lyon's crystal blue eyes.

She abandoned any semblance of control she had over her own emotions. Demandingly, she slanted her full-lipped mouth down over Lyon's, thrusting her tongue deeply into his mouth. As her tongue entwined with his, she held his face tightly in her hands, holding him steady, seeking to control his movements. In the past, when they made love, Jade had been the passive recipient of his attention. She accepted his kisses and his sensual caresses gladly, taking them as a gift, without saying to Lyon precisely what she wantd from him.

That was before. She was no longer that frightened young widow, quaking at the shadowy forces around her.

She pushed him backward onto the cape-covered straw, following Lyon down, her mouth never separating from him. She flattened herself upon him, trying to press every inch of her body against him as his hands roamed over her back, along her thighs and buttocks.

He smiled slightly while Jade kissed him, and for an instant she knew fear. Was she going too far? Did he find her abandonment amusing?

Jade didn't want to think about it. Perhaps Lyon was experienced enough in the ways of the flesh to be cavalier about such matters, but she wasn't. With everything else that she had been through that day, she wanted to know that Lyon was not merely with her physically, but emotionally as well. And if she had to lie to herself, to pretend to herself that she was something unique and special in Lyon's life, then that's what she would do.

She felt her dress being raised. When her legs were free, she trapped Lyon's thickly muscled thigh between her own. The pressure of his leg against the juncture of her thighs fired a pleasing sensation, heightening and simultaneously feeding her deep-fevered hunger.

There was a part of Jade's mind that was angry with Lyon. She wanted him to be as frantic, as yearning and urgent for her touch as she was for his. She wanted him to be as affected by the events of the day, and by her beauty, as she was affected by him and the things that she had seen.

This was all so new to her! Her only regret was that she had not met Lyon earlier and that she had been forced at an early age to marry an egotistical fool like Prince William. Because of William, she had mortgaged her youth for an old man's dream.

As she kissed Lyon, feasting on his mouth, on his lips, an idea slowly took shape inside Jade's mind. She would show Lyon that though she undoubtedly was not the most experienced of his numerous lovers, she was the most ardent, the most willing to learn all the sensual subtleties of passion. She was the one woman who loved him for all that he was, both good and evil.

Taking him by the shoulders, Jade pushed down as

207

forcefully as she could, holding Lyon prone upon the straw. Then she quickly released his leg from between her tensed thighs, and before he could say anything, straddled his torso, sitting up.

"Don't move so far away," Lyon murmured, raising up, his mouth searching for the exposed, responsive nipple that he had pleasured just moments earlier.

Jade placed her hands upon his shoulders again and forced Lyon back down upon his cape. Her eyes sparkled with amber fire, a fire that had been locked away within her bosom for much too long. Now that it had been set free, it would never become shackled again. Not by Lyon, not by the Fates, not by anyone!

"This time . . ." Jade began. For a moment trepidation cut her words short. She paused, moistened her lips with the tip of her tongue, inhaled deeply, then continued. "This time *I* will say what we will do, and how we will do it."

She saw the spark of amusement shine in Lyon's eyes, and as before, it annoyed her slightly. He *still* was not taking her completely seriously, but she would change that.

"You mock me?"

Lyon rolled his head from side to side, his gaze dancing from Jade's face down to her exposed breast, then back again. He rested his hands upon her legs, sliding his fingers beneath her dress to stroke her warm, smooth skin.

"No!" Jade snapped. She caught Lyon's hands and pulled them from her, leaning forward to pin his wrists against the straw mattress. "Not until I say you can."

He laughed. "And I need your permission?"

Her eyes bore into Lyon as she replied, "As a matter

of fact, yes, you do."

Lyon smiled then, more with pride than amusement. He saw the determination in Jade's eyes, saw the confidence and the inner sense of who she really was shining through powerfully. He had watched her blossom, and he could only hope that he was partially responsible for the rare, magnificent flower before him.

"As you command, Lady Jade, my princess," he said in his rich, baritone voice, the one he used for formal occasions.

Jade released his wrists, but she did not take her hands from him. Instead, she let her fingertips trail drom his arms to his throat. Lyon kept his arms over his head, resting them with the fingers curling inward toward the palms, as though waiting impatiently to touch Princess Jade Crosse again.

Though her fingers trembled slightly, Jade was determined that nothing would stop her. She unfastened the first stud of his fine white shirt, then the second, and a third. She dared not look into Lyon's eyes. Whenever she did that, strange emotions came to life within her, and she did not want to become a slave to her emotions now.

Acting much more bravely than she felt, Jade pulled hard at Lyon's shirt, pulling the long tails out of his breeches, unfastening all the studs until she was able to push the garment aside to expose his naked chest.

His arms were still above his head, which made him appear even more gaunt than he actually was. Jade was able to distinguish the rippled line of his ribs, as well as the multitude of crisscrossing muscles that moved sleekly just beneath the surface of his skin. They defined in exquisite and erotic detail his strength, his power, his manliness.

Jade placed her hands lightly upon his chest, sighing softly at the touch of his skin against her fingertips, the heat of his body against her palms.

He's flawless, she thought.

Then she saw again the scar on his chest, jagged and partially hidden by the sparse hair that grew on his chest. At that moment it seemed a crime that anyone should mar such masculine perfection, and in the dizzying illogic of passion, she contemplated making it a royal edict punishable by something suitably severe.

"How did you get that?" she whispered, running the tip of her finger along the line of the scar. "Does it still hurt?"

Lyon shook his head. She watched his throat work as he swallowed. Lying passively on his back upon a mattress of straw was not in accord with his command-ing nature, and the strain of it showed upon his features.

"It happened long ago," Lyon said in a hoarse voice as Jade ran her fingertip over the scar. "In a battle. One of so many."

Jade whispered, "You fight too much." Then she bent down and kissed the scar, running the moist pink tip of her tongue along the length of it.

She heard and felt Lyon's sudden intake of breath. She had shocked him, she knew, and that pleased her. She would shock him, excite him, and satisfy him more than any woman he had ever known.

He shifted beneath her. Jade felt him move as she kissed his chest, and the newly discovered impish side of her nature wondered how long she could continue this tantalizing exploration before Lyon Beauchane, man of action, demanded to take charge of the situation.

Jade knew Lyon wouldn't be patient much longer, and knowing that she was erotically torturing Lyon pleased her so much.

She kissed his nipple, flicking her tongue against him in serpent-like fashion. Beneath her, Lyon nearly lifted off the mattress. When he moved, she felt the hard, thick line of his manhood brush against her thigh.

He wants me just as much as I want him. But if I make him wait, he'll want me even more! she reasoned.

Lyon started to reach for Jade again, but she stopped him. When she leaned forward to return his hands over his head, her breasts swung near his face, brushing against him. Jade felt the raspy stubble of a day's growth of beard against her one exposed nipple, and she moaned softly. As she sat on Lyon, she responsively wiggled her bottom slightly from side to side, feeling the throbbing undulations of his passion.

"You can't touch me until I say you may."

"I do not take orders from a woman."

"You will from this one. I am your princess," Jade reminded Lyon with a twinkle in her eyes. She slid lower on his body, her heart hammering with the fiery passions that grew hotter and more demanding with each passing second.

"But must I obey you even in matters of desire?"

Jade purred throatily as she tugged the buckle of his breeches loose. *"Especially* in matters of desire!"

She opened his breeches with trembling hands, and when Lyon raised his hips in silent invitation, she lowered his garment.

He sprang free instantly. Jade looked at him, then looked away. She did not know what to think. She didn't know what to do. The passion that had driven her forward suddenly vanished as the reality of this little game overwhelmed her.

She had never really looked at him before, without his caresses igniting the desire in her soul. Now she was able to think clearly, and everything within her was screaming, *He's too big!*

Another little voice reminded her, *No, he's not! He's perfect!*

Very slowly, as though his masculinity were potentially dangerous unless she was careful, she reached for him, taking him in both hands. He sighed, and the reassuring sound further emboldened Jade.

He seemed to leap in her hands at her touch, becoming even larger. His size no longer evoked a frightened response from Jade.

As she squeezed him, feeling his hardness, sensing his suppressed desire for her, she thought about their first passionate encounter together, when he had kissed her low, teasingly, in a way she had not thought possible. He introduced her to a summit of physical ecstasy that was at once frightening in its power and addicting in its influence over her emotions and her body.

Does he want me to kiss him like that?

She sensed that he did, but she was too unsure of herself, too afraid that she would do something wrong and dispel the magic aura in the cave. As she held Lyon in her hands, feeling him throbbing with life, she knew that one day she would have the courage to risk failure . . . but that day was not this day.

212

"Don't move," Jade whispered.

She stood then and shed her clothing, resisting the urge to turn away from Lyon to hide herself. She could feel his eyes upon her, and it seemed as though he could look straight into her soul. Though Jade wished she could do that to Lyon, she did not want him to do the same to her.

Completely naked, she turned directly toward Lyon, resisting the urge to cover herself with her hands. Kneeling near his feet, she pulled his boots off slowly, then removed his stockings, breeches, and undergarment. Then she removed his shirt, and when he rose to allow her to push the cloth from his arms, she pressed against him, her breasts brushing his face.

Lyon captured her nipple, hard and distended with passion, between his lips.

With a startled cry of ecstasy, Jade guided him into herself, trembling from head to toe as she felt him pushing deeper and deeper. He helped her establish a rhythm that was pleasing to both of them. Jade was not surprised that she again reached the pinnacle of ecstasy with Lyon, but the swiftness at which she reached that mysterious land.

The sound of her voice echoed off the walls of the cave as Jade cried out Lyon's name while the fire of culmination swept over her.

Chapter 18

He held her close, her head on his shoulder, her breathing even and steady. Lyon couldn't be sure that Jade was sleeping, but he suspected she was.

But sleep was not possible for him. His eyes were wide open as he stared at the ceiling of the cave, thinking about what must be done.

He believed that Jade was innocent of the atrocities she had been accused of. But if she was innocent, then someone else needed to be guilty, but who? How would it be possible to find out?

Jade had to be brought to Lord Charles Frederick's. Once she was there, she would be safe. Any plans that had to be made should include Lord Charles and Baron von Mueller, so hiding Jade away in the castle made perfect sense. Lady Shannon, Lord Charles's wife, would take perfect care of Jade. Knowing that Jade was safe would put Lyon's mind at ease while he did whatever was necessary to rid Castle Crosse of the parasites that had infected it.

"What are you thinking of?" Jade asked quietly, not

raising her face from Lyon's shoulder.

"I thought you were sleeping."

"No, just enjoying the quiet. What were you thinking?"

"Of what I've got to do now. I know you're not to blame for the murders and everything else that has the peasants howling. There are decisions that must be made."

Jade abruptly pulled her knees beneath her, rising up so that she could look down into Lyon's face. "Decision? And just who do you think should be the one to *make* those decisions?"

Lyon smiled consolingly. "M'lady, men are killing other men, and doing this in your name. The peasants think that you're responsible. Do you really think that you are in a position to learn who is guilty of destroying the peasants' faith in your judgement?"

"Yes, I most certainly do!" Absently, Jade reached for her clothes, and began putting them on. "Need I remind you that the land is mine? That the villagers who have been murdered are villagers who are living on *my* land? That the men who are responsible for these murders are probably part of *my* inner circle?"

"You don't need to remind me of what I obviously know," Lyon said, the edge of his voice sharp and jagged, like a blade.

"Obviously, I *do* need to remind you, since you seem to have forgotten that you work for me."

No knight would ever calmly accept anyone questioning his loyalty, especially not Lyon Beauchane, a man whose word of honor was the only law that reigned above all in his world. He swore savagely through clenched teeth, drawing the horrified gasp

215

from Princess Jade that he had sought.

"I am returning to Castle Crosse immediately," Jade said, stepping into her dress which looked only slightly worse for the ordeal that she had been through since that morning.

"You will not," Lyon said, pulling on his own clothes hastily. He had no experience at all in arguing with women, especially not one with greater authority than he possessed.

"I would appreciate it if you would escort me to Castle Crosse. If you don't wish to do so, I will understand." She shot Lyon a damning look as she struggled with the fasteners of her gown. "You are not the only one who knows this forest."

Now that she was certain Lyon was convinced of her innocence, Jade was sure that the only way to find out who was behind her troubles was to be where those troubles were generated. If she had any chance of recovering the respect of her people, and the control of her castle and lands, then she must be where her enemies were. Only then could she learn their identity, and fight them with whatever weapons of intelligence and courage that she possessed.

"You can't go back," Lyon said. He fingered the handle of his dagger, suspecting before this night was through, he would need it to save Princess Jade's life, and probably his own, as well.

"Don't tell me what I cannot do. You don't know what I'm capable of."

Lyon smiled, mentally twisting the meaning of her words, and letting Jade know he had done just that with nothing more than the look in his eyes. She scowled at him.

"I've got to return," Jade said, not looking at Lyon. It was easier to stand her ground when she did not have to look into his eyes. "I have to learn exactly who my enemies are. As a military man, surely you can understand that."

Lyon would not take the bait. He looked at Jade as she fidgeted with the fasteners of her robe. A powerful, insistent voice said that he must get her as far away from all danger as possible. But what would Lord Charles Frederick think if he brought her there? Hadn't Lyon received specific orders that Lord Charles and Baron von Mueller were to be insulated from his activity?

For the first time since he had reached the age of eighteen, when Prince William had touched a sword to his shoulders and bestowed upon him the honors of full knighthood, Lyon felt the urge to have a home of his own, something permanent and stable and safe where he could seek a haven.

But it wasn't for himself that he wanted a home, it was for Jade. He recoiled physically, shocked at the realization.

Lyon Beauchane, knight, warrior, man of action, lover . . . wanting something as mundane as a home?

The thought of it was so absurd that he couldn't help but smile. The absurd things that go through a man's head when he's recently made love to the most beautiful woman ever to walk the face of God's earth! Absurd!

"Perhaps you'd care to include me in your thoughts," Jade said acidly. "They seem to amuse you so very much, mayhaps they'll have the same effect upon me."

Shaking his head, Lyon stepped away from Jade,

trying to control the suddenly chaotic ramblings of his once-disciplined mind.

Absurd and laughable to think of settling down with Jade? Aye, it was absurd, he told himself . . . and he would keep telling himself that until he believed it.

But beneath the laughter he didn't believe it was abusrd. Lyon had schooled himself to spot self-delusion, knowing it was a reprehensible personal weakness. He could not pretend that the idea of seeing Princess Jade's lovely face on the pillow beside him every night, seeing her face with every sunrise, was a notion that disgusted him.

"Well?" she prodded.

The hard edge to Jade's voice pleased him enormously. She was very strong deep inside, where the heart and soul were. The years in Castle Crosse, the myraid of servants and the jewels and expensive gowns had not weakened the fire of her spirit.

"Trust me, my lady, when I tell you that I do not find anything about you laughable. You please me in countless ways, and that is why I smile."

"Lies come easily from your lips," Jade said.

She refused to be pulled in by his charms, but the edge to her voice wasn't as lacerating as it had been. No woman could be entirely immune to Lyon's flattery, especially when he put the full force of his dazzling blue eyes behind his words.

"The truth comes even easier." He smiled, but his brain was working feverishly, hoping to convince Jade that she mustn't return to the castle, where he could not protect her. "Can't you see how dangerous it is for you to return to Castle Crosse?"

"Return with me. It is your home as well as mine. If

you're there, you can protect me."

Lyon grit his teeth. If he returned with her, he wouldn't live a full day, not if the castle was as riddled with enemies and spies as Lyon believed. He would find himself outnumbered and cornered at some point, either in a barracks or perhaps on the training fields, where something would go awry. An arrow would mysteriously miss its target and land in his chest, or he would commit suicide by hanging himself, and no one would ask too many questions about the bruises on his face and body.

No, Lyon thought, if I openly entered Castle Crosse, where Garth Rawlings is in charge of all the knights and mercenaries, I would never leave the castle alive. Accompanying Jade might even put her in more danger, not less.

"I cannot," Lyon said at last.

"And I cannot stay away. We have reached an impass." Jade swallowed, emotion constricting her throat. "Will you escort me back to the castle? Not all the way, of course."

Very formally, as training for the knighthood dictated, and with a very heavy heart, Lyon replied, "As you wish, m'lady. As my princess, you need only ask to make it so."

To see Bishop Nathan Fields's violent temper unleashed was a frightening thing, even for someone who had fought and won as many fearsome battles as Garth Rawlings.

"And you can't find her? You can't find one woman you were following all day?" the bishop bellowed, his hands balled into white-knuckled fists.

Garth Rawlings said nothing, but in his heart, he prayed for two things; the safe return of Princess Jade, and for the opportunity to personally learn if Bishop Nathan Fields bled red blood, and whether great pain would make the towering man of the cloth crawl and squirm on his arrogant knees. Pity, Garth thought, that Bishop Fields would not survive the instructive taste of his own vile medicine.

"My men will find her," Garth said, repeating the hollow words for perhaps the thirteenth time in the thirty minutes he had been in Bishop Fields's chambers. Although he'd like to think of something else to say, his brain just wouldn't seem to work properly when Bishop Fields was screaming the way he was.

Nathan Fields slammed his fist down upon the table, sending the ink and quills, the blotter and the rather lethal-looking gold charm, bouncing on the hard, flat surface. His eyes, small and black, stabbed into Garth, skewering him with imperious hatred.

"Listen to me carefully, my idiotic friend," Bishop Fields said slowly, as though he was talking to a very stupid man incapable of understanding quickly spoken speech. "This is not the time for Princess Jade Crosse to die. If she dies, then the Crown will send someone to investigate her death. London gets very panicky whenever a member of the royalty dies. It makes everyone nervous, and we don't want them nervous."

Garth looked away and said under his breath. "We're going to kill her anyway."

"Yes, you fool, we *are* going to kill her."

Bishop Fields was literally quivering with rage. Oh,

how he hated having to deal with inferiors! If only he could find one person in all of England with an intelligence to match his own!

"But *when* we kill her is critical to the success of my plan," the bishop continued. "If we kill her before the stinking peasants thoroughly hate her, then London will turn its damned suspicious eyes toward us! If we wait until all the villagers want to kill her themselves, then we can kill her and blame the filth that lives beyond the walls of Castle Crosse for her murder, and the Crown will believe it!"

Bishop Fields slumped into his chair, sinking his face into his hands. How he prayed for the day when he could issue the order to have Garth Rawlings executed, and it wouldn't affect his plans one whit!

"Now do you see why she mustn't be murdered yet, you fool?"

Garth was spared the indignity of having to respond when there was a soft rap of knuckles against the door. Upon the bishop's acknowledgement, the door opened and Mary Ellen walked in, holding the broken end of an arrow in her hand.

"You'd better hear this," she said to the bishop. Her eyes darted over to Garth, silently asking Bishop Fields if it was acceptable to speak in front of the knight. When Bishop Fields nodded, Mary Ellen continued. "Three men have been found dead. Killed hard and quick, and by the looks of the tracks, by just one man."

"Who were they?"

When Garth heard the names, it surprised him. He knew the men weren't the most able fighters in the world, but they were killers nevertheless. It seemed unlikely that they could outnumber a foe three-to-one and still die without bringing their quarry down with them.

"Two with a sword, you say, and one with an arrow?" Garth asked.

Mary Ellen turned for the first time to face him. "The one got it in the back," she explained. "Haven't found his horse yet, but it appears as though he was trying to ride away from the others. This was sticking out of his back."

Taking the broken arrow from her, Garth inspected the three feathers at the tail end of the shaft, which guided the arrow's flight. The feathers were especially long, and the notch in the very end of the shaft had a queer U-shape to it.

In the pit of his stomach, a chill expanded inside Garth Rawlings. Helpless to stop it, he felt the blood drain from his face. Slowly, pretending that nothing was wrong, he took several deep breaths, forcing himself to be calm in the face of pure, primal danger.

"What is it Garth? Speak up, man!" Bishop Fields demanded irritably.

"The killing has begun," Garth said simply. He handed the broken arrow back to Mary Ellen. It felt good to know something that Bishop Fields did not. "He's back. It's not just a rumor anymore. He's back, and he's drawn the first blood."

Bishop Fields simply stared at Garth.

Mary Ellen breathed a single name. "Lyon Beauchane."

For a long time, no one in the room spoke, each contemplating privately what this new revelation meant to them personally.

Finally, Bishop Fields leaned back in his chair and kicked his foot up upon his desk.

"An arrow in the back, eh? Well, it's pretty clear to me, than, that Lyon Beauchane ambushed these fine men. Shot in the back without a warning! How cowardly can you get? The peasants will vilify the name of Lyon Beauchane! They won't find him to be such a handsome rogue when they hear about this!"

Garth shook his head. "If you try to tell them that Lyon Beauchane ambushed a patrol, shooting an arrow into one man's back without so much as a warning, they'll know you're lying."

"Know I'm lying? Even *you* can't say for certain that I'm lying! You weren't there! Nobody was there except Lyon!"

"The peasants won't believe he would do something like that."

"What did happen then?" Bishop Fields asked. Despite his contempt for Garth Rawlings, he had to admit to himself that Garth knew Lyon better than he did , and that knowledge was valuable.

"If I were to hazard a guess, I'd say that those men chanced upon Lyon, and thought they'd make quick work of him." He looked at Mary Ellen. "You say two bodies were close together, killed by a sword?" She nodded. "They were the first to attack, and he cut them down. The man who got shot in the back was running from the fight. He'd seen enough, and he wanted no part of Lyon Beauchane."

Bishop Fields uttered an obscene curse that Mary Ellen found amusing from a man of the cloth. Only her expertise at keeping her thoughts to herself enabled her to prevent showing her amusement.

223

"Whatever the story, whatever the truth, the fact is that Lyon Beauchane has now killed three men, and so he's an outlaw! I want a rider sent for London immediatley saying that we've got problems here with Lyon Beauchane. He's become a madman! I'll write the letter myself, asking for advice. The Crown will love it! They love feeling important!" Bishop Fields bolted to his feet, his mind spinning with thoughts, alight with excitement. "Garth, I want you to gather your finest men. I want a village razed. Burned to the ground! I want everyone slaughtered! Everyone, except a child or two. We'll want someone alive who will publically blame Sir Lyon Beauchane. This has to happen tonight, do you hear?"

"Most of my men are searching for Princess Jade," Garth said. He was getting swept up in the excitement of the moment, and being able to play a part in the destruction of Lyon Beauchane made his pleasure all the greater.

"Find them. Bring them back. For right now, finding that frigid wench is secondary." He looked straight into Garth's eyes. "Do the job properly. I want everyone killed, the village in ashes by morning. A child or two should be spared. Make them too young to give accurate descriptions of you and your men, yet old enough so they won't forget the name of Lyon Beauchane. You've failed me once tonight, Garth. Handle this personally, and you'll go far in redeeming yourself."

"I will," Garth said, and though he hated Bishop Fields, he was excited. For reasons unknown to him he really *did* want to earn the man's respect.

Bishop Fields was in a state of high excitement by the

time he finally pushed Garth out of the room. He then turned to Mary Ellen, and she knew by the glistening look in his eyes what he wanted. She started for his bed, but he caught up with her before she reached it, tearing at her nightgown even as she tried to remove it herself.

Chapter 13

They crouched at the edge of the treeline, holding hands in the darkness, neither saying a word. In the distance, at the drawbridge of Castle Crosse, riders were streaming out, most of them carrying torches.

"They are looking for you," Lyon said quietly.

Jade watched the tiny specks of light moving into the darkness. Was it possible that she could be so hated when so many men would ride into the night in search of her? She didn't want to believe it was so, but then . . .

"You don't have to go," Lyon said, giving Jade's hand a ressuring squeeze. "We can turn around right now and no one will be the wiser."

Jade shook her head, sending her wavy, blond tresses shimmering over her shoulders. "No, I must return. But we will see each other again soon, and when we do, I will know who the spies are within Castle Crosse."

In the moonlight, she looked again at Lyon's face, marvelling for the hundredth time how comely he was in any light, under any circumstance.

"Trust no one, m'lady. Believe only in your-self . . . and in me."

She tried to speak, but the pain in her heart made words impossible. Why was it their time together could not be longer? Why must the loving moments that she spent in his arms always be followed by painful hours and days of separation and sorrow?

Leaning toward him, Jade kissed him quickly, then rose to her feet.

"Three days," she said, a slight tremble in her voice. "In three days I will again be in your arms."

Then she stepped out of the shadows and began walking toward Castle Crosse, her home and the home of her enemies.

When Jade returned to Castle Crosse, an immediate and heartening roar of approval from her staff greeted her. She doubted the sincerity of these people who feigned loyalty to her and plotted behind her back.

Bishop Fields, as Jade's personal advisor, was called for immediately. Knowing she would be asked hundreds of questions by the bishop, Jade thought the best lie to explain her absence was to say that she had been thrown from her horse and bumped her head. She explained she had walked a long way, confused and dazed from the fall. Then suddenly, everything came clear to her once again, and she made her way back to Castle Crosse. She was never in any real danger, she explained to the stern-faced bishop. During the entire time she walked, she did not see a soul, and she doubted that anyone saw her.

Bishop Fields, though he claimed to be overwhelm-

227

ingly happy that his princess had returned to the castle safe and healthy, held a darkness in his eyes that suggested the presence of many angry thoughts and violent desires. He did not entirely believe Jade's story, but he could not say so without openly calling her a liar. Even if Princess Jade Crosse was only nominally the leader of Castle Crosse, she still had enough clout to make his life difficult, if not entirely impossible. Directly insulting or challenging her honesty and integrity might not only be imprudent, but devastating to his master plan.

It had gone so smoothly, Jade could hardly believe her luck.

The next morning, she realized her luck had run out.

First, as she tried to leave her bedchamber, Mary Ellen informed her that she was to stay in bed "until the good bishop says you can leave and still be of a healthy spirit." Jade wasn't at all sure what that meant, and had no intention of simply taking her maid's word. Then Bishop Fields arrived and explained that since Jade had been dazed by her fall, it would only be prudent to stay in bed a couple days to ensure her continued good health.

If Jade wanted to maintain her lie, she would need to follow the bishop's orders, at least temporarily. She returned to her bed and tried to pretend that it didn't bother her that Mary Ellen was annoyingly smug about being right concerning Bishop Fields's orders.

Then the next horrifying surprise landed right in Jade's lap, along with the silver tray that held her evening meal, delivered by Mary Ellen.

The village of Tewsbury had been attacked the previous night by Lyon Beauchane and a contingent of his soldiers and mercenaries. The village, Mary Ellen explained, had been burned to the ground. There were few survivors, two very small boys and a teenage girl. The boys had done most of the talking, telling the horrifying tale in gory detail which Mary Ellen was happy to pass on. The girl did not say much of the incident because she had been attacked, apparently by Lyon Beauchane himself.

Jade felt the blood drain from her face. She was thankful that she was sitting down and in bed because she doubted that she would have been able to stand. Lyon a rapist? Impossible!

"W-what time did all this happen?" Jade asked. She picked up her tea cup, but her hand shook so badly the tea sloshed over the hand-painted gold rim. She abandoned the attempt.

"I heard it happened an hour or two before dawn," Mary Ellen explained, already wiping up the spilled tea on the silver serving tray. "That's the time to attack, I've been told, if you want to kill people. Sir Garth Rawlings told me so. It's the time when folks sleep the soundest. Tsk! Tsk! That poor dear, having to live now after a murdering monster like Lyon Beauchane forced himself upon her, soiling her like that! Tsk! Tsk! Such a shame when bad things happen to good girls like her."

"But Lyon couldn't have done that," Jade said, a certain pleading quality in her tone that was not at all like her. "He couldn't have, don't you see?"

Mary Ellen took a step away from the bed. Her eyes narrowed as she looked closely at Princess Jade. "No . . . I don't see, m'lady. Why couldn't Beauchane have raped that poor child? She wasn't the first one to suffer his beastly lust, you know. There was another poor child he violated some days ago. It's been told all through the villages. Everyone knows of it."

In that instant, Jade hated Mary Ellen, and any doubts that she'd ever had concerning the fealty of the young maid vanished. She knew then, just by looking into Mary Ellen's eyes, that she was an evil person, and that she enjoyed her evilness. Throughout the fiefdom, Lyon Beauchane's name had been held in awe, in respect. Now Mary Ellen was taking great pleasure in seeing that name sullied, and her only reason was because she was malicious and spiteful.

Jade began to explain again that Lyon couldn't be responsible for what he had been accused of, then she bit her tongue and shrugged her shoulders. She could not defend Lyon without admitting that she had been with him during her absence on the previous eveing.

It had been a long, painful week for Jade. She missed her *rendez-vous* with Lyon, and spent that week thinking of him and defending him. She tried to find out what she could from the servants concerning the activities of Lyon Beauchane, but she learned very little. The peasants had formally complained to Sheriff Dunne about Lyon's murderous activities. Sheriff Dunne had assembled a group of his finest men to ride the forest in search of Lyon. Also, Garth Rawlings had taken the finest knights from Castle Crosse to conduct his own search.

Jade was assured that, between Sheriff Dunne and Garth Rawlings, Lyon Beauchane and his men would be found, and they'd be slaughtered on the spot like the dogs that they were.

When the villagers spoke Lyon's name, they spit on the ground afterward to get the taste of his name out of their mouths.

There was nothing Jade could do to still the destructive tongues, to silence the false stories. There was nothing she could say that would convince anyone that Lyon was not a rapist, not a murderer. There was nothing she could do that would convince anyone that there were murderers within the high, protective stone walls of Castle Crosse, murderers who hadn't traveled afar to fight wars, but men who now surrounded the Princess Jade Crosse and offered her their sound advice.

But who were those men?

"Can you believe what is being said?" Lyon bellowed, his voice echoing off the thick walls of Baron von Mueller's vast study.

"You needn't shout," Lord Charles said, sitting in a huge chair at the long table, which was strewn with maps of the area.

Baron Timish von Mueller, not given to raising his voice, narrowed his eyes at the impetuous young man. "We can believe what is being said because we have heard what is being said," the baron explained. "What we need to know is who is really behind the razing of Tewsbury. Your ranting and raving will not bring us one bit closer to discovering the true culprits."

Lyon Beauchane had been a military man his entire life, and he understood protocol and position. He withdrew a chair from the table and sat down facing the maps, determined to keep his temper in check.

The baron was right, he concluded. It would do no good to scream about what had already happened. The best course of action was to determine what they could do to change the future.

"The first thing I think we need to consider is whether or not we go straight to the Crown with what we know," Baron von Mueller said. "As a foreigner, I don't feel I am the one to write such a missive."

He looked to Lord Charles. The big man wiggled a palm, undecided as yet.

"The other possibility," the baron continued, "is that we handle the problem ourselves. But if we do choose to be in control of our own destiny, we must realize that the Crown will not look favorably upon us if we fail."

"The Crown may not look favorably upon us if we succeed," Lord Charles commented dryly.

Silence embraced the three men. If they involved London, it would mean disgracing Princess Jade Crosse. She would almost surely lose her lands and castle to the London nobility if it was felt that she could not keep her lands and peasants in order, or could not pay her taxes. But if nothing was done, the peasants, already angry with the land-owning lords, would lash out. Eventually, their anger would spill over to the neighboring lands. No matter how fairly von Mueller and Lord Charles treated those serfs living and working the land, the conflicts would increase until there would be a bloody insurrection of devastating scope. Then the Crown would *have* to get involved . . . and no one would be happy about that.

Lord Charles sipped his ale, then said, "We can safely say, then, that Princess Crosse is not responsible. Correct?"

'Aye, that is correct, m'lord," Lyon replied forcefully.

"Then we've got to get her out of there. In the past four days I have sent as many letters to Castle Crosse, asking if there is anything I can do to help Princess Jade, or to catch that traitor, Lyon Beauchane. I've received two letters in return, both of them written by Bishop Nathan Fields. Each says that the princess has everything under control, and that any day now they expect to catch the errant knight and bring him to justice."

Baron von Mueller smiled. "Bishop Fields would sell his soul, I wager, to find out that you are staying under my roof, Lyon."

"Bishop Fields *has* no soul," Lyon replied.

Lord Charles raised a huge hand to draw attention back to himself again. "I have spies within Castle Crosse. I can get word directly to Princess Crosse informing her that we plan to get her out of the castle. Once she is out of the Castle, we can act more freely, since at the point an accidental noble death seems unlikely."

"You have spies within Castle Crosse?" Lyon said, his brows furrowed together.

"And so have I," Baron von Mueller said matter-of-factly. "When you stand at the top of the mountain, the only direction you can move is down. Be aware of that, young man. I am a solid judge of character, and I'd say that someday you, too, will stand at the peak of the mountain. And when you do, and you have a Castle Crosse beside you, you, too, will have spies in your employ."

Lyon realized there was much he had yet to learn, and he got the feeling that there would be no better teachers than Baron von Mueller and Lord Charles.

"So we get Princess Jade out of the castle, then we shake the walls," Lord Charles continued. "Whatever and whoever rises to the top is likely to be responsible for our troubles."

Lyon asked, "And if the Crown is informed of our actions, then what?"

"I have a man in London. He can delay many things," Lord Charles replied.

"And if a rider is sent from Castle Crosse, it is likely he will have to cross my land. I'll have men watching the roads. A little detention for a week, or so, shouldn't cause much of an incident."

It was Lyon's first lesson in how a handful of powerful men could direct the lives of many others, and he was thankful that the power rested in the hands of men of character such as Lord Charles and the baron. But what of the power and wealth of Castle Crosse? Who really held the power there? Lyon would find the answers to those question later, after he had Jade safely tucked away.

Then he would shake the walls of Castle Crosse, and be ready to kill whoever rose to the top of the trouble.

He placed his elbows upon the long table, leaning close, not wanting to miss a single word as their plans for action were made.

Bishop Nathan Fields leaned back against the headboard of his bed, a sated smile on his lips. On the bed beside him, Mary Ellen was breathing softly, sleeping after their harsh coupling.

On the small table beside the bed was the letter he had received several hours earlier. Immediately upon receiving and reading the letter, Bishop Fields had called for Mary Ellen to be escorted to his quarters. There he practically ripped off her clothes and threw her upon the bed, satisfying his lust in a celebrating way.

The letter was from London, written by an assistant to King Henry, addressed to Princess Jade Crosse of FitzPatrick. It stated that the Crown was not responsible for the insurrection and turmoil that was happening within the Crosse fiefdom, and that it was Princess Crosse's own actions that had caused the problems. Furthermore, the Crown would not be at all surprised if the peasants broke into open revolt because of the conditions that had been foisted upon them. Then, in a caring and gentle tone, the letter went on to explain to Jade that the peasants are really rather easy to control, and that they need actually quite little to keep them quiet. However, once their anger has been aroused, it often proves quite difficult to calm it again. Therefore, it is recommended that Princess Jade relax some of the restrictions, at least temporarily, that she has placed upon the peasants. This would quite likely satisfy some of the more vociferous of the insurrectionists, and would please Princess Crosse's closest neighbors, Lord Charles Frederick, and Baron Timish von Mueller. Each of those men had written terse missives to London complaining that Princess Crosse's gross mismanagement of her property and people was causing problems in their own fiefdoms.

Bishop Nathan Fields read the letter one more time, then refolded the single sheet of paper and returned it to the envolope.

He had everything in order now. The Crown believed that Jade had become extremely greedy, and that she was personally responsible for the peasants threatening violence and open insurrection. Lord Charles and Baron von Mueller had even helped set the trap by writing to the Crown to complain about Princess Jade. He smirked. Their complaints gave invaluable validity to the lies the bishop was spreading about Jade.

As he lay in bed, his lust for women satisfied, his lust for power freshly piqued and rising with each second, he decided that it would be best to act immediately. He would have Jade killed, and he would blame Lyon Beauchane for her death.

A slow, sadistic smile curled his thin-lipped mouth as another thought entered his brilliant, savage mind. He could even write a letter to the Crown asking for help after Jade Crosse's murder, stating that Lyon Beauchane and his men had become so powerful and so murderous that they appeared unstoppable. With help from London, Bishop Fields could again restore order to the area, and the taxes to the Crown would resume unchecked.

It was all so perfect, he could hardly believe it. At first he had seen Lyon Beauchane's return from the wars as a problem. But now it was the best thing that could have happened, since it made Princess Jade Crosse's murder that much more plausible.

Almost giddy with excitement, Nathan Fields pushed against Mary Ellen's shoulder. He wanted her again. Such days deserved celebration, and he liked being serviced by women who had no choice but to heed his wishes.

*　　　*　　　*

Garth knew instinctively that if he handled this task expertly, he would vastly increase his standing with Bishop Nathan Fields.

Along with a dozen of his finest men, as well as Sheriff Sean Dunne and two of his men, Garth was accompanying Jade to the village of Esselex, at the very outskirts of her property, bordering Baron von Mueller's fiefdom. Jade had been told that Lyon Beauchane and his men had attacked the village, burning much of it to the ground, killing many of the men and raping many of the women.

That was the story that Jade had been told, though in truth none of the woman had been raped, none of the men murdered, none of the huts and homes burned.

None yet, that is.

When Jade heard the rumor, she demanded to see Esselex herself. Even though it was quite a long ride from Castle Crosse, she said she simply could not believe that a knight that her husband had bestowed such responsibility upon could turn into a vicious monster. She went storming up to the bishop and refused to take no for an answer, even though Bishop Fields appeared to do his best to convince Jade that it wasn't safe yet for her to travel so far from the castle.

As Garth thought about this, a smile pulled at his mouth, and a sadistic light shone in his eyes. Even though he hated the biship, there was no denying the fact that the man was a genius. He had planned the assault on Esselex, as well as Jade's murder, and all he had to do was get the princess to the village *prior* to razing it. Then everything, from the attack on the people to Jade's murder, could be blamed on Lyon Beauchane and his men. As long as everyone in the village was murdered, there would be no voice to speak out against them.

The plan really was deliciously diabolical, and Garth was envious that he had not thought of it himself.

Bishop Nathan Fields had told Garth that it was his personal responsibility to see that the princess did not live to see another day.

"I'll kill her myself," Garth promised. "You can count on me, m'lord."

"I am," Bishop Fields replied, looking straight into Garth's eyes. "I am holding you responsible for the success of this day's work."

Riding easily in the saddle, Garth admired the delicate curve of his princess's hips. It didn't bother him at all that she rode her horse like a man, spreading her legs to sit straight ahead. Before the day was over, she would be spreading her legs for him!

The thought of it made him shiver with anticipation. He had often dreamed that one day she would realize his true worth, that his princess would spot him at the games, or doing some manly task within the walls of Castle Crosse. Then, she would understand, with just a single glance, that he alone was man enough for her.

The truth was that she had never once cast him a flirtatious glance, not even after her foolish husband had been killed. She didn't realize the raw, masculine perfection so near at hand, living in the castle with her. For that oversight, Princess Jade Crosse would be punished by Rawlings.

Very soon, they would arrive at Esselex, and Jade would be happy that the village was intact. And then Garth's men would begin rounding the peasants up to be slaughtered, and while that was going on, Garth would force himself upon Jade. Once finished, he would kill her, leaving her body behind so that Lyon Beauchane could be blamed for her murder.

A high-pitched giggle, sick and maniacal, tittered out of Garth's throat. It was a glorious day! He would, in a single afternoon, have sex with a princess, kill a member of the nobility, and plant evidence to have Lyon blamed and ultimately executed for it all!

This was the most magnificent day in Garth Rawlings's life, and he knew it would never again be quite this lovely.

Chapter 20

Jade had been to villages that had been razed before, so she thought she knew what to expect. For miles downwind, the odor of burning homes should be carried on the breeze.

As she approached Esselex, she could not smell that fetid stench of burning death. Raising up slightly in the saddle, she sniffed the air, not caring that she received a questioning look from the young broadswordsman who rode beside her. Very faintly, she did smell something.

Sniffing again gave her the information she needed, and it surprised her. Instead of detecting the harsh scent of a village burning, she smelled the mouth-watering aroma of roasting mutton, which reminded Jade of how little she had eaten that morning when she'd broken her fast.

She had been too anxious in the morning to eat, and now she was paying for it. Her heart felt as though imprisoning steel bands surrounding it had suddenly sprung open. If the village of Esselex was still intact, if the people there were still hale and hearty, then that would prove Lyon was not the dragon that rumor painted him to be.

Though she tried not to dwell on it, the rumors about Lyon did make Jade question what she knew about him. She didn't want to believe that he was a brutal rapist and murderer, and she believed that he wasn't. Still . . . now and then . . . one couldn't help but wonder if maybe there was more than just a hint of truth about those awful things that had been said. The truth of it was that Jade couldn't be with Lyon every minute of the day, so there was always the possibility that he might . . .

The sound of a male voice beside her snapped Jade out of her own thoughts. She was happy for the distraction, since she never enjoyed it when her thoughts began to question Lyon's innocence.

"Pardon?" Jade said, blinking her eyes. She had been disturbed by Garth, who had ridden so close beside her that his knee was nearly touching hers.

"I asked if you were feeling well, m'lady," Garth repeated.

He was smiling in a way that was unpleasantly different for him, and Jade found it distinctly unsettling. She wondered what could make him so happy, though there really wasn't joy in his smile. It was more like satisfaction, but what could Garth be so satisfied about?

Garth added, "You had a troubled look on your face."

"I'm feeling well, thank you," Jade replied formally. She looked straight ahead, hoping that Garth would leave. When he didn't, she was forced to turn her attention back to him. "Is there anything else you wanted to know?"

"No, m'lady. We'll be arriving at Esselex soon, and I wanted to be with you when we do."

His eyes went up and down over Jade, and it made her feel as though she should bathe. Never before had any of her subjects been so openly disrespectful of her in a lustful manner, and Jade made a mental promise to tell Bishop Fields what the captain of the knights had done.

There were four riders ahead of her, so Jade's view of Esselex was initially blocked. When she saw the faces of the children, and their parents standing behind them, Jade's emotions soared.

The villagers were looking on at the approaching riders with a certain amount of trepidation, but that was to be expected. They were alive! And the village was intact! She could hardly wait to talk to the village elders. If she could speak to them privately, without Sheriff Dunne or Garth Rawlings hovering about at her elbow, then she could convince them that the hideous rumors concerning Lyon Beauchane were all lies! And those stories about people being executed under Jade's direct orders would get corrected, too!

Before the sun set, Jade would have at last gotten the word directly out to her people that she and Lyon weren't the evil people many wrongly believed them to be.

The parents began pushing their children toward their huts, and the obvious fear in their actions tore into Jade's heart. They had reached the outskirts of the hamlet, and though no one said anything directly, it was clear that the women and children were going into hiding.

"Don't run! Please! I only want to talk to you!" Jade called out.

At her side, Garth Rawlings began laughing, a steady, loud, eerie sound.

When Jade turned to look at him, his eyes glowed with feral passions that at last could be set free.

"Oh, my God, you're mad!" Jade gasped.

Garth grinned wider, nodding his head. Then he raised his hand high, his eyes never leaving Jade's. It was the signal the soldiers had been waiting for. They drew their swords and battle-axes.

When Garth dropped his hand, the men shouted as one and began the attack upon the helpless villagers.

"What are you doing?" Jade screamed, holding on tightly to the reins as her horse pranced about this way and that, made nervous by the destriers that raced past her. "Knight Rawlings, call your men back! Call them back this instant!"

He leaned over in the saddle, trying to grab her. Jade's mare, already skittish from the sudden burst of action, leaped sideways, enabling Jade to partially avoid Garth's outstretched hand. But he caught the billowing sleeve of her dress, and pulled hard. Had Jade's thighs not been strengthened by so many hours on horseback as a youth, she would not have been able to remain in the saddle.

The tearing sound was sharp and pleasing to Garth, and when he realized he had torn the sleeve of his princess's gown off at the shoulder, he howled with glee and held the white, torn cloth to his nose. He inhaled deeply to get the scent of her, as a hunting animal might get the scent of his prey.

The madness she saw in Garth's eyes, combined with the hideous, savage war cries of the knights as they attacked the villagers, told Jade that she knew nothing at all about what was truly going on within the confining stone walls of Castle Crosse.

"I'll see you hanged for this!" she shouted.

Her threat only brought forth another peel of hideous laughter from Garth.

There could be no doubt that the attack upon the village, and the attack upon her, had been orchestrated well in advance. She had played into Bishop's Fields's hands, and into Garth Rawling's, an insane murderer who was merely the physical arm of the savage greed and desires of his leader.

The fact that Garth had not drawn either sword or dagger told Jade that he did not intend to kill her . . . at least not right away. That was enough to freeze the blood in her veins. She watched as he tossed aside the sleeve, and stared with building horror as the pure white silk was trampled beneath the muddy hooves of the soldiers' horses.

"The last thing you'll ever see is my face, you wench!" Garth shouted madly. "My face as I show you what a man I really am!"

He spurred his horse forward. Jade, rather than turning her mare around to flee, struck her heels against the mare's ribs, urging her mount forward. The two horses shot past each other, moving in opposite directions like destriers during a jousting match.

Garth was caught by surprise by Jade's bold move. He swung an arm out hoping to catch her, but his move was a fraction too slow. By the time he had stopped his mount and turned, Jade was riding away from the road leading into Esselex at a swift gallop, moving deeper into the forest for protection.

Jade's heart hammered in her chest, just as her mare's hooves hammered against the ground. She found what appeared to be an animal trail and jerked hard on the reins, turning to the right, heading the frightened mare in that direction.

Time seemed to take on new dimensions for Jade. Everything seemed to happen so quickly, and though she thought she had been riding for quite a long time with Garth chasing her, the whispering voice of logic told her that only a few seconds had elapsed. But a couple seconds was all she needed to become aware that the horse she rode was no match in speed, stamina, or courage, to the strong, battle-hardened destriers that the soldiers rode. And Garth, she guessed, would keep the swiftest war horse for himself.

Jade leaned over her mare's neck, urging the frightened animal on, but she knew it would do no good. Behind her, not ten yards away, Garth was riding easy in the saddle, apparently not in any great hurry to end the chase.

Glancing quickly over her shoulder again, Jade looked at her pursuer. Icicles of fear stabbed her heart as she saw the look of primal, feral bloodlust shining in Garth's eyes.

She turned in the saddle again, kicking her heels hard against the mare's panting ribs, urging the old animal on to more speed, though there was no more to give.

And then she felt Garth's hand on her shoulder, and though she tried to scream, a paroxysm of fear constricted her throat so that she couldn't even make a sound.

The crackle of Garth's laughter rang hollow and deafening in her ears. She felt herself being pulled backward, and though she tried to keep hold of the reins, they were ripped from her fingers.

An arm whipped around Jade's waist, lifting and dragging her from the saddle. She tried to hold onto the mare with her legs, squeezing with all her might. As Garth slowed his own destrier, Jade's mare ran out from underneath her. This time, when Jade tried to scream, the sound of her voice echoed through the forest.

"Scream, you little wench!" Garth hissed, holding onto his captive with one arm. "Scream your bloody head off! There's nobody here who'll help you!" He laughed then. "Bring us an audience if you want! When I'm finished with you, maybe I'll give you to the others."

Jade did not at first comprehend the full magnitude of the threat. It was difficult to breathe with Garth holding her with an arm pressed hard against her stomach while she bounced against the side of the heavily muscled destrier.

He released her suddenly before his stallion had come to a complete stop. A moment after Jade's delicate slippers hit the ground, she landed hard on her hands and knees, sliding and bouncing in the groundcover of leaves and pine needles. She heard the tearing sound of her gown once more giving way to greater force and saw a huge hole had been ripped in the cloth near her knee, and the left shoulder of the gown had been torn nearly in two.

Garth was still laughing as he whipped his destrier around to face Jade once more. In her dishevelled, frightened state, with her gown tattered and dirty, her hair strewn every which way in a satiny profusion, she had never looked more desirable to Garth. He felt the blood running hot in his veins, an explosion of raw adrenaline whipping his senses into a frenzy that was oblivious to fear or danger, and certainly mute to the faintest hint of human compassion.

When Jade turned and began running, Garth tossed his head back and howled like a wolf. He then leaped off his horse. He would run down Jade on foot. It was more personal that way, and he wanted this to be very personal. He wanted her to know that it was Garth Rawlings who was doing this to her, not some mere stranger. He *needed* her to know that she was being bested by the man that she had paid so little attention to over the years. He needed Princess Jade Crosse to know that she had slighted the wrong man, a man of courage and strength and ultimate virility. She wasn't an innocent victim picked at random, she was the intentional target of Garth Rawlings. She would pay a terrible price for not realizing how manly he really was.

It would be the last lesson he would teach her; the last lesson she would ever learn.

He was a strong man, and though he could not defeat Lyon in the competitive games during their training, he was still much stronger and faster than Jade. He gained on her quickly as she ran through the forest, dodging low-hanging branches. He watched as her hair streamed over her shoulders, flying behind her like the mane of a golden pony, her legs pumping madly as she ran. When he was nearly at her side, he watched her breasts rise and fall inside her gown. Then, in profile, he saw the fear in her expression. That last stimulus was too much for a man like Garth Rawlings to ignore or deny for even a second longer.

With saliva glistening upon his mouth, Garth's lips peeled back to snarl in a display of yellow teeth. He tossed himself at his princess, tackling her, tearing at her clothes even before they'd struck the ground.

Chapter 21

She used every weapon her body possessed, and managed to spin on the ground beneath Garth, even though his weight was a burden to her. Jade's right knee slipped between Garth's thighs to connect solidly with his groin. As the breath gushed from his lungs and pain doubled him over, Jade curled her fingers like talons, and brought her fingernails clawing down the sides of his face. Red lines formed on Garth's face, and he squeezed his eyes tightly shut to protect them.

He cocked a gloved fist back and tried to strike Jade, but she moved too quickly for him. His powerful fist only thudded harmlessly into the ground. Pain still roiled within him, and breathing was difficult because the knee to his groin had struck with astonishing strength.

Garth reached for Jade's long hair, knowing that once he had her tresses wrapped around his heavy, gloved fist, she would be powerless to fight him.

He'd no more than touched her long blond hair when Jade stabbed her thumb into his left eye.

Garth let out a howl of rage and rolled away from the wildcat, needing just a few moments to gather his wits about him before he resumed the attack. He had no doubts that he could defeat Jade. He just had to wait until he could see clearly before he resumed the attack. Then he would make her pay dearly for all the pain that she had caused him.

Scrambling to her feet, Jade wheeled to face her attacker once more. She was surprised to see the red welts running down his cheeks, even more surprised to see how he held a hand over his eye. Had she blinded him? Though Jade loathed violence, she hoped she had.

"You'll wish you'd just laid down and spread your legs, wench woman!" Garth hissed, a hand still cupped over his eye, slightly bent over from his bruised testicles. "For every drop of blood I've shed, you'll spill a thousand. I promise you that, woman!"

The way he said *woman* made it sound like being one was an insult. Jade looked at the man she had once considered the leader of the knights of Castle Crosse. She realized that all of her initial instincts concerning Garth had been correct. Before, she hadn't been able to say why she never trusted him, only that she didn't. As she bounced on the balls of her feet, prepared to run from Garth's next charge, Jade promised herself that if she lived through the day then she would always listen to what her heart and her instincts told her about people.

She did not have enough experience at fighting to know what she should have done in the situation. By waiting and watching Garth, she allowed him time to compose himself. The pain in his groin quickly lessened, and before long he was able to see clearly with both eyes again. Had Jade continued her attack while he was blinded in one eye and crippled up with pain, she might have been able to incapacitate him permanently.

When Garth finally took his hand away from his eye, he was smiling again in that sadistic way that Jade had come to know.

"I like a good fight," he said quietly as he began advancing slowly on Jade. "It heats my blood."

Jade looked at him, remembering suddenly what Lyon had said. There *was* evil in this world, even if she didn't want to believe in its existence. Looking into Garth's eyes and seeing the hatred he felt for himself, for her, for all of humanity told Jade more than she ever wanted to know about the potential for evil within the hearts of a few people.

In the distance, Jade heard the cries of the villagers of Esselex. She could smell the smoke now, hear the crackle of flames eating away at homes that sheltered good men and women who wanted nothing more out of life than a fair chance at happiness.

"Come to me, Jade, you wench!" Garth whispered. A dribble of saliva rolled from the corner of his mouth down his chin. "Come to me now on your knees!"

The response that Garth got was not the one he wanted. Instead of fear, he saw defiance. Instead of Jade's tremulous voice, he heard the deep baritone voice that he had not heard in years. He recognized it instantly.

Lyon Beauchane!

251

"No princess—no *woman!*-kneels for swine!" Lyon repeated, advancing slowly, moving so that he stood between Jade and Garth.

He held his sword in his right hand, a dagger in his left. He spared only a glance at Jade to reassure himself that she was not mortally injured, although she was certainly shaken and frightened.

"You've been a swine all your life," Lyon whispered to Garth, sizing his opponent up. "Surely you must be accustomed to being treated like swine by now."

The changes in Garth's expression, in his demeanor, were swift and appalling. No longer faced with an enemy that he could surely defeat, he now faced an armed foe who possessed skill even greater than his own. He had been denied the chance to satiate his twisted desires, and being denied anything always enraged Garth Rawlings.

Garth drew his own weapons, but there was a furtive look in his eyes as he studied Lyon. Garth did not like fair fights; he like a sure thing. As he squared off with Lyon, he wondered what the odds were that one of his men might have followed him into the forest after Jade.

They began to circle slowly, both men holding a weapon in each hand. They had both been to the same school, taught to fight in the same way; they had battled each other many times using blunt wooden daggers and practice swords that would not draw blood.

"I've always beat you before," Lyon whispered. "I'll beat you again."

"Not this time," Garth replied. "This time, the hour belongs to me. And any second now my men are going to come running, each of them hungry for a taste of that wench!"

Lyon shook his head slowly. He made sure that Jade stayed directly behing him as he circled with Garth, moving just a little closer with each step. "Listen carefully, Garth. Does that sound like your swinish criminals engaging in a battle against unarmed peasants, or like your men falling under the swords of my brave knights?"

Garth listened. What he heard disturbed him greatly. The metallic clang of swords meeting swords drifted over them, riding the warm night breeze. By now he should have heard the screams of the women as they were carried off by his mercenaries, and the death cries of the old peasants as they were cut down mercilessly. He only heard the sounds of battle, of armed men against armed men.

At that moment, Garth wanted very much to turn and flee. He could run from Lyon, and no one in Castle Crosse would tell of his cowardice. He could run, and no one would ever know that he was afraid of Lyon Beauchane. No one would know but himself. He had known that for a long time already.

Garth was thinking about his chances of running away successfully when Lyon attacked. It was the usual opening charge, one that had been taught to both of them in their days in training. Lyon raised his sword high overhead, then brought it down the brutal force. A moment after the attack was blocked, he lunged forward with the dagger, aiming for the midsection. Garth leaped sideways, tossing his hips backward. The point of Lyon's dagger cut the cloth of Garth's shirt at his stomach, but did not reach his flesh.

Once the initial attack had been averted, Garth's confidence began to return. After all, Lyon wasn't that much better. Maybe the wars had taken some of his edge off, and that was all the advantage that Garth would need to turn defeat into a beautifully bloody victory.

Jade kept her distance from Lyon, but always stayed behind him, sensing that this is what he wanted her to do. She was so frightened that she couldn't even speak a word of encouragement to her lover. But he had come for her once again, arriving to stand between her and the most immediate source of danger.

As the men fought, swords ringing out as they collided, daggers missing flesh by inches, she promised herself that if Lyon lived through this battle, she would do whatever was necessary to put an end to the fighting for all time. She could not imagine another woman watching the man she loved fighting against pure evil.

And it was at that moment, as Lyon and Garth alternately advanced and retreated in their running swordfight, that Jade realized with pristine certainty that she loved Lyon Beauchane. She loved him as she had never loved anyone, more than she had ever loved even her own father. If she did not have him at her side, her life would be pale and immeasurably bleak.

The battle, as with the chase that Jade had lost, seemed to go very slowly, lasting hours, though in truth it had gone on for a little more than a minute. Then the odds changed when Sheriff Sean Dunne and his deputy burst into the small clearing, weapons in hand.

Lyon sized up the situation in a glance, and knew

that time was swiftly running out for himself and Jade. Unless he made his move immediately, he would have no move to make at all.

Rather than waiting for Sheriff Dunne to attack, Lyon feigned a lunge toward him, apparently leaving his side open for attack. The young soldier who had accompanied the sheriff into the melee immediately saw the opening, and went for it . . . exactly as Lyon knew he would. As a warrior, Lyon was older, wiser, and much more experienced. He almost regretted sidestepping the sword that slipped harmlessly past his stomach, then burying his own dagger into the young man's body.

Death, swift and final, shocks even the most callused of men, including Sheriff Dunne and Garth Rawlings. They hesitated only a second to look at their fallen comrade, each thinking that it could just as likely have been himself bleeding on the ground with sightless eyes still open, the look of horror and surprise frozen upon his face for all time.

Garth's destrier was long accustomed to the sights and sounds of battle, of the smell of human blood. He had been trained to remain close if his reins were allowed to dangle to the ground. Jade's mare, on the other hand, had fled in panic and was nowhere to be found.

In the instant that Garth and Sheriff Dunne were contemplating the corpse on the ground, Lyon whipped up the reins of Garth's destrier and leaped into the saddle. The stallion reared up on its hind legs at first, protesting the unusual rider now sitting in the saddle. However, the harsh command, the firmness with which the rider held the reins, and the way the rider stayed securely in the saddle, all let the horse instinctively know that this man was in command.

"Stop him!" Sheriff Dunne screamed, already reaching for the dagger at his hip, hoping to throw it at the fleeing knight.

Lyon kicked his bootheels against the stallion's ribs, spurring him on as he leaned far to the side, one arm hanging low. Jade raised her arms to him, and he swept her up smoothly, dropping her onto the stallion's rump.

It was fortunate for Jade that she had spent so much time riding as a child. If her equestrian skills had been any less developed, she never would have been able to stay on the madly galloping stallion as it rushed through the forest. It dodged trees, occasionally followed trails, but more often rushed pell-mell through the thick foliage.

She wrapped her arms around Lyon's waist and hugged him tight, wanting desperately to kiss him, to say all the things that her heart demanded she say.

"I knew you would come," she said when the mad gallop had slowed to a steady canter, after it was clear they were safe momentarily.

"Then you knew more than I did," Lyon replied.

He turned his head a little and grinned, looking at Jade out of the corner of his eye. He dropped a hand from the reins onto her leg. Her dress was pushed up high, and he slipped his hand beneath the garment to touch her bare thigh.

Lyon's smile vanished when he said, "You can't go back to your castle. Not yet. But someday soon you will

256

be able to, and you won't have enemies within the castle walls when you do. I promise you that, Jade. I give you my word as a man, and as a knight, and your loyal servant. You'll have your castle, your lands, and you'll be able to travel wherever you want to, whenever you want to."

"I don't care what I have or where I go . . . so long as I have you beside me," she said softly.

News travels swiftly, especially during troubling times. It was not surprising that before nightfall, many of the peasants near Esselex had already heard of the attack, of the counterattack, and of the ensuing carnage.

What was said about the attack and the defense of Esselex, however, was anything but consistent.

One story had it that Jade and her men, led by Garth Rawlings, had attacked Esselex at dawn, and had murdered many of the villagers because they had voiced opposition to her taxes. Lyon Beauchane and his soldiers had defended the villagers, and the last anyone had seen of Sir Lyon, he was riding away with Jade, having successfully taken her prisoner. According to this version, Lyon intended to ransom Princess Jade to Bishop Nathan Fields, who was quite likely her lover. This would explain why even a greedy man like the bishop would pay a premium ransom for her safe return.

In another version of the story, it was Lyon's men who had attacked the village of Esselex. In a thoroughly uncharacteristic move, Garth Rawlings and Sheriff Dunne, working in accord, mounted a powerful counterattack against the marauding military force. When the fighting had finally ended, Lyon had escaped into the forest. Many of his men had been killed, and Princes Jade had been mortally wounded. She was, at that very moment, on her deathbed in Castle Crosse, clutching onto life with the last of her strength while Bishop Fields held a prayer vigil over her weakened body.

Yet another tale fought for the ready ear and the vivid tongue. The third rumor held that Jade had led a contingent of men into the hamlet of Esselex. Without warning, the soldiers turned on the villagers, and upon their own princess. The murder and mayhem was horrific, and would have been much worse if Lyon Beauchane and his band of fighting men had not been following the soldiers, and by counterattacking had foiled the assault. Most interestingly of all, it seemed as though Garth Rawlings had actually attacked Princess Jade, and that it was Lyon Beauchane who had come to her defense.

It was this story that was most fervently embraced by those who still believed in the potential for goodness within Castle Crosse.

"How . . . how much further . . . is it?" Jade asked, panting, clinging to Lyon's hand like it was the only lifeline that kept her from drowning in a sea of doubt and depression.

"Not much further, darling," Lyon replied. In the past hours he had taken to using endearments to Jade, something he had never done with a woman before. "The Baron's land starts just on the other side of that river." He pointed through the trees. Jade could faintly see the blue twinkle of moonlight upon running water. "Once we get past that, it's not much further. I promise you, not much further."

But Lyon had been saying "not much further" for an hour now, and Jade knew he was just trying to keep her confidence up. Now, though, she wanted the truth. She had been running for two hours almost without rest, and had been fleeing from Garth Rawlings and his men for four hours.

The stallion that had carried them to safety had been felled by a lucky shot by one of the sheriff's men. An arrow struck the magnificent beast, and though he regretted greatly having to do it, Lyon was forced to put the animal out of its misery.

There was no guessing where his own destrier was. When the battle had suddenly erupted, Lyon had entered the fray on foot.

He knew, too, that his men would survive the battle, even though they were dramatically outnumbered. Lyon had issued commands on the run that they were to engage the enemy only as long as necessary, then lead them into the forest. Lyon had no doubt at all that his men could run Garth's soldiers in circles and escape at will. Lyon had trained his men to be the supreme experts at forest fighting, skilled at the hit-and-retreat tactics that were so successful against enemies of greater numbers.

When they reached the edge of the stream, Jade, in a most unladylike fashion, dropped down onto her stomach at the stream's edge, cupped her hands, and drank freely of the cool, clear water.

As Lyon watched, his heart went out to her. On many occasions he had known great privation and hardship, but he saw no reason why delicate Jade should have to endure similar hardships.

Watching his princess drinking from her own cupped hands at the edge of a stream, one sleeve of her dress torn off, and the rest of her dress in rags from the mad rush through the forest, made Lyon feel as though he had failed in his duties as a knight to Castle Crosse . . . and as a man.

Jade finally pulled her knees beneath her, looking up at Lyon. She pushed her long blond hair away from her eyes. Her hair was in tangles, and there were twigs and leaves caught in the thick, wavy strands.

"How much longer?" she asked, and her simple honesty made Lyon want to tell her the unvarnished truth.

"An hour from here, perhaps. Not longer, I swear."

"Aren't you going to drink?"

He looked down at her, and from his vantage, saw much more of her bosom than she intended. The gown was badly torn, and what Lyon saw made him red with anger. She had been brutally treated by Garth, and her torn dress was just the outward sign of that savage treatment.

When Jade saw the direction of his gaze, she adjusted her bodice a bit more modestly. What she did not understand was why Lyon's eyes did not reflect the pleasure, and the undercurrent of desire, that she usually saw whenever he looked at her. It was a

260

troubling question, and one that Jade forced to the back of her mind, something that she could ponder when the more pressing problems in her life had been addressed.

Silently agreeing, Lyon dropped down, drank deeply and quickly, then got back to his feet, helping Jade up. He dared not let his guard down for very long.

He looked at the river, smiling, thinking of how in his youth he would come here, strip off all his clothes, and swim for hours. Back then, he came to this area to escape from the world for a while. Now he was crossing the river to escape literally with his life.

"There's a low spot over here," he said, again taking Jade's hand. "It's about waist deep. I can carry you."

The independent streak in Jade came to the fore, and she stubbornly replied, "I can walk on my own two feet."

Lyon held her hand as they crossed the stream. When they were halfway across, at the deepest point, Jade murmured, "Waist deep for you, maybe."

They started laughing then, because the water came much higher on her than on Lyon. It felt good to laugh, and they both embraced it, taking pleasure in the sound of their own dampened merriment.

"Let me help you," Lyon said when they'd reached the far bank.

"I'm fine, truly."

"It's no trouble." Lyon got down on one knee before Jade and, very slowly and patiently, wrung the water out of the skirt of her dress. "It's the least I can do."

"You've already done more than enough."

Lyon tilted his head back to look up at Jade. She

smiled at him, and a tear formed in her eye. Who was this deadly knight who killed men who opposed him, yet was so gentle that he would kneel like a common servant to wring water from her tattered dress?

Sheriff Sean Dunne reined in his horse, raising his right hand to stop the three riders following him.

"This is as far as we go, men," he said, as much to himself as to the others as he looked out over the slender, winding stream that marked the boundary between the Crosse fiefdom and Baron von Mueller's lands.

The youngest of the soldiers, a savage young whelp with a taste for the hunt, growled. "We know they've gone into that bloody foreigner's territory, m'lord, so why not follow? We've got the men to chase the murdering thieves wherever they run."

Sheriff Dunne smiled crookedly. There was a time when he, too, was young, energetic, headstrong, and abominably foolish. Now he looked upon the world, seeing it for exactly what it was without pretense or romanticism. He knew his power had limits.

"*We* are the murdering thieves," the sheriff said without any trace of remorse or sarcasm in his tone. "And we have no rights whatsoever on Baron von Mueller's land. You do no one any good, least of all yourself, pretending to be inestimably virtuous young men of reason and high moral character."

The young soldiers exchanged glances. They had no understanding of what the learned Sheriff Dunne had just said.

"Come on," the sheriff said after a long pause, suddenly feeling world-weary, disturbed by being forced to endure the company of the young, uneducated soldiers. "We'd better get back to Castle Crosse. The bishop's plans have been thwarted, and his temper is positively ungovernable when he doesn't get everything he desires."

Though he had gone out of his way to make the young soldiers aware of their inferior education, Sheriff Dunne was not feeling superior in any way. The plans to murder Princess Jade Crosse had gone hideously awry. Not only was she still alive, but the sheriff and his men, and Garth Rawlings and his knights, had all been disgraced in the attack on Esselex. Many soldiers had died under the sword of Lyon's formidable warriors. And those who did not die were disgraced, because now there could be no confusion over who the real villains were. The peasants would surely realize that neither Lyon Beauchane nor Princess Crosse were behind their troubles. When they inevitably realized that they were being hideously abused by people who did not have the sanction and authority of the Crown behind them, they would surely rise up in angry, armed revolt!

Perhaps, with luck, Garth Rawlings could be blamed for everything. After all, most of the men in the raiding party were knights under his command.

He tried to avoid thinking about Lyon Beauchane, but tearing those images out of his mind was next to impossible. Over and over he kept seeing in his mind's eye the young man attacking Lyon from the side, and over and over he saw how easily Lyon had killed the soldier. It hadn't been any great struggle at all to dispatch him. Lyon had killed the mercenary quickly, cleanly, and without a backwark glance . . . and if he could do that with such ease, then no one who opposed him could be considered safe.

Sheriff Dunne had been ready to do battle with Lyon, but only so long as the odds were in his favor. When it was just himself and Garth Rawlings against Lyon, the odds were not favorable enough to risk. In fact, they were damnably bleak.

Lyon Beauchane may not have known it, but he had fled with Jade only seconds before Garth and the sheriff had run.

Now the blood will surely flow, Sheriff Dunne thought as he led his men back to Castle Crosse. The only way to silence that truth is to kill it, so everyone who knows what really happened at Esselex must be killed. It is what Bishop Fields will demand, and it is what I will do.

One thing bothered Sean Dunne more than anything else: his fight with Lyon had become personal. Lyon had looked into his eyes and had seen him as the enemy. Sheriff Dunne could no longer pretend that he was an innocent man. Sooner or later, Lyon Beauchane would make him answer for his murderous behavior.

A shiver slithered through Sheriff Dunne as he rode back toward his home.

He hoped none of the men saw the shiver. He didn't want them thinking that he was frightened. But in the deepest part of his soul, he was frightened to death of Lyon Beauchane. The only way he would ever be spared was if enough men could be put together to find and confront Lyon, and cut his heart out once and for all. Only then would Sheriff Dunne again feel safe.

Baroness Christina von Mueller and Lady Shannon Frederick were in a state of high dudgeon as they walked hurriedly down the long, dimly lit hallway. Servants scurried away at the sight of them, accurately spotting the grim, resolute expressions of the two women.

A young cook, who hadn't yet heard that the baroness was furious, had the misfortune of stepping into the hallway. As soon as she was spotted, the baroness asked, "Have you see the baron?"

The cook, not yet seventeen, was momentarily dumbfounded. Under Baroness Christina's glare, her senses returned. Silently, she extended a hand, pointing a trembling finger toward the thick oak door at the end of the hallway.

Lady Shannon and the baroness started toward the door when the cook at last found her voice and said, "Everyone's been tol' they aren't to be disturbed, m'lady!"

The baroness and Lady Shannon exchanged glances. "I'm not under my husband's orders," the baroness ground out through clenched teeth.

Christina opened the door without breaking stride, and she and Lady Shannon stepped into the room, daggers shooting from their eyes.

At the huge oval table, Lord Charles Frederick and Baron von Mueller were sitting on either side of

Princess Jade. The men had been questioning her for over an hour. Princess Jade's face was drawn and pale, her hands folded in her lap. When the two women burst into the room, Jade gasped, half-rising from her chair. Her nerves were taut as a lute string, her reserves of strength and fortitude nearly depleted.

"We're occupied," Baron von Mueller said, grinding the words out, rising from his chair, anger making his accent more pronounced.

"Not any more you're not!" his English wife shot back without hesitation.

Baroness Christina and Lady Shannon went directly to Jade, pushing their husbands aside. The baroness took Jade's hands lightly in her own and searched her eyes. "All will be well soon," the baroness said softly. "How about a hot bath for you? Perhaps a little good wine? They always make me feel better when the day has been a bit much."

Lady Shannon added, "There's a feather mattress that's just waiting for you. After a good nap the world will look much better." She turned slightly to glare furiously at her husband, Lord Charles. "I imagine this big cad has about frightened the very wit from you."

Princess Jade replied, "They were questioning me. They keep insisting I knew that my men were charging a crossing tax. That's what they think."

"They're men," Christina explained in a long-suffering tone. "Most times, they don't think at all."

Lady Shannon added, "We've been married to these menfolk a fearsome long time. We'll teach you all about men and how you don't need to tolerate their foolishness."

Lord Charles and Baron von Mueller stood by silently while their wives escorted Jade protectively out of the room. The men knew better than to cross their wives when they were this intractable. Men who defied Lady Shannon and Baroness Christian had a way of regretting it for a long, long time.

Chapter 22

"I'd like to speak with Sir Lyon, if I may," Jade said, sitting on the edge of the thickest goosedown mattress she'd ever seen.

"You can speak with him later, after you've rested and you've taken some nourishment," the baroness replied. The look in her eyes, though, said she felt Jade had been through enough trouble because of men. If Jade had a proper amount of common sense, she wouldn't have anything to do with Lyon or anyone else of *that* gender.

Jade was pleased that the two women had come to her rescue, saving her from answering the same questions, thinly rephrased, posed over and over again by Lord Charles and Baron von Mueller. Just the same, despite her exhaustion, she wanted Lyon at her side now. She had been through so much, she desperately wanted to share Lyon's strong body beside her own, to feel his strength and courage. When he was near her, she felt braver and more courageous.

But no matter how forcefully Jade asked to see

Lyon, she was refused. Lady Shannon and Baroness Christina, like the aunts Jade had never had, declared they knew what was best for her, and for now that was plenty of good food, lots of rest, and absolutely no men whatsoever. Not even a knight as handsome as Sir Lyon Beauchane!

Jade was left alone in the guest room, which she appraised visually. She was awed by the size and opulence of the room, its thick wine-colored curtains, magnificent furniture, ornately carved frame around the looking glass, and the beautiful carpets on the floor. She realized that the von Mueller's were at least as wealthy as she was, and quite likely much wealthier.

Baroness Christina and Lady Shannon were right when they demanded that Jade eat, take a bath, then get some sleep even though it was the middle of the afternoon. All the things that had happened in the past twenty-eight hours suddenly weighed like an anvil on Jade's shoulders. She stripped out of her clothes, tossing her soiled and torn dress aside, leaving it on the floor. It was ruined beyond repair from her flight from Garth Rawlings and his foul men.

The tub had been brought into her room by four of the largest, strongest men Jade had ever seen. The water was steamy hot, and even though it was a warm day, the thought of letting her troubles soak away for a while sounded wonderful to Jade.

From a small glass bottle that had been brought in with the tub, Jade poured a thick liquid into the water, then swirled the water around with her hand. Bubbles foamed on the surface of the water in an inviting white blanket.

Jade tested the water with her foot, sighed dreamily,

then stepped into the high-walled, slope-backed wooden tub.

"Heavenly," she sighed aloud as the bubbles swirled around her chin. She was covered completely except her head and her knees, which poked up through the soap suds.

"I'm delighted you think so."

At the sound of the male voice, Jade half-burst out of the tub, rising and spinning toward the door to the guest bedchamber.

Entering, Lyon was frozen in mid-stride. To see Jade on her knees in the wooden tub, her beautifully rounded breasts swaying from her frantic movement, soap lather running down her body . . . to see the way her waist narrowed beneath her ribs and her flat stomach . . . to see her honey blond hair swirl in loose waves around her wet shoulders . . . it was enough to test the willpower of any man.

As soon as Jade recognized Lyon, she relaxed, realizing that she was much more tense than she had thought. She sank back into the tub, only a little embarrassed that Lyon had seen her naked, and issued a weary smile.

"You've really made a habit of sneaking into my bedchamber, and I must say, I'm not at all fond of it." There was no rancor in Jade's tone despite the words.

Lyon approached slowly, with a slight swagger to his step, mentally recovered from the shock of seeing Jade wet and gloriously naked. Fatigue born of flight from assorted enemies and enduring many hours without sleep hung on his features.

"I had to sneak in like a thief," Lyon explained. He

270

picked up a small towel from a table, then sat on the edge of the tub, only slightly disappointed that he could not see through the soapy bubbles. "I was given notice by Lady Shannon and Baroness Christina that you were *not* to be disturbed. Lord Charles and the good baron himself told me that if I valued my freedom, I wouldn't see you until after you had eaten and rested. Even then, I should not see you in your bedchamber."

A throaty laugh rumbled from Jade. "They are concerned about me. No doubt, your reputation as a seducer of women has reached their ears."

"I'm hurt you'd say such a thing, m'lady," Lyon replied with false innocence. "You know I am your humble servant, and live only to grant your every wish."

Jade laughed again. It felt good to laugh, wonderful to see Lyon smiling again. He was, she thought looking up at him, ridiculously handsome, much too handsome for any one man to be. She thought, too, of all the women he had shared his body and his passion with. She immediately tried to block that from her thoughts. She could not change the past, could not rewrite history. The most she could do was influence what happened each day. Though she was often frightened of hoping for too much, she hoped that each day from this day forward would be spent with Lyon.

Lyon reached into the water, lifting Jade's foot. She did not resist as he rubbed a fragrant block of soap against the towel, then began washing her.

"When you said you were my servant, I never expected this."

"I've done many things that you haven't expected."

Jade's smile radiated pure sensuality. She nodded, resting her head against the high, sloping back of the tub, relaxing under the pressure of Lyon's strong hands and the soothing effects of the warm, soapy, fragrant water.

When Lyon had finished with her foot and calf, Jade eased it from his grasp. Then she raised her other foot out of the water, pointing her toe, smiling sleepily, seductively. The sensation of Lyon washing her, running his hands over her legs, massaging her tension-knotted muscles and rubbing her flesh with the cloth was distinctly sensual, but only because it was Lyon who was touching her. Jade had had female servants wash her feet for her before, but it had meant nothing to her. She'd felt their touch only on her skin; with Lyon, she felt his touch in her soul and in her heart.

"I could get accustomed to this," she murmured sleepily.

"I wouldn't let you get accustomed to this."

"Mmmm. Then this is a rare, unrepeatable experience?"

"Not at all, m'lady. I merely indicate that whenever it would appear as though you were growing accustomed to having me bathe you, I would do something deliciously different. When I bathed you the next time, you would be wondering the whole time if I would do that again, or do something . . . else."

Jade sighed as Lyon's soapy hands reached her knee. She slipped just a little lower in the tub to get her leg higher out of the water. The heated water had warmed her skin, but Lyon's massaging touch had warmed her in much deeper places.

She thought briefly of getting out of the tub, taking

Lyon's hand, and leading him to the huge goosedown bed where they could make love. She resisted the temptation, waiting to see what erotic game Lyon was now playing with her, knowing that she should just put herself in his hands and trust her intuition and senses.

She moistened her lips with the tip of her tongue, blew a blond curl away from her mouth, and cleared her throat. Lyon's hands were now very nearly at her thigh, at the surface of the soapy water. "And what are these deliciously different things you hint of?"

"Oh, m'lady, I mustn't tell you. If I did that, then you'd know and wait rather than guess and anticipate. And anticipation, my lady, is a spice of life."

"Yes . . . yes . . . of course," Jade whispered.

She was willing at that point to say anything, agree to anything. Lyon was the tonic she needed, the mysterious elixir that stripped reality away and freed her from the problems of her mortal world. In his arms, she was not a frightened or disillusioned widow; she was not a young woman who had been stripped of her home and her lands. She was only Jade, not even *Princess* Jade, and that was exactly the way she wanted it to be.

When Lyon eased her foot back into the water, Jade fully expected him to lift her out of the tub. She would let him take her to that big bed, and once there she would do everything he wanted, and even more. At last, she would let her imagination run free, casting aside all her inhibitions and vague notions of what was or was not proper for a lady.

But Lyon didn't take Jade out of the tub. Instead, he worked a fresh lather of soap into the towel, then took

273

her hand and began washing it slowly, paying attention to each individual finger before working into the palm, and finally going over the wrist and forearm. As he bathed Jade, his eyes went over her slowly, though she was mostly hidden beneath the water and the soap suds.

Lyon walked around the tub to sit on the opposite side so that he could wash her other hand and arm. When he was hidden from Jade by the back of the tub, he discreetly adjusted himself within his breeches in a wholly unsuccessful attempt to hide his excitement.

"So perfect," he whispered as he ran the soapy cloth over Jade's biceps and shoulder. "All of you is perfect, flat where you should be flat, firm and round where you should be firm and rounded."

"And what will happen to your passion for me when that which is flat becomes rounded, and that which is firm and rounded becomes soft and sags? Is it only my looks that appeal to you?"

"As long as my eyes can look at you, they will see only perfection," Lyon answered.

Though Jade wanted to believe she was above the petty need for flattery, she adored hearing Lyon saying pretty things about her.

It was not easy for Jade to close her mind off to the horrors that she had witnessed that day, to avoid thinking about the hideous fact that Garth Rawlings had intended to rape her, and probably murder her as well. It was almost impossible for her to stop thinking about Sheriff Sean Dunne, the man sworn to uphold her law within the boundaries of her fiefdom, and how that man had proven himself to be a criminal of the lowest and most savage ilk. But with Lyon touching her softly, washing away her fears and tensions, anything was possible.

He ran the cloth along her neck, and Jade tilted her head far back, arching her back slightly. She felt her breasts rise above the surface of the water, heard the soft intake of Lyon's breath as she became visible to him.

Tonight I'll give him everything . . . all of me . . . everything that I have will be his. I'll take him to that special place where he has taken me, she thought.

The cloth ran lightly over her neck and shoulders, then down to her chest. Jade kept expecting Lyon to run his hand down further, to cup her breast in his hand, or at the very least to touch her with the soapy cloth.

But he did not do what Jade expected. Moving off the edge of the tub, Lyon walked behind her and eased her forward so that she did not lean against the back of the tub. Then he ran the block of soap over the cloth again to work up a thick froth, then began washing her back.

The disappointment she felt was fleeting. Could there be another sensation quite like this in the whole world? To be slowly, lovingly bathed by a handsome knight who had sworn unwavering fealty to you?

Jade wrapped her arms around her legs as Lyon washed her shoulders, then worked his way lower, below the surface of the water even. She put her chin on her knees and sighed dreamily. Was it possible to be both passionately amorous and thoroughly fatigued at the same time? It must be possible, for that described Jade's state perfectly.

I'll turn toward Lyon, raise myself out of the water,

275

reach out for him, and be carried to bed, she planned.

With her chin still resting on her knees, she smiled. It would be so easy, and she was so very ready!

And that was exactly when she heard the soft knock upon her bedchamber door.

"God's bones!" Lyon hissed through clenched teeth. He dropped the cloth into the bath water, moving away from Jade.

"Yes?" Jade called out, quite suddenly aware that she was not in her own castle and did not have the authority to which she had long ago become accustomed.

"My lady, may I enter?"

It was Baroness von Mueller. Jade didn't really want to let her into the bedchamber with Lyon there, but the edge to her hostess's tone suggested she would not take *No* for an answer.

"We shant take long," Lady Shannon added.

Lyon and Jade exchanged a look. "Those two are beginning to vex me in a most unsettling way," he said quietly.

The door had been opened just enough for Christina and Shannon to hear him. "And we will continue to vex you," the baroness said with a certain tone of imperious authority that Lyon had been trained to respect.

Lady Shannon added, "Vexing is what we do to young knights who visit bedchambers that are not their own." Her eyes met Lyon's unwaveringly. She raised a hand, pointing to the open door she had just passed through. "My husband would like to speak with you. When we did not find you in the knight's quarters, the baroness and I came directly here."

Baroness von Mueller added under her breath,

"Your reputation with attractive young women is well-deserved, but, alas, *not* well-respected."

There just wasn't enough anger and sanctimony in Christina's tone to deliver the full impact that she wanted. When Lyon Beauchane walked out of Jade's bedchamber, everyone in the room was smiling slightly, some more than others.

"That man is much too handsome," Lady Shannon said, addressing both Jade and Christina.

Christina replied, "Aye, that he is."

Jade, who at first thought she had violated the laws of propriety which would earn disfavor from her hostess, now realized the baroness was acting more out of obligation to convention rather than any self-righteous desire to keep her and Lyon apart. It made her feel much better, though it was still terribly disconcerting to have been just seconds away from asking Lyon to take her to bed, to finding herself suddenly sitting in her guest bedchamber with two matronly women of sizable social stature.

Lady Shannon picked up a large, thick towel for drying and held it out for Jade. "Out of there now," she said. "I've bathed myself, my children, and on occasion, my husband. You're none of those three."

"That I am not," Jade said stifling the smile that pulled at her mouth. She took the towel from Shannon, sensing that the older women, in an unspoken way, rather envied her budding romance with Lyon Beauchane. They would never admit it, particularly since Jade and Lyon weren't betrothed.

"We have much to discuss," the baroness said then. "There is much you should know, and the truth is always easier spoken when the menfolk aren't around."

The three laughed then, and Jade got the distinct impression that here were two friends she would have her entire life.

Spending time with Baron von Mueller and Lord Charles was not how Lyon had intended to pass his afternoon. Not after he'd seen Jade in that big, soapy tub, not when his erotic imagination had invented magnificently stimulating notions of the possibilities that could be tried with two people together in that big tub.

But then, it wasn't up to Lyon to decide who he was to spend his time with; not when the problems to be faced encompassed as many vital issues as those now concerning the leadership within the stone walls of Castle Crosse.

Baron von Mueller said, "We can field an army strong enough to crush anything they put against us. I don't care how many mercenaries and soldiers have been put in with the ranks."

"Do we have exact counts of how large the Crosse army is now?" Lord Charles asked. The baron shook his head. "Then I suggest we think of another tactic. My spies tell me the number of men in arms grows almost daily. Many of them are not even paid by Rawlings; they just rob to get whatever they want or need."

"And Sheriff Dunne does nothing to stop this?" von Mueller asked.

"Of course he doesn't," Lyon said bitterly, jumping into the conversation. "He's in this with Garth! And if you ask me, it's that bloody bishop who's behind this

278

all! Garth's not smart enough to be a leader; the sheriff's got the brains, but he lacks the charisma to be a real leader."

"And that leaves only Bishop Nathan Fields, doesn't it?" Lord Charles said, scratching his beard, his gaze distant and unfocused as he thought. He liked the way Lyon's mind worked, admired its logical progression.

If it had only been an errant knight, like Sir Garth, or an outlaw sheriff, like Sean Dunne, Lord Charles wouldn't have hesitated to take matters into his own hands. A small, elite, group of men could be formed to ride to Sheriff Dunne or Garth Rawlings, and either kidnap the men, or execute them on the spot. Either way, it would put a quick and final end to their villainy. But having a bishop behind the problems that they faced made it much more difficult. Although von Mueller had lived in England for many years, and had married a woman of high-ranking English blood, he was still a foreigner, and still suspect. Lord Charles himself, though knighted, had been outspoken on many edicts and laws that had come down from the King and his court in the past. Though considered by many to be a businessman of extraordinary acumen, he was also considered something of a firebrand, an itch that the Crown was not particularly happy about having to scratch.

"Whatever decision for action we come to," Lord Charles continued after a long pause, "I think it is clear that von Mueller and I must remain behind the curtains of secrecy. If we get directly involved, we'll need to answer for a hundred other things that have nothing to do with the particular problem we are now faced with."

"I've got good men," Lyon said. It had been some

time since he'd seen his men, and though he would never tell his men, he missed their companionship. They had been so much a part of his life on a daily basis, that it was odd now to go days on end without seeing them. "They're all we need to fight Bishop Fields."

Baron von Mueller said with a growl, "You'll be hideously outnumbered! Not even greater skill can make up the difference!"

"I don't intend to fight them face to face, or indeed in any way that will allow them the advantage of their larger number," Lyon explained. "I believe that the peasants will soon understand that I am not responsible for their troubles. When they believe in my innocence with their hearts and souls, they will be happy to work with me and my men against Bishop Fields." Lyon leaned back in the chair and stared at the high, thick-beamed ceiling, concocting a plan of action as he spoke. "The peasants will be my eyes and ears. They'll keep me informed about where Garth's men are. They'll let me know everything I need to attack Garth's soldiers. We'll hit them hard, fast, then be gone before they can mount a serious counterattack."

It wasn't the kind of fight that either Lord Charles or Baron von Mueller appreciated. They preferred confronting their enemies directly, affecting a quick and decisive end to conflicts. But under the circumstances, it was an excellent battle plan, perhaps the only viable one for a badly outnumbered outlaw army without a castle to call home.

The baron realized that though he could not play a direct role in opposing the forces that had caused murder and mayhem in the area, he could provide invaluable assistance to the one man capable of effectively fighting the forces of evil. "We will provide you with the finest destriers, the best food and weapons, with everything you and your men could ever possibly want or need. We'll arrange for additional supplies of food and weapons to be secretly placed at various places on Crosse land."

Lyon chewed on his bottom lip, thinking about what the baron and Lord Charles were saying. On several occasions, he added his own ideas to the battle plans, but he mainly kept his silence, listening to the wisdom of the two elderly gentlemen who had planned and plotted many more battles than he.

Plans were put forward, some agreed upon, others challenged and discarded. It was decided that a series of letters had to be written to the Crown immediately. If, in fact, Bishop Fields was the man behind the treachery at Castle Crosse, then he would have given *his* version of the conflict to the Crown. Though it was doubtful that with just letters alone Lord Charles or Baron von Mueller could counteract the damage done, it would be possible however to open the specter of doubt concerning the bishop's veracity. If that alone was accomplished, then they would have accomplished a great deal. From what Lord Charles had heard, Bishop Fields currently was held in rather high esteem among those in royal power.

As he listened to Lord Charles and von Mueller speak, a sadness crept slowly, coldly through his bones. When the battle began, he would have to leave Jade behind. It would be too dangerous to bring her along with him. Once he left von Mueller's castle, he and his men would be on their own. To preserve the secrecy of

Lord Charles's and von Mueller's involvement, Lyon would not again be able to seek refuge on their land or in their castles.

He hated the thought of leaving Jade, but he knew his duty was paramount . . . even if it meant leaving behind the woman he loved.

Chapter 23

The high drawbridge leading into von Mueller's castle presented a formidable barrier to Garth Rawlings and his men. This did not mean that Garth was in any way stopped by the drawbridge. If the little German inside the walls did not want to cooperate and answer questions, Garth was certain Bishop Fields would approve of him using whatever force he felt was necessary to make Baron Timish von Mueller cooperate.

Garth called out to the guard, demanding a personal visitation with the baron and baroness. The guard said it wasn't possible. Garth replied that the baron himself would be in grave personal danger if Garth was not allowed to speak with him privately.

Ten minutes passed, then twenty, and finally the drawbridge was lowered. Garth made no effort to hide his smile. He looked at the soldiers and knights who rode with him as though to say, *See what a big and powerful man I am?*

"Only you," the broad-shouldered guard at the gate said, standing on the drawbridge holding a huge battle-ax in his massive hands. "The others stay out there."

Garth hesitated only a moment. He did not like proceeding on his own. He much preferred leading a phalanx of savage killers who would protect him. But the powerfully built guard had read that in him, and maneuvered him so that if Garth backed away, he would appear cowardly.

"Stay here," he told his men. Then, in a lower voice, though still loud enough so the threatening guard could hear, he added, "If these fools can't have a man-advantage, they fill their breeches. I'll be back in less than an hour."

As Garth rode his horse over the drawbridge and past the stony-faced guard, he knew he had made yet another enemy for life. One day he would need to answer, one way or another, for the insult.

Eventually, Garth was ushered into a large room where the baron was seated, with his guest, Lord Charles Frederick. Garth was surprised to see Lord Charles there, but not disappointed. He had long found both men annoying, and having them together gave him the opportunity to insult them even more effectively.

"Good day, Baron," Garth said with little enthusiasm or respect in his voice. The baron did not respond, and Garth was all too aware of the effrontery. "I have come to ask you questions. Where is the baroness? I want her here, too."

Garth saw a muscle tick in the elderly baron's jaw. He liked that. He liked being able to insult the nobility, and he especially hated wealthy foreigners like von Mueller.

"You should be very careful of what you want," the

baron said slowly, anger thickening his accent. "If you're not lucky, you just might get what you're asking for."

Garth grinned crookedly. He did not have to worry about whether the German liked him or not. With the bungled murder of Jade, the hierarchy of the whole area was in peril. Until the killing reached some kind of logical stopping point, it was every man for himself.

There were several empty chairs in the large chamber, as well as a small table between Lord Charles and von Mueller. Garth waited to be invited to sit, but wasn't surprised when the invitation never came. There would come a day when men like von Mueller couldn't snub him, couldn't turn a condescending eye toward Sir Garth Rawlings—at least not without paying a heavy price for it.

"Why have you come?" the baron asked.

When Garth had rehearsed what he intended to say to the baron during the ride over from Castle Crosse, he had intended to phrase his words as questions rather than accusations. But now, with the baron so obviously contemptuous, Garth decided there was no need for even the veneer of civility.

"We know you've shielded Lyon Beauchane, and probably Princess Jade Crosse as well," he began. As he spoke the words, he felt the emptiness in the pit of his stomach as fear curled inside. These were serious, deadly accusations he was about to make; he was alone, without his men to back him up. But his caution was mistimed; he'd gone too far to back down now. "Lyon Beauchane is a murderer, and the wench Jade Crosse is helping him. They're outlaws, and if you do anything to help them, you'll be branded an outlaw, too." He paused and let his gaze drift to Lord Charles. As long as he'd gone this far, Garth wasn't going to miss the opportunity to insult and threaten the big Englishman. "You too, m'lord. We know all about you and what you really stand for."

Von Mueller replied, "You say that Princess Crosse is an outlaw. The last I heard, she was *your* princess. Isn't it true that you have sworn an oath of loyalty to her? Perhaps *you* are the outlaw."

Deep inside himself, Garth felt his courage slipping. To combat the loss, he cloaked his cowardice with savage indifference to any semblance of polite behavior.

"And *you* are a little man, a runt pig!" Garth sneered, looking down at the seated baron. "If you give Lyon or Jade any help at all, you'll swing from your neck, and so will your wife! We know Lyon and Jade crossed the river onto your land, and we've got sound suspicion that they came here. So this is your warning, little man, and heed it well. If you don't, I'll be back again to burn this pig sty to the ground . . . with you and the baroness in it!"

Outwardly, the baron seemed almost completely unaffected by Garth's insulting words. Inside, though, he was sizzling. He clapped his hands together twice in rapid succession, and the door opened. Two large guards entered the room.

Von Mueller did not rise from his chair as he looked up at Garth. He stood only a little over five feet tall, and Garth was very nearly six feet tall. He had no intention of playing into Garth's hands by helping him show the difference in their heights.

"You call me little man. Runt. By what power do you say these things to me?"

"By the power in here," Garth replied, tapping his chest with a forefinger. Then he tapped his biceps. "And here."

"That is mass, not power, and it certainly isn't a right to be claimed by a man such as you."

Garth laughed. He didn't like the two guards standing behind him, but he had already breached proper conduct so dramatically that the best he could hope for was a forceful threat.

"Little man, you have been warned," Garth said, puffing his chest out. "If you stand in our way, you will be crushed."

"*Our* way? You talk as though there are many of you. Who stands behind you, Garth? Is it Bishop Fields? Sheriff Dunne?"

"Runt, I ask questions, I don't answer them."

Baron von Mueller's face reddened with explosive anger. He made a subtle move with his hand and the two guards moved behind Garth.

"Allow me to explain the difference between sheer mass and power," von Mueller said in a low, superior voice that quivered slightly under the strain of self-control. "You have mass; I have power."

"You have *nothing!*" Garth shot back, then spit upon the marble floor at the baron's feet.

The two guards moved in unison, slamming their fists into Garth's kidneys with awesome force. Garth's body arched hideously backward. He squealed out in agony, dropping to his knees as he lost control of his bladder. He fell to the floor, soiling himself, writhing in pain.

"I have nothing?" von Mueller asked, still seated in his chair. "You have just wet yourself like an infant, and you tell me I have nothing? You come into my home and insult me, threaten me, and then say I am nothing?" He swore then in German. To his guards, he said, "Throw this swine out. And be careful when you do, lest he wet on you like he did himself!"

Lord Charles rose from his chair, then bent low to tell Garth quietly, "It's best to not get the baron angry. He has a way of winning arguments when threatened. And don't mention the baroness. It'll get you hurt every time."

Garth was still curled into a ball on the floor when the guards grabbed his arms and dragged him from the room. He was hit occasionally in the face as they hauled him to the drawbridge, where they threw him in the dirt before his waiting men.

Bishop Nathan Fields could hardly believe what he had just heard. Sir Garth Rawlings beaten by Baron von Mueller's men! Though Garth tersely explained that the attack came from behind, and that it had been entirely unexpected, Nathan didn't believe him. More likely, Garth had said something insulting that the proud baron had responded to, prompting the violence.

The problem now was whether or not to believe that von Mueller was hiding Jade and Lyon. The violence could simply be a response to Garth's offensive behavior. Or it could mean he had something to hide, and he didn't dare keep Garth at the castle any longer.

The bishop swore again to himself. Sitting in his private chambers, he sipped good wine and picked idly at a loaf of bread that had just been baked.

Many days had passed since Garth had bungled the execution of Princess Jade Crosse. In that time, more than a dozen riders had been sent to London with letters written in the bishop's own hand. The letters accused Lyon Beauchane of treason and debauchery of the vilest sort; it blamed Jade for everything imaginable, accusing her of conspiring against the Crown, and acting as an agent for foreign governments.

If Bishop Fields was to turn this nightmare into his dream of glory, he had to have Jade killed. Pity, he thought, that it was so difficult to find competent killers these days!

The longer Jade stayed alive, the greater the chances were that she would find an ally to help her regain her position within Castle Crosse. Bishop Nathan Fields understood this as an irrefutable fact. He had even sent Garth to von Mueller to make sure that the German kept himself and his formidable private army occupied with other matters. But, once again, because of Garth's stupidity and his savagery, the bishop's plans had not achieved the results that he had hoped for.

What was happening *Out There?*

He looked upon the world beyond the walls of Castle Crosse as simply *Out There.* Somewhere *Out There* Lyon Beauchane was probably sharpening his sword, testing his bow, preparing himself for war. Somewhere *Out There* Princess Jade Crosse was probably sitting with a council of elders, explaining in that clear, trustworthy tone of hers that she did not know that the peasants had been treated hideously and forced to pay monumental taxes since the death of Prince William Crosse of FitzPatrick.

Closing his eyes, the bishop could picture what was

happening *Out There* so clearly that he could almost feel the sharp edge of the executioner's axe against his neck.

It was all so very clear, really, what needed to be done. First, Jade had to be found and dealth with; then Lyon Beauchane. And once those two problems had been buried, the secondary problems of the Baron and Baroness von Mueller could be similarly solved. Then, just for the sake of neatness, Lord Charles and Lady Shannon could feel the sting of the axe.

All in due time, of course. Once Jade's and Lyon's blood had been spilled and their corpses buried, all the other problems would just drift slowly away. Bishop Nathan Fields could rule his enfeoffment however he wanted to, without interference from anyone.

"It won't take long. Truly it won't," Lyon said.

Jade kept her face turned away. She blinked rapidly, feeling the tears threatening.

They sat on a blanket near a cool spring that cut a diagonal path through von Mueller's land, a basket of food and wine between them. Somewhere, hidden in the trees that surrounded them, the finest archers in von Mueller's command kept a watchful eye on the visitors.

Von Mueller had been in power too long to believe that there were no spies in his camp. He suspected that if the ruthless devils within Castle Crosse thought they had the chance, they would send a team to kill Jade and Lyon. Von Mueller had assigned the archers to prevent that.

It was knowing that hidden eyes were watching them

that had prevented this afternoon feast from becoming an afternoon of outdoor lovemaking. Rather than making love, they talked, and Lyon was now angry with himself for having brought up the subject of his impending departure.

"I still don't understand why I can't go with you," Jade replied at last, when she was certain she'd regained control of her emotions.

"It would be too dangerous," Lyon explained again. "Besides, we'll be on the run constantly. You'll be much safer here, infinitely more comfortable. It's going to be war, my darling." He reached out to touch her hand, but she pulled away from the contact. "If it were possible for me to stay with you, I would. Believe me, I would. But it isn't possible. Not as long as you're kept from your own home and land."

"I don't care about *land*," Jade shot back. "I care about you, and I don't want to see you killed!"

Her words came out fast and honest, and once they had been spoken, there was nothing that Jade could do to bring them back. She curled her knees beneath her, determined then that the meal would come to an end, but as she began to replace the foodstuffs back into the basket, Lyon caught her wrists in his large hands.

"I love you," he said.

Jade looked straight into his eyes. Had she really heard those words? Was her mind playing tricks on her?

"I love you," Lyon repeated, his face close to Jade as they knelt on the blanket. "I have, I think, since the first time I saw you in your bedchamber, maybe even before then. I can't say when, exactly, that I fell in love with you, but I have. I have with all my heart and soul.

291

That's why I've got to fight to get your land and castle back."

"I don't care about *things,* Lyon, I only care about you."

The tears came to her eyes then, and this time Jade did not try to restrain them. It felt wonderful to say the things that were in her heart, to not have to hold them back, to let her true feelings for Lyon show without being afraid of what he would think of her.

He cupped her face lightly in his palms, smoothing away the tears that trinkled down her cheeks with his thumbs. Lyon knew that Jade believed his words, but he didn't entirely believe them himself. How long would it be before the comforts of the castle would be all she could think about? How long could Jade stay living in a camp, constantly on guard for an enemy that could ride up at any second?

No, Lyon thought, no matter how much she believes that physical comforts mean nothing to her, she has been a wealthy princess for her entire adult life. Eventually, unless she regained her land, her castle, and all the wealth and power they represented, she would resent her life with Lyon, and that would inevitably lead her to resent him.

"It is my duty to fight your enemies," Lyon said at last. "When I have defeated them, then we can live in peace in Castle Crosse."

Jade cried softly. She turned her face slightly to kiss Lyon's palm, hating the fact that there were strangers who were watching them from the trees. She felt spied upon, her privacy violated. All she wanted more than anything else in the world was to hold Lyon's naked body close to hers, to feel the warmth and strength of him moving into her, making her feel safe and secure and loved once again.

"Don't go," Jade whispered, fighting back the sobs. "There will always be enemies. You've fought so many wars already."

"One more war, m'lady, and then we will live in peace. I promise you this."

Jade began sobbing then, unable to restrain her emotions. She melted into Lyon's arms, not caring if there were men watching her from the trees. She wrapped her arms around Lyon's lean waist and pressed her cheek to his chest.

"I love you, my princess," Lyon whispered, stroking her long, wavy, blond hair. "Never, ever forget that. And very soon I will return for you. I promise you. I swear upon it as a man, a knight, and your devoted servant."

I don't want you as my servant, I want you as my husband, Jade thought. Hardly had the thought entered her consciousness when she wondered if it would ever be possible for Lyon to put aside their class differences and claim his equal role beside her.

Several days later, even before the sun had risen, Lyon stood beside a huge bed, looking down at the sleeping princess who lay partially hidden beneath the blanket. With her blond hair streaming out, spread across the pillow, her lips slightly parted, she looked lovelier than ever. Lyon, though, resisted the temptation to kiss those lips.

He must leave this morning, while she slept. If he looked into her eyes and heard her pleas that he must not leave von Mueller's castle to fight the new rulers of Castle Crosse, there was a very real possibility that he would do as she asked.

Leaving Jade was the hardest thing that Lyon had ever done. Not until he had fallen in love with Jade had he ever seriously questioned the meaning of honor and duty, and their true significance to his life. As he looked at her now, watching her chest rise and fall with her shallow breathing, he wondered once again if all this fighting was really worth it. Was there ever any just reason to meet violence with more violence?

He closed his eyes for only a moment, willing the questions silent. He had made his decision to leave. It was the honorable thing to do, the noble thing to do, and he wasn't going to think about it another second.

Another image sprang into his mind. This one was of the young girl who had been attacked and violated under Bishop Fields's orders. She had been told that it had been Lyon Beauchane who had attacked her. The pain, the fear, the distrust of all men . . . Lyon had seen all these emotions in her eyes. It was something that he would never forget. Until that wrong was righted, until he rid the world of the men responsible for teaching that poor child the true meaning of fear and distrust, he would not rest.

Sir Lyon Beauchane knew that his duty was, where his loyalties were, and what he must do. This was one conflict that would not be solved by politics and politicians, not by the reasoned approach of rational men. Countless letters had already been sent to London, both by Bishop Fields and by Baron von Mueller and Lord Charles. Worthless accusations abounded.

Lyon shuddered. It would do no good to think longer about how unjust this conflict was. It was futile to wish that the hand of God would suddenly appear and slay the guilty parties responsible for the blood-shed and greed that had been the hallmarks of life within Castle Crosse for the past six months.

With clarity of purpose, he placed the brief letter to Jade upon the small table near her bed. Saying a silent prayer asking for her safety while they were separated, Lyon left the bedchamber, closing the door gently so the princess would not awaken.

Chapter 24

"What do you mean he's not here?" Jade demanded.

Baroness Christina reached across the table to pat Jade's hand. She smiled sympathetically at the young woman, saying, "It's for the best. The men discussed it last night. You'll have everything you could ever want while you're here as our guest."

"Everything but Lyon," Jade shot back, speaking from the heart.

The bluntness of her words caught Baroness Christina and Lady Shannon by surprise. It was an open declaration that she had been intimate with Sir Lyon, to whom she was not married and unacceptably outranked socially.

Lady Shannon said in a whisper, "Yes, Princess, but soon you will have him back in your arms. There are matters he must attend to, and that's the only reason he's left you with us."

"The Baron has arranged for Sir Lyon to have everything he could ever possibly need," Baroness Christina added.

"But he's just one man against so many!"

Lady Shannon said, "He's probably rejoined his own men by this time. There's safety in numbers." She exchanged a look with Christina. "Leave the fighting to the men, Jade. Charles and Timish will do everything they possibly can to help Sir Lyon win the battles he faces."

Jade didn't want to hear any of it. She didn't want excuses, she wanted Lyon, plain and simple. Last night, she'd made love to him, abandoning herself to the pleasure and joy she felt in his arms. This morning, he was gone. She was alone with people she hardly knew, and the man she loved was fighting in a war, on her behalf, against an army that was large, strong, and ruthless.

"I'm going to him," Jade said suddenly, bolting out of her chair. She looked contemptuously down at the spread of food that had been laid out for her morning meal. It looked and tasted wonderful, but she could take no pleasure in anything until she was confident that the man she loved was safe.

"You can't," Baroness Christina replied.

"The hell I can't!" As expected, as she had intended, the obscenity shocked the older women. Jade, always sensitive to others, immediately regretted her behavior. "I'm sorry, I don't mean to offend you. It's just that I know that Lyon's in danger and I want to be there with him. Mayhap there's something I can do to help him."

"I know you want to, but don't you see that it's best for everyone if you sit quietly and wait for him to return to you?" Lady Shannon asked. "It's what Sir Lyon said he wanted for you."

Jade nodded, as though in agreement, but she was

thinking, Lyon doesn't make my decisions for me. I will travel upon my land whenever I want to!

Vance Raymond chewed his fingernail, squinting his eyes in the afternoon sunlight. He was at his perch, looking out over the valley, keeping an eye on the small flock of sheep that was collectively owned by his village. Wolves had been known to steal away with lambs, and it was Vance's job to make sure that such theft didn't occur.

He had another job, though, and it was more important than keeping a watchful eye out for wolves. He was looking for Garth Rawlings and his men. For the past two weeks they had been terrorizing villagers, wantonly killing peasants, destroying homes and lives with calloused, even gleeful, indifference to the suffering they left behind. The attacks, Garth always explained, had been ordered by Princess Jade Crosse, but none of the villagers believed this anymore. At one time they did think that their princess was behind the destruction of their lives, but now they knew better, no matter what lies savage men like Garth Rawlings spoke.

Rolling the long, smooth shepherd's cane between his palms, Vance counted the flock. There were twenty-two lambs and ewes, and two rams, just as there was supposed to be. Last week, there had been twenty-seven, but Garth and his knights had taken several lambs, slaughtering them on the spot, stealing the valuable meat.

Garth had claimed the meat was for Princess Jade, but an ambitious and mischievous youngster from the village had followed the knights. He discovered they

298

had ridden with the meat only several hundred yards before making camp. The meat was cooked and devoured in animalistic fashion; the knights gorged on the meat, not sharing the bulk of it with anyone back at Castle Crosse.

What they brought back to the castle would feed twenty or thirty men, provided they ate sparingly.

It mattered little to Vance Raymond whether Garth and his men were outlaws, or officially sanctioned murderers given the full authority of the Castle Crosse and Queen Mary herself. As far as he was concerned, a thief was a thief, a murderer a murderer.

Movement, far off, caught Vance's attention. Something instinctive in him made him sit up and take notice. Squinting more, he at last made out the figures that had drawn his attention. He didn't have to look twice to know that it was Sir Garth and his knights, all mounted on fast destriers, moving at a rapid pace across the valley, headed straight toward the village.

"Bloody bastards!" Vance cursed under his breath.

He moved away from his look-out position, his heartbeat rapidly accelerating. The soldiers weren't on a raid looking for food, he sensed. They were determined to do far worse than steal livestock, though he couldn't say why he knew this.

Holding his staff tightly in his hand, the young man, not yet twenty-years-old, did what he promised the village elders he would not do. He abandoned the flock, for there were more important lives to be protected. Human lives, the ones of his father and mother and brothers, the ones of his cousins and other villagers were in danger. Vance Raymond simply wasn't going to let his concern for the sheep endanger the lives of the people he loved.

When Garth pulled his gelding to a halt, he knew already that he wouldn't be able to find a soul in the village. Though it was midafternoon, he couldn't hear a single human sound. Chickens cackled in their pens; a lone sow grunted, wallowing in the mud of her pen, nursing nearly a dozen piglets. Beneath the shade of a tree, a butter urn had been abandoned, clearly within the last fifteen or twenty minutes.

"They're out there somewhere," Garth said quietly, to himself, though two young mercenaries sat in their saddles on either side of him. "In the trees. They're looking at us right now, I'll wager."

"Should I go and roust them out?" the young killer on Garth's right volunteered.

"You probably wouldn't even see them. None that count, anyway."

Garth sighed wearily. This campaign was not going as he had thought it would. Bishop Fields never for a moment let him forget that he had failed to kill Princess Jade. Furthermore, Lyon had rejoined his men again, and for the past two weeks had been making raids against Garth's men. So far, twelve of Garth's men had been killed. The only damage that Lyon's forces had suffered was the loss of one horse.

There was no doubt in Garth's mind that Lyon was being helped by the villagers. How else could Lyon seem to know every move that Garth made, almost before he even made it? The lies that had been told about Lyon and Jade had worked with the villagers for only a little while. The truth soon circulated among the villagers; Bishop Fields had ordered Garth and Sheriff Dunne to hunt down and kill Lyon Beauchane.

300

The mercenary to Garth's left said, "You want me to find one of the elders? We'll sin 'im alive, then we'll see how long the rest of 'em stay hidin' in the woods, eh?"

Garth shook his head. The murderous impulses of these young mercenaries surprised even him. They were among the most cold-blooded killers that Garth had ever known, even though for many years now he had surrounded himself with killers.

"That won't be necessary," Garth said at last. "They can hear me, and that's all that I really need."

"They can hear my knife goin' into 'em, too," the young man said, clearly unhappy that he had been denied a chance to kill again.

Garth stood in the stirrups and called out loudly, "From this day forward, anyone who helps Lyon Beauchane or his men will be executed, along with everyone in his family! If I hear that Lyon has been given food, I will lock up your people and let them starve to death in the dungeons! From this day and time until the end of time, Sir Lyon Beauchane is to be considered a murderer, an outlaw, and an enemy of God. All who help him will be treated accordingly!"

Garth sat in the saddle again, and for only a moment, he closed his eyes. There were times when maintaining the pretense of having some kind of higher authority for his debauchery was difficult. It seemed so ridiculous to him to have to scream to the peasants that he had been given the power to kill them summarily when they didn't believe it, and he knew they didn't. It had all the feel of a parent listening to a child greatly exaggerating some adventure, all the adults in the room patiently waiting for the child to finish his story, everyone knowing there was little more than a grain of truth in the fantastic story.

The young mercenary to his right began to say something, but Garth cut him off short with an icy glare. Garth wasn't in the mood to listen to anything the mercenary had to say. Quite suddenly, Garth was angry and tired. He had been denied the pleasures that he'd thought were his for the taking, and it bothered him greatly. Princess Jade had escaped his clutches in two ways; he hadn't managed to rape her, he hadn't killed her. In the process, she had dangerously discredited Garth in Bishop Fields's estimation.

"Let's get out of here," Garth said suddenly, jerking hard on the reins to turn his destrier around. "I need a tankard of ale and a wench."

The dress was made of cheap cloth, and just feeling it brought back a wave of nostalgic feelings for Jade. Not since she had been a little girl had she worn anything but superior quality fabric. Before her happy but poor childhood had been cut short by Prince William Crosse's entrance into her life, she had worn dresses exactly like this one every day.

Jade brought the dress to her face and inhaled deeply. The cloth had that same smell that she remembered, hinting at strong lye soap that had been rinsed from the fabric with plenty of clean water.

This will be perfect, Jade thought confidently. And for the first time in the week that she had been living secretly in von Mueller's castle, she felt confidence surge through her veins. She was meeting a problem directly, taking action herself instead of waiting for someone else to come by and rescue her from her troubles. This gave her an inner sense of well-being and empowerment that surprised her.

She shoved the coarse dress into a small leather bag, then stepped out of her guest bedchamber. At the end of the hall, a large, stony-faced guard stood on duty, cradling a battle-ax in his arms. When he noticed Jade walking toward him, his eyes narrowed. He hadn't been notified that Princess Jade would be going anywhere, and he didn't like anything to happen without being forewarned.

"Do not worry, good sir," Jade said, waving a hand to dismiss any worries the guard might have had. "I am only going to see the baroness. We have not had tea together in three whole days, and I'm positively starved for her companionship."

Jade smiled sweetly at the man, privately condemning herself for turning on the charm. She suspected he would suffer for what she was about to do, but she saw no other way around her problem. Some day, when she had her land and her castle back, she would reward the young man appropriately.

"You're supposed to stay here and pretend that I'm still in the guest bedchamber," Jade said, letting her voice dip just enough to give it a conspiratorial tone. "That way, if there are enemies of mine within the castle, they'll think I'm still there instead of with Baroness Christina."

The guard clearly was not impressed with what he thought was a poor plan to protect Jade, but he had been told that she was to be protected under all circumstances, and given everything she wanted. The fact that these orders seemed contradictory appeared to be lost on everyone but himself.

"Try not to be too bored, and I'll see you upon my return in an hour or two," Jade said. She smiled again, a little amazed that the guard was going to do what she said. "Remember, if anyone asks, I'm still in the guest bedchamber. And don't be surprised if the baroness herself comes to check on you. She's going to test you, so all you're to say is that I'm in my room, and that I do not wish to be disturbed."

The guard nodded, showing his appreciation for the forewarning. It was just like women to come up with these silly games, he thought. No man in charge would spend time testing the guards in such an ineffective way. And even if a man *would* devise such a test, he'd take steps to make sure that the person tested couldn't be forewarned.

Though not a liar by nature, Jade discovered that, when pressed, she could lie with conviction. Since the "test" lie had worked once, she used it three more times, all with the same effectiveness. At last she was in the grain storage hut located near the rear of the castle grounds, between the castle and its high, surrounding wall.

She was scared, her hands shaking, but she was also excited. After having sat in her bedchamber waiting and worrying about Lyon, it was magnificent to at last be taking charge of her own life and actions.

After a quick check to see if anyone had spotted her slipping into the shack, Jade stripped out of her immaculate green velvet gown trimmed with gold braid as quickly as her fingers could remove it. Next came the snowy white underdresses, which were tossed on top of the green gown that hung over a wooden railing within the shack. Lastly, Jade removed her soft kid slippers.

Completely naked, certain that someone would enter the shack at any second, Jade frantically pulled the old dress over her head. Only then did she breathe a temporary sigh of relief.

The fabric was a little scratchy against her flesh, particularly since she wore no underdresses. But if this ruse was to be successful, she could not afford to make a single slip. Peasants simply didn't wear the fine silk underdresses that Jade had been given by Baroness Christina von Mueller.

Finally, she pulled the velvet ribbons from her long hair, another luxury unavailable to peasants. She tied an old brown scarf around her head to hide her honey blond hair.

She had intended on going without footwear. Her kidskin slippers were too fine, delicate, and expensive for her to wear if she was going to pretend to be a commoner. But she did not have any other footwear. After deliberating a moment, Jade quickly put her slippers back on.

Then, with her heart hammering faster than ever, she stepped out of the grain shack.

A few minutes later Jade walked over the drawbridge and past the four armed guards. The men all gave Jade more than just a glance. That was because they thought she was an extremely attractive peasant, not because she was the woman that they had all been commanded to protect.

Jade smiled broadly as she continued on past the outlying village that surrounded the castle. She didn't know where to search for Lyon, but she felt confident that somehow, some way, they would be together soon.

305

Fate had brought them together the first time; it would bring them together again.

Vance Raymond sat with his legs folded beneath him, holding his shepherd's staff loosely in his hands. His mind was at ease as he watched the sheep grazing along the treeline.

It had been a good week for him. Since he had been able to warn his village of Garth Rawlings's approach, nobody had been hurt. To award his quick thinking, the village elders had given Vance a new wineskin filled with the very best wine produced in the village, three laying hens, and a brick of magnificent cheese. And, since his quick thinking was considered an act of bravery by many, if not outright heroism, he suddenly appeared much more handsome to the maidens in the village. Though Vance had not previously given matrimony much consideration, he was thinking about it now, and liking the mental images he was getting.

When he became aware of movement to his right, Vance leaped to his feet, instantly assuming that Garth had returned, bent on vengeance for being thwarted the last time he was at the village.

When Vance saw that it was just a very beautiful peasant with long blond hair, wearing an old sack dress, he smiled. Perhaps word of his intelligence and heroism had spread to other villages, he mused, since he did not recognize the young peasant woman who approached.

"Hail," he called out as she approached.

"Hail," she replied.

Vance wished that the woman wouldn't wear the

scarf around her hair. It detracted from her beauty, and there really didn't seem to be any reason for the scarf, a muddy brown color that did nothing to enhance the maiden's beauty.

With his finger, Vance smoothed his moustache. He wanted to give this woman a favorable first impression. If she had travelled far just to meet him, he figured it was the least he could do. Since she walked alone, it seemed entirely unlikely that she was simply a traveller. Women did not travel alone, especially since the death of Prince William, because there were roving gangs of men who preyed upon unescorted women.

He rose slowly to his feet and leaned upon his staff, affecting a jaunty posture. It was best, he knew, not to appear too enthusiastic with the young maidens. For some reason, they seemed to like it when a suitor didn't fawn over them.

First he noticed that her slippers had mud staining their surface, and Vance assumed that the maiden had crossed the river from von Mueller's fiefdom to come see him. Then he got a closer look at the peasant woman's face, and Vance Raymond, dutiful peasant, dropped to his knees before her.

"Princess, I am your servant! Do with me as you will!"

Jade approached the young man, laying her hand lightly upon his head. She smoothed a thick lock of dark hair across his forehead.

"What is your name?" she asked.

"Vance Raymond, m'lady," he replied, keeping his eyes cast down.

Chaotic questions danced in his head. He had heard that Princess Jade was innocent of the atrocities that had been blamed upon her. Seeing her now, dressed as a peasant, was a powerful shock to his senses. Had her enemies brought her this low?

"Rise, Vance, and take me to your elders."

"Yes, m'lady. Whatever you wish."

When he got to his feet, Jade studied his features. She did not have to ask him if he believed she was a murderess. One look into his eyes assured her that he knew the truth. She saw respect and love in the dark brown depths of his eyes, joined by a touch of sadness when he looked at her tattered old dress.

"Tis a long tale to tell," Jade explained, guessing at least some of the questions that Vance was too polite to ask. "Perhaps some day, you will be invited to the castle, and I will explain why I am dressed in this manner. And after that, you can repeat the story to the good people in your village. They will repeat it to others, and then everyone will know the story, and of the young man who had heard it first, from the princess's own lips."

"I would be honored," Vance said with a tone of awe. To receive a private audience with Princess Jade in Castle Crosse would elevate his social standing astronomically.

Chapter 25

Lyon approached the village slowly, waiting for some sign from one of his men that it was safe. Across the rump of his horse lay the fresh carcass of the wild boar that Lyon had killed cleanly with a single arrow from sixty yards. The large boar would feed Lyon, his men, and the villagers. He hoped this would offset the inconvenience of his intrusion into their little hamlet.

He had sent his men on ahead to the village, remaining behind the hunt. He had learned over the years that his men were magnificent soldiers, but not particularly gifted hunters. Whenever success was critical, Lyon always hunted alone. Besides, Lyon had long since learned that he had a way of unintentionally intimidating people. It was best if he sent his men into the village first. Lyon Beauchane didn't like to intimidate people unless he absolutely had to.

Ian of Buchwald, a soldier of valor from Lyon's forces, stood along the roadside, a ridiculously broad smile on his face. Lyon approached him slowly, curiously.

"I've had a successful hunt," Lyon said to his soldier.

"Aye, m'lord," Ian replied from his sentry position, his unexplained grin unchecked.

"The village is safe?"

"Aye, m'lord. Safe as safe can be, an' waiting for your arrival, I might add."

If Lyon didn't know better, he would have thought that his man had been drinking spirits. It wouldn't be entirely out of character for Ian to have become drunk, but Lyon hadn't been gone long enough for that to have happened. Even if he *had* tarried long on the hunt, Ian wouldn't imbibe while he shouldered the important responsibility of being an alert sentry.

The village lay fifty yards down the road from where Ian was positioned. As Lyon walked his horse that final fifty yards, he realized that virtually everyone in the village was awaiting his arrival, a fact that caused him much puzzlement. If there would have been something amiss, if Garth or Sheriff Dunne had set a trap, Lyon's men wouldn't be grinning so damned stupidly, as if they knew something that their leader didn't.

"I suppose this will all become clear to me shortly," Lyon said as he dismounted. He helped two of his soldiers remove the boar from his horse. The men just continued to grin, saying nothing.

Lyon turned and faced the handful of villagers who had gathered near. "Are any of you going to explain what is so bloody funny?"

"I will," a feminine voice said from the crowd.

Lyon's mouth dropped open. He was shocked speechless to see Princess Jade Crosse, dressed in peasant garb, step through the crowd. His speechlessness was short-lived, and his shock was nothing compared to that of the peasants' when he hissed through clenched teeth, "Jade, you bloody fool, I'm going to take you over my knee and spank your behind for this!"

He closed the distance that separated them in a heartbeat, then scooped Jade up in his arms. It would have been romantic, Jade thought, if there hadn't been twenty people watching. And if Lyon didn't look like he was so angry that he would explode at any second.

"What the bloody hell do you think you're doing?" Jade asked, quite suddenly feeling very embarrassed at being carried away. She heard an elderly woman gasp, and knew that she had better keep a more careful check on her tongue or her reputation would be besmirched all over again.

"I'm going to put some sense into that beautiful but addlepated head of yours!"

"Addlepated? What? I ought to . . ."

Jade had laced her fingers together at the base of Lyon's neck while he carried her, but now she balled her hand into a fist and reached back to punch him in the nose. Since Lyon had one arm beneath her knees and the other beneath her shoulders, there wasn't a thing he could do to protect himself . . . except drop Jade. This is exactly what he did, right onto a pile of hay used to feed the village milking cows.

"And what the dried Devil's bones do you think you're doing *here,* dressed like *that?"*Lyon demanded, glowering down at Jade. However angry he was, it didn't keep him from noticing—and appreciating—

the fact that Jade's legs had flown up in the air and the skirt of her tattered peasant's dress fell up above her knees.

"I don't have to answer to you!"

Jade got to her feet as quickly as she possibly could, standing was better than being in such an ignominious position.

A small crowd of soldiers and villagers had gathered, some looking very nervous, others amused. The soldiers had sworn to protect Jade against all enemies. But what were they to do if the man manhandling her was Sir Lyon, their leader?

Once on her feet, Jade smoothed out her hair as best she could with just her hands, removing the few strands of hay that had become entangled in her tresses. She then turned dismissively away from Lyon toward the audience.

"You may leave now," she said in a calm, regal voice. "I'm afraid that Sir Lyon and I have had a misunderstanding, which we must resolve privately. I assure you, I will be safe in his hands."

The moment that last sentence left her mouth, Jade regretted it. Only their respect for Jade kept the soldiers from laughing out loud, and the young women of the village did not resist smiling knowingly. Jade wondered if any of them had been "safe in Lyon's hands," as she had inappropriately put it. Whenever Lyon was concerned, jealousy was never far below the surface with Jade, despite her desire to rid herself of the maddening impulse.

She did not turn to face Lyon again until she was certain that they were alone. Then she turned slowly, sensing Lyon's gaze upon her, feeling the heat of a two-week separation sparking the ever smoldering passion between them.

"I had to come to you, don't you see?" she began slowly, unsteadily.

She could see from his stony expression that he was furious with her decision to join him. She also knew that she could change his attitude with little more than a smile, a joke, a soft laugh that carried the promise of sensuality in it. She was not in any mood to fight with Lyon.

"It's not safe to be with me." Lyon stepped forward to look down at Jade. There was the slightest softening of his features, the first fissures in the icy wall of his anger. "You should have stayed with the von Muellers. They would have protected you."

"I've been protected from life for ten years now, Lyon. Now I want to live life." It was Jade who took a step toward him this time, moving close enough to reach out and place her hand lightly over his heart. She felt his warmth through his shirt. "I want to live it with you, Lyon. Is that so difficult to understand? How long could you live in a gilded cage and be happy?"

The very thought of it made them both smile. It was a truly ludicrous notion. Lyon was much too virile to ever tolerate such a serene lifestyle.

"But you're *not* me," Lyon said, struggling to hold onto his anger, which was fleeing quickly, chased away by the gentle amber eyes that gazed at him so lovely. "You're the mistress of Castle Crosse, the owner of all the land that we can see. As a knight of Castle Crosse, I have pledged my loyalty to you."

Jade never liked it when Lyon brought up the differences of their station in life. It was true that she outranked him, but in her eyes that shouldn't make any difference in how they looked upon each other.

Softly, her throat tightened with emotion, she said, "I do want your loyalty, but not because you are a knight of Castle Crosse. I want it because you are the man I love, and the man who loves me."

Jade fought the tears brimming in her eyes. She didn't want to weep. It seemed, suddenly, a weak thing to do. She stood there, shoulders square, openly defying Lyon to say anything other than that he loved her.

"You are a stubborn fool," Lyon replied, and though his words were insulting, there was a slight quiver to his voice. He, too, was fighting to control his emotions. "But you are *my* stubborn fool, and I love you as I could never love another." He cupped her face gently between his palms. "You are my mistress. You are my goddess."

Jade's tears, held back by sheer stubbornness, were set free. Jade melted into Lyon's arms, pressing her face into his chest. She inhaled, loving his scent, his touch, the blissful safety she felt when his strong arms surrounded her. It didn't matter whether she lived in a castle or a hut, whether she slept on a downy mattress or a pile of blankets; the only possession worth having, the only thing she needed, was Lyon's love. If she had that, then she had as much as she could ever hope for. Anything more would be a gift from the heavens that she should be thankful for, but must never covet.

Some time later, the boar was turning on the spit above the fire. Jade at last felt truly at peace. She sat on

314

a blanket, with Lyon at her side. Sentries had been posted because there was a constant fear that Garth and his men would show up.

"Tell me, Sir Lyon, exactly how much *do* you love me?" Jade purred, unabashedly fishing for compliments and vows of love.

Lyon laughed lightly, leaning to the side to nuzzle Jade's neck. Her satiny hair tickled his face and he felt a stirring within him down low, but he was determined to keep his physical desires in check for a little while longer.

"There is a vanity to you, m'lady, that I did not know existed," he teased.

"Tell me."

"I love you more than all the world. You don't just make life worth living, you are life itself." He pressed his cheek against hers again, the tip of his tongue dancing briefly against her earlobe. "And later this evening, I will show you exactly how deep my love for you goes."

Jade blushed then, the warmth of passion rippling quickly through her. Lyon was truly devilish, she thought. And he had taught her to appreciate and revel in his wickedness . . . and for that she would be eternally grateful to him.

The sun had just set, so there was still enough daylight, combined with firelight, for the village peasants to see them clearly. Jade, noticing that several villagers were looking covertly at her, moved a little further away from Lyon. She was determined to show at least some degree of decorum, if only as long as there were others watching. As soon as she got Lyon alone, she

315

would strip herself of inhibitions and decorum as quickly and completely as she would strip herself of the scratchy peasant's dress.

Feeling the need to change the topic of conversation, Jade looked sternly at Lyon. "Tell me now, Sir Lyon, all that has happened while we have been separated."

Lyon smiled, loving the sudden formality to Jade's tone, knowing that when the time was right, she would be anything *but* formal with him.

"I have heard from messengers that within Castle Crosse, all is chaos and confusion. Some of the merchants believe that you have been killed by me, some believe that Bishop Fields had you murdered. The stories abound, and the entire matter is a continuous topic of conversation and rumor. The knights have formed into small bands to search for me and my men. Two weeks ago, Garth had seventy men in his ranks; now he has sixty-one."

Sorrow darkened Jade's mood. She didn't like to hear of anyone dying, not even her enemies. "How many men have you lost?" she asked, half-afraid of the answer she might receive.

"None. Some wounded, but all will heal." Lyon made no effort to hide the respect he had for his men, or the pride he took in his battle plan. "We engage the enemy on our own terms, fighting as *we* decide to fight. Garth and his men greatly outnumber us, so we have chosen to attack rather than run, hitting them hard, then disappearing into the forest. We stay constantly on the move."

Jade didn't have to be told what was going through

Lyon's head. He was afraid for her safety, afraid that she would slow his troop movements down. Speed and mobility were key ingredients in ensuring Lyon's continued victories against Bishop Fields, and the forces currently controlling Castle Crosse.

After a long silence, Jade asked, "How long do you think the fighting will continue?"

"It could last for many weeks, months. I cannot say because I cannot guess exactly what it is that madman Fields will do next."

"Bishop Fields? You are sure it is Bishop Fields behind the atrocities?"

"I've received messages from Lord Charles and the baron. Their spies confirm that it is Fields who gives orders now that you are no longer in the castle."

Jade sighed. She had hoped that it wouldn't be Bishop Fields who turned traitor. There had been times in the past when she'd turned to the bishop for comfort, and he'd been there with a kind word and a sympathetic shoulder.

"I do not think this war will last very long," Lyon said, his tone indicating that he was coming to the conclusion as he spoke. "Fields is isolated from real power. He's sent missives to London attempting to place blame for the insurrection on you, on the peasants, on everyone but himself. King Henry will soon be expecting its tribute, and if it does not get it, someone will be sent here to find out why."

"And nobody wants that to happen?"

"Precisely. London has a way of finding a problem, then getting rid of that problem by simply usurping all the land of whoever caused the problem."

Jade looked away briefly, turning her gaze toward the fire. She remembered back when Prince William was alive, and how he would make certain that taxes sent to London were always sent in advance. The awesome power that rested in King Henry and his minions was best left in London, Prince William believed.

"Baron von Mueller and Lord Charles have sent their men to intercept messengers and missives from Bishop Fields to London, but one can never be absolutely certain that a letter hasn't slipped through. So the baron and Lord Charles have written missives of their own to the Crown, giving their version of what has been happening within your fiefdom."

The circles within circles of this deception surprised Jade. She had known all along that politics could be a sordid business, but this was much more convoluted than she had suspected.

"So the Crown has been told of Bishop Fields trying to murder me?" she asked.

"Nay, m'lady. If the Crown suspects that you are weak, you'll lose your land in a heartbeat. Of that you can be sure. Lord Charles and Baron von Mueller have related their own set of lies, avoiding the truth whenever possible." He laughed then, clearly pleased with the machinations that had been going on since he left von Mueller's castle. "If the Crown can figure out what has been truly happening in your fiefdom, it will be a miracle worthy of the heavens."

Lyon laughed aloud, and this surprised and disturbed Jade. There was a strong part of Lyon that enjoyed this particular war. He was indeed a man of action, and he loved a good fight. Could a man like that ever be satisfied with being a husband? Could a man like that grow old and gray gracefully? Or would he clutch foolishly to his youth and end up dead on the field of battle, fighting in a war that never should have been fought, clinging to a past best left buried?

A murmur went through the camp, interrupting Jade's thoughts. Lyon was instantly alert. A few seconds later, Ian rushed to his side, knelt, and whispered in his ear.

"What is it?" Jade asked. Without meaning to, she was clutching onto his cape.

Lyon issued a soft command to Ian, then turned to Jade. "Mounted soldiers are moving this way."

"Garth?"

"Possibly. Garth's men, anyway. Rather than engaging them, we'll disperse. When the men find the boar, they'll go no further."

Jade looked at the boar. Peasants were hacking huge chunks from it. They would leave behind just enough meat to keep the soldiers occupied. No one would get fat on what was left behind.

"Stay here. I'll be back in just a minute or two."

Lyon was gone before Jade could say a word. She followed him with her eyes, watching the way his men looked to him for leadership, and how he carried that mantle of responsibility easily upon his broad, powerful shoulders.

The soldiers acted with an economy of movement, hurriedly without being frantic. When Lyon returned to Jade, he carried his bow and quiver full of arrows.

"Come, m'lady, it is time for us to leave."

"Garth's men will follow us." Jade was frightened of witnessing more violence, especially against the villagers.

"My men split up whenever we're being followed. We know where we'll meet up later." He reached down to take Jade's hand, helping her up. "A horse is being prepared for you."

Fear curled inside Jade, and she tried to calm its strident voice as best she could. Lyon did not seem at all frightened by the approaching soldiers, but then she had yet to see him show any fear at all.

"You're not leaving me, are you?"

Lyon smiled then and quickly threw an arm around Jade's shoulders, briefly enveloping her beneath his cape. She knew that he was trying to chase away her fears, and for this she was grateful. Her love for him heightened, even though she had not thought it possible.

"No, m'lady, I'm kidnapping you!"

Despite the circumstances, Jade laughed then, letting Lyon lead her to a medium-sized destrier. As they approached the horse, men were busy shortening the stirrups.

"Whose horse is this? If I take this animal, someone will be without one," Jade said.

A handsome young man who was working on the saddle turned a smile to Jade. "Do not worry about me, m'lady," the young man said. "I will be content to remain here. It should be easy enough for one man to hide in this village."

Jade was about to protest more when she noticed an attractive young woman standing behind the soldier. It was clear that the maiden was waiting to take the soldier with her, and Jade smiled because she could well remember those first frantic, passionate encounters she'd had with Lyon.

"Treat her well," Jade said to the young man, keeping her voice low so that only he could hear.

"I will, Princess. I promise my life upon it."

Moments later, Lyon and Jade rode into the night, moving slowly and steadily away from the villagers and the soldiers and the problems and responsibilities inherent in the positions of power that Sir Lyon and Princess Jade held.

Chapter 26

"Begone, I say! Get out of here, you ugly wench!" Bishop Nathan Fields hissed through clenched teeth, pointing a finger at his chamber door.

Ashen-faced, Mary Ellen walked backward toward the door. She was afraid to even turn her back on Bishop Fields. In the past two weeks since the ill-fated attempt on Princess Jade's life, Bishop Fields's behavior had become increasingly erratic. Lately, he had called for Mary Ellen, telling her he needed the relief from the tension that she could provide. A moment later he'd turn her away, usually with insults chasing her to the door.

"Yes, m'lord," Mary Ellen whispered, stumbling slightly. She rushed out the bedchamber door, ignoring the smirk she received from Garth Rawlings, who stood just outside in the hallway.

Bishop Fields was quivering from anger. The cords in his neck stood out prominently. It was especially ominous-looking because he had lost more than ten pounds in the past fortnight. When violently angry, he appeared almost cadaverous.

When Garth Rawlings entered the chamber, followed immediately by Sheriff Sean Dunne, the bishop turned his back to them for a moment to force himself to relax. It was not easy to be calm when tension gripped him so severely that he could not think of anything but Jade; not even when Mary Ellen did her level best to arouse and excite him. He had sent her away because she had failed at the only thing Bishop Fields had felt she was any good at.

"You sent for me?" Garth asked. Privately, he was enjoying Bishop Fields's growing unease.

"Yes." Bishop Nathan Fields turned slowly, and when he faced Garth and Sean Dunne, his composure was again rock solid. "I've called you here for explanations."

"Explanations?" Garth asked.

"Explanations as to why you haven't found and killed Jade and Lyon."

Garth noticed that in the past two weeks *Princess* Jade and *Sir* Lyon had become simply Jade and Lyon. He noticed, too, that the whites of the bishop's eyes had become muddy yellow in color.

"I've kept Lyon on the run constantly," Garth said. "He and his men have got to be on the brink of exhaustion. They can't run much longer. The moment he stumbles, he's a dead man."

"So you say." Bishop Fields reached for the pitcher of wine on his desk, then stopped. He had already drunk three goblets of the strong red wine that day. If he drank much more of the heady brew his judgement would surely be impaired.

"Don't pay Sir Lyon too much thought," Garth

323

continued. "He doesn't dare cross onto von Mueller's land, nor Lord Frederick's."

"He did before."

"Aye, that he did. But he did not stay long with von Mueller, and none of his men went with him. As you said before, he went to von Mueller's looking for help. He got an audience with the little man, but nothing more than that. Now von Mueller won't even let him into the fiefdom."

Bishop Fields was still worried. He didn't trust Lyon, von Mueller, or Lord Charles.

"I've had every available man looking for Sir Lyon and Princess Jade," the sheriff said, his voice reedy with tension. "It's only a matter of time before they're caught."

"Time! How much time do you need?" Bishop Fields bellowed.

As the bishop flew into a tantrum, cursing Sheriff Dunne's heritage, intelligence, and loyalty, the sheriff remained silent, taking the foul comments without rebuttal. But as the insults were heaped one upon the next, he knew that his time was quickly running out. Garth Rawlings had chosen to tell the bishop the silliest of lies, but they were lies that the bishop wanted to hear. Sheriff Dunne chose instead to tell the truth, and for his honesty he had earned the bishop's disfavor.

For an instant, Sheriff Dunne looked at Garth, and saw that Garth was greatly enjoying the insults being hurled at him by the bishop.

To ingratiate himself to that monster, Garth will promise to kill me.

The truth of the thought hit Sheriff Dunne hard. He realized then, with absolute clarity, that he was the only

324

truly educated man among Bishop Fields's immediate circle of advisors. Men like Garth Rawlings had never liked him, he knew. Before, such enmity had not bothered the sheriff a whit, but now he realized that his life was ensured only as long as he maintained Bishop Fields's good graces.

It was only a matter of time before he was killed, and Sheriff Dunne knew it. Fields, his tenuous grasp on reality becoming more frail by the moment, would demand that someone be held accountable for the failure to kill Princess Jade. Since Dunne was more likely to tell Bishop Fields the unadorned truth instead of the sweet-sounding lie, he would be the one held accountable.

Eventually, Bishop Fields's vitriolic assault trickled to an end. He reached for the wine pitcher at his desk.

"Get out of here," Bishop Fields said, pouring the goblet with wine so quickly that some of the red liquid splashed onto the papers on his desk. "Both of you, get out of here now, and don't come back unless you bring Jade's head with you."

Sheriff Sean Dunne bowed low and said, "Aye, it will be so."

As he left the room, the sheriff realized that the longer he stayed at Castle Crosse, the more his life was in jeopardy. There was no telling how much longer Bishop Fields would be able to hold onto his sanity. Once he lost it entirely, there would be total chaos within Castle Crosse.

London. The name of that blessed city sounded like the name of a loved one to Sheriff Dunne. It was in London that he had received his education. And it would be in London that Sean Dunne could give *his* version of what had been happening at Castle Crosse to King Henry and his advisors.

And it was in London where he could start a new life.

Garth Rawlings was saying something to Sheriff Dunne, but he refused to listen. Now that he knew what he must do, he would allow nothing to stand in his way. He wouldn't be safe until he was ensconced in London . . . far away from Garth Rawlings, the vicious right hand man of Bishop Nathan Fields!

On his hands and knees, Lyon blew slowly and steadily at the small red glowing ember. He nearly had the fire going, and soon he would be preparing the meal to break the fast. Jade was nearby, only her head above the blankets. The morning air had a chill to it, and Lyon knew that soon winter would be upon them. No longer would it be so easy to camp outside and brave the elements while fighting with Garth and his men.

Lyon put the water on for Jade's morning tea. He wished he had sweet honey to give her for the tea, but such luxuries were impossible for two people on the run.

He stepped over to where Jade lay sleeping. Someday soon he would give her the sun, the moon, the stars, Lyon promised himself.

He hated not being able to shelter her from the cold, or from the influences of people like Bishop Nathan Fields. But one day, after Fields had been exposed and punished, after Garth Rawlings had been disposed of, after Sheriff Sean Dunne had been stripped of power and thrown into the streets . . .

Shaking his head angrily, Lyon returned to the campfire. It did no good to think about what *someday* would bring. He had to think about the present problems that rested upon his shoulders while he sat watching the fire.

Lyon Beauchane couldn't give Jade the sun, the moon, or the stars, but he could present her with hot tea in the morning when she awoke. That's exactly what he did.

"Good morning, sunshine," Lyon said quietly, getting down on one knee near Jade. He held the steaming cup in his hand, waiting for her to awaken sufficiently to hold it herself. He didn't want her to burn herself accidentally because he gave her the cup while she was still groggy with sleep. "Did you sleep well?"

Her long, wavy, blond hair was tussled from sleep. Jade pushed the tresses from her face, and propped herself up on her elbow. She smiled sleepily at Lyon, having no understanding at all of how beautiful she looked to him in her dishevelled state.

The morning chill made her shiver slightly as she accepted the tea. He pulled the blanket up around her shoulders again.

"Good morning," Jade at last said. She smiled again sleepily, tilting her head back to invite his kiss, which she received. "And bless you. I've become really quite cosseted, getting my tea in the morning like this."

"It seemed the least I could do." He studied Jade's face intently as she tested the tea. "I have nothing with me to sweeten it."

"It's the best tea I've ever had in my life." Jade smiled again, rather theatrically puckering to invite another kiss.

I could get used to seeing his face first thing in the morning, Jade thought sleepily.

She sipped the tea again. It really was quite horrid, the water tasting a bit brackish, especially without anything to sweeten the strong brew. But Jade didn't care. The gesture was sweet, and pleased her palate more than any honey.

Jade, at last fully awake, suddenly became aware that there were many thoughts whirling through Lyon's head that he didn't voice. She reached up, and with the tip of her finger pushed a thick lock of blond hair away from his eye.

"You really are too beautiful," she said softly, knowing that strong emotions were about to affect her. "Last night, when I wanted to feel you next to me, but I was too torn apart by all that had happened to make love to you—"

Words were impossible for Jade quite suddenly as she remembered how Lyon had instinctively known that she needed only his arms around her last night, in lieu of further intimacy.

"Shhh! You needn't talk about it," Lyon cut in. His statement didn't surprise Jade at all. Only on the rarest of occasions did Lyon appreciate any conversation that came straight from the heart.

"Yes, I do," Jade replied after a moment. "There are a thousand things that I should say to you. When I'm alone, I always tell myself the things that you should hear, but then when we are together again my courage fails me. You always do everything you can to silence me. This time, I'm going to say what need be said."

Lyon smiled indulgently, but Jade was not at all

insulted or put off by his reaction. She knew him well enough to realize that he simply had no experience whatsoever in dealing with matters of the heart. Consequently, whenever such matters came up, he did everything he could to avoid the subject.

"I love you, Sir Lyon," Jade began. "I love you more than either you or I could have imagined. I love you so much that I think it's silly that you're worried about what will happen between us when this conflict is over." She looked him straight in the eyes. "Yes, I know all about that. All about how you're worried that when this grand muddle is over I'll just look at you as another of my servants whose sole purpose is to serve me."

She was able to see into Lyon's eyes then, and it surprised her. Some of the things that she was saying were nothing more than guesses. From what she could see behind Lyon's eyes, she could tell that each and every word was hitting the mark.

"You spend so much time worrying about whether you're properly shouldering all the responsibility you think you must," Jade continued. As she spoke, she slipped her right hand beneath Lyon's cape to touch his muscled chest through the sheer fabric of his shirt. She could feel his heart beating. "Haven't you ever wanted someone to just take care of you? Haven't you ever just wanted to let all the affairs of the world go on without you . . . if only for a few days?"

Lyon had wanted that very thing to happen, but hearing the idea spoken aloud made him squirm with discomfort. He had too long a history of running from such words and facing such emotions to remain calm and detached.

He leaned down, trying to kiss Jade, hoping that she

329

could be diverted, silenced by seduction. However, she had spent too much time thinking about the matter to be so easily diverted.

"Don't now," she said. "You need to hear this."

"No, you just need to *say* it."

"No more and no less than you need to *hear* it," Jade said with unwavering determination. "So listen, bonsier, and listen well." Jade set the cup down, then curled her knees beneath her, very subtly moving closer to Lyon. She never once took her hand from his chest. "You have saved my life and my reputation more times than I can count—"

"I fear, m'lady, that I have done more harm to your reputation than good, especially with taking you away without a chaperone from the village."

Jade laughed lightly. It was wonderful when Lyon was chivalrous, even though both of them were intensely aware of the physical and spiritual intimacies that they shared.

"That's not true. There isn't one single decent person from that village that doesn't want to see the two of us together as—" Jade cut her words off short. She had almost said *man and wife,* but to do that might force Lyon into a proposal of marriage. Unless he gave it of his own free will, then Jade didn't want it at all. "Together as *one,*" she said at last, completing the sentence and silently praying that Lyon hadn't noticed the hesitation in her speech. "You do so much for me, so much in so many different ways. . . ."

Lyon had noticed the subtle change in Jade's tone, and it surprised him. Part of him wanted to stop her. He was afraid that she was going to try to seduce him.

330

and that was something that he didn't want, only because they should really be breaking camp, and getting on horseback again.

One glance into her amber eyes told Lyon that Jade most definitely was in a romantic mood on this fine morning. A second glance told him that she would not be easily dissuaded from whatever course of action she had chosen.

When she knelt and hooked her hand behind his neck, Lyon chuckled softly. There was something almost comical about Princess Jade Crosse being sexually forward. But then she pushed him hard on the chest, knocking him backward so that he landed on his backside, his booted feet kicking forward, nearly hitting Jade. She moved quickly, staying on her knees beside his hip, looking at him with amber eyes that smoldered with mischief and promised mayhem of the most delightful kind.

"After all you've done for me, isn't there anything that I can do for you?" Jade asked theatrically. Her eyes told a truth that shocked Lyon, one which none of the fiefdom ever would have believed.

"Jade, I don't know if this is the right time for you to become so . . . *adventurous,* " Lyon said, choosing his words carefully, suddenly at war with a twisted image of how ladies were meant to behave. The times he found Jade most exciting, he realized, were the times she had flouted such a narrow definition of womanhood.

I don't know if this is the right time, either, Jade thought, struggling to maintain the bold colors of her courage. But if I wait for the right time for everything, if I wait until there's no chance at all of failure, then what thrill will there possibly be in achieving success?

"My darling," Jade purred, sliding up so that part of her weight was upon Lyon, "I never dreamed I would say this, but right now, you're talking too much."

Jade squirmed, raising her knee to slide her thigh against Lyon's, moving up on his body so that she could kiss him full on the mouth. When their lips met, she boldly thrust her tongue into his mouth, looping one arm around his neck so that he could not pull away from her.

"Jade?"

"Shhh! You don't need to say a word," she whispered in a breathy rush of words, afraid that her courage would fail her at any second. "Just allow me. Lay back, my darling, and let me take care of everything."

It was not in keeping with Lyon's character to simply lay back and be passive. But under the circumstances, he did exactly as he was told without further question or comment.

Jade stretched her body out so that she was pressed along his tall, muscled body. With a trembling hand, she unfastened his breeches, keeping her eyes down, afraid of what she would see if her gaze met his. Was she being too forward, too wanton for his enjoyment?

Don't think about it now! she mentally upbraided herself, forcing herself to continue, even though her confidence was quickly failing.

She remembered how Lyon had silently coaxed her forward before when they had shared a moment of passion, but she had stopped him, unable to do what he wanted. Now, however, she would let nothing prevent her from continuing. With newfound courage, she opened his breeches, and he sprang out, long and fiercely aroused. She gasped softly, looking at him, aware of what she had caused and how she must complete what she had begun.

She took him into her palm, curling her fingers around his throbbing length. Lyon's low groan of pleasure told her that he enjoyed being touched.

"I've never . . . I don't know what you'll expect . . ." she whispered, courage failing her.

Lyon said nothing. Instead, he pushed his fingers through her silky blond hair at the nape of Jade's neck and turned her face to him. Doubling up, he brought her face to his and briefly, but fiercely, kissed her mouth. Then he lay back again, twirling a long lock of hair around his forefinger.

It was the approval, unleavened by stipulations or qualifications, that Jade wanted. She stroked her fingers up and down, feeling the lusty pulse of his blood flowing through him, hardening and heightening his arousal.

"Let me make you happy," Jade whispered, kissing the nape of Lyon's neck, then his chin before working his way slowly down his body.

She loved his scent, and the way his body responded to her touch. She loved everything about him and she intended to show him that.

Slowly, timorously, she brought her lips to the crown of his manhood. She kissed him lightly, then let her tongue play briefly over the enflamed flesh. Lyon gasped with pleasure, and his body tightened from head to toe. Made more bold by Lyon's obvious approval, she inhaled deeply, then gave him the wet warmth of her mouth.

Sighing, Lyon stared at the leaves of the trees overhead, trying unsuccessfully to remain calm, feeling himself being pushed at a furious pace toward the edge of ecstasy.

"So-o-o good," he whispered, continuing to twirl Jade's hair slowly around his forefinger as the rising pressure within him became greater.

Chapter 27

"I love it when you're this way," Jade said softly, her cheek against Lyon's chest.

"What way is that?"

"At peace. All the angles and sharp edges softened into curves. It's such a nice change from the way you usually are."

Lyon laughed softly, and Jade enjoyed listening to the sound as it rumbled through his chest. She snuggled a little closer to him, idly wishing that they didn't have their clothes on, since it was always so much more intimate to feel his body, warm and naked, against her own.

He was stroking her hair, twirling it in circles. Jade raised her knee so that her thigh rested against his. When he sighed softly with contentment, she wished that she'd given him such pleasure much sooner. She was so silly to be so insecure in her own ability to give Lyon satisfaction!

"What am I usually like?" Lyon asked after a moment. "Am I really that reprehensible?"

"Oh, it's not that you're bad. That wasn't what I meant. It's just that so often you've got this intense look in your eyes, and you're always ready to fight, always looking for trouble or danger."

"Mayhaps that's because there's been so much trouble in my life."

"And mayhaps it's because you like the knight's life. You may not admit it, but you like the fight, Lyon. That's something about you that's difficult for me to understand."

"Then don't try to understand it."

The brittleness in Lyon's tone told Jade that he didn't appreciate what she had said. Though he hadn't moved even a single inch, he suddenly seemed to be far, far away. Jade damned herself silently for bringing the subject up. Lyon hated it when she tried to get deeper into his being than he had invited her to go.

A silence enveloped them. Then, swiftly, Lyon moved Jade away and stood. With an economy of movement, he retrieved his cape and swirled it around his shoulders, then reattached the sword belt around his trim hips.

"We've got to keep moving," he said sharply. There wasn't the faintest hint of warmth in his tone. "Whenever the men and I are separated, we have a plan to regroup in two days. The men will be expecting me at the Camden Pass by the morrow's dawn at the latest. Since travel is apt to be slow, we mustn't tarry."

He turned then and began saddling the horses. Jade got to her feet, smoothing out her hair as best she could without a comb or brush, and then folded and rolled the blankets so they could be tied to the horses.

Would it always have to be this way? Would prickly

unhappiness always follow their ecstasy and that blissful sense of oneness between them? If war and violence and conflict did not follow Lyon, then he would follow it. Living in peace was a foreign state of being to Sir Lyon Beauchane.

Could a man like that ever be any woman's husband? Would he ever be able to accept a princess as his bride? If so, would it change him so much that Jade would soon be unable to recognize him as the man of magnetic allure that she had learned to love?

Lyon strode over to her when he'd finished readying the horses. His face was set in a hard, implacable expression. In one hand he held his quiver and bow, and in the other he carried his dagger and sheath with a slender belt made of rope.

"Here, put this around your waist," he said, extending the sheathed dagger toward Jade. When she didn't voluntarily accept the weapon, Lyon forced it into her hand, but she let it fall to the ground. "There may come a time when you'll wish you had that weapon with you. These are not peaceful times in which we live. Princess, of all the fiefdoms on this island of England, none is going to be more violent in the coming days than yours."

The words bit into Jade's conscience. She hated the fact that she was proprietor over a fiefdom that, of late, had known many deaths and few births. Her villeins had endured far more pain and hunger and suffering than happiness and laughter and the warm-belly satisfaction of finishing a productive day's work with one's family.

Hot, stinging tears of frustration brimmed in her eyes. These were triggered by the truth of Lyon's words, and the fact that he seemed to take a certain sadistic pleasure in saying them.

She bent down to retrieve the dagger and belt, noticing that it was the same dagger that Lyon had held to her throat on that very first night when he had climbed into her bedchamber. When she bent over, she felt her long hair fluff out momentarily as something whispered past, tugging at the strands. A fraction of a second later, she heard the *thud* of an arrow hit the trunk of a tree behind her, and she realized that she had missed being pierced by a deadly arrow literally by a hair's breadth.

"Lyon!" she screamed.

If she had frozen with fear rather than reacting to the threat immediately, the man she loved would have died. As it was, the two arrows intended for Lyon cut harmlessly through the air where he had stood only an instant before.

Sadly, it was not the first time that Jade had witnessed hideous violence that seemed to erupt from nowhere. How did one even attempt the foolhardy task of negotiating with a thunderstorm of violence, trying to appeal to its mighty, lethal illogic?

Wheeling toward her attackers, pulling the dagger from its sheath, Jade crouched, bending her knees, and held the dagger out in front of herself threateningly.

Four men rushed toward her, though Jade could hear that there were many more. She recognized the colors that the soldiers wore and knew they were quartered at Castle Crosse. Since she did not recognize any of their faces, she knew they were soldiers-for-hire who had only recently been added to the ranks to help in the fight against Lyon and his men.

Within the bosom of every person is the self-protective instinct, the uncivilized, primordial self that will do whatever is necessary for the preservation of self and family. It was this instinct that rose like a shield before Jade as the men attacked.

None of the four men, she noticed, carried a bow. None of them had tried to ambush her with an arrow from the woods. The closest of the four grinned hollowly as he rushed toward her. He looked contemptuously at her dagger, and tried to grab Jade. She thrust the blade at him, but he was an experienced fighter. He deftly sidestepped the attack.

"You're a spirited wench, that you are!" he shouted, still grinning wickedly, holding a broadsword in his hand.

"I am Princess Jade Crosse of Crosse Castle, and I command you to leave!" Jade shouted.

The only response she received from the soldier was a cackle of sadistic laughter. He reached for her a second time, his powerful hand calloused from years of hard work, dirt embedded beneath his cracked fingernails.

The soldier never really thought that Jade would do it. She stabbed at his midsection a second time, exactly as he expected her to, but both moves had been tentative, cautious, more defensive than offensive. What the man never dreamed of was that Jade would, after missing the second time, step inside the swinging arc of his clutching hand, and thrust straight forward with the dagger a third and final time.

Lyon kept all his weapons in perfect, deadly working condition, and the dagger was no different. The blade cut cleanly through leather and flesh, not slowing its forward plunge until the haft thudded into the hired killer's body. His eyes burst open wide, and the heavy broadsword dropped from his hand.

"You wench, you've killed me!" he hissed, his face close to Jade's.

She did not have time to think about it. She pushed at the killer, clutching tightly onto the handle of the dagger at the same time. The man was dead before he hit the ground, and Jade turned away from him, willing herself not to look at the corpse. She knew that she had no choice but to defend herself and Lyon from these foul men, hating what she had just done nevertheless.

By the time Jade was able to turn her attention back to where Lyon stood, three more men were on the ground, all of them bleeding, none of them dead.

If Jade ever had any doubts of Lyon's strength, they vanished as she watched him fending off two men with his broadsword. The heavy sword was intended to be used with two hands, but Lyon held it in just one. As he swung it furiously from side to side, it was obvious that the retreating soldiers did not want to challenge the tall, blond knight.

The hunting party had originally had eight men in it. Jade had killed one soldier, and Lyon had felled three more. Two other soldiers were trying to prevent being vivisected by Lyon's broadsword.

Whatever instinct had first prompted Jade to fight back, briefly supplanting her abhorrence of violence with the deeper instinct of self-preservation, also made her suddenly throw herself face down on the ground.

It was listening to that instinct, that inner voice that she was learning to trust, that saved her life once again. The archer's deadly, iron-tipped arrow nicked the shoulder of Jade's peasant dress, cutting the fabric, but failing to cut her skin.

She rolled on the ground, screaming a warning at Lyon. If there was an archer aiming at her, then surely there was one aiming at Lyon as well.

Lyon's reflexes were lightning fast. Just when it seemed as though he had the soldiers in a position from where they could retreat no further, he did the unexpected by leaping sideways, disengaging from the fight.

It was the unexpectedness of the move that saved his life. The arrow, aimed at Lyon's back, missed its mark but continued on unchecked for another four feet until it pierced a soldier's chest. Lyon had tricked the archer into killing his own ally.

"The horses!" Lyon shouted to Jade, at last able to take a second away from his own fighting to see how Jade fared. "Get to the horses!"

Jade ran as fast as her legs could carry her to the horses. They were well-trained animals, accustomed to the harsh clanking sounds of fighting and the rich smell of blood. They had remained in place during the skirmish. Jade grabbed the reins of both animals and, positioning herself between them, led them quickly to Lyon.

An arrow ricocheted off the stiff leather saddle of Jade's horse. The arrow nicked the horse's neck, drawing blood. The animal reared up on its hind legs. It took all of Jade's strength to maintain her hold on the reins.

She was still struggling to control the animal when she felt hands at her waist. Before she could spin to see who had grabbed her, she was hoisted high in the air

341

and unceremoniously dumped onto the saddle by Lyon.

"Go! Go! Go!" he screamed, bringing the flat of his broadsword down with a stinging slap against the mare's rump. The animal lunged forward. A moment later, Lyon was in the saddle of his own destrier, crouched low over the animal's neck, following close behind Jade as arrows chased them.

The morning meal at Lord Charles Frederick's was always an extraordinary event. The huge, stately man lived life to the fullest, and he believed that a good day began with a spectacular meal. Consequently, the morning fast was broken by enormous quantities of chicken eggs, sliced ham and beef, fruits and vegetables, hot tea and even cold ale, all piled high on the trestle table.

That morning, those gathered round the table included several of Lord Charles's grandchildren, as well as Baron and Baroness von Mueller.

Lord Charles and the baron sat at one end of the huge, oblong table, their heads bent low as they discussed the continuing conflict with Bishop Nathan Fields. They kept their voices muted, not wanting the troubling topic to be overheard by their wives, and certainly not by the children present.

"Apparently, chaos still reigns inside the castle," von Mueller said as he munched on a piece of sliced melon. "Laborers haven't been paid for their work, not even when their payment was to have been in food."

"The peasants within Castle Crosse are starving?" Lord Charles asked, his bushy brows rising. The thought of those good people starving rankled his sensibilities.

"Not quite starving, but they're being cheated daily. Of that you can be confident," von Mueller explained. "The entire structure seems to have collapsed. Those barbarians that now wear the colors of Castle Crosse and heed Garth Rawlings's orders have taken to stealing directly from the peasants to get what they want, even from the commoners living inside the castle walls."

"It's only a matter of time before it all collapses," Lord Charles said quietly, shaking his head in disbelief. "Before it all comes down around his shoulders, you can believe that Bishop Fields is going to cause as much bloodshed and damage as he possibly can."

"Does he even realize that he can't possibly triumph?"

"Probably. He's an intelligent and shrewd man. He *must* know that he lacks the support from within and without to succeed."

For a moment the two men were silent, reflective, each thinking of Bishop Nathan Fields, and what could be done to staunch the escalating, needless bloodshed. A servant approached Lord Charles and bent low to whisper in his ear. The old leader's eyes shot over to von Mueller, the smile creasing his bearded face carrying victory.

"Lady Shannon, Baroness von Mueller, if you will pardon us," Lord Charles said, rising swiftly. The baron rose, too, though he did not know what had been spoken by the servant.

"But Charles! You promised that you would keep Christina and I company this morning!" Lady Shannon

343

complained. She had seen precious little of her husband since the disruptive arrival and departure of Sir Lyon and Princess Jade.

Lord Charles bent low to kiss his wife's cheek, and his open display of love brought giggles of approval from the grandchildren seated at the table.

"I do apologize, m'lady," he said. "But we really must take our leave. I'll make this up to you, I promise."

"So you have often said," Lady Shannon replied, sighing, though it was clear that she was not truly angry with her husband. She had been married to him long enough to know the heavy burden of responsibility he carried.

As Lord Charles left the room, he was thinking that a new carriage for Lady Shannon was in order, harnessed to a new four-horse team. He'd search throughout England for white horses, Lady Shannon's favorite, and present her with the carriage and horses as soon as the situation in Castle Crosse became stable.

They made their way swiftly to the basement of the castle. The air was damp and cool, smelling of old rope and tallow, odors that failed to hide another scent: fear.

Von Mueller said nothing. He knew that when the time was right, he would be told what was necessary. Something within him whispered that critical decisions would be made within the next few minutes.

Two guards stood outside the heavy locked wooden door. As the guards saw the approach of Lord Charles, they lifted the solid bolt locking door. Lord Charles entered the room, which was illuminated by a single torch. There wasn't a single window in the underground room to allow in either sunlight or fresh air.

"Mein Gott!" von Mueller exclaimed when his eyes adjusted to the dim light. At last he knew what had caused such a stir at Lord Charles's table.

Sitting in a chair, looking a little bruised and rumpled by the scuffle of his capture, was Sheriff Sean Dunne.

"You're to be commended," Lord Charles said to the two guards who had positioned themselves inside the room. "How many people knew about this?"

"Less than a dozen, m'lord," the soldier replied quickly.

"Keep it at that. I need absolute secrecy."

"Yes, m'lord."

"Everyone who has had a hand in the capture of this man will be rewarded accordingly, including yourselves."

"Thank you, m'lord!"

The young men left the small room quickly, leaving the door ajar so that light and air could enter. With four heavily armed guards stationed just outside the door, Sheriff Dunne stood no chance whatsoever of escaping.

"I understand that you were on the road toward London," Lord Charles said, looking down contemptuously at Sheriff Dunne. "What were you going there for?"

"What I do is none of your—"

Lord Charles had already heard of too many murders, too many pointless deaths, to grant Sheriff Sean Dunne much sympathy. He cut the man's insult off short with a powerful backhand swing that knocked Dunne off the chair and sent him toppling to the dirt floor.

345

"You and your men have been responsible for rape, murder, and untold misery," Lord Charles said slowly, obviously having difficulty controlling his tone and his temper. "It is my personal opinion that the moral thing to do is to have you executed immediately. You do not make this a better world by your presence in it. Therefore, if it is my wish that you die, then you will die. I suggest you keep a civil tongue in your head, answer every question I ask of you, and pray that you live long enough to see another sunrise."

Sheriff Sean Dunne picked himself slowly up off the floor and sat down once again on the short, three-legged stool. All the defiance, all the false courage and anger that he had shown just seconds earlier, had completely vanished. He was a guilty man who knew he was guilty. All he had to do was look into the eyes of Lord Charles and Baron von Mueller to be assured that the threats against his life were not idle ones.

In a slow, even, defeated tone, the former sheriff told of how he had intended to ride to London to give his personal version of the events at Castle Crosse.

"Bishop Fields isn't paying the tax to King Henry," he said, fixing his gaze upon the dirt floor. "He's figuring that the King will get angry, then blame Princess Jade."

Lord Charles smiled. It was a clever plan. He had to give that much credit. Once King Henry got really angry over not receiving tribute from Castle Crosse, Bishop Fields could step in and pledge to pay all taxes due if he was allowed to usurp the reins of power.

It was all so simple, it was truly a work of genius. And though Lord Charles had no respect for the bishop, this last bit of information reaffirmed his belief that Nathan Fields was an enemy who should never be underestimated.

"Why were you leaving?" von Mueller asked the seated man. "Seems to me you have much to gain, as one of Bishop Fields's closest advisors, with the overthrow of power from Princess Jade."

Without lifting his face, Sean Dunne spoke of Bishop Fields's increasingly erratic behavior, and of Garth Rawlings's deepening treachery.

"You were running for your life then?" Lord Charles asked. Sean Dunne nodded, never raising his eyes. Lord Charles laughed softly. "It doesn't surprise me to learn what a coward you truly are. No loyalty to Princess Jade nor to Bishop Fields and no courage, that's the man you are. More a worm than a man! You crawl on your belly! You act and talk like a strong man only as long as you're the sheriff. Alone, on your own, you're nothing!"

Sean Dunne turned his face up then, and though he was not crying, his face was pale white, and his eyes begged for sympathy.

"I never meant for this to happen," he cried out. "I'm a man of letters! I'm a scholar, really. It wasn't until Prince William made me his sheriff that . . . that . . ."

"That you started losing control of the good man inside you?" von Mueller asked.

"Yes! Yes, that's exactly it!" Sean Dunne replied rapidly.

The expression on Baron von Mueller's face did not in any way indicate that understanding brought forgiveness. He cared little no matter how or why power had muzzled the better part of this man's judgement; all that mattered is that it had.

"You can understand, can't you?" the sheriff pleaded.

"I have more power than you can imagine," von Mueller said slowly, fighting against the anger that raged in him on behalf of the great suffering the man had caused. "I would never so much as *dream* of doing what you have done."

The interrogation continued. Sean Dunne held nothing back, answering every question to the best of his abilities. Baron von Mueller and Lord Charles received their first truly accurate picture of what had been happening inside Castle Crosse since the death of Prince William.

By the time Sean Dunne had finished, one surprising fact was inescapably clear. Bishop Fields *did not* believe that his failure to capture control of the fiefdom was inevitable. He believed deep down that if enough enemies were killed, then only victory was inevitable. If only enough peasants were murdered, if enough land-owners silenced, then the keys to the fiefdom would be *his!*

When the baron and Lord Charles locked themselves in an upstairs room with goblets of ale, their hearts were heavy and their brains afire.

"We've got to stop that madman *immediately,*" Lord Charles said. "He's going to step up the killing, and the longer you and I do nothing, the more peasants will die."

"I agree," the baron replied. "And you know that this means total war."

"I see no other way, my friend."

"Neither do I, *bonsier* . . . neither do I."

348

Chapter 28

It was the way the men treated Lyon that most impressed Jade. Every man, no matter what his rank, treated Lyon with absolute respect. It wasn't merely the respect given a soldier of higher rank. Jade had witnessed often enough the scornful words spoken of Sir Garth by his men when he wasn't present, so she knew the difference. Lyon's men seemed to respect him genuinely, to believe in his abilities and judgement, and followed his commands without question or hesitation.

It had been a harrowing escape through the forest in daylight. Since that early morning attack by the hunting party organized by Garth Rawlings and paid by Bishop Fields from Jade's own personal funds, they had been followed on two different occasions. At last, they reached the elbow of the River Abodanto, where it had been arranged that the soldiers and knights would meet up if they were ever separated.

Many concerns prayed on Jade's mind, niggling away at her sense of ease. She could not forget the look on that man's face when she'd plunged the dagger deeply into him. Over and over again she could see his lifeless eyes, dead and yet still showing the surprise that he had known on the last beat of his heart, in her mind's eye. No matter how hard she tried to concentrate on other matters, she could not forget that she had taken another man's life. He was an evil man, but still a man of flesh and blood, his vitality forever stilled by her hand.

She kept a close watch on Lyon from a discreet distance, trying to divert her thoughts. It was enjoyable to watch him while he worked with his men. She was able to see him in a natural setting, in a completely male world. He took his responsibilities as the commander of men seriously. His principal concern was always the safety of his men, though the objective of raiding Castle Crosse to rid it of the usurpers was also of great importance.

Shortly after Lyon and Jade arrived at the camp, a mercenary in Lord Charles's employ rode in. When he was able to have a private conversation with Lyon, he said that the *former* sheriff, Sean Dunne, had been captured. Bishop Nathan Fields was planning attacks on several villages, intent on burning them to the ground and killing all the peasants. Bishop Fields believed that the villagers had offered havens of safety and replenishment for Lyon and his men, providing food and water in their generosity of spirit. For such generosity, the good Bishop demanded that every man, woman, and child be slain.

Lyon relayed the information to Jade and his men. Something had to be done immediately to stop Bishop Fields, delaying meant allowing dozens of innocent peasants to die. Even if the peasants were warned of the impending attack and were able to escape into the forest, their homes would still be destroyed, and their livestock most assuredly stolen or senselessly slaughtered.

"We've got to attack," Lyon said quietly, sitting on the ground, Jade at his side, his troops surrounding him. "We all know that Bishop Fields will not be able to maintain his power much longer. He's mad, and madmen cannot hold sane men at bay indefinitely. Until we put an end to the terror that is Bishop Nathan Fields, good, decent, innocent people will be jeopardized."

He paused for a moment, then quickly stood. He withdrew an arrow from his quiver and held it loosely in his hand, rolling the smooth, straight shaft between his fingers as he examined the arrowhead.

"Right now, Garth and his knights are all separated into smaller hunting parties searching for Princess Jade and myself. Collectively, their numbers are much greater than ours, but they are scattered across this fiefdom. Many in their ranks are mercenaries with no loyalty to anyone but themselves, and no heart for a strong fight."

Lyon replaced the arrow in his quiver slowly, knowing that Jade and his men were watching his every move. When he turned his attention back to the men and resumed speaking, he made a point of briefly looking into the eyes of each and every one of his men. He gave them all the same feeling that he was talking to them individually, privately, personally.

"They outnumber us, but we have skill and discipline on our side. What I suggest—"

The word *suggest* brought a momentary disruption

of his speech as the men laughed softly. All knew that a *suggestion* from Sir Lyon carried the weight of a direct order.

"—is that we send men out to infiltrate the enemy ranks. We want the mercenaries, the men who are fighting only to fatten their purses with stolen gold, to know that if they leave now, they may live. But they must leave immediately. At the same time, we still send riders, men on our swiftest horses, to all the villages. The men of the villages will be told to take their hay-forks and wood axes, their bows and arrows, and anything that can be used as a weapon, and march upon Castle Crosse."

Jade gasped when she heard Lyon say he wanted the serfs to attack her home. Had Lyon completely lost his mind? Was he as intent upon destruction as his nemesis Bishop Fields?

Sensing the questioning disapproval from both Jade and his men, Lyon raised a big hand to silence any comments. He was formulating this plan in his head as he spoke, and he did not want any opposition yet. Later, he would listen to his men, but only after he had finished.

"The head and the fiery tongue of this dragon lives in Castle Crosse. It is not the hunting parties riding through this fiefdom who are our real enemies. It is men like Bishop Nathan Fields and Sir Garth Rawlings who are our real enemies!" The murmur of acceptance told Lyon that he was on the right track. "The hunting parties are only the arms of the dragon. We all know the dragon will live, even if we cut off an arm or two or even three. But if we cut off the beast's head, the heart will stop beating, and the arms will fall limp and not hurt us."

"To Castle Crosse!" a young soldier suddenly shouted, raising his sword high over his head. "We'll kill this dragon tonight!"

Lyon let the men shout and scream for a while, their blood flowing hotter and hotter. He then raised his hands for silence once again. Jade, not at all impressed with displays of violence, studied Lyon, watching the way he controlled his men. He was, she realized once again, a born leader, a man destined to be the leader of men in battle.

"We must not act foolishly," Lyon continued when his men again had quieted and were listening to him. "Innocent people must not be killed, and within Castle Crosse, there are *many* innocent people." Lyon drawled the word out to give it greater significance. "There are only a handful of men behind our troubles, and it is those men we seek. The innocents living in Castle Crosse are our brothers and sisters and cousins, our aunts and uncles, our family." His voice went low, serious, as he continued, "We cannot kill them without killing ourselves."

A soldier nodded, saying quietly, "And we will not kill ourselves, m'lord. We know who our family is, just as we know who our enemy is. Our family will live; our enemy will not."

It took only minutes for the best riders to be teamed with the fastest horses. The villagers would be warned of what was to happen that night at dusk, and the individual hunting parties would be sought out and warned. If they followed the advice given, the chances of success by Lyon and his men improved. If the mercenaries held true to their code of greed and violence, their chances of being slaughtered in the attack was more than likely.

Silently, Lyon prayed the mercenaries that he had always despised would prove to be cowardly, willing to run away from a war they'd been paid to fight.

The sun had nearly set, and by the looks of the dusky evening, the moon would rise full and bright. Though certainly no military tactician, Jade realized the bright moonlight might well hurt their chances for success.

But what were their odds of success, under even the most favorable conditions?

For the entire day, Jade had tried to keep her mind occupied with other matters so that she wouldn't ponder the consequences of failure. Attacking Castle Crosse would be dangerous for Lyon, herself, their soldiers, and for the serfs and merchants living inside the high, protective wall surrounding the castle. It still seemed so utterly absurd that she would have to storm her own home that Jade had a difficult time believing this all wasn't some horrible nightmare.

Jade suspected that if she thought too much about failure, she would somehow bring it about. So whenever her worries came to mind, she immediately threw her heart and soul and all her energy into a new task that would somehow help the men who would be doing the actual fighting.

"You've done a fine job, m'lady," a battle-scarred knight said, inspecting the razor's edge of an arrowhead that Jade had just sharpened.

"Thank you," she replied. "It seems the least I can do to help you men."

"M'lady, you do not need to help us. It is for you we go to battle."

The seriousness of his tone took Jade aback. She studied the man, surprised to see that he was in his late forties or early fifties. He seemed much too old to still be an active soldier. It struck her as odd, as well, that such a soldier of advanced years and obvious experience should be taking orders from Sir Lyon Beauchane, a man many years younger.

"To your health," Jade said, shaking away her internal questions. She handed the knight the arrow, and he proudly placed it into his quiver.

The knight stood looking down at Jade for several seconds, silent, brooding. Finally, she said, "Please speak freely. Tell me what it is that troubles you."

The knight smiled crookedly, showing a thin white scar through his graying beard. "On the morrow, m'lady, you will have Castle Crosse back. I pledge my life upon it."

Emotion tightened Jade's throat. She nodded silently, and the knight stepped away.

She hated the fact that she was sharpening the iron arrowheads that would soon be aimed at her enemies. In so doing, she could not help but feel that she was party to lethal violence. She hated, too, the fact that if she simply abdicated her castle, her position, her possessions, it would not help the lives of the people living in her fiefdom one whit.

No matter how she looked at it, it appeared as though Lyon's analysis was correct. Bishop Nathan Fields had to be attacked directly, immediately, and removed from power.

There was no other way, and the unbending reality

of this truth tore Jade's heart.

Lyon stepped near, then knelt on one knee beside her. "I can see from the look in your eyes that this is difficult for you," he said. When Jade picked up another arrow to sharpen the point on the sharpening stone, Lyon took the arrow from her. "Perhaps you are more suited to making and rolling bandages, Jade. You will help us by doing that, and your delicate hands will not have to touch weapons."

Jade looked deeply into his eyes, wondering at first if he was being sarcastic with her, teasing her because she hated war and violence and weapons. But looking into his fierce blue eyes, she saw only sympathy, concern, and understanding.

"I love you," she said. The words spilled out of her mouth quickly, without her even being aware of thinking them. Once the words had been spoken, she moved away from Lyon, as though shocked at herself for what she had done, and was afraid of his response.

"Do not move away." Lyon's deep, resonant voice was rough-soft with love. He was aware that he could be intimidating, even when he didn't mean to be. "You must never hold fear in your heart for me. I am a soldier, and it is true that I fight wars. But in my heart I am not a violent man. I do not kill for pleasure, or for personal profit. Tonight, I fight so that others who cannot fight for themselves will have a better life." He closed the distance between them, touching her cheek softly, delicate as a feather with his fingertip. "I love you, Princess Jade."

The simple honesty of his declaration struck Jade with astonishing force. She took his hand in hers, turning the palm toward her, and placed his hand over her heart. No words were spoken between them; words were not needed. In that moment, their hearts were one, joined together by invisible bonds that could not be severed by external forces or circumstances, or even by the surge of time.

She wanted to take him into her arms then, to hold him close and listen to his whispered promises that all would be well. But one of Lyon's knights came forward, needing Lyon's decision on a matter of preparation. She watched Lyon's entire attitude change, going from caring lover to rational military leader in one armoring heartbeat.

"I must leave now," was all Lyon said before he rose and walked away, leaving Jade feeling disoriented and confused.

What would happen when this evening was over and the war had either succeeded or failed? Would Lyon's love remain undiminished? Would his strength of will be powerful enough to marry a woman of greater standing in the kingdom of England? Women simply did not marry below their station, just as men did not marry above it. Would their marriage be accepted, even if they *could* make it to the altar?

She pushed all doubts from her mind, and went to where several young men were tearing apart all unnecessary clothing, turning the fabric into bandages.

Given her choice, Jade would rather live a life constantly on the run and in perpetual poverty if she had Lyon at her side. She had already lived a life of wealth and leisure that was devoid of love, and she knew how hollow and false that life was.

* * *

Garth placed his hands together over the pommel of his saddle and stared off into space.

Something was wrong. Exactly what it was, he couldn't say. But he could feel something chilling the marrow of his bones . . . and he didn't like it at all.

Early that day, he had ridden from Castle Crosse with a contingent of twenty men. His mission for the day was to attack a village, burning and killing everything and everyone, stealing anything that even remotely had value. Bishop Fields had given him the orders directly, and Garth sensed that this was his chance, in some measure, to redeem himself for failing to murder Princess Jade.

But everywhere Garth and his soldiers went, the villagers seemed prepared for them. The first village was completely deserted. All people were gone; not a single pig or chicken had been left behind. Infuriated, Garth torched the buildings, and even killed the single mangy dog that had been found.

It wasn't until he reached the second village that he knew that the peasants had a strong notion of what was going to happen. Even in the fields, where their crops had been planted that would sustain them through the difficult English winter, Garth hadn't been able to find a soul.

Everyone had gone somewhere. But where? And why? How could the simple peasants of this fiefdom have known that their time of retribution for assisting Sir Lyon was at hand?

The men weren't happy about being denied the pleasure of drawing swords against peasants, either. Garth looked at his men briefly, despising them for their lack of discipline and understanding of protocol, hating them because they seldom showed him the kind of respect due their commanding officer, and a knight of Castle Crosse.

"We might as well go back for all the good we're doin' out here," a soldier-for-hire grumbled, not talking to Garth, but speaking loud enough so that the commander couldn't help but hear. "Where the 'ell did they all go? Might as well go back to ol' Castle Crosse and pour ourselves a pint, eh?"

Garth turned in the saddle to fix the complainer with a steely stare. The man immediately fell silent. As Garth stared at the man, an idea struck him with such force that he clutched onto the pommel of his saddle to remain seated.

The peasants weren't in their villages, and they weren't tending their crops or their livestock, but they had to be somewhere. If that somewhere happened to be at Castle Crosse . . . and they were all there together. . . .

"Back to the castle, men!" Garth hissed, jerking hard on the reins to turn his destrier around.

He felt a cold emptiness in the pit of his stomach. Was it possible that Lyon had organized the peasants into a fighting force? Impossible! But Lyon had done the impossible before. He'd done it enough times for Garth to suspect that for Sir Lyon Beauchane, *nothing* was impossible. And because the likelihood of anyone organizing the peasants into a unified fighting force was so unlikely, it made perfect sense that it was something Lyon would do.

Garth dug his spurs into his destrier's ribs, urging the animal to a full gallop.

Mary Ellen sat on the hard stone floor of the cellar,

hugging her knees to her chest. Tears dribbled down her cheeks. It wasn't *her* fault that Bishop Fields had been unable to perform in bed, but she was the one being punished for it. Bishop Fields had accused her of witchery, saying that she had stolen his manliness with spells and incantations. No matter how frantically she denied his accusations, he refused to believe that the problem could be his own. No, someone else had clearly victimized him, and logic deemed that Mary Ellen was the guilty party.

She was hungry and thirsty. Not even a complete day had passed since she had been locked away in the cellar of Castle Crosse, but already Mary Ellen knew that if she stayed within the dark, cramped confines much longer, she would surely lose her mind.

She hugged her knees tighter, wondering if anyone would bring food and water, part of her wanting desperately to stay alive, part of her beginning to think death was a positive alternative to the despair of incarceration.

Bishop Nathan Fields's long, flowing robes slapped against his legs as he strode furiously back and forth along the length of the room. The tables were strewn with maps of the fiefdom, as well as reports and journals of expected crops, and various other records of the collective value of Princess Jade Crosse's fiefdom.

The pungent smell of wine permeated the room, though the bishop had drunk very little of it. Earlier, in a fit of rage, he had cast his wine goblet against the wall, splattering the red liquid everywhere, and dousing a new round of letters to King Henry and his court that he had been composing. Furious that such a thing should happen, the bishop immediately ordered a servant to bring him a fresh goblet with more wine. Then, when he disliked the taste of the wine, Bishop Fields accused the servant of trying to poison him, and sent that jewel-encrusted goblet smashing against the wall as well.

Within a two-hour period, four large goblets, all of them thick with jewels, had been thrown against the hard stone wall. Wine pooled on the floor of the bishop's chambers, and the air had grown thick with the overlaying smells of fear and perspiration and stale wine.

Incompetents! He was surrounded by incompetents! First that traitor, Sheriff Dunne, had ridden off without a word to anyone. His betrayal was made even worse by the fact that he couldn't keep himself from being captured by von Mueller's guards.

What had the sheriff told von Mueller?

All the conversations, everything that had been said in Sheriff Dunne's presence, came back to Bishop Fields in a single vortex of words. There was no denying the fact that the sheriff knew all of the plans that Fields had made, or at least most of them. And since he had been captured while riding toward London, fleeing like the sniveling coward he was, it made little sense to assume that Dunne wouldn't yield the truth under questioning. If Baron von Mueller knew what Bishop Fields had planned, then it stood to reason that Lord Charles Frederick also knew, which meant that there could be no denying that an open war would soon be necessary.

361

Bishop Fields sat at his desk and picked up his quill, inhaling deeply to summon a sense of calm. Before him was a long sheet of paper, fresh and clean, upon which he began writing down the names of the people who had to die. He started with Princess Jade Crosse, and followed it immediately with Sir Lyon Beauchane. From there, he wrote Baron Timish von Mueller, then Lord Charles Frederick. Then, for good measure, he followed those names with Baroness Christina von Mueller, and Lady Shannon Frederick.

And there was Mary Ellen! Yes, mustn't forget about Mary Ellen and her treachery. And Sir Garth. Yes, indeed, Sir Garth Rawlings had to be murdered. No doubt about his name being on the list. He knew far too much to live.

And Walter, the servant who had brought him the wrong wine. Yes, Walter had to be taught one final lesson. Such swinish behavior had to be punished accordingly.

And who else should go on the list . . . ?

Bishop Nathan Fields walked to the window of his chambers and looked down into the courtyard. It was dusk, almost night. He hoped that Garth had successfully taught the other peasants a lesson that they would not soon forget. The order had been given that Sir Lyon mustn't be helped, and yet food and shelter had been provided. So the peasants, swine to the last wretched child, must be killed. And after Garth finished with the peasants, Bishop Fields would find someone to put an end to Garth. Bishop Fields didn't want his favorite murderer to become too powerful; a dagger in his back would make sure that wouldn't happen.

In the distance, Bishop Fields saw a few lights. Were they torches? It was difficult to see, since the torch bearers were along the distant treeline.

He turned away from the window, not worrying about what the points of light in the darkness might mean. He was surrounded by stone walls, completely protected within Castle Crosse. Whatever was happening out there couldn't touch him, so Bishop Nathan Fields went back to his desk, adding more names to the steadily growing list of people who needed to be killed.

Chapter 29

What impressed Jade most was the willingness of the men, young and old, to put their lives in jeopardy to protect their families, to protect their way of life. As she looked at the men as they huddled in the growing darkness, she was aware that unless she treated the serfs properly when—and if—she regained power and control of Castle Crosse, they could just as easily rise up against her.

"We'll be starting out soon," Lyon said, kneeling beside Jade. "I want you to stay here until I come back for you."

"Yes, I know that's what you want," Jade said, an impish yet defiant twinkle in her amber eyes. "But it isn't what you're going to get. I'm coming with you. We've gone this far together. There's no reason we can't see this through to the end together."

"God's bones, Jade, don't you realize how perilous it's going to be?" Lyon clenched his fist in anger, though it wasn't a threatening gesture toward his princess. He was simply angry with her stubbornness.

He was listened to and obeyed by powerfully built soldiers who had fought many wars, but he could not give orders to a wisp of a woman who had never wielded anything mightier than a tapestry needle until meeting him.

In the face of Lyon's anger, Jade was determined to remain perfectly and annoyingly calm. "Yes, I am quite aware of the dangers involved. That is why I *must* be there with you, and not only because of you. If the soldiers and the village men all know that I am with them, in body and not merely in spirit, then it will strengthen their courage. They will know that the battle they are fighting is for the greater good of every man, woman, and child in the fiefdom."

Lyon glowered at Jade, fixing her with his most damning and crucifying blue stare. She looked back at him, serenely calm, supreme in her conviction that her actions were right, just, and honorable.

"You *are* stubborn," Lyon whispered, the words coming out through clenched teeth.

"And you are right," Jade replied, implacable, smiling.

She saw then that several men were standing behind Lyon, apparently waiting for instructions from him. They had listened in on their argument, and apparently every one of them found it vastly amusing that she had stood up to Sir Lyon's wrath and had emerged the victor.

The march of the last hundred yards by fifty-six men and one woman to the outside wall of Castle Crosse began.

Jade felt her heart pumping, her blood flowing fast, but along with the fear was a new sensation. She felt a responsibility and love for the villagers who lived on her land, and who swarmed around her. In the past, she had always considered their welfare whenever she had made decisions. Seeing them now defending her, jeopardizing their own lives to see that she would once again sit in the big chair in the receiving hall at Castle Crosse, warmed her heart and prompted her to resolve to bring them great happiness and prosperity. She would use her sense of judgement and fairness to end disputes among the villagers, and to make the decisions that would serve the best interests of everyone, no matter what rank in society they held.

Lyon led the march, holding his huge broadsword in one hand, using his left to point where he wanted his men to go. The peasants, though untrained, listened to every direction Lyon gave. They followed it immediately, sensing that their only hope for success rested in the tall, blond knight's capable hands.

"What if the drawbridge don't come down?"

Lyon shot a deadly look at the soldier who had asked the question. The man instantly backed away. With a circular wave of his hand, Lyon summoned the man to his side once again. It was obvious that the soldier wished now that he had kept his doubts to himself.

"Good men have promised me that at sundown the drawbridge will come down and the gate will come up. If they say it will be so, then it will be so."

"Of course, m'lord," the soldier said, backing away again. "If you believe it, then surely it will be so."

"I believe," Lyon said, smiling encouragingly, motioning him into his position in line.

He had been promised by Baron von Mueller and

Lord Charles that the drawbridge would be lowered, the gate raised, and that opposition to the soldiers and villagers would be minimal. Spies within Castle Crosse were still in place, and mercenaries working for Sir Garth should have been bribed to abandon their posts at exactly sundown.

If all went as planned, opposition to the "invading" troops would be negligible and any casualties minimal. What couldn't be overlooked was that the plan had been both hastily conceived and implemented.

From the sentry positions on the high wall that surrounded Castle Crosse, Lyon saw men watching the advancing, ragtag army. Were they soldiers loyal to Bishop Fields and Sir Garth? If so, the drawbridge would not be dropped, nor would the heavy gate be raised. From outside the battlements, Lyon could do nothing against Bishop Fields. The surrounding, unbreachable wall had been built to protect the castle, and it served its purpose indiscriminately.

They slowly approached the castle, and still the drawbridge remained in position. The upper edge of the wall was anchored snugly against the surrounding wall. The moat surrounding the wall provided a final barrier to the castle defense.

"Good sirs," Lyon whispered aloud, though he spoke to the absent Lord Charles and Baron von Mueller. "Do not fail me now."

It was at that precise moment that Lyon heard the scream of rage. He turned to look in the direction from which the sound had come, and his heart froze in his chest.

Sir Garth, riding tall in the saddle and brandishing a sword, followed by many of his knights and soldiers-for-hire, rode toward the castle at a dead gallop with murder in their eyes.

Lyon sized up the situation in a glance. Within a minute or two, Garth and his men would be upon them. With the moat at their backs, and several of Garth's men moving to cut off a retreat back to the forest, they were trapped. And if archers positioned themselves high on the wall, it would be savage child's play to kill the so-called "invaders."

"Prepare to fight!" Lyon shouted, pushing through the throng of soldiers and villagers so that he would be the first to meet the charge from Garth's men.

The creaking sound of the drawbridge coming down was sweet music to Lyon.

He decided the greatest danger to his men would come from inside the castle walls, so he turned away from Garth's attack, running back to the slowly raising gate. The courageous shouts of the villagers rang in his ears, and it tore into his heart that so many of them were armed with nothing deadlier than crude pitchforks.

Each passing second brought Garth's soldiers closer. The drawbridge was finally lowered enough for Lyon to leap upon it, and he saw that the last barrier to the castle defenses, the interior gate, had been raised no further than two feet. Merchants inside the wall were fighting with Bishop Fields's mercenaries.

"Attack! Attack!" Lyon shouted, rolling beneath the gate.

He was met instantly by a mercenary he did not recognize. With scorn, Lyon dispatched the ill-trained man, cutting him down with his broadsword. He realized that though Bishop Fields may have hired many killers, he had hired woefully few quality soldiers.

Inside the walls of Castle Crosse, tension and suspicion had yielded to mass disruption. Some of the merchants and servants had been told of the impending attack while others had not. Few people were certain who their enemy was, whether there were soldiers fighting on their side, or if simply everyone was against them.

Lyon quickly realized that the lowered gate, and its opening gap of only two feet deep, had an advantage. It forced people to get down on their hands and knees to crawl through, which left them momentarily vulnerable. And the lowered gate also made it impossible for Garth and his men to ride into the castle. On foot, Garth would not have the many advantages inherent in being astride his mighty destrier.

An arrow struck the ground at Lyon's feet, missing him by inches. He spun in the direction the arrow had come from just in time to see an archer, atop the wall, restringing another arrow into his bow. Before the archer could send off a second shot, a peasant, armed with only a shepherd's cane, clubbed the man over the head. The archer's knees buckled, and he fell off the walkway, dropping fifty feet into the stone courtyard.

Lyon took the time to give the man a brief wave of thanks for possibly saving his life, then turned his attention back to the battle. He watched as Jade rolled beneath the gate, her blond hair swirling after her, her moves graceful and voluptuous. Rushing to her, thankful that she was still alive, Lyon grabbed her by the arm and hoisted her to her feet.

"Stay out of the fray," he said.

"Don't worry about me!" She raised high on her tiptoes quickly, kissing Lyon flush on the mouth. "I'll meet you in my bedchamber when this is over!"

She turned away from Lyon, shouting warnings to the peasants as they fought with soldiers, giving directions during the battle almost as an experienced commander would.

Lyon watched her for only a second before he had to resume the fight. He felt more confident now that when the bloodletting finally ended, his Jade would be safe.

Still outside the gates, Garth was screaming as loudly as he possibly could, cursing his men, hating them for their cowardice. Yet, he knew *he* would never follow his suicidal commands.

Already he had issued orders for three of his men to crawl beneath the gate to raise it. Each soldier, crawling through the gap on his hands and knees, had ben easily dispatched by the peasants, using pitchforks and a scythe. Now Garth's men had drawn their bows and waited to shoot the peasants as soon as they showed themselves, which, of course, the peasants failed to do.

"You there! Beneath that gate *now!*" Garth shouted at one of his younger mercenaries, glowering down at the man.

"You want the gate open so bloody bad, do it yerself!" the mercenary shot back.

Garth allowed no man to talk to him that coarsely. With a jabbing thrust of his sword, he cut the young man down, killing him on the spot. When he looked at his men again, he saw that he had gained their fear, though not their respect. Sighing, he realized that fear was a greater motivator anyway.

"Now under that gate and raise it, or I'll kill you all myself!"

They hated Garth, but they also knew that if he promised to murder, he would do exactly that. Realizing too that there was some safety in numbers, the mercenaries rushed the gate, many trying to roll beneath it at the same time while others used their arrows to fend off the scythe-wielding peasants.

High within Castle Crosse, unable to fathom quite fully what was happening, Bishop Nathan Fields stood in his chambers, hands tucked into the pockets of his robe, watching the fighting wage far below. His thin, hawkish face was set in a twisted scowl as he watched the poorly dressed, badly equipped peasants fighting armored soldiers and mercenaries.

It seemed impossible to him that the peasants could win. He harbored not an ounce of love in his breast for the commoners that he so often had preached to. He despised them all as low-born vermin, worthy of nothing, certainly not worthy of his precious time. They were merely a commodity, like cattle or sheep, for him to tally in his account ledgers.

As he watched the peasants moving snakelike into the castle, he could not really believe that they would pose a threat to him. He was Bishop Nathan Fields, a man of superior education, learning, and intelligence. He was confidant to many of the most powerful and privileged people in England. Surely, God could not allow a man of his value, his standing, to be harmed by an unwashed, illiterate rabble of common peasants.

He walked slowly but confidently from his own chambers, moving down the hallway to Princess Jade's bedchamber. He noted with some consternation that it was deserted of all servants. There he would know some measure of comfort while his men conquered this meddlesome, petty insurrection.

He closed the door behind him, pulling a face when he realized that he'd had the bolt removed from the door so that Jade could not lock him out. Sometimes, late at night, he liked to quietly sneak into her bedchamber and watch her while she slept.

The bishop went to the small room off the bedchamber, where the clothes that Jade had once worn still hung along the walls. Mary Ellen had been helping herself to Jade's wardrobe lately, but she left some dresses in tact. He picked up a garment and brought it to his face to inhale the lingering scent of the princess who had once worn it.

Yes, it would have been gratifying to feel his fingers tightening around Jade's throat as he held her down, begging for mercy that he would not show her. It would have been satisfying to feel her naked body writhing beneath him. It would have been . . .

It hadn't quite worked out that way, and this now disappointed him.

Several floors below, he could hear the echoing shouts of the peasants, hear their hurried footsteps as they approached. They wouldn't hurt him though. He was their bishop, and they looked up to him as their spiritual leader. They were peasants, little more than penned-up domesticated animals, and they knew their place in the grand scheme of things.

Bishop Nathan Fields smiled confidently, secure in his power and position, enjoying the sense that he was mightier than all he had even known, soothed by the fragrance of the young woman who had worn the silken nightgown he held to his nose.

He was sitting on the bed that Jade had used when the door burst open. A dozen peasants streamed into the bedchamber, their faces flushed with exertion and excitement, their eyes wild with the hunt.

"Leave. I wish to be alone." Bishop Fields spoke the words calmly, quietly. He sensed their primitive, sweaty fear. He felt no fear whatsoever.

"Tonight, you bloody bastard, you no longer can tell us what to do," an older peasant said. He held in his hands a pitchfork, but he cast it aside. His hands were thickly calloused from many years of hard labor. "Tonight, you get what you have long deserved!"

"Leave my sight, you swine! The smell of you nauseates me!"

The old peasant had been beaten down by Bishop Fields in one way or another a dozen times since the death of Prince William, but the beating would end here and now. He walked toward the bishop, his thick-fingered hands extended.

"Swine, I command you to *leave!*" Bishop Fields said, his voice raised imperiously. He pointed toward the bedchamber door.

The bishop's look of utter revulsion was all it took to snap the other peasants from their fearful stupor. The old man grabbed Bishop Fields by the lapels of his robe and shook him.

"Swine! How dare you call me swine!" the proud, old peasant shouted, enraged beyond any anger he had ever known.

It was all so impossible, but it was true. Bishop Nathan Fields was actually being touched by these vile commoners! When they raised him up high over their

373

heads, their wretched, filthy peasant hands holding him strongly, he could not understand why God Himself did not immediately smite the hellish pack down.

Then he knew this was merely one final test for him to pass, one final chance for him to prove his worthiness of the almost godlike power he wished to wield within the forbidding walls of Castle Crosse. His face broke into a gracious, not-quite-humble smile. When he was carried out of the bedchamber to the balcony, Bishop Fields knew that God would act at any moment, praising him for his supreme aplomb.

He continued to smile graciously and patiently as the peasants tossed him over the balcony railing to the rocks and ocean far below.

As that battle ended triumphantly, another battle was just beginning in the courtyard. Lyon had just spotted Garth rolling beneath the gate. But before Lyon could attack his longtime foe, another of Garth's men rushed into the melee and was about to stab a fiercely fighting peasant in the back. Lyon interceded and confronted the mercenary. Though his superior fighting skills enabled him to quickly dispatch the man, Garth had already made his way through the ruckus and was about to enter the castle.

"Don't run, you coward!" Lyon screamed, hoping that Garth's pride would prevent him from rushing into the castle. The hatred Lyon felt for this man demanded they meet in a final, face-to-face confrontation.

But Garth, ever pragmatic, even amidst the chaos of warfare, hardly paused a beat when he heard Sir Lyon's challenging insult. He rushed into Castle Crosse, sword in one hand and dagger in the other, heading toward the knight's chambers. New passageways had been built since Lyon had left to fight in the wars. In the labyrinthine hallways and tunnels, Garth would have the advantage, and he wanted every advantage he could get when it came to fighting Lyon Beauchane.

Outside, at the entrance to the castle, Lyon paused, pressing his back against the stone wall. He watched the fighting for a second, seeing if there was anyone in particular who needed his assistance before he went to settle a personal score with an evil man who had lived too long already.

Pausing to watch the fighting, Lyon saw that his plan had worked. It appeared that only Garth's core legion of soldiers had returned to Castle Crosse. Though the peasants had vastly inferior weapons, they outnumbered their opponents. Also, the peasants fought because it was *their* fight; the mercenaries fought because they had been paid a paltry sum to fight the peasants.

The tide was turning, and the peasants, though falling at a rate equal to the mercenaries, would prevail in the end. Numbers were with them, and so were their hearts. Lyon knew that in battle, that was the only weapon that was truly essential.

He found Jade near the base of the surrounding wall, helping a young man who had been cut on the thigh by a sword. She was wrapping a bandage around his wounded leg, and a wave of pride swept over Lyon. She was safe, out of harm's way for the most part, yet still she was doing something vital to help them achieve a successful outcome to the battle.

Lyon turned away from the carnage in the court-yard, at last fully focused on a single goal, convinced

375

that the battle would be won, and that the woman he loved would live through it.

Inside the castle, it was dark, and slightly warmer than outside. The air held a faint dankness, and Lyon wondered if it was the smell of impending death. All his senses tingled with the possibility of sudden violence.

With a shrug of his shoulders, Lyon slipped off the harness of his quiver, letting the arrows clatter to the floor. Next he rid himself of his bow. Whatever fighting he had to do would not be done in such an impersonal manner, not done from a distance crossed in the blink of an eye by an arrow. This enemy that had tried to rape Princess Jade needed to die, and to know why he was dying. Lyon would look into Garth's eyes at the moment of truth and put a curse upon his soul that he prayed the heavens would hear.

Behind him, the fighting continued, but as Lyon moved deeper into the castle, he could hear less of the clang of sword striking sword, fewer screams of pain. From ahead, he heard nothing at all. Not even the hurried footsteps of his quarry.

"Garth . . . are you there?"

Lyon asked the question softly, in an almost conversational tone. His voice echoed through the stone hallways. No returning voice greeted him as he moved through deeper, darker passageways. Silence closed in around him, broken only by the soft grating sound of small pebbles being pressed into the stone floor by the soft soles of his boots, and the racing whir of his own blood.

It came from nowhere, without warning. Lyon had just checked down one hallway when a sword swept

376

toward him. It came from what *had* been a solid wall when he had lived in the knight's quarters. The blade cut through his black silk cape and the tight leather vest, through the fine linen shirt, through flesh.

Lyon lashed out with his own sword, swinging it frantically at an enemy he could not see. His sword rattled against the stone wall harmlessly. He tossed himself to the floor, rolling to his left, seeking to avoid the second assault he was sure would come.

But the second assault did not come.

Lyon rose slowly, feeling the burning sensation where Garth's sharp sword had split flesh, feeling his blood, warm and sticky, running down the side of his body. He felt his clothes sticking wetly to him. The thrust had been intended for his heart, but had missed. It sliced instead the inside of Lyon's biceps, then glanced off his ribs, high on his side just beneath his arm. The wound was painful, and would cause much bloodshed, but it was not fatal. Unless he was weakened by the loss of blood, unless his cut arm lost some of its strength, and that loss was all that Garth needed to turn the Fates to his favor, unless . . .

Lyon stilled his fears ruthlessly. Later, after Garth was dead, he could waste time listening to such unworthy babble.

He studied the wall from where the sword had been thrust into him and discovered that a single stone had been removed. This gap allowed either a sentry to watch all who came and went, or a sword to be stabbed straight forward through the hole.

Lyon inspected the hole in the wall. How many other changes had occurred at the castle since he had been gone? On the opposite side of the wall was the small, locked room where the knights had kept their ration of wine.

Lyon continued on, moving deeper into the castle, deeper into the stale darkness. Fewer torches now lined the walls to light the way, and he had only his memory to guide him. But was his memory accurate? After what had just happened, he could no longer be confident that he knew where he was going.

"Fight me, Garth," Lyon said. He had heard no sounds of glee from Garth after the attack, and that now surprised and worried him. The passing seconds sapped his strength. The blood loss was worse than he had originally suspected. He felt perspiration dew the sides of his face, although it was cool in the lower recesses of the castle.

"Show yourself and fight me," Lyon said as he walked slowly forward, now keeping to the center of the hallway to prevent another surprise attack.

He knew Garth was watching him. He knew it by the prickle of his skin, and by the intuitive awareness curling in his gut that had long warned him of such things.

In an exaggerated move, he wiped sweat from his brow with the back of his left hand, which held a dagger. He staggered slightly then, grimacing as though severely crippled by pain. He pressed his elbow against his side to staunch the flow of blood. After taking two more steps, he stumbled, falling to one knee. With a groan, he staggered back onto his feet.

"Come out, you bloody swine!" Lyon called, only now when he spoke there was the distinct sound of fatigue drawing his words down.

Lyon believed in his instincts, and they had not let

378

him down. Garth had been watching him from a hidden vantage point similar to the one he had used in his first ambush. In the flickering torchlight, he had seen the dull sheen of blood on Lyon's left side, watched as the once powerful knight staggered and fell to one knee. Clearly, his sword had struck Lyon much more effectively than Garth had first thought. Sensing that his foe was badly injured and weakened to such an extent that he would not possess any real threat, Garth stepped out of the shadows. A smile dominated his face a tittering, high-pitched laugh escaped from his lips.

"And *you* call me swine?" He laughed contemptuously as he sized Lyon up for the kill. "Brave talk is all you have left! I'm not going to kill you straight away, Lyon. No, that would be much too heroic a death for the likes of someone like you. I'm going to cut tiny little pieces from you and watch you die by—"

Garth's words were cut off when Lyon, who had been slightly bent over to the left, stood straight up, smiled, then spread his arms a bit in the classic sword-and-dagger stance that was taught to all the knights of Castle Crosse.

"Coward . . . pathetic, stinking coward," Lyon whispered, advancing slowly on Garth. "You come out from hiding only when you think victory is assured. I could feel your eyes upon me. That's why I fell to a knee, knowing that an animal like you would be watching for some sign of weakness. You're afraid of strength. I'm not weak, Garth, nor will I play yet another easy victim for you." Lyon laughed derisively, moving forward, almost within fighting range now. "You couldn't even defeat Jade, you wretched cur. What makes you think you could defeat me?"

Lyon was trying to goad Garth into attacking, into letting his emotions overrule his knowledge of warfare. For all his bravado, the truth was that Lyon could feel his strength slipping away rapidly. Unless he fought Garth soon, he had no prayer for survival. If Garth knew that time was on his side, he would delay the fight until Lyon was as weak as he had only pretended to be.

They circled each other slowly, just as they had before in the forest when Lyon had prevented Garth from raping Jade; each man armed with a sword and dagger, each man trained in the same style of warfare.

Lyon knew that he could not fight long, and he was certain that with his injuries he was no longer stronger than Garth. But he was wiser. He did have an intellectual edge, and he was determined to use that to his fullest advantage.

"You were never strong enough to defeat me," Lyon said challengingly.

In response, Garth attacked with a roar of rage, stepping in and slashing down hard with his sword, then jabbing forward with his dagger. His slashing sword was blocked by Lyon's, and though he came nowhere near flesh with the deadly tip of his dagger, he was able to judge Lyon's strength and swiftness by his reaction.

Lyon also knew what Garth had hoped to accomplish by the first attack. Had his strength been sapped enough that Garth could feel it? Had he leapt away from the stabbing dagger swiftly enough to give the impression that his wounds were insignificant?

These questions hounded Lyon. He circled with Garth, neither man leaving any opening in his defensive posture. But as he circled, Lyon felt another stream

380

of blood trickle down his side. The movement to defend himself had opened the wound even more. Time was now critical. His strength would not last another full minute.

"You can do better than that, can't you, swine?" Lyon taunted, needing his foe to attack in a rage rather than with practiced skill.

Garth said nothing in response.

The sword in Lyon's right hand felt monumentally heavy, and seemed to be growing heavier with each second. Did he have enough strength left? Would he die here in the bowels of Castle Crosse by the hand of the man he despised?

He sensed gray defeat closing in on him, surrounding him like a cloak of darkness. He needed to strip Garth of his intelligence, and it was at that moment that he knew what must be said.

"Sometimes, after Jade and I have finished making glorious love, we lie in our bed together and laugh about you," Lyon said quietly. He watched Garth's eyes, not his hands. Even in the dimness of the torchlight, it was the truth in his eyes that was most critical. "We laugh at you, Garth! She knows you desire her, and she finds it so amusing that an ugly, impotent worm like you would ever be so foolish as to dream of being with a princess of her beauty. And she is beautiful, isn't she, Garth? Much too beautiful for—"

Garth attacked with a howl of rage, his ego sundered by Lyon's words. It was bad enough to know that Princess Jade had never fully appreciated him, but to be laughed at by her and her lover was much more than he could sanely accept.

The end came quickly, without any final parting

words, without the enemies looking into each other's eyes, without curses. Garth attacked, leaping forward, slashing and hacking with sword and dagger. Lyon parried the thrusts, stepped back away from the second wave of the assault, then moved in. By this time the sword in his hand felt so heavy he could only use it to block Garth's blows, but his dagger, much lighter and certainly sharper, arced upward and found Garth's vulnerable, black heart.

Death was instantaneous. Garth fell face down and did not move.

Lyon stumbled back through the corridors. By the time he reached the courtyard, a strange white light hovered inside his head, just behind his eyes.

With a single exception, the fighting in the courtyard had ended. Lyon stepped out just in time to see villagers dragging a vile mercenary named Edward away. He had raped a young girl, and though he was still alive, what the villagers had done to him would make it impossible for him to ever rape again.

His ears were ringing, and that strange, yet soothing, white light was brighter than ever. A voice called out, high and clear, and Lyon turned his head to see Jade running toward him, her blond hair flying behind her. She was smiling joyously. Lyon smiled back.

Then he fell face down in the courtyard and, like Garth, did not move.

Epilogue

"There, there, no one will notice," Lady Shannon said, putting needle and thread to a side seam of Princess Jade Crosse's wedding gown.

Baroness Christina added, "It's just bride jitters. Nothing more than that."

Jade was too nervous to speak. She placed her hand lightly over her stomach, which was not as flat as it had been two months earlier, when she had her suspicions confirmed. Not as flat as a month ago, when Lyon knelt on one knee before her and proposed they spend their lives together as husband and wife.

"Every guest will know," Jade said quietly. "The villagers will all know." She had never intended on being with child on her wedding day, but then she never really thought she would marry again, much less marry a man as virile as Lyon Beauchane.

"As for the nobility, what do you care what they think? You never have before, and this is not the time to change your views. As for the villagers, I believe they love Sir Lyon as much as they love their princess. If two people they love create a child, well . . . what could make them happier than that?"

The wedding was to take place outside, and though it had caused quite an uproar among the landowners and the nobility, all the villagers had been invited to attend the ceremony.

"It's time," Baroness Christina said quietly, a maternal light shining in her blue eyes as she looked at the splendidly gowned princess.

The women laughed then, the nervous laughter of people about to be standing in front of hundreds of people during an ornate ceremony. There were still huge problems that Jade and Lyon had to surmount, and she knew it. Lyon was not her social equal, and though this did not bother her, it did affect Lyon's moods on occasion. It disturbed him greatly that Jade was marrying "beneath herself." Jade, too, had her fears: would Lyon be as pleased with fatherhood as he claimed? Could he settle down sufficiently to be a husband, and not a knight errant, nor warrior at large?

But they would challenge these problems together, strengthened by their love for each other as friends, as man and woman, as husband and wife, and soon, as a family . . . together.